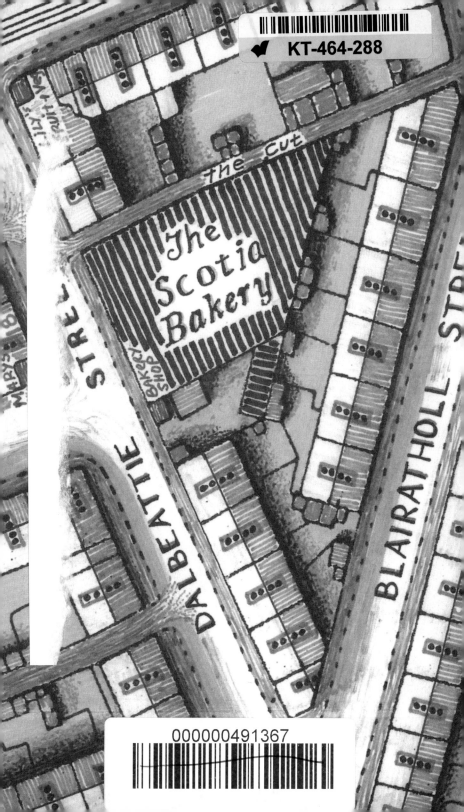

Staying On Past the Terminus

Also by Robert Douglas:

Night Song of the Last Tram
Somewhere to Lay My Head
At Her Majesty's Pleasure
Whose Turn for the Stairs?

Staying On Past the Terminus

ROBERT DOUGLAS

hachette
SCOTLAND

First published in 2011 by
HACHETTE SCOTLAND, an imprint of
Hachette UK

1

Cataloguing in Publication Data is available
from the British Library

ISBN: 978 07553 8028 2

Typeset in New Baskerville by Palimpsest Book Production Limited,
Falkirk, Stirlingshire

Printed and bound in Great Britain by
Clays Ltd, St Ives plc

Hachette Scotland's policy is to use papers that are natural,
renewable and recyclable products and made from wood grown
in sustainable forests. The logging and manufacturing processes
are expected to conform to the environmental regulations
of the country of origin.

HACHETTE SCOTLAND
An Hachette UK Company
338 Euston Road
London NW1 3BH

www.hachettescotland.co.uk
www.hachette.co.uk

In memory of the late Archie Hind who, sadly, never gave us his second novel.

ACKNOWLEDGEMENTS

With many thanks to my publisher, Bob McDevitt who IS Hachette Scotland. To Myra Jones, copy editor extraordinaire. And to Leah and Jo and all at Euston Road. Yet again, thanks to Michael Melvin for his splendid jacket design. And also the faithful members of our original writing group – Gellie Draper, Christine Lowes, Jadzia Race, Chris Raetschus and David Wedderburn (sounds like we meet in Berlin!).

Finally, my wife Patricia. The Manageress. The source of many good story lines – whether I want them or not. Love ya!

A GLASGOW GLOSSARY

Giving it laldy: Having a great time

Gonny no' dae that: Desist

It wiz dead mocket: It wasn't very enjoyable

Away and bile yer heid: Don't bother me

Send fur the polis: I require a Policeman

He's bothered wi' the duke of argylls: A chap with
haemorrhoids

Gie ye the boke: It's enough to make you sick

Screw the bobbin: Keep Calm

Mair troubles than a doacter's book: A person who is
often ill

A right wee scunner: A somewhat annoying person

Her hoose is always manky: An acquaintance who is
unlikely to win 'Housewife of the year'

Hauled ower the coals: Get into trouble

THE RESIDENTS OF 18 DALBEATTIE STREET IN THE YEAR 1961

'The Top Landing'

Archie CAMERON, age 44.
Ella CAMERON, age 42.
Archie jnr., age 21.
Katherine, age 15.
Archie served in Paras during Second World War. Captured at Arnhem 1944.
Archie is metal turner at Howden's. Ella works at Cakeland as confectioner.

Frank GALLOWAY age 48.
Widower. Tram driver.
Frank served in Royal Navy during Second World War, in minesweepers – North Sea and Atlantic.
Wife, Josie, died 1960.

Agnes DALRYMPLE, age 53.
Shop assistant at the City Bakeries.
Was in the Land Army during the Second World War.

'Two-Up'

Jack MARSHALL, age 53.
Marjorie MARSHALL, age 47.
Jane, age 5.
Jack is storeman at Goldberg's Department Store in Candleriggs.
Marjorie is a clerk/typist in City Chambers.

Ruby BAXTER, age 32.
About to move into close. Going through an acrimonious divorce. Moved from house in Hyndland to Maryhill. No children. Unemployed.

Alec STUART, age 61.
Irene STUART, age 63.
Alec is still Manager at Andrew Cochrane's, Grocer's, on Maryhill Road.

'One-Up'

Dennis O'MALLEY, age 60.
Teresa O'MALLEY, age 58.
Dennis and Teresa are southern Irish. Lived in Glasgow since 1920s.
Dennis is a brickie's labourer. Teresa is a charlady.

'Granny' THOMSON, age 86.
Long a widow. Everybody comes to Granny for advice.
The 'Wise Woman' of the close. She has lived there since 1910.

Robert STEWART, age 33.
Rhea STEWART, age 33.
Sammy Jnr., age 10.
Louise, age 9.
Robert is foreman mechanic at Rossleigh's Garage on Maryhill Road. Rhea still at Macready & Co., Solicitors, in charge of office.

The Close

Bert ARMSTRONG, age 41.
Irma ARMSTRONG, age 34.
Arthur H., age 10.
Bert is from Newcastle. Served in Durham Light Infantry during War.
Irma is German.
Bert is a van driver.

Billy McCLAREN, age 47.
Drena McCLAREN, age 41.
Billy Jnr., age 21. Policeman.
Charles, age 10.
Billy captured at Dunkirk, 1940. POW 5 years.
Billy is a painter and decorator.

Samuel STEWART, age 59.
Mary STEWART, age 61.
Samuel built Spitfires during the war. Now works at Singer's factory.

CHAPTER ONE

A Flitting

A May afternoon in 1961. The blue Pickfords van has barely halted outside the tenement close before three removal men climb down from the cab, make their way to the rear and open the large doors. Seconds later another figure emerges from the vehicle. He stands on the pavement, looking around while smoking a cigarette. Just under six feet tall, he wears the bottle-green uniform and peaked hat of Glasgow's Corporation Tramways. As he takes a last draw he stares again at the close, at the entrance to what is about to be his new home – 18 Dalbeattie Street, Maryhill.

From behind a first-storey window, an old woman looks down through her net curtains. 'Huh! Ah don't think that fella huz his troubles tae seek,' she murmurs. 'He's no' a happy soul, that yin!' Two of the removal men appear from the back of the van carrying tea chests. Their voices drift up . . .

'Huv ye got the key, gaffer? It's the top storey, in't it?'

'Aye, it is. Ah'll away and get something to bring up. Nae good going aw' the way up there empty-handed.' As he makes for the back of the vehicle the two men enter the close. A third Pickfords man climbs down from the rear toting a table lamp and a vase. He follows the others. For a moment, the man in the Tramways uniform is alone in the body of the large vehicle. He glances at his furniture. It just doesn't look right in this unfamiliar setting. His eyes are drawn to a candy-striped mattress. It stands upright, held by a canvas strap. How many nights did Josie and I sleep on that? A wave of sadness floods over him. He stares at the sideboard. He knows if he opens its doors he'll find the wartime Utility Mark stamped inside. Like a birthmark. Standing next to it is a well-worn pine table. How long did that dominate the middle of oor kitchen in Dalmarnock? Twenty-five years? One of the first things we bought. He runs the tips of his fingers along its surface. Can ye call a table a Jack of All Trades? How many meals did the three of us eat sitting round this? Daniel wi' his homework spread over it. Playing table games wi' his pals. Josie's sewing machine sitting on top of it, whirring away. Me using it tae paste wallpaper. He looks round the other objects. These should aw' still be in oor hoose in Allan Street, not piled up in a removal van. And there's aw' the stuff Ah've had tae give away. Ye cannae fit a room and kitchen intae a single-end. He looks at his belongings. And aw' this upheaval caused by a kiss. An innocent kiss. Desolation, like a cloak, drapes itself over him. Oh God! Ah could sit doon on the floor o' this van and fuckin' howl like a bairn for what's been lost. C'mon, gie yerself a shake! It's done – and it'll never be right. Them lads are waiting for ye. He lifts a cardboard box. His eyes take in the kitchen utensils sticking out of it. More memories triggered. With a juddering, tired-to-death sigh, he heads for the close.

He hears the sound of a window being raised. Looks up in time to see a snowy-white head of hair emerging from it. 'Is that you jist movin' in, son?'

He smiles at being called 'son'. At forty-eight, it's a rare event nowadays. 'Aye, Ah'm moving intae the single-end on the top storey.'

'When you've got aw' yer stuff intae the hoose, jist lock the door and come doon for a dish o' tay. Ye can sort yerself oot later. It's the middle door oan the first landing. Thomson's the name.'

'Right. That'll be smashing, Mrs Thomson. Ah should . . .'

'Never mind the "Mrs". It's Granny Ah get called. Fae weans tae auld yins, everybody ca's me Granny.'

'Okay, Granny. It'll no' take long. Mibbe half an hour. Ah've jist got a few sticks o' furniture.'

'Nae matter. The kettle's alwiz on the bile in this hoose.' The head is withdrawn, the window slides shut. His spirits rise slightly. Frank Galloway enters his new close.

Ten minutes later, emerging onto the street to fetch another box, he almost collides with a woman . . . 'Oh! Sorry.'

'Zat you movin' intae wan o' oor empty single-ends? Two-up or three-up?'

He smiles. 'I'm for the top storey.'

'That's good. Ah'm yin o' your neebours up top. Agnes Dalrymple's the name.'

'Oh, pleased tae meet ye. Ah'm Frank Galloway.' He offers his hand.

Agnes blushes, suddenly shy. She's not used to men who offer to shake hands with a woman. She takes the proffered hand, blushing all the more as she does. Frank looks at her;

fairly tall, slim, mid-fifties at a guess. Ah'll lay a pound to a penny she's a spinster.

'Eh, oh, Ah'm pleased tae meet you tae,' she says, then pauses, obviously trying to think of something else to say. It comes to her. She glances upwards. 'Huz Granny gave ye yer official welcome tae the close yet?'

'She has. Ah'm comanded tae come doon for a cup o' tea as soon as the van's unloaded.'

'Aye, naebody gets intae number eighteen without an invite fae Granny.' Agnes pauses, then hastens to add. 'Oh, but mind, she's a good auld sowel. Oh, God, aye. She's the mainstay o' the close so she is. She likes tae get tae know any new tenants. Never fails tae make them welcome oan their first day. Anywye . . .' she fiddles with her shopping bag, 'Ah think you'll find it's a good wee close tae live up. In fact, Dalbeattie Street's no' a bad street. Fairly quiet. Right. Well, Ah'll away. Cheerio the noo.'

'Yeah. Ah've nae doubt we'll see each other quite often. Cheerio.' He watches as Agnes Dalrymple, terminally shy once more, backs up, turns and makes haste up the stairs. He watches her go out of sight. Ah'm almost certain that was sherry Ah smelt on her breath. Jist like ma Auntie Bessie.

Frank approaches the middle door of the three on the landing. F. THOMSON is boldly engraved on the brass combined letterbox and nameplate. The door is open. He gives a gentle knock. Then another; louder. No response. He enters the small lobby. The door into the single room is ajar. He knocks it. When there is still no answer, he pushes it. With only slight protest from its hinges, it swings open to reveal the Glasgow of his childhood. Granny Thomson, surrounded by bric-a-brac from an earlier age, lies fast asleep in a chair by the range. Just above her mantelpiece, on either side of the chimney breast, two gas bracket lamps hiss gently to themselves. A pair of china dogs (wally dugs, his granny would have called them) stand guard. He smiles, Ah could have forecast those. He knocks harder.

'Eh? Who . . . Oh, aye. In ye come,' she clears her throat, 'the kettle's bileing. Have ye got yer stuff moved in?' She gives a little grunt as she eases herself out of the chair, moves stiffly over to the range. 'Whit dae they call ye?'

'The name's Frank Galloway.' At just that moment she has lifted the kettle off the hob, so he doesn't offer his hand.

'Ah'm Isabella Thomson. Sometimes get "Bella" from them that's known me fur years, but maist o' the time it's Granny.'

'Right! Well, Ah'll join the "Granny" brigade.' He pours a spot of milk into his cup. 'How long have ye lived up the close, Granny?'

She brings the teapot over to the table, places it on its stand, stirs it, puts the lid on. 'We'll let that mask a wee minute. Right! Ah moved in here in nineteen-ten. This is 'sixty-wan. Fifty-wan years. Jesus-johnny! It's a lifetime when ye say it like that, in't it?'

Frank nods up towards the gas brackets. 'Have you nae notion tae get the electric put in?'

'It's in!' She points. 'Had it connected a few year ago.' He looks up. Twisted brown flex wriggles down from the ceiling, ends in a schoolroom-type, green plastic shade with a white interior. 'Ah hud tae get it in. Could'nae find anybody tae charge the accumulator for ma auld wireless. So Ah hud nae option. Got the electric put in, then bought a mains radio. Ah could'nae live withoot ma wireless.' Frank laughs.

'Ah never noticed the electric fitting. All Ah could see was the gas burning when Ah came in. Dae ye jist use the electric at night?'

'Ah don't use it at aw' – except fur the wireless. Ah like the gas. Ah'm used tae it. If Ah did'nae need it for the wireless, Ah wid'nae huv bothered gettin' the bugger put in.' She sniffs, adjusts her bosom with a forearm. 'The electric man's alwiz playing hell. The maist Ah've ever burnt in a quarter is one-and-tuppence. That wiz only because the shop ran oot o' gas mantles, so Ah hud tae use the electric till he got them in. Ah don't like it for light. Too bright.'

He smiles, shakes his head. 'Dae ye mind if Ah smoke?' In answer, she slides an ashtray in his direction. Frank produces a twenty-packet of Senior Service from inside his uniform jacket. Extracting one, he holds it loosely between two fingers and thumb while rapidly tamping one end up and down on the side of the pack. The tobacco compressed to his satisfaction, he reaches into a trouser pocket, brings out a Ronson Varaflame lighter. Rich blue smoke twists and curls its way up towards the ceiling. In spite of all the tamping, he still has to pick a loose piece of tobacco from inside his lip.

'When Ah saw ye standing oan the pavement, jist before Ah opened the windae tae speak tae ye, Ah could'nae help but notice, ye did'nae look ower happy.'

He draws deeply on the cigarette. 'Is it *that* obvious?' He dislodges some ash neatly into the ashtray.

'It's mibbe no' obvious tae everybody. But efter eighty-six years o' practice, Ah'm pretty good at reading folk. The way they look, an' move, an' stand. It can tell ye a lot. But maistly it's in their faces – especially when they don't know somebody's watching them.'

Frank takes a sip of tea. 'Ah certainly could'nae argue with ye, Granny. From living a quiet life, which is the way I like it, all of a sudden, well, ma life's been turned upside doon this last twelve months. Last year Ah lost ma wife, Josie. Then earlier this year, March, if ye remember, we had a big fire at Dalmarnock depot. Lost sixty caurs. So Ah've decided tae transfer tae Maryhill depot so Ah can carry on as a tram driver.' He takes a draw on his cigarette, lifts the cup to his lips again.

The old woman has been watching him closely. The aura of sadness around him is tangible. Frank Galloway sighs heavily, takes another deep draw on the cigarette. 'This time last year Ah was the most contented man in Glesga.' The smoke spills upward out of his mouth.

'Aye, it's amazing how oor lives can change fae wan year tae the other. Sometimes fae yin day tae the other. Dae ye have a family?'

He delicately gets rid of the ash again. 'A son, Daniel. He's twenty-four. Married. Him and I hav'nae spoke a word since the day his mother died,' he pauses, 'and for a terrible reason. He believes Ah was responsible for his mother's death. Ah wasn't. It was just a misunderstanding on her part. But there's no way Ah'll ever get him tae believe that. He refuses tae talk tae me.'

Isabella Thomson decides to change the subject. She leans forward, points to the silver and blue enamel badge on the breast pocket of his uniform. 'Ye must have been oan the trams for a while. That's a long-service badge, isn't it?'

'Aye. This is the twenty years award. Ah've been with them for twenty-two up tae now. That was interrupted wi' five years away in the Royal Navy during the war.'

'Are they really daeing away wi' the caurs, next year?' she asks. 'Huz it been decided?'

'Aye. If it runs according tae plan. September 'sixty-two and that'll be it. We're the last city in the land who've still got their tramway system. Nearly everybody else got rid o' them in the fifties. Except for Blackpool, of course. They just keep them as a part of the attractions.'

'So is that why you're flitting intae Dalbeattie Street, 'cause we're handy for Maryhill Depot?'

'Exactly. It's jist a ten-minute walk. But also,' he sighs, 'too many memories in our auld room and kitchen in Dalmarnock. Ah had tae get away from it. This wee single-end up the stairs will dae me fine. Less rent, easy tae keep tidy . . .' He shrugs his shoulders. 'And nae ghosts in every corner. A fresh start and aw' the rest of it. At least, that's supposed tae be the idea.'

'Ah hope it works oot for ye, son. Ah would definitely think getting away from your auld hoose is a good idea. You'd never shake off the past if ye carried on living in it.'

Frank carefully stubs the cigarette-end out in the ashtray. 'Ah think it's a sensible thing tae do. Unfortunately, there's nothin' can be done aboot the trams finishing next year. Ah'm a tram man through and through. Ah'm gonny drive them for as long as Ah can, but eventually Ah'll have tae go ontae the buses. Ah've nae intention of leaving Glasgow Corporation, so Ah'll jist have tae make the best of it. Anyway . . .' He rises to his feet. 'Ah'll away up, Granny. Make a start. Thanks for the tea.'

'Noo listen. Anytime you're feeling browned off, whitever. Jist come doon and knock that door. Don't sit up there on yer own. Dae ye hear? And don't be thinking Ah'm jist a nosy auld wumman who wants tae know yer business. Anything ye tell me, wull'nae go any further.'

'Ah'll probably take ye up oan that. Thanks, Granny. Ah'll say cheerio for the minute.'

Frank Galloway opens his 'new' front door. The stale, unlived-in smell hits him again. He takes two steps in, reaches a hand out, switches the light on. He stands for a minute in the small lobby, looks into the single room. After the comfort, the homeliness of Granny's flat, this suffers cruelly by comparison. The shadeless bulb shines a weak sixty watts down onto his scattered belongings. Table, chairs, carboard boxes and tea chests look as if they don't belong. They don't. The flat has been empty for months since its previous tenant died. You can tell. It feels, looks, abandoned. Unloved. Reluctantly, he steps into the small room. Reaches into his pocket for the twenty-pack. You're smoking far too much, Frank. So what? He sits on a kitchen chair under the stark bulb. Goes into his tamping routine, but less energetically. Flicks the lighter. In the silence, the wheel grinds noisily against the flint then sparks the Varaflame into life. The flowing gas sounds loud. He looks at the beautiful blue-tinged flame for a moment. Lifts his thumb. The cover snaps shut, the living flame gone in an instant. The smoke, grey in the poor light, curls up to caress the bulb. Next month. June the eighth. Josie will be gone a year. A year already. The great weight of loss and loneliness presses down on him once more. Tears brim in his eyes. 'Oh, Josie. Why did ye have to turn up that day? At that minute? And see what wiz'nae there.'

CHAPTER TWO

So What Else Is New?

'Are ye in, Drena?' Ella Cameron doesn't bother knocking her pal's front door. It's half-open anyway.

'Aye. In ye come.' Drena McClaren is peeling potatoes under a stream of cold water from the brass tap. She turns, keeps her dripping hands over the large Belfast sink. 'Zat you just in fae yer work?'

Ella looks heavenward. 'Ye ask me that every night that God sends.'

'Dae Ah?'

'Aye. Dae ye never think o' changing the record?'

Drena deftly winkles an eye out of a potato. 'Okay then. Where huv ye been the day, Ella?'

'Jeez-oh!' Ella shakes her head. 'Ah've been at ma work doon in Cakeland.'

'Aw! That's nice. Is this you jist gettin' in?'

'Up yer pipe!' Ella gives her a two-fingered salute.

*   *   *

'Right! We'll jist leave that fur a wee minute.' Drena puts the lid on the teapot. 'Ah'll jist go next door and see if Irma's got time fur a cup.' She pauses at the kitchen door, turns. 'Before Ah go. Can ye gie's a lend o' thirty bob till Friday, Ella? Ah'm pink lint!'

Her friend sighs. 'You're always skint, you.' She reaches a hand into her Rexine shopping bag; it emerges holding her purse. Drena watches her extract a pound note, then a red ten-shilling one. 'Here y'are. Ah jist hope *ah've* got enough left tae dae me till Friday.'

'Thanks, Ella. You're a pal.' She folds the notes together, slips them into her peenie pocket. 'Right! Ah'll away and gie Irma a shout.' She steps out into the close, chaps the Armstrongs' outside door, opens it. 'Ella and me's gonny huv a cuppa, Irma. Have ye time fur wan?'

'Yah, I'll be right ower the noo.'

Drena comes back into the house. 'Aye. Eva Braun will be ower the noo.' She takes another mug from the press, places it on the table, lifts Ella's lit cigarette from the ashtray and takes an appreciative draw.

Ella sniffs. 'The next time Ah hear ye saying ye don't smoke, Ah'm gonny point oot that ye don't *buy* the buggers. Ye jist smoke your favourite brand: 'OPs' – Other People's!'

'Noo, Ella, remember, whit a friend gets is never missed.' She puts the cigarette back in the ashtray. 'Huv ye seen anything o' the new man that's moved intae Donald's auld hoose?'

While she has the chance, Ella takes a draw from her cigarette. 'Ah've jist seen him in passing. Said "Hello", but that's as far as it's went. He works oan the caurs as ye probably know. Talking aboot hooses, Ah wonder when that auld single-end o' yours, on the second storey, is gonny be let tae somebody.'

'God! Ah know. Billy and me were in it fur years. Yet since we moved doon tae the close, tae get the room and kitchen, naebody seems tae huv stayed up there fur long.'

'You were pregnant wi' Charles when ye flitted doon here, weren't ye?'

'Aye. So that makes it ten years ago since we moved oot. Ah think it's had a new tenant very near every year. It's strange, in't it? Naebody seems tae bide in it fur any length o' time!'

'Though mind,' says Ella, 'some o' them huv hud a good reason. There's been two, mibbe three, who fell aff the perch no' long after they moved in!'

'Ah know. Eeeh! Mibbe it's haunted,' says Drena.

'Yur knickers are haunted! Ye don't believe in aw' that baloney, dae ye?'

'Now ye never know. It could be the ghost o' Donald McNeil.'

'Donald lived in the single-end oan the *tap* storey!' splutters Ella. 'Why the bloody hell wid he come back an' haunt the single-end doon the sterrs? That flat hud nuthin' tae dae wi' him.'

'Aye, but if ye remember, Ella. The last couple o' years of Donald's life, wi' him huvin' the arthritis, he hud an awfy joab gettin' up the last two flights o' stairs. So mibbe he's haunting the single-end doon below 'cause he cannae make it tae the top storey anymair.'

Ella's mouth falls open, she shakes her head. 'Ah'm no kidding. Sometimes Ah worry aboot you. That's yer best wan yet. Whit a load o' keech! An arthritic auld ghost that cannae get up the sterrs tae where it *should* be haunting – so it jist haunts the flat doon below!'

'It's possible. Jist common sense when ye think aboot it.'

'Yur arse in parsley!'

It's a few minutes later. Order has been restored. 'This is Monday, in't it?' enquires Drena.

'Uh-huh. The whole day.'

'Oh, good. This is the night *Rawhide* is oan the telly. Ah jist love that guy who plays the trail boss. Whit's he called, again?'

'Gil Favor,' says Ella.

'Ah'll tell ye whit. If Ah got half a chance Ah would'nae mind daeing *him* a favour. Ah'd huv him intae the back of wan o'them covered wagons as soon as look at him!'

Ella tuts. 'Dirty bizzum so ye are!'

Irma enters. 'Halloooh, girls!' She sits next to Ella. 'Is Drena McClaren being a dirty girl again?'

'You've got it right in wan, Irma. Ye know the trail boss oan *Rawhide*, Gil Favor?'

'Yah.'

'She says she'd let him huv a ride at her, if she got the chance.'

'Jings! Mmm, he is very braw, mind,' agrees Irma.

'*See*! Ah'm no' the only wan,' says Drena. 'Ah'll bet ye Irma wid'nae say naw tae a wee bit of von rumpy-pumpy wi' Gil. Zat right, hen?'

'Och aye, he is very nice. But you know who I fancy the best? My *nummer eins* for a quick jigajig?'

Drena interrupts. 'Whit would that be in German, Irma? A *schnell* jigajig?' As usual when they are together the three of them start to get carried away.

'Ah, but let me tell you who I would fancy the best.' Irma looks around, she has their attention. 'The man in *Sea Hunt*. The blond one. Lloyd Bridges.'

'Och, you jist like him 'cause he's blond, German-looking,' says Ella.

'Aye, but also 'cause he's an aulder man,' suggests Drena. 'Remember, Bert's aulder than her. She likes the mair mature man, that yin. Anywye, whit aboot you, Ella? Who dae you fancy from stage or screen for a quick poke up the nickers?'

By now Ella is filing a jaggy bit on one of her nails. She doesn't look up. 'Errol Flynn,' she says. She manages to keep control of herself.

'An' you're calling *me* a dirty bizzum,' says Drena. 'Eeeh! Yah radgie-arsed bugger!'

Ella nonchalantly continues filing.

Irma looks from one to the other. 'Surely Errol Flynn is okay? He is handsome. Yah?'

'Don't ye know why she's picked him, Irma?'

Ella seems absorbed in her manicure. The side of her mouth twitches imperceptibly.

'No. Why?' asks Irma.

''Cause he's supposed tae huv the biggest tadger in Hollywood!' exclaims Drena.

'The *world*!' mutters Ella. She concentrates hard on her nails.

'Michty me!' says Irma. All three, as usual, become helpless.

Irma is first to recover. 'But how do we know this is really true?'

Ella leans forward, as though to impart a confidence. 'When Archie wiz a POW there wiz an American compound next tae them. Wan o' the Yanks hud been a taxi driver in Hollywood before the war. He said it wiz common knowledge that Errol wiz, as he put it tae Archie, "hung like a donkey"!'

'Crivvens!' says Irma, eyes wide open in wonder. 'Can you imagine such a thing. Hung like *ein Esel*. *Wunderschon!*'

Two heads turn as Drena falls off her chair.

CHAPTER THREE

Happy Families

It's bedtime in Jack and Marjorie Marshall's flat – for five-year-old Jane. 'C'mon, hen, a wee visit tae the toilet then a wash in the sink. It's baw-baw time.'

'Awww, Mammy.'

'Ah! Now never mind "Aw, Mammy." Everybody has to go tae their bed when it's night-time, darling. Take the lavatory key and make a wee visit.'

'Well, you'll have tae watch the door.'

'Mammy always watches the door for you.'

As Jane descends the flight of stairs, Marjorie stands at the flat door, keeps an eye open for any monsters or bogeymen in the vicinity. Jane gets to the half-landing unscathed, then tentatively opens the door to the small water closet. It's unoccupied. Just before she closes and snibs the door, she looks up to check her mother is still on guard.

Five minutes later, the next stage in their nightly ritual begins. The child stands naked in the Belfast sink while

Marjorie sponges her down. 'Oh, you're getting to be such a big girl, Jane. You'll soon be too big for the sink. It'll have to be a tin bath in front of the fire, I'm thinking.' Marjorie turns her head towards Jack, 'Isn't that right, Daddy?'

Jack Marshall looks up from *The Evening Times* for a moment. 'Def-in-ately! And when she steps oot o' the bath every night, Ah'll have tae gie her a rub doon wi' the *Daily Record*!'

The child laughs, 'You're silly, Daddy!'

'Dae ye hear the cheek o' that yin tae her Daddy? Jist you remember, Jane Marshall, you're in your bare nuddy at the minute. It'll be easy for me tae gie ye a scud oan the bum wi' a teaspoon!'

'No you won't,' says Jane, giggling.

'Will Ah no'? We'll see aboot that, ma girl!' Jack makes a great fuss of rustling his newspaper and rising from the chair. 'Where's a teaspoon? Somebody gie me a teaspoon!'

Jane squeals with excitement, 'Quick, Mammy! Quick!' Marjorie lifts her from the sink and stands her on the floor. She manages to wrap her in a towel just as Jack approaches, brandishing a teaspoon. Amid shrieks from his daughter he attempts to lift a corner of the towel to carry out his threat. Marjorie and Jane fight him off until all three are weak with laughter. Then this big man, over six feet in height, eventually has to admit defeat. He trudges back to his chair, returns to his newspaper. Jane puts on her pyjamas and wanders over to the sink. She opens a round, pink tin of Gibb's Dentifrice, wets her child's toothbrush under the flowing cold tap and rubs it on the solid block of toothpaste until it foams. She then proceeds to brush her teeth.

Minutes later she appears at the side of Jack's chair, freshly washed, a few damp blonde curls sticking to her forehead and smelling of soap, toothpaste – and little girl. He looks sternly at her.

'What do *you* want?'

She places both hands on his forearm, 'Story, Daddy.'

'Och! Ah've nae time for stories. Ah've got the paper tae read.'

She stamps her foot, presses down on his large forearm with both hands, 'Daaadyyyyy!'

Jack makes a great show of reluctantly putting the paper down. He suddenly sweeps her off her feet and she lies in his lap, her head on his chest, looking up at him. 'Right then, Daddy's wee scone. Whit's it tae be?'

'*Snow White and the Seven Dwarfs.*'

'Aw! No' again?' He puts on a look of anguish.

'*Yes*, Daddy!'

'Would ye no' like another yin for a change?' Jack winks at Marjorie. She sits in the chair on the other side of the fireplace.

'*Noooo*! Snow White.'

'Aw, man man!' He gives a sigh. 'Okay, then. Anything tae keep the peace.'

As Jack reads the story to his daughter she snuggles into him. Her thumb sneaks into her mouth. 'Aw, look! Wee sooky thumb is back. Can ye believe it? Five years of age. You're too big tae sook yer thumb, Jane Marshall. Big school lassies don't sook their thumbs.'

'Don't care. Story, Daddy.'

Jack resumes the oft-told tale.

Marjorie looks on in pleasure. She loves to see her smaller than average daughter nestling, safe from harm, in Jack's brawny arms. Those same arms which once protected me, she thinks, just eleven short years ago. Married to Richard Sneddon. Knocked about almost every weekend, sexually abused. Then Jack, literally, comes to my rescue. Within weeks of leaving, Richard obligingly comes home drunk one night, falls down the stairs and fractures his skull. Three months later I marry Jack. She looks at him and remembers . . . I didn't think it was possible to be so happy, yet fate held more good fortune. Five years later I'm pregnant. Forty-two years of age! Never even considered it a possibility. Our wee miracle – come December she'll be six.

She looks again at husband and daughter, feels her eyes mist up. Jack has just finished the story. Jane is almost away. Her eyes are closed, but the thumb is being sucked intermittently. He now goes to his emergency plan; starts singing his silly wee song. Two lines, repeated for as long as is needed . . .

'Shoogy, shoogy ower the glen,
'Daddy's pet and Mammy's hen.'

As ever, it has the desired effect. Jack sings softer and softer until, finally, Jane's head lolls against his chest. Out for the count! Some evenings, if Marjorie's had a busy day in the office at the City Chambers, it often claims her too. Such a simple bedtime routine. Yet it never fails to give her pleasure. Makes her count her blessings.

Her man rises effortlessly from his chair, gently carries his daughter through to the room. A couple of minutes later he returns, ducking his head automatically as he comes through the door. He walks to his chair, picks up the paper, sits down again.

'Did she waken up when you put her down, Jack?'

'Naw. Sound as a wee top.' He finds his place, starts reading.

Marjorie sits for a while longer, takes little glances at him now and again. Her man. And through in that room, their daughter lies fast asleep. From being, at one time, the unhappiest lassie up this close, for the last eleven years she's been the exact opposite. She sighs in contentment.

CHAPTER FOUR

Slow to Change

Robert Stewart is preparing veg at the sink when he hears the staccato clip-clop of Rhea's high heels as she enters the close. As both kitchen and outside doors are ajar the sound carries easily up to the first storey. He turns to Sammy and Louise. 'Here's your mammy coming. When you finish that game don't start another one. You can set the table ready for dinner. Okay, pals?'

'Okay, Daddy,' says nine-year-old Louise. 'Ah was'nae gonny play another one anyway, 'cause he's a big cheat so he is.'

'Ah'm not!' says ten-year-old Sammy.

'Are SOT!' accuses his sister. 'He always cheats at Monopoly, Daddy. He threw a nine and should have landed oan my hotel, but he went an' jumped ower it intae Community Chest.'

Robert tries not to laugh. 'Listen, you two should think yourself lucky you've got somebody tae play wi' on rainy days. Ah was an only child, so Ah had tae just amuse myself on days like . . .' His attempts at diplomacy are interrupted, as Rhea bustles into the kitchen. 'Mammy's hame!'

'Hiyah, Mammy!'

'Hello, hen.' As happens every evening without fail, Robert Stewart's heart lifts when his wife walks through the door. He watches her place her bag on the chair by the sideboard, take her coat off, step back into the lobby to hang it up. She re-enters the kitchen. 'You're a wee bit later the night, aren't ye?'

Rhea gives both kids a kiss on top of their heads, then gives her man a kiss on the lips which approaches lingering. 'A caur came aff the rails at St George's Cross, so we aw' hud tae get aff. Then aw' the men passengers helped the driver and conductor shove it back oan again. Whit a carry-oan.' She stands for a moment, lost in thought. 'Well, it wiz a laugh, really.' She turns to the kids. 'Whose turn wiz it tae watch ye last time Mammy and Daddy had a night oot, Granny O'Malley or Granny Stewart?'

'Granny O'Malley.'

Rhea turns to Robert. 'Ruth gave me a ring at the office this morning. George and her would like us to come tae the club oan Saturday night. Roon' aboot seven. Have a meal wi' them first. Oh! And Ah'll tell ye whit else. When Ah wiz coming hame oan the caur, as usual Ah wiz reading people's newpapers ower their shooder. There wiz a man in front o' me wi' the *Citizen*, and there wiz a bit oan the front page,' she sighs, 'Gary Cooper huz died!'

'Aw! He has'nae.'

'He huz!'

Robert stops slicing carrots for a moment. 'Aww! Hey, I really, really liked Gary Cooper.'

'Me tae. Remember when we went tae see *High Noon*?' Robert is about to reply, but doesn't get the chance. Rhea continues, a faraway look in her eyes. 'Mind yon Sundays when the Blythswood used tae show auld films and you took me tae see *For Whom the Bell Tolls*, wi' him and Ingrid Bergman?' As Robert looks at her he sees her eyes fill with tears.

'Remember it?' he says. 'Ah'll never forget it.' He laughs.

'Shut up, you!' She slaps his arm.

'Whit happened, Mammy?' asks Sammy.

'Gary Cooper and Ingrid Bergman faw in love and there's a war oan somewhere and he gets wounded.' She turns to Robert, 'Remember her hair? It wiz short and curly and *blonde*. It did'nae half suit her. Ah wonder why she never had her hair like that in any other pictures?'

'Get oan wi' the story, Mammy,' demands Sammy.

'Anywye. Gary cannae go any further 'cause he's wounded too badly. So he tells them tae leave him wi' a machine gun and some watter and he'll haud the enemy back at this wee bridge so's the rest of them can get away.' She pauses, 'Ah think he hud a few hand grenades, tae. But oh! Ye should see the state Ingrid's in. She's no' wantin' tae leave him. They huv an awfy joab dragging her away, she's greetin' and sobbing and at the finish-up they actually huv tae tie her ontae a hoarse. And as they're riding away she's screaming Gary's name an' trying tae throw herself aff the hoarse. Heart-rending, so it wiz.' She reaches for the tea towel hanging on a nail by the sink, dabs her eyes. The sound of laughter brings her back to reality. Robert is leaning on the coal bunker, choking. Young Sammy is also in kinks. But Louise wipes away tears. Rhea rounds on husband and son.

'You've nae heart, you two. Haven't they no', hen?'

'Ah! But your mammy has'nae told you the *full* story,' says Robert.

'Never mind the full story!' Rhea tries to put a hand over Robert's mouth. A wrestling match ensues which ends when Robert enfolds his wife in a bear hug and manages to finish his tale . . .

'Your mammy was in such a state at the end o' the fillum, that efter everybody had gone hame she was still sitting in her seat, wi' two usherettes trying tae get her tae stop greeti—'

'Ah wiz'nae!'

'And at the finish-up, the manager had tae invite her intae his office for a cup o' tea before she pulled herself thegither, and Ah could take her hame.'

'It wiz a really sad fillum,' says Rhea. She sighs. 'Poor Gary. Ah'm no' half gonny miss him.'

Robert Stewart drives along Woodlands Road, then spots a space barely fifty yards from Le Bar Rendezvous. He drives the one-and-a-half-litre Riley into it, switches the engine off. Rhea and he climb out, lock the saloon car then walk along the pavement, looking up, as if drawn by the glow of red neon above the entrance. Rhea tingles with anticipation. She knows she's in for a lovely evening. She takes Robert's arm. 'When ye think of it, it's nice that after aw' these years, George and Ruth still like tae see us two.'

'Well, whit it is,' Robert tries to keep his face straight, 'they've got that many posh customers, it helps to keep their feet on the ground tae have somebody common, like yerself, stoating in and oot noo and again.'

'Ah'll "common" ye, Robert Stewart! Wait till Ah get ye hame the night.'

'Yes, beloved.' Robert opens one side of the Art Deco double doors and they step into the small vestibule. He pushes a matching inner door and the familiar brasserie cum nightclub is revealed. Rhea's glance takes in the blue plush banquettes – recently changed from red – the bijou dance floor and bandstand, the subdued wall lights shining upwards from the shelves behind the bar. She loves it all. As is to be expected, at just turned seven p.m. there are less than ten folk in.

Ruth already sits on her high stool at the far end of the bar. Her trademark tortoise-shell cigarette holder lies in an ashtray. The lit Black Sobranie fixed into it surrounds her with its pungent, exotic aroma. Her face lights up. 'Robert! Rhea! I'm *so* glad you've got here early. We can enjoy a bite and a good blether before we get busy.' Robert kisses her on both cheeks. While she and Rhea talk, he takes the opportunity to look at her. She may be in her late forties, but Ruth Lockerbie can still only be described as 'a stunner'. As she asks Rhea how the children are and they exchange small talk, Robert continues to stare unashamedly at her. She becomes aware of it, turns in his direction, a smile on her face. 'You're staring at me again, Robert Stewart!'

'Aw, he's crazy aboot you, Ruth,' says Rhea. 'Huz been since the first day he met ye. He's alwiz saying you should huv been a film star.' She turns to Robert. 'Dain't ye?'

He laughs. Blushes. 'I was just looking at you while you were talking to Rhea. I think I've finally managed to put it into words, Ruth. You are the female equivalent of Cary Grant. The *older* you get – the better-looking you become. Seriously!'

Ruth gives out with her wonderful, throaty laugh. 'What a lovely compliment.' She turns to Rhea. 'I'm glad you don't get annoyed at your man saying such things about another woman.'

'Oh, Ah agree wi' him! First time Ah seen you – when ye were at the Bar Deco oan the Byres Road – Ah said tae Robert, "She should be a fillum star, that yin." And Ah'll tell ye whit else Ah said, Ruth. Ah told him that you fancied George.' She breaks off for a moment, pokes Robert on the chest with a forefinger. 'And he would'nae believe me. But Ah was right. Ah could tell by the way ye looked at him when he spoke to ye. And Ah'll tell ye something else. Back then, George wiz totally unaware of how you felt aboot him.'

'Hah! You are *so* right,' says Ruth. 'Do you know, *I* had to finish up telling *him* that I had feelings for him. Can you believe it?'

Rhea holds herself upright. Bristles. 'Of course Ah believe it. He's a man. They're aw' numpty-heided buggers! Cannae see whit's in front o' them.'

Robert and Ruth go into a fit of laughter at the vehemence of Rhea's dissertation on the shortcomings of men – and are eventually joined by Rhea herself. George Lockerbie walks over to join them, a smile on his face. 'You're all having a great time. What's the joke?' He's nonplussed as three fingers point at him and Ruth manages to say, '*You!*'

Robert looks at his watch. Just gone eleven o'clock. The place is jumping. As usual Rhea has had him up on the dance floor for most of the evening. He looks around. Good music from the little combo up on stage, the small dance floor crowded, coloured lights trying hard to penetrate the cigarette smoke. No wonder George and Ruth only open Thursday, Friday and Saturday nights. They'll easily take enough on those three evenings to give them a good living. Three nights on, four off. Nice work if you can get it! His musings are interrupted when Ruth raises a hand in the air, waves with her fingers. There's Johnny McKinnon and Veronica just come in.'

The burly figure of Johnny approaches. 'Hello, friends! How are you all?' Ruth and Rhea are hugged and kissed to within an inch of their lives. Veronica is dealt with likewise by George and Robert. The men shake hands warmly. Johnny turns to Robert.

'There's a Riley parked a few yards along the road. Is that the one you were telling me about?'

'Yeah. That's it. My new pride and joy.'

'I had a look at it as best I could under the streetlights. It does seem to be in great shape.'

'Yeah, as I was telling you last time, Johnny, this old guy traded it in at the garage. It's a '46 model. Fifteen years old and only got twenty-three thousand on the clock. Been garaged all its life. Soon as I seen it, I thought, "I'm having that!" That's the best about being foreman. I have first refusal.'

Rhea chimes in. 'Oh, Ah jist love it as well, Johnny. Ye can keep yer Ford Zodiacs and Vauxhall Crestas. When Robert brought it hame and Ah climbed intae it for the first time . . . OH! The smell of that leather upholstery. And the lovely, walnut dashboard. Thank goodness Robert's a mechanic. He should be able tae keep it running fur years.'

Johnny smiles. 'I don't suppose it'll happen, but if ye ever get another one, or something similar, I'd definitely be in the market for it.' His eyes take on a dreamy look. 'I'll tell you what I'd *really* be up for, Robert, a pre-war Jaguar SS.'

'Ah, but the trouble is, Johnny, that makes two of us!'

*　　*　　*

Rhea looks at her watch. Twenty past one. She loves it when George and Ruth suggest everybody comes back to their flat in Hillhead. And all the better when Johnny McKinnon and Veronica Shaw are in the company. Not that Rhea contributes much to the conversation. The topics are usually way over her head. But Robert enjoys it and always seems able to hold his own, no matter what's being discussed. She looks at him. Glass of beer in hand, he's involved in a three-way conversation with George and Johnny. Ruth and Veronica are in the kitchen rustling up some sandwiches. An LP plays on the radiogram. Al Bowlly. It's at low volume so as not to intrude. He's singing, 'Love is the Sweetest Thing'. It is *so* thirties. Rhea looks slowly round the Art Deco flat. Recalls Ruth telling her of how she'd bought all the fixtures and fittings from the lady who'd previously owned it. Ruth was living here before George came on the scene. A 1930s flat in 1960s Glasgow. And they've no intention of altering a thing. Ah don't blame them. Rhea's eyes take in the furniture, fittings, carpets. Al Bowlly has seamlessly moved on to 'Have You Ever Been Lonely?' This is a time machine so it is. Ah feel as if Ah'm sitting here and it's . . . what? Choose a year. Okay, 1936. Every time Robert and I are doon the toon, if he sees a shop front or a building that's Art Deco, he always points it oot tae me. He loves it, tae. Ah'll bet Robert would move intae an Art Deco flat in a minute if he . . .

'Sandwich, Rhea?' Ruth has appeared at her side.

'Oh, aye. Yes, please.'

'Would you like tea or coffee?'

'Coffee would be lovely, Ruth. You always have real coffee up here. Even the smell of it is gorgeous.' Rhea sits up straighter on the sofa. 'Ah've been listening tae the music and looking roon' your flat. It happens every time. Efter a few minutes Ah could swear blind Ah've floated back tae 1936!'

Ruth laughs. 'It has that effect on me on a regular basis. That's the whole idea of it. Transport folk back in time. I'll go and fetch your coffee. One sugar, if I remember correctly.'

'Yes, please.'

Veronica crosses the room to sit beside Rhea. 'I was just watching you. I think you're like me, Rhea. I never, *ever* tire of being up here.'

'Ah'll tell ye, Ah could move in here the 'morra, Veronica. And it really suits Ruth, doesn't it? Her style, her personality – and this flat. They jist aw' go thegither.'

'They certainly do. What about you and Robert? You still live in the same close you were brought up in, don't you? Don't you fancy moving to a nice, red sandstone flat like this?'

Rhea takes a sip of coffee. 'Ah think we'd like tae. We've got oor room and kitchen nice, mind you. But the trouble is, we live up the same close as both oor parents. In lots of ways it's so handy. We're in and oot each others hooses aw' the time. When the weans come hame fae school, they go tae one or other of their grandparents till Robert and me comes in fae work. And also, just like tonight, we've got ready-made babysitters.'

'Yes. I can see why that's a big plus. But I'd really miss not having a bathroom. And I'd hate having to share a lavatory on the landing with another two famiies. I really would.'

'It's no' that we cannae afford tae move. Robert's foreman at Rossleigh's on the Maryhill Road and Ah'm in charge o' the office at Macready's the solicitors. Ah've been there since Ah left the school. But baith oor parents would be huffed if we moved oot the close. They really would. Though mind, Veronica,' she raises the coffee cup to her lips, 'there's wan good thing tae be said aboot sharing a lavvy oan the landing. In the winter – the seat's alwiz warm.'

CHAPTER FIVE

Boring? We Love Boring!

As Irene Stuart busies herself round the kitchen, the wooden-cased radio on the sideboard plays softly. It's always tuned to the Light Programme. The window nearest to the sink is raised a few inches. Now and then shouts or laughter drift up from weans playing in the back courts. She likes the window open. 'Mmmm.' Twenty-five past five. Alec should be turning the sign on the shop door round to 'Closed' any minute. Better get the tatties on. She lights a gas ring, slides a pan of already peeled potatoes on to it. The opening bars of 'Stranger on the Shore' float out from the radio. 'Oh! Ah like this.' She reaches a hand out, turns the volume up. The evocative sound of Acker Bilk's clarinet floats out of the second-storey tenement window, drifts into the back courts and surfs over middens, wash houses and weans playing shops and sodjers. Somehow, it doesn't seem out of place.

The potatoes are simmering gently when she hears his footsteps on the stairs. They halt. The brass door handle chinks as it's turned. This is followed by the sound of his feet on the lino as he steps into the lobby; these are then muffled as he walks onto the carpet runner. Alec Stuart pushes the kitchen door open as he closes the outside one. 'Hello, sweet-heart!' He still hasn't appeared yet.

'Hello, darling! How were things at the shop today?'

'Fine, fine. The usual Friday.' She listens to the rest of the familiar noises as he goes through his six-days-a-week routine. Jacket and boots are taken off. Slippers put on. He enters the kitchen carrying his piece tin, walks over to her for a kiss. 'Anything out of the ordinary for you, Irene?'

'Well.' Even though both doors are closed and there are only the two of them in the house, she lowers her voice. Alec tries not to smile as she goes into her 'for your ears only' ritual. 'Agnes fae upstairs gave me a wee knock at quarter past five. She was jist hame fae her work. Oh, Alec, ye could smell the drink on her breath. In fact, ye could hear the sound of two or three bottles clinkin' the gither in her bag. That'll be her getting her stock in for the weekend. The soul handed me in a Swiss roll and a couple o' fern cakes.'

Alec grimaces. 'Poor lassie. It's livin' on her own that's doing it. She's going melancholy so she is. How old is she, anyway?'

'She's early fifties. Och, she misses Donald McNeil, you know. Even though he was twenty-odd years older than her they were good neighbours, company for yin another. After Donald died she was aw'right when she used tae huv a night oot wi' me and oor Mary.' She looks Alec in the eyes. 'Then you spoiled it when ye came oan the scene and snapped me up. Mary's sort of dropped off seeing her, too. Poor Agnes. She huz'nae got anybody nooadays. Goes doon tae Granny's for a wee blether. That's about it. Ah'm worried aboot her losing her job at the City Bakeries because of the drink.'

'Hah! Came oan the scene and snapped you up, is it? Rescued ye from the shelf more like!'

'Oh! You beast, Alec Stuart.' Irene lifts the fish slice and chases him round the table a couple of times. He grapples with her, then kisses her. Looks into her face. 'The best thing that ever happened tae you, Irene Pentland, was the day you walked intae Andrew Cochrane's and saw me behind the counter. By good luck for you I took a bit of a fancy to ye. Began to pay ye a bit of attention – and in due course, allowed ye to become Irene *Stuart*! I think that's a more accurate description of what went on, is it no'?'

Irene looks heavenward, shakes her head. 'Talk aboot "Ah love me, who dae you love?" Ah could give ye a different version. But tae save the tatties being overcooked and your fish sticking tae the frying pan, Ah'll just say, yes darling, that's pretty much how it happened.' Alec lets her go. As she walks towards the cooker she says, in a stage whisper, 'Ah *don't* think!' then skips away from him, giggling like a schoolgirl.

Alec places his knife and fork neatly on his cleared plate. 'You can't beat a piece o' fried haddock in breadcrumbs with boiled tatties. So. What's on telly the night, hen? It's usually good on a Friday.'

'Ah had a look in the paper. Half-eight is *Take Your Pick*, then *No Hiding Place* at nine thirty-five.' She begins to clear the table; looks everywhere but at Alec.

'Aye? And what comes in between them two? Could it be *Bootsie and Snudge* maybe?'

Irene tuts, casts her eyes ceilingwards. 'You and that *Bootsie and Snudge*. Oh! Ah've just remembered. There was a postcard this morning from Mary. Will it be aw'right for her and James tae come over on Sunday?'

Alec gives a broad smile. 'Ye know it will. Ah enjoy your James's company. And Mary's a smasher . . .'

'Another glass of beer, James?'

'Hi doan mind if Hi do!' says James. Both men laugh.

'Aye, Colonel Chinstrap, eh?' says Alec. 'Those were the days. *ITMA*. Tommy Handley.'

Irene winks at Mary. 'Awww, is that who ye were doing, Colonel Chinstrap? Ah thought it wiz Snudge oot o' *Bootsie and Snudge*. You make them sound the same.' She and Mary avoid looking at one another. Irene lifts her brother's glass and expertly pours some more pale ale into it – just as she used to during all the years she kept house for him, spinster sister looking after bachelor brother.

'There's still some left in the bottle, Mary. Will Ah do you and me another wee shandy?'

'Go on then. Though mind, this is our third.' The two women giggle.

Alec looks at his brother-in-law. 'Ah think that was the first giggle o' the night.'

The normally serious James Pentland regards his wife and sister, then turns to Alec. 'Mmm. As Bette Davis said in yon picture, "Fasten your seat belts. It's gonny be a bumpy ride!"'

'Jeez-oh!' Irene shakes her head, 'Daeing impressions a few meenits ago – noo he's quoting bits oot o' fillums. Ah'll tell ye whit, Mary. Ten years o' being married tae you huz brought this man oot o' his shell. At one time, his sole interest in life was jist tae be timekeeper at NB Loco.'

Mary looks at her husband. 'Aye. He's a ball o' fire nooadays!' The women are convulsed. The men feign indifference. Alec puts his glass down. 'Ah'll tell ye what, James. There's no' half been a lot happened since we last saw you. You've got tae hand it tae the Russians, puttin' that Gagarin fella in space. Did'nae half steal a march on the Americans, eh?'

'Didn't they just. The Yanks wouldn't be ower pleased. It'll spur them on, mind. They'll no' sit still for the Russians taking over in space.'

'Definitely. But even so, James. That's now *two* historic "firsts" the Russians have got tae their name.' He counts them off on his fingers. 'The first satellite in space, wi' yon Sputnik – and now the first man. That must really rankle wi' the Yanks.'

'Ah'll bet it does. Ah wonder whit the Americans will do tae try and catch up? They'll put hundreds o' millions o' dollars intae it, whitever it is.' The two men sit silent for a moment, lost in thought. Irene and Mary look at both of them, then avoid each other's newly twinkling eyes.

'Ah was reading in a magazine,' says Alec, 'that the Americans will probably attempt tae put up the first permanent space station. Then efter that, they'll send a man tae the Moon.'

James laughs. 'Ah don't think so, Alec. No. It'll be thirty, maybe even forty years, afore that's possible. Be about the end of the century. Minimum!'

Irene nudges Mary's foot under the table, but doesn't look at her. 'Whit aboot us? Britain? We could mibbe attempt tae put the first, ohhh, the first tram intae space!'

Mary lets out a squeak, but recovers well. 'Oh! That's a good idea, Irene. But whit number would it be? Trams alwiz have tae have route numbers.'

The two men glance at one another. Shake their heads. 'Pay nae heed tae them,' says Alec.

'It would huv tae be a number twenty-three. That route used tae run oot tae Airdrie, if ye mind. It was the longest tram ride in the city. Then last year they withdrew the twenty-three all together. So it wid be nice tae bring it back. Mind ye, Ah think the Moon's a bit further oan than Airdrie.'

Mary attempts to answer but can't get it out. The two women become helpless, made worse every time they look at their men's faces.

'It's impossible tae have a serious conversation in this hoose when these two get the gither.'

'You're right there, Alec. We are now entering whit's called "daft time".'

'Ah'll tell ye something else,' says Mary, 'the Americans are gonny have a job finding an astronaut as good-looking as yon Gagarin fella. He was a bonny wee lad so he—'

Irene interrupts. 'Oh, isn't he jist, Mary. He's got a lovely, smiley face so he huz.'

'Ah know. Ah wid'nae mind daeing a few orbits wi' Yuri.' The two of them go into fits again.

James pulls a face, shakes his head. 'There'll be no more serious conversation the night, Alec. We've got two choices. We either sit here listening to these two trying to see who can be the silliest – or else it's hame time.' He winks.

Irene coughs. Attempts to control herself. She doesn't look at her sister-in-law. 'Okay. We'll behave oorselves. Win't we, Mary?'

'Nae chance!' She tries to say something else, but grows weak again. She shakes her head. Both women sit, silently quivering, frightened to look at one another. Mary eventually points at Irene. 'Ohhhh! Ah cannae help it, James. It's your sister. She's a bad influence oan . . .'

James looks at his gold Waltham pocket watch. 'Anyway, it's five to ten. We'll get no more sense oot o' these two the night.' Both men regard their red-faced, wet-eyed wives. 'It's like being married tae a couple o' Chivers Jellies, in't it?'

'It wiz the third shandy done it,' says Alec, 'tipped them ower the edge.'

'Say goodnight, Mary,' says James.

'Goodnight, Mary,' says Mary. 'Oooooh!' She holds her side. 'Ah'm in pain so Ah am.'

CHAPTER SIX

New Places, New Faces

I t's a bright morning with a cool breeze as Frank Galloway
strides up the Maryhill Road. As he nears the end of his
short journey he looks at his watch. Just eight minutes from
Dalbeattie Street to the Depot. Good. He turns left into Celtic
Street, then stops. Aye, Ah think they might be right when
they say this is the shortest street in the city. Celtic Street is
formed by the gable-ends of two tenement blocks which are
part of Maryhill Road. Facing him, maybe twenty yards away,
a tram emerges from the large doorway of the depot.

He takes a few steps into his new workplace, stops for a
moment to take in the vast shed. Facing him are the various
bays. A few are empty, but most have one or more trams in
them. New ones, old ones, 'works' cars used by the repair squads,
a tower wagon for reaching up to the overhead lines. There are
quite a few ex-liverpool trams, of the type known as Streamliners
– though not by Glaswegians. On arrival in the city a few years
ago they had been pressed into service at once, still sporting
the green paintwork of their city of origin. Glasgow folk had

immediately christened them Green Goddesses. Designed in the same Art Deco style as the Corporation's own Coronations and Cunarders, they'd been bought from Liverpool when it began to run down its tram system in the late fifties. Though the Streamliners now sport the green, cream and orange livery of the rest of the fleet, it makes no difference to the citizens of Glasgow. They continue to call them Green Goddesses.

Frank breathes in. 'Ahhh!' God, I love it. The smell . . . no, the *aroma* of a tram depot. Oil, grease and . . . what? There's the smell of hot electric motors. Another ingredient is when the bow collector on top of a tram 'shorts' on the overhead wires. Large sparks shower down like golden hail, bounce along the ground, then lie glowing for seconds until, reluctantly, the life goes out of them. They leave behind a scorched metallic smell. Boilersuited engineers busy themselves servicing motors and four-wheeled bogies, a welder's torch twinkles, green uniformed drivers and conductresses exchange banter as they pass one another going to or coming from their trams, the canteen, the office, the cashier . . . Frank feels a pang of sadness. And dread. How can they throw all this away next year? Since the days of Queen Victoria the trams have been a major part of the city's life. Glasgow *is* its trams. He sighs. It won't be long until this will be a bus depot. Full of the poisonous stink of exhaust fumes. Pure carbon monoxide. The corporation and its transport department are committed to it. Trams are old-fashioned so they . . .

'Hello, Frank!'

He turns. 'Eric! Ah knew Ah'd be bumping into you sooner or later. How are you?'

'Fine. So Ah take it that, jist like maself, you're determined tae drive a tram up tae the last possible minute?'

'Oh, God, aye. Postpone the evil day for as long as possible, Eric. They'll have taken the last tram tae the breaker's yard before Ah give up. In fact – Ah want tae drive it there!'

'Huv ye reported in yet?'

'No. Where is the manager's office?'

Eric points. 'Jist ower there.'

'Right. Ah'd better away over and show face. Ah'll see ye later.'

As Eric Hutchman watches him head for the office, he wonders if he should have asked him how things are since he lost Josie. No. Might be best tae let Frank bring the subject up. It'll still be a bit raw. It's just aboot a year Ah think.

'Come in, come in.' James Forsyth, the depot manager, half rises from his desk to offer his hand. 'Sit yourself down, Frank. I hope you're going tae be happy with us.'

'Well, I'm sure I will be, Mister Forsyth. Until the change-over tae buses comes along.'

'Oh, aye. I'm with you there. I'm a tram man, myself. It'll be a sad, sad day when they go. Not a thing we can dae about it. The powers that be have made their minds up.'

They talk for a few more minutes, mostly about friends or workmates they've known in common, then, 'I'll just give a wee ring tae the duty inspector. Get him to bring along the conductress we've teamed you up with. She's waiting in the Staff Room. I think you'll find she's a nice wee lassie.' Frank watches and listens as he makes the brief call. Minutes later the office door is knocked. 'Aye, just come in.'

Frank stands up as the two enter. He looks at the girl. Well, not exactly a girl, probably in her thirties. She appears a confident young woman. He notices she's wearing a five years service badge. The manager does the introductions. 'This is

Wilma Ballantyne. Wilma, this is your driver, Frank Galloway. Frank's come tae us from Dalmarnock. And this is Inspector Joss.'

Frank offers his hand to both, 'Ah'm very pleased tae meet you, Wilma. Ah hope we're going to work well together.' He's pleased to feel a firm handshake.

'Aye, me too.' He's also glad to see she hasn't blushed. Good for her.

'Right,' says Mister Forsyth. 'We've got a car allocated to you. Inspector Joss will take you to it. Once again, welcome tae Maryhill, Frank.'

'Thank you very much, Mister Forsyth.' They leave the manager's office. Outside, Frank pauses. 'Now, as all wise tram staff should do before starting their shift, Ah'm just gonny pay a wee visit.'

'Aye, Ah suppose Ah'd better dae the same,' says Wilma.

'Whit? Visit the gents?'

'No' until Ah know ye better.'

Frank looks at Inspector Joss. 'Ah'm glad tae see this depot is up tae scratch with the standard of repartee expected from its clippies.'

'Oh, aye. We've got more than oor fair share o' feisty lassies at Celtic Street right enough,' replies the Inspector. It's said with a smile.

The trio head over towards the bays. Wilma carries the green tin box containing her T.I.M. ticket machine and spare paper rolls. A leather cash bag is slung round her shoulders, the float chinks as she walks along. The Inspector stops, points. 'That's yours, ten-twenty-four. As you'll know, we have quite a few ex-Liverpool Streamliners at Maryhill.' He looks sad.

'She's on the twenty-nine service of course. That's the only route we have now. The rest have gone.' He manages a smile. 'Enjoy yourselves.'

As they head towards 'their' tram, Frank takes a glance at Wilma now and again, trying to weigh her up. In the office he'd liked her on first sight. Now, as they make casual conversation, he continues to study her. Maybe five feet four inches tall. Brown hair. He notices lighter, fairer streaks here and there. Certainly not a plain Jane, but not a raving beauty either. He hides a smile. You're no' exactly an oil painting yourself, Frank. I bet if she was made-up and dressed for a night oot she'd look quite, well, attractive. It's hard to weigh-up clippies. The uniform tends towards the masculine; the hat doesn't do them any favours. And if they don't bother with make-up at work, a guy could be forgiven for no' giving them a second glance. He recalls the number of times he's been caught out over the years. Some lassie or other at Dalmarnock – whom he thought he knew quite well, seen her round the place all the time. Then, one day she comes clip-clopping into the depot on high heels to pick up her wages. All made-up, hair done, smartly dressed. Just as he's walking past a familiar voice has said, 'Are ye no' speaking the day, Frank?' The times he has, literally, done a double-take. 'Jeez-oh! Ah never recognised ye!' Aye. Be nice if fellas could improve themselves to that extent.

It's nearing the end of their shift. The ex-Liverpool tram stands isolated, all lights blazing, at the end of the line – Maryhill terminus. Time for a blaw. A break. Frank sits on a bench seat at what will be the rear of the saloon for the return trip back to the city. Wilma sits opposite. He takes out the twenty-pack of Senior Service, flips the end open, offers it to her. 'Do ye smoke?'

'No. Ah tried them in ma teens; Ah could'nae get away wi' them.'

'Think yerself lucky.' The gas lighter ignites, the blue flame dancing for a second. 'So where dae ye live, Wilma?'

'Ower in Possilpark. Crombie Street.'

'Oh, Apache territory!'

'Cheeky bugger!' She laughs.

'Are ye daeing a bit o' courting?'

'Naw. Still on the shelf.' He detects a slight blush as she says it. 'Ah live wi' ma mother. She diz'nae keep too well. Ah'm, sort of, her support. Though sometimes Ah think it's me that could dae wi' the support. Ah'm afraid it's jist work and hame, work and hame. Aw' ma pals have long since stopped asking me tae come on nights oot.'

He takes a draw on the cigarette. 'Oh, that's a shame. You're still a young lassie. Ye know whit they say aboot all work and no play.'

She sighs. 'Aye, Ah'm beginning tae know *exactly* whit that means. Life's jist passing me by. Ah turned thirty-four a few weeks ago. Ah've nae social life at aw'. The only laughs Ah get nooadays are when Ah'm at work. There's not many tae be had at hame. Anywye, what aboot you, Frank? You'll be married?'

He picks a shred of tobacco from his lip. 'Ah was. Lost ma wife last year in a road accident. She got knocked down . . .'

'Oh, how awful! That must have been terrible for ye. Do ye have a family?'

'Ah've got a son, Daniel. But he's married and away fae hame. Ah'll tell ye all aboot it sometime. It's no' as straightforward as you'd think.' He looks down the line. 'Here's another caur coming. Time we were away.' He rises to his feet, makes his way along the saloon towards what is now the front of the tram, for the return trip. Just before he slides open the door to the driver's compartment, he turns. 'Did you swing the bow collector over the other way when we stopped, Wilma?'

'Aye. Did it the same time as Ah wiz changing the destination blind.'

'You're on the ball, kid.' He takes a last draw of his cigarette, flicks the stub out of the open door, watches it land on the cobbled setts midst a shower of sparks. Wilma makes her way to the rear of the car, steps down onto the platform, leans back into the little alcove formed by the curve of the stairs above her head. She stares out of the open door into the dark, deserted road. Mmmm, he seems quite a nice fella. Seconds later the tram hums into life. Up front, Frank moves a lever, the doors rattle shut in front of her eyes. He bangs his heel twice on one of the metal studs set into the floor, the warning bell dings to no one in particular. Then he swings the solid bronze lever in front of him. With barely a tremor the Art Deco tram glides off. Wilma seems a nice wee lassie. Her and I will get on fine. Just like Rosemary and me at Dalmarnock. Well. Like Ah've always done wi' my conductresses. Treat them aw' as equals. He accelerates along the deserted road into the falling dusk, leaving the empty terminus and glowing cigarette end to the oncoming tram.

CHAPTER SEVEN

The Newcomer

It is a fine July day in 1961 when Ruby Baxter moves into the close. The hours preceding her arrival, as far as Granny Thomson is concerned, are just like any other morning. No premonitions, no portents – except that it's going to be a scorcher. The sun is blazing through her net curtains and falling on the *Daily Record* spread out on the table. She sits back in the kitchen chair, looks around her room. The single-end is filled with light and warmth. Dust motes float between her and the windows. Ah *love* mornings like this. 'Ah'm no' gonny light the fire the day. Ah'd be melted. Jist boil a kettle on the gas when Ah need it. Ah think Ah'll get a bit o' that sun oan ma face.' As she's alone in her single-end, this has been said out loud to no one in particular. At eighty-six years of age she does this often nowadays. She refutes the idea that she is 'talking tae herself'. Not a bit of it. Jist thinking aloud. 'Right! Cushion, pillow – and chair.' She raises one of the two windows, slides the chair over beside it. The pillow is placed on it to act as a cushion. The actual cushion is laid on the window ledge. She leans forward onto her folded arms. 'Ahhh!' Turns her face up to the sun. 'Oh, that's braw.' It's barely a minute later when the back of her neck begins to ache. 'Ach!' She opens her eyes, looks left, then right, along Dalbeattie Street. No' many folk aboot. Ah've seen the day there would be wee groups o' weemin sitting ootside their closes oan kitchen chairs. Taking the sun an' huvin' a rerr laugh. She gives a sad smile. Nearly aw' at work nooadays, the young hoosewives. She looks straight down at the pavement. Thinks back. Ten, maybe fifteen years ago, there would huv been five or six of us sitting doon there oan a row o' kitchen chairs. Legs stretched oot, heids leaning back against the wa' . . . Ella, Drena, Irma, Teresa O'Malley, Irene Pentland. Well, Irene Stuart she is noo. She can almost see them. Hear them. Laughing and cackling and hee-hawing. Eh, God! We hud'nae twa pennies tae rub thegither, but whit laughs we used tae huv. The memories are so clear. In her mind's eye she can see the tops of their heads all in a row. It's funny. We're mibbe better aff, but we don't laugh as much as we used tae. Ah wonder why? Well, at least they're aw' still ma neebours. Nane o' them has died oan me.

As she dozes in the hot sun, this train of thought stays with her. Them years efter the war and intae the fifties. They were the best of it. Did'nae think sae at the time. Yet they were. Ah've had some grand neebours ower the years. Faces come to her from her earliest days at number 18. Only one or two names. But it's the faces. Yon two lads who were killed in the Great War. She can see them, clear and sharp. Their coarse uniforms, puttees round their legs, in and oot the close wi' their wives and bairns when they were oan leave. Then back tae France. The Western Front. Killed within a month o' yin another.

She gives a heavy sigh, blinks away some tears. At least the Second War wiz'nae sae bad. Naewhere near as many killed. We never lost anybody from the close during that yin. 'Mmmm.' That sun is nice oan ma face. She closes her eyes . . .

'Granny! *Granny!*'

She wakens with a start; wonders where she is for a moment. Looks down. Teresa O'Malley, as usual laden with shopping, looks up at her from the pavement. 'Were ye havin' a bit kip?'

'Ah wiz – till you woke me up, yah Irish bugger!'

Teresa laughs. 'Sorry, hen.'

'Anywye,' the old woman clears her throat, 'are ye coming in for a drink o' tay?'

'No' at the minute, Bella. Oi've got a bit of ironing t' do. Oi'll come in when it's done.'

She watches her long-time friend and neighbour disappear into the close. Yawns. Still tired. Looks to her left, to where Dalbeattie Street joins the Maryhill Road. Cars, lorries and buses, liberally sprinkled with trams, constantly go by. The cream, green and orange livery of the Corporation's vehicles seems extra bright in the sunshine. Pedestrians, mostly women trailing weans, also pass up and down the main road as they 'go for the messages'.

The matriarch is giving some thought to coming in off the window, having a proper doze in her fireside chair, when a removals van turns in from the Maryhill Road, immediately cuts across the street at an angle and pulls up directly below her. 'Ahah!' Are we finally gonny get a tenant for that single-end, two up? Now wide awake, she plumps up the cushion on the window sill, settles down again. The driver and three mates emerge from the cab. As they make for the rear of the large van she hears one say, 'Huv you got the key?'

She calls down, 'Is yin o' you lads the new tenant?'

The oldest man, the driver, looks up. 'Naw. She'll no' be long. She's away for the rations.'

Oh, so it's gonny be a wumman this time. Granny looks at the driver. 'Right, Ah'll catch her when she arrives. Ah always ask new folk in for a cuppa and a biscuit the day they move in.'

'Aye. She'll be alang shortly.'

Bella decides to stay at the window until the newcomer shows up. As she watches the men unloading the van, now and again her eyes are drawn to some items of furniture. Mmmm. Yin or two good quality bits and pieces. After a while, she begins to feel certain there's going to be *too* much stuff for a single-end. Jeez-oh! She'll no' be able tae swing a cat in there! In fact, if they don't stop soon she'll no' get a cat through the door!

Less than five minutes later her eyes are again drawn to the Maryhill Road end. A taxi has turned in. 'My! We're busy the day.' No sooner has the hackney cab entered the street than it also crosses over, pulls up behind the van. Goodness! Surely that's no' somebody arriving by taxi – tae move intae a single-end? Must be an heiress. She looks on in interest, keen to get her first glimpse. But the cab just sits there. No movement. The removal men are upstairs. Dalbeattie Street is quiet. Only the summer's day murmur of traffic from the main road. Her eyes never leave the taxi. Curious. At last, with a 'put upon' sigh that can be heard thirty feet away, the driver reluctantly climbs out of his vehicle. With a pained expression on his face he reaches for the handle of the passenger door nearest the pavement, opens it wide. Granny watches with great interest. There's a pause, then, a patent-leather high-heeled shoe appears – leading the way for a silk-stockinged leg. As this long, long leg reaches for the pavement its owner's black skirt rides halfway up her shapely thigh. The skirt is closely followed by the hem of a pale fur coat. Chinchilla. Only after the second leg has stretched out to join the first, does the rest of the passenger emerge – as from a chrysalis. She stands upright; the expensive fur coat drops in slow-motion to knee height, sways seductively, then settles. The redhead glances disdainfully at her new address. The look on her face is easy to read. It says, 'There *must* be some mistake.' A couple of shakes of her head makes the long Titian hair cascade and fall into place, barely touching her shoulders. Ruby Baxter has arrived.

'How much do I owe you, driver?'

The man leans into his cab, looks at the meter. 'Four shillings, Ma'am.'

She pouts her glossy, red lips. Nods in the direction of the rear of the vehicle. 'My luggage?'

'Oh, aye.' Making it obvious that it's a trouble to him, he retrieves two suitcases and a brown paper carrier bag, stands them on the pavement.

Ruby Baxter takes exactly four shillings from her purse. 'If you'd opened the door without being asked, you'd have got a tip. However, I only tip *good* service.' She presses the money into his hand. Without another word she lifts her luggage and makes for the close. The driver looks at the coins in his palm, then at the receding back of his former passenger. Having finally got the message he decides it will be in his best interest to say nothing. Climbing into his cab, he engages gear and drives off.

'Humph!' Without a word Granny Thomson bangs her window shut, takes a last glance through the net curtains, begins putting the lids back on the biscuit tins. 'A redhead, is it!' She bristles. 'Aye. And she's nae better than she ought tae be, that yin!'

CHAPTER EIGHT

Light and Shade

'And the next *Tonight* will be tomorrow night. Goodnight.' As Cliff Michelmore signs off, Billy McClaren pushes his empty plate away, leans his elbows on the table. As designated man of the house Billy has the place at table which faces the television. 'There's alwiz something interesting oan that show, i'nt there?'

'Aye.' Drena starts clearing the table. 'Ah like auld Fyfe Robertson the best.' She goes into an impression, 'Here we arrrrrr, somewherrrre in Merryhilllll about to watch a wumannnn wash the dishes on her ownnnnnnn, jist like she dizzzzz every niiiight.'

Her husband looks at their son, William. 'You no' gonny gie yer Ma a hand?'

'Whit aboot you?'

Drena lays the dishes on the draining board. Stretching an arm out she presses one of the channel buttons at the front of the TV.

'Aw, God! Zat you puttin' oan that *Coronation Street*?'

'Ah like *Coronation Street*.'

'Whit dae ye see in it? It's set doon somewhere roond Manchester wye. Whit possible attraction is there fur somebody that lives in Glesga?'

'Plenty,' says Drena as she pours a kettle of hot water into the basin. 'They're living the same sort of lives as oorselves. Jist speak wi' a different accent, that's aw'.'

Billy shakes his head. Turns to William junior. 'Dae you like that serial, William?'

'It's aw'right. Ma always huz it on, so Ah jist watch it along wi' her. Ah like auld Ena Sharples best. She's a wee bit like Granny Thomson. Alwiz telling aw' the women whit they should dae. She's the matriarch.' The melancholy signature tune comes on.

Drena turns her head. 'Whit's a mate-re-arch when it's at hame?'

Her husband looks at her. Keeps his face straight, 'It's an English sort of nickname, for a friend who lives under the railway arches.' William Jnr looks everywhere but at his father.

'It is'nae' says Drena.

Billy points to the screen. 'Look! There's a shot looking alang the street. Ye can actually see the railway arches – there, at the end. Ena lived in one o' them jist efter the war, before she got a hoose. That's why she's called the "mate-re-arch" – oor friend from the arches.'

Drena looks at the two of them in turn. They concentrate on the screen; frightened to look at one another. 'Mmmm. Ah'll ask Ella when she comes doon. She'll know. Oh! That reminds me, William. Ella and Archie are coming doon at eight o'clock – efter they've finished watchin' *Coronation Street*.' She gives Billy a dirty look. 'We aw' want tae see ye in your uniform.'

'Awww, Ma! What for? You still treat me like Ah wiz a wee boy. Dressing up in ma cowboy outfit oan Christmas morning so's the neighbours can see me. Jeez! Ah'm twenty-one noo!'

Drena tuts. Looks at Billy. 'Can ye believe this yin? Jist graduated from the training college as a polis. Went an' picked up his uniform yesterday. He's tae report tae Maryhill polis station the morra fur his first shift. Huh! And naebody's tae get a look at him! The four of us huv watched him grow up. Took an' interest in him. And therr's aw' the thanks we get, eh?' She looks heavenwards. 'Well, Ah don't know whit Ah'll say tae Ella and Archie.' She pointedly looks at the clock on the mantelpiece. 'They'll be coming through that door in aboot twenty minutes. Ah'll jist huv tae tell them straight. He cannae be bothered his arse tae put his uniform oan!' She adjusts a bosom with the inside of her wrist. 'If ye want tae see him, you'll huv tae go up tae Maryhill Polis Station the morra, jist before two, catch him afore he starts his shift.'

Billy turns to his son. 'It'll be easier if ye jist gie in, William. Otherwise we'll never hear the end of it.' He turns to his youngest boy. 'In't that right, Charles?' The ten-year-old looks up from the *Dandy* he's reading.

'Might as well, William. Anywye, Ah want tae see ye as well.'

The older boy shakes his head. 'Okay. Ah'll away through the room and get changed.'

'Aw' that's good, son.' His mother smiles.

As the kitchen door is closed and they hear the bedroom one open, Drena turns to Billy. 'And remember, Billy McClaren. If ye don't mind, could we dae without you and Archie Cameron talkin' tae wan another in buggerin' German half the night? Especially if youse get a couple of wee haufs doon yer necks.' She carries out further bosom adjustments. 'This

55

is nineteen-sixty-wan. The war's been ower fur sixteen years in case ye don't know . . .'

'But Drena, ye don't know how it is fur us auld Kriegies when we get thegither . . .'

'Aye, but we *dae* know how it is. Ella and I huv tae suffer it every time the two of ye meet.' She holds her left arm akimbo, puts its index finger along her top lip in lieu of a moustache, raises her right arm in the Nazi salute. 'Von klugen stumpen, humpen, jumpen,' she intones.

'Oh! Thanks very much, hen,' says Billy.

She keeps her finger and arm still in position. 'Whit fur?'

'You've jist asked me tae huv a bit o' the auld jigajig the night.'

'Ah huv not.'

There's a knock on the kitchen door followed by it being opened. 'It's just us!' says Ella.

'Aye, in ye come.'

'By, there's a lot of hilarity going on in here.'

'Oh, it's alwiz a laugh-a-minute at the McClarens,' says Drena.

'Billy! *Alte freund. Wie gehts Du?*'

'Bugger me!' says Drena. 'They're off already.'

'Aw, it's aw'right, girls.' Billy turns to Archie. 'Nae German the night.' He inclines his head in Drena's direction. '*Streng verboten!*'

'*Ach so?*' says Archie.

'You're daeing it,' says Drena.

'Ah'm jist telling him.'

'Well tell him in English.'

'Zat no' terrible.' Billy McClaren shakes his head. 'Couple of auld POWs and were no' allowed tae keep oor German sharp. Anywye, where's this new polisman?'

'Ah'll go and get him,' says Drena. She makes for the door.

William McClaren finishes buttoning his tunic. As he reaches for the peaked hat with its black and white check band, he hears footsteps in the lobby, voices from the kitchen. Butterflies take off in his stomach.

The room door is knocked. 'Are ye ready, son?'

'Aye. Just!'

'Can Ah come in?'

'Naw, Ma. Away through the kitchen. Ah want youse all tae see me at the same time.'

Drena retraces her steps, sits on a chair in the middle of the room so she's facing the door. 'He'll be through any minute. This is oor first time seeing him, tae.'

They hear tackety boots. 'Ready or not, here Ah come!' He gives an embarrassed laugh as he intones the childhood saying. It seems no time at all since he was saying it as he played round the street with his pals. He opens the kitchen door, forgets he's wearing a peaked hat, 'Oh! Jeesus-johnny!' The hat is knocked off his head by the lintel, bounces off his shoulder. He manages to catch it. Looks at the smiling faces of those waiting. Knows his cheeks are burning. 'Well, so much for a grand entrance, eh?'

'Aaaach! There's worse thing happen at sea.' says Archie.

'Put the hat back oan, son,' says his dad. 'We want tae see ye in the full message.'

'Therr ye are, then.' He doesn't quite know where to put his hands.

'Aw! Dizn't he look smart?' says his mother, a catch in her voice. 'Jist like a real polis.'

'He *is* a real polis,' says Ella. 'It's the morra afternoon ye report for yer first shift, in't it?'

'Aye.'

'Well, Ah think a wee toast is in order,' says his father. 'Tae wish ye all the best an' that.'

'You alwiz think a wee toast is in order,' says Drena.

Archie looks at his watch. Ten past ten. 'Huv tae be gettin' up the stairs soon, Billy. No' wanting tae be going tae work in the morning wi' a sore heid.'

'Jist a toaty wee wan for the road, pal.' Billy reaches for the bottle of Haig's Dimple. As he does so there's a knock on the kitchen door, it opens. '*Irma!*' exclaim Billy and Archie.

'Jeez-oh!' says Ella, 'we're in trouble noo, Drena. Here's Eva Braun!'

'Halloooh, everybody. I just open my door to put the milk bottles out. And so much laughter from my neighbour's house.' She looks at William. 'Oh, William. ZO smart!'

Billy McClaren regards her through the rose-coloured specs he and Archie always wear when she appears. 'Isn't he jist, Irma. *Mein sohn* the *Herr Wachtmeister.*'

'Oh, crickey jings, *Ja. Er ist bestimmt ein* braw polisman.'

Ella sits back, nudges Drena. 'Here we go – "The Broons and Oor Wullie visit Colditz!"' The two men and Irma stop talking, turn their heads as Ella and Drena go into such a state they can hardly get their breath.

Archie puts an arm round Irma's shoulder, Billy leans in confidentially. 'Irma, *unsere Frauen gesagt das wir mussen* nae mair *Deutsch sprechen*. Zat no' terrible?'

'Oh, *schade!*'

'You're right, hen. It's *bestimmt* a buggering *schade*, so it is.'

Ella and Drena, partly recovered, sit side by side, arms folded as they watch proceedings.

Ella stands up. 'Archie Cameron, it's quarter tae twelve. You were gonny go tae yer bed nearly two hours ago.'

'Ella, darling. The night's young. We're celebrating wee . . . well, *big* William joining the polis.' He looks around. 'Where is William anywye?'

'Went tae his bed an hour ago.'

'Hey, Billy!' Archie taps the side of his nose. 'Ah think it's mibbe *zeit* that *wir schlafen gehen.*'

'Dae ye think so?' Billy looks at his watch. 'Oh, *Du hast recht*, Erchie. Aye, *mein alte kamerad*, s'time we were in *unsere* scratchers.' He looks at the faces of Ella and Drena. Leans confidentially in the direction of Archie's ear. 'Ah think we might be in trouble. A wee bit *Storung*. You huv'nae been using the German, huv ye?'

'Not me, pal. English *dem ganzen* evening. Ah might possibly huv slipped a few words in early oan – *aber niemand* noticed. Ah'll ask *meine Frau*. Ella! *Liebchen*! Huv Ah been guilty of *manchmal* fawing intae the German noo and again?'

'*Ja!*' says Ella, 'aw' fuckin' night!' She and Drena began to vibrate as they try to keep their faces straight.

'Help ma Boab!' says Irma, 'Ah'll huv tae *schnell* zum lavvy *gehen!*'

CHAPTER NINE

Progress Reports

––––––––––

'Are ye in, Bella?'
'Aye. In ye come Mary.'

Granny listens to the footsteps in the lobby, watches the inside door open to reveal Mary Stewart from the close.

'Teresa no' in yet? She usually beats me to it.'

'Ah've nae doot she'll have heard ye, Mary. She'll be in any minute. Ah'll brew the tay.' With what is increasingly becoming an effort, the old woman heaves herself out of her chair and limps to the range. As her hostess makes the tea, Mary sits at the table, looks around. Although they've been neighbours for more than thirty years, she never tires of coming into Granny Thomson's. Without fail it always takes her back to her childhood. Before the First World War every house was like this. Gas brackets on either side of the chimney breast. Staffordshire wally dugs on the mantelpiece, heavily embossed wallpaper on the walls, framed prints hanging by long cords from picture rails. A china match-striker – still in daily use – lies in the hearth. Next to it, a slim green tin with 'Price's

Coloured Spills' on it. Mary smiles. Queen Victoria's alive and well as far as Granny's concerned. The thought occurs to her – Ah wonder if Queen Victoria smelled like Granny when she was eighty-six? That 'old woman' smell. Ah suppose it's from always washing at the sink, wearing the same clothes every day for far too long. My ain granny smelled just like that. It's not unpleasant. Well, maybe on a really hot day. Ah don't suppose the auld Queen washed herself at the sink . . . another thought occurs – Ah'm sixty-one. Jeez! Maybe I smell like that? Ah'll ask Sam tonight. Her reverie is interrupted as they hear a door open, then close, out on the landing. Granny is pouring hot water into the teapot, stirring as she does. 'This'll be herself.' It is.

'Good afternoon, girls.' Teresa O'Malley enters, joins Mary at the kitchen table. The cups and saucers are already out. And the biscuit tins. The two women watch their hostess hirple over to the table, place the teapot on its matching stand. They know better than to offer to lend a hand.

Granny places a cushion on a kitchen chair, sits herself at the table. 'Ahhh!' She smooths out non-existent wrinkles on the multi-coloured chenille cover. 'We'll jist leave that tae infuse. Then we'll have a cuppa and a bit biscuit – and put the world to rights.'

'Ah'm needing a cup o' tea to put *me* to rights,' says Mary Stewart. 'Do ye know what it is, Ah've never done a hands turn the day – and Ah've got the cheek tae be tired! Choking for a drink o' tea.'

'Jayz! Ye don't have t' tell me, Mary. There's nuthin' more tiring than doing nuthin', I'm telling ye's. Takes it out o' ye.'

There's a pause in the conversation while the matriarch goes through the tea-pouring ceremony, moving the strainer from cup to cup. Lids are then removed from biscuit tins. 'Now, c'mon. You're at yer Granny's. Don't be shy.'

Teresa sits back, plate in hand. 'Well, what ye got t' tell us about the new tenant, Granny?'

There's a sniff, 'Not a thing!'

Her guests look at each other, then heads swivel back.

'Have ye not had her in?' enquires Mary Stewart.

'Indeed Ah haven'y. And she'll no' be getting asked, either.'

'Eee, Granny, you *always* have new folk in. Did she upset yer in some way?' asks Teresa.

'Ah've never spoke a word tae her. Nor her tae me. And Ah'm not likely to!'

Teresa O'Malley draws her breath in, looks at Mary. 'We'd better take heed. We both know this one's fey. In fact, is there anybody knows *better* than us, that she has the Gift? Remember when your Robert was missing in Korea? Sure an' all, I'll never forget the state o' my Rhea with the worry. Child didn't know where t' put herself. Then she came runnin' into the house one night, "Mammy! Mammy! It's gonny be okay. I was about t' leave Granny's there, and she came over aw' strange. She took me by the shoulders and said, 'It'll be aw'right. Your Robert will get back hame. Don't worry.'" And Jaysus, didn't we get word the next day he'd been picked up. Remember, Mary?'

Mary Stewart, eyes brimming, can only nod.

'So what's happened, Bella? The new one. Have ye been gettin' bad vibrations from her?' Teresa wants all the details.

'It was something like that. Dolled-up in a fur coat. Huh! Arriving in a taxi . . .'

'A *taxi*! Rolled up in a taxi tae move intae a single-end!' says Mary.

'To be sure,' says Teresa. 'And there's even less of them in fur coats. Fur coat an' no drawers I'm t'inking!'

'Exactly whit Ah thocht,' says Granny. 'But there's more. She has a look aboot her. An air. Oh! And the strut of her. Take note of whit Ah'm telling youse. This yin could be ruthless! Don't get involved wi' her. She'll eat ye up and spit ye oot, that yin.' They watch Granny's eyes narrow. 'And mark ma words – there is not a man in this close safe! Don't say ye hav'nae been warned!' She sits back, vibrating with indignation.

Teresa nudges Mary. 'Don't ye be forgetting that.'

'Don't be forgettin' it yerself.'

'Though mind . . .' Teresa gives it some thought. 'She'll have the divil of a job enticing Dennis out from behind the *Evening Citizen* after he's had his dinner!'

Mary laughs. 'Aye, and Ah'll tell ye. Marilyn Monroe could'nae coax Sammy oot o' the big chair once he's settled for the night.'

'Sure, there's no danger,' mutters Teresa. 'The old bedtime shenanigans are low on Dennis's list of "things to do" nowadays. Jayz! Can't remember the last time he caused any bother. The femmy fat-alley will have her work cut out if she sets her cap at himself.'

It has just gone five o'clock. Granny dozed off shortly after her two friends left and now, forty minutes later, lies sound asleep in her fireside chair. The next pair of visitors have to knock the inner door twice before she stirs, 'Granny! *Granny!*' Five-year-old Jane Marshall, accompanied by her mother, Marjorie, can't wait any longer.

'Eh? Oh, Ah jist drapped aff there for a few minutes. Oh,

it's me little darling' from upstairs. In ye come, hen. Come in and let me see ye.'

Jane comes running over, stands at the side of Granny's chair. 'Got something tae show ye, Granny. Mummy bought it for me the day.' She holds out the item.

The old woman sits up straight. 'Now jist let me see. *Oooh!* Isn't that wonderful. It's a kaleidoscope! Jane Marshall! What a *lucky* girl you are. Oh, Granny must have a look through it.' The child becomes even more enthusiastic because of Granny's obvious pleasure in her new toy. She watches as her friend looks closely at it, strokes the varnished wooden case with her hand.

'Isn't it lovely, Jane? It's beautiful on the *outside* as well as the inside.'

'Yes!' The little girl dances in her excitement.

'Now, Ah'll jist slide ma chair roond a wee bit so as tae get the light from the windae. You know you see it best when you can hold it up to a *bright* light, don't you?'

'Yes. Mummy told me.'

'Eeee, Ah can hardly wait to see through it.' Granny makes a great show of getting her chair into a good position then, at last, raises the instrument to her eye. There's sharp intake of breath. 'Oh, my! Isn't that jist beautiful.' She moves it an inch or so away from her eye, turns it, then brings it back again. '*Hah!* Oh, my goodness!' She holds the kaleidoscope still, turns her head toward Jane. Whispers, 'It's like looking into a fairyland, isn't it?'

'Yes!' The child is struck by this thought. 'It's like a fairy-land inside.'

'See,' says Granny. 'I haven't changed it yet, have a look at this one.' She slowly moves the instrument to the side so

Jane can look into it. Smiles at the little girl's reaction . . .
'Oooooh!'

'Did you know, Jane, that every time you turn it, you not
only get a *new* scene. You get one that nobody in the world
has ever seen before? It *never* shows the same picture twice.'

The child's eyes have a faraway look as she thinks about
that. The old woman can tell she doesn't quite grasp it. She
points to the other end of the case, 'See all the little coloured
pieces of glass inside, Jane. Watch this.' She turns the kaleidoscope round and round in her hands. 'Can you see
how they roll and spill over one another?'

'Uh-huh.'

'Well, because they keep falling into different places all the
time, that means that when you look through the eyepiece
you always get a *brand new* picture. Isn't that wonderful?'

'Yes.' Jane's eyes are still far away. Thinking.

'Try this. Hold it to your eye. Now, while you're looking into
it, slowwwwly turn it. See what I mean? The picture keeps
changing and it's *always* a new one. For ever and ever and ever!'

Granny and Marjorie watch her face light up as she at last
grasps what her friend has been at pains to explain to her.
After a minute or more, she reluctantly takes her eye away
from the viewing end. 'It does, Granny, it makes new pictures
all the time.'

'Yes. Because it's a magical world in there.' Granny leans
forward. 'It's the fairies' secret cave,' she whispers. Jane holds
the kaleidoscope in both her hands for a moment. Looks at
how small it is. Yet she knows that inside it, there lies a large,
jewel-like fairyland.

'It looks as if it's an auld yin, Marjorie. Victorian Ah would
think.'

'Yes, I think so. We saw it in the window of that wee antique shop next to the Methodist Church on the Maryhill Road.'

'Oh, Ah know the one ye mean. Just past the Blythswood. The fella runs it wi' his mother. He sells some nice bits and pieces in there.' She turns to Jane. 'Well, what a nice surprise for Daddy when he comes hame fae work the night.'

'Yesss! Let Daddy see the magic land inside it.' The adults smile as they watch her return to the wonders of the kaleidoscope.

Marjorie laughs. Lowers her voice. 'You know, I've never got on with my mother. She could best be described as a difficult woman, and she's not mad about children, either. Anyway, last Sunday we were coming back on the tram, having called in on her for ten minutes. Well, Jane thinks she has three grannies, you know. Jack's mother. Mine – and you!' They both laugh. 'Her nibs here, says to me, "My favourite Granny is Granny that lives down the stairs. She's the best one." So there you are. You're Top of the Grannies' Pop charts.'

'Well, is that no' lovely. Ah'm honoured. Anywye, ye know what I think of her, Marjorie. She's ma wee angel. She lights up the hoose when she comes in.'

'Right, c'mon darling. We'd better get upstairs and start Daddy's dinner. Say bye bye to Granny Thomson.' Jane runs over, her new wonder toy in one hand, puts her arms round Granny's neck. She likes the smell of Granny. She gives her a kiss and a hug, 'Bye bye, Granny.'

'Cheerio, sweetheart. Probably see ye tomorrow. Cheerio, Marjorie.' Smiling, she watches the pair make their exit. Marjorie has remembered not to close the outside door. The old woman listens in pleasure as Jane chatters to her mother about the wonders to be seen inside the kaleidoscope. Her little girl's voice echoes down the well of the stairs as they climb, hand in hand, to the next landing. The closing of their door cuts Granny off from this childhood world. She sits back in her chair. 'Ach, Ah never really missed oot by no' having bairns.' She closes her eyes, gives herself up to the whispered lullaby of the gas lamps. 'Mmmm, not a bit of it. They're aw' ma bairns.'

CHAPTER TEN

A Helping Hand

'Whit wiz that? Did you hear a noise, Katherine?' Ella Cameron stops stirring the pan of steak mince.

'Aye. It was like a thump, wizn't it?' Fifteen-year-old Katherine sits at the table trying, yet again, to understand the enigma that is algebra. She is no further forward than the day she was introduced to the subject. 'It sounded as if it wiz oot on the landing. Will Ah go and see, Ma?'

'Aye. Jist open the door a wee bit, hen. Ah don't want folk thinking we're spying on their visitors.'

Glad to escape the mind-numbing equations of her homework, Katherine enters the lobby and quietly opens the outside door. 'Haaah!' The drawing in of her breath is followed by the door being banged shut.

Ella turns to face her as she runs back into the kitchen. 'Whit's the matt—'

'Oh, Mammy! Auntie Agnes huz collapsed on the landing up against her door. Ah think she's deid!'

Ella shakes her head. 'She'll be deid aw'right. Deid drunk!'

Katherine's hand goes to her mouth. 'Auntie Agnes?'

'Aye. The soul's been drinkin' a bit mair sherry than is good for her, lately. Ah'd better go an' have a look. C'mon. Ye might huv tae gie me a hand tae get her in.'

'Well, aw'right. But if she really *is* deid, Ah'll no' be able tae touch her. Ah'll have tae come back intae the hoose.'

'Don't worry, hen. She'll no' be deid.'

Katherine watches her mother pat Agnes's cheek. 'C'mon, Agnes. Waken up! Ye cannae lie there.' The only response is an occasional low moan. Her eyes remain shut. Ella tries again, shakes her by her shoulders. 'C'mon, Agnes. Let's be having ye.'

'Jiss wannie shleep. Leave's alane.' She slumps lower into the corner by her front door. Ella straightens up. 'Well, at least her key's in the lock. That'll save us raking through her bag.' She looks at her neighbour. 'Ah don't think we'll manage her between us. Ah'll gie Frank a knock. Ah think he's early shift this week.' She goes to the middle of the three doors, knocks on it, tries the handle. It opens. 'Frank? *Frank*! Are ye in?' She's relieved to hear 'Aye. Just a minute.' Seconds later the inside door opens, Frank Galloway appears. He's wearing a collarless shirt, his studs showing. Braces hold up his uniform trousers. He looks sleepy-eyed.

'Oh, hello, Ella. Ah was jist having a wee half-hour in the chair.'

'Sorry, Frank.' Ella beckons him out onto the landing, points. 'Can ye gie me a hand tae get her intae the hoose? Drunk as a puggy.'

He gives a wry smile, lowers his voice. 'It's a shame. But

Ah've been expecting something like this. Ah've seen her come hame the worse for wear, two or three times.'

'Me tae.' Ella also speaks quietly. 'Anywye, her keys are in the door.'

'Okay!' Frank rubs his hands together. 'Let's get tae work. Where does she usually sleep, the kitchen or the room?'

'Kitchen. She likes the recess bed.'

She watches him step into Agnes's lobby then open the door to the right. He takes a quick look into the kitchen. 'The way's clear. Let's get her ontae her bed and she can sleep it –'

Ella interrupts him as she hears a noise, 'Oh! Jist a minute, Frank, this might be Archie. He's due hame aboot noo.' She looks over the bannister, peers down through the narrow well of the stairs. 'It is him. Good!' She leans on the rail, 'Archie!' she hisses. 'Hurry up and gie us a hand.'

The two-step of Archie Cameron's tackety boots becomes a quickstep as he begins to take the stairs two at a time. As he comes onto the last half-landing he looks up, spots Agnes. 'Whit's the matter wi' her?'

'Elephant's trunk!' states Ella. Katherine stifles a giggle.

'Poor soul.' He looks at the crumpled heap that is Agnes Dalrymple. Fails to hide a smile.

'S'nuthin' tae laugh at, Archie Cameron.' Ella gives him a dirty look.

'Ah wiz'nae. No' at Agnes. It wiz the way you said "Elephant's trunk!"' He winks at Frank when his wife isn't looking. 'Right, we should manage her between us. We'll jist stand her up and sort of half-walk, half-carry her. Whit dae ye think?'

'Yeah, that should do the trick.'

'*Uuuh-hup*! Jeez! Folk are'ny half a dead weight when they're paralytic, urrn't they, Frank.'

While the two men negotiate front door, lobby and kitchen door, Ella picks up Agnes's large shopping bag. They all hear the heavy clink of full bottles. 'Oh, my God! Ah know whit this'll be.' A look inside confirms it. She shakes her head, turns to Katherine. 'Two full bottles o' sherry.' She investigates further. 'The usual assorted cakes and a Swiss roll. Oh! And a couple o' bridies.' She sniffs. 'At least her diet's improving.'

With the assistance of the men, Ella manages to get Agnes's coat and shoes off. 'Right, boys. Get her oan tae the bed and we'll make her comfortable. Then we'll jist huv tae leave her tae sleep it aff.' She pauses for a moment, looks at Agnes, sprawled on the recess bed. She feels a lump in her throat. 'We'll need tae try and dae something aboot her. She's a good soul, ye know. Kind-hearted. She's lonely. That's the cause of aw' this.' Ella shakes her head. 'Anywye. We'll leave her be for a while.'

As they are about to leave the kitchen, she takes hold of Frank Galloway's arm. Points to the framed photo of an RAF sergeant on the sideboard. 'That was her fiancé. Was oan the bombers. Never came back fae a raid.' There's a catch in her voice. 'Would be a different Agnes if that fella had lived. He wiz an English lad. Arnold something.' She looks at the photo again. 'They aw' seemed tae be called Arnold back then.' Ella puts the snib on the lock. 'Ah'll come in and oot during the evening until she's able tae look efter herself.'

The two men and her daughter wait for her on the landing. Ella's on the point of closing the door when she hears a noise. She listens for a moment, then softly closes the door. Agnes has started to snore.

*   *   *

Next day. Since yesterday evening there have been a couple of meetings and much to-ing and fro-ing at Granny's single-end. These have involved the usual suspects: Ella Cameron, Drena McClaren, Mary Stewart, Teresa O'Malley and Rhea. Part-time delegates are Irene Stuart and Irma Armstrong (representing West Germany). As could have been forecast, Granny Thomson is eventually nominated to meet with the subject of these discussions and convey the findings to her.

It's almost twenty minutes to six when Agnes Dalrymple enters the close at 18 Dalbeattie Street. As she sets foot on the first-storey landing she hears the familiar voice, 'Is that you, Agnes?'

'Aye.'

'C'mon in a wee meenit. Ah want tae see ye.'

'Right ye are.' Agnes walks through the already open doors into Granny's single-end. The Grand Convener sits at her kitchen table, facing her visitor. 'Sit yerself doon, Agnes.' She points to a kitchen chair, pulled out in readiness. 'We'll have a dish o' tay.' Agnes leans her bag against a leg of the table, obligingly sits on the designated chair. She watches the matriarch rise, hirple over to close both doors, then begin to brew the tea.

It's a couple of minutes later. 'Ahhhh!' The old woman drops heavily onto her chair, places the strainer on Agnes's cup. 'Right, hen. A nice cup o' tea.' She looks knowingly at her guest. 'The drink that enervates but does not intoxicate!'

Agnes smiles. 'Aye, so the temperance folk used tae say.' In the silence that follows this, the only sounds to be heard are of the tea being poured, and Granny's chesty breathing. The teapot is clunked down on it's stand, the cosy placed over it. 'Dae ye want a biscuit?'

'Naw thanks. It would put me aff ma dinner. Ah try no' tae eat between meals.' Agnes takes a sip of tea. 'So whit huv ye got tae tell me, Granny?'

'Can ye no' guess?'

'Naw.'

Isabella Thomson looks at her. 'Ah hope you're no' gonny be difficult, Agnes. Aw' your freens and neebours are worried aboot ye.'

'Worried aboot me? Whit aboot?'

'Well For a start, the state ye were in when ye came hame fae your work, last night.'

Agnes looks quizzically at her friend. 'You're gonny have tae tell me whit you're on aboot, Granny. Ah have'nae a clue.'

'Okay, if that's the way ye want tae play it, Agnes. We'll dae it your way. Jist aboot this time last night, ye were lying drunk, conked oot, on the landing in front of yer door. Archie Cameron and Frank Galloway had tae carry ye intae the hoose. Ella took your coat and shoes aff and they laid ye on top o' the recess bed. Remember?'

Agnes's eyes widen, her hand goes to her mouth. She sits very still. Tries to remember. She looks at Granny's unsmiling face. 'That really happened, Granny?'

'Ah'm afraid so, hen.'

They sit in silence for a minute, then Granny watches as tears, big tears, begin to roll down her friend's cheeks. Agnes reaches into her pocket for the gent's handkerchief she always carries. She clears her throat, swallows hard. 'Ah woke up last night, oh, must huv been efter ten. Ah wiz lying on top o' the bed, fully-dressed. Ah could'nae remember going for a lie doon when Ah came in fae work, but Ah thought tae maself, ye must huv, Agnes. Ah don't even remember coming hame, coming intae the close.' She pauses. 'When Ah left work Ah went intae the Solway Bar for a wee schooner of, well, red biddy.' She blushes. 'It's cheap, and . . . it diz what it's supposed tae dae. Makes ye feel, well, a bit better. Cheerier.' She stops as the tears begin to flow again. 'Oh, Granny, is that no' awfy. Ah'm that embarrassed. Ah'll never be able tae look they folk in the face again.' Granny reaches out, takes one of Agnes's hands in both of hers.

'Don't talk keech! Last night Ah had aw' yer neebours in and oot this hoose. The sole topic of conversation wiz you, Agnes Dalrymple. We're aw' worried aboot ye. We don't want tae see ye losing your job. Or losing your hoose if ye cannae pay yer rent . . .'

There's a knock on the inside door, it's opened. 'It's just me!' Teresa O'Malley comes bustling in, sits on the chair next to Agnes, noisily scrapes it under the table – and sideways – so as to sit closer to her. 'Oh! Yah bugger! Trapped the old fingers there so Ah did.' Agnes laughs in spite of herself. Teresa reaches a hand up behind her, gently rubs her back. 'Don't you be worrying yerself, darlin'. We'll all help ye t' get sorted out. But mind! You'll have t' keep well away from that red biddy. Jayz! Could strip paint wit' that concoction so ye could.'

'How dae you know she's been drinking the red biddy?' enquires Granny.

'Sure, and haven't Oi been standin' in the little lobby this last five minutes. Waiting for the right moment t' come in Oi was. Didn't want t' be interrupting yeas.' Agnes manages a smile. 'Oi'll take a wager – it's the loneliness, Agnes. Would ye t'ink so?'

'Aye. You've got it right first time. It wiz'nae so bad when Ah hud ma auld pal, Donald McNeil next door. The last few years, as Donald got aulder, we were more and more in and oot wan another's hooses. But when Ah lost him last year,' she becomes tearful, 'it wiz jist like the shutters came doon. Ah don't half miss him. Nearly every weekend he'd bake soda scones and – specially for me – treacle yins. We'd huv a proper high tea every Sunday, jist him and me . . .' She breaks down, racked by sobs. It's some minutes before she can continue. 'Dae ye know whit he did? He left me jist over a thousand pounds. And his medals fae the First War. Did ye know he had a bravery wan? Now, whit is it again?'

'The DCM,' says Granny.

'Now, Oi didn't know that,' says Teresa.

'Ah did.' Granny reaches for her cup. 'He telt me many a year ago. Made me promise no' tae tell anybody else. Aye, he was a grand man. You don't get many Donald McNeil's in a dozen.' Her face softens. 'He was always oor first-foot at the New Year, Agnes. Wizn't he?'

'He wiz. And then he'd go back tae his ain hoose and away tae his bed by one o' clock.' She is near to tears again. 'Oh, he's such a miss, Bella.'

'Well. Ah'll tell *you* something, Agnes Dalrymple. And you'll know it's true.' Granny leans forward. 'Donald McNeil did *not* leave you that money tae waste oan drink!'

Agnes looks shamefaced. Nods. 'You're right, Granny.'

'Jayz! Now I would second that. He definitely would not. Last t'ing he'd want ye t' do with it.'

'Right! Before ye go, Agnes – now this is only a suggestion.

As Ah've told ye, all your freens met in here last night. We were aw' agreed you're needin' company, and you're needin' to get oot and aboot. But, most important of all, you need an interest, hen. Something you'll enjoy. You are good wi' people, Agnes. You've worked aw' these years behind the coonter at the City Bakeries. Do ye know whit we think would be jist the thing for you?'

'Naw, what?'

'Becoming a hospital visitor. Ah'm sure you'll know whit that is. It entails ye going tae see folk who don't have anybody tae visit them. Even if ye jist did wan evening a week, and mibbe a Sunday efterninn. Not only would it get ye oot the hoose, but we think you'd get tae meet some really interesting people noo and again. We were aw' agreed that you'd enjoy that, Agnes.'

'Sure, and it wouldn't get boring,' says Teresa, 'you'd be forever meeting new folk. Specially when the ones you've been seeing for the last wee while, well, sort of . . . keel over!'

'Jeez! Will ye listen tae cheerful Charlie Chester,' says Granny.

Teresa and Agnes rise. 'Now, Agnes. There's only Dennis and me in that house nowadays. There's nuttin' t' stop ye coming in for a cuppa now and again.'

Granny remains sitting at the table. 'If you don't know by now, Agnes Dalrymple, that you can come intae this hoose at any time o' the day or night for a dish o' tay and a blether . . .'

'Ah know that, Granny. It's maistly ma ain fault. Ah've been wallowing in ma ain misery since Donald went.' She gives a heavy sigh. 'Naw, youse are right. Ah'm gonny have tae gie maself a shake.' She picks up her bag. 'Thanks a lot.' They hear the catch in her voice. She looks at both her neighbours. 'Youse really are good pals.'

'Ach! Away wit' ye,' says Teresa.

'Mind,' says Granny. 'Don't be expecting me tae supply the treacle scones like Donald used tae. Ah'm the worst baker up this close. That is yin skill that Ah never, ever mastered.'

CHAPTER ELEVEN

A Refusal Often Offends

Though it's barely six weeks since Ruby Baxter moved in, Granny Thomson already knows the sound of her footsteps. It isn't difficult. None of the other women at number 18 wear such high heels. The old woman has been sitting for nearly an hour. Listening. Waiting. At last she hears the metallic clip-clop as the Baxter woman enters the close. From out of nowhere comes a memory of her Uncle Isaac. My God! Ah have'nae thocht o' him for years. Now whit would he have called Ruby Baxter? Aye. A high-stepping filly! The smile fades from her face as the 'Cantata For Heels' steps onto the landing. 'Mrs Baxter?'

The étude stops. 'Yes?'

'Can Ah speak tae ye a meenit? Jist come in.'

Ruby walks through the front door, stops, pushes the inner one further open to see into the room. She remains in the lobby, framed in the doorway. Without moving her head she does a quick inventory: lit gas lamps, electric light fitted, a radio on the sideboard. No TV. She looks at the old woman.

'Yes, Mrs Thomson?' Damn it! She feels somewhat apprehensive. Has an idea what this 'audience' might be about.

During these same moments, Isabella Thomson appraises her. She's well made-up. The coiffured red hair flows down and ends in an inward curl, just touching her shoulders. A light green, well-cut woollen coat. Mmmm, Ah would'nae mind the price o' that. The chinchilla's mibbe at the vet. Or mair likely up the pawn. Granny looks her straight in the eye. 'Ah've been asked tae point oot tae ye, in case you've never lived up a close before, that every third week you're expected tae wash your stretch of stairs and landings. It's known as "taking your turn". Your neighbours on the seond storey tell me you've missed twice.'

Ruby returns the same unblinking gaze. 'Oh, have I. Well, to be honest, I can't see me going down on my knees. It's something I've never had to do up to now.'

As Granny looks at her, she can't suppress the thought . . . I'd think there are some activities where it wid'nae bother ye tae go doon on your benders! Instead she says, 'My, you've been lucky. But now you're living up a close, it's a case of "When in Rome". Ye know whit Ah mean?'

Ruby Baxter pauses. 'Mmmm, I hope you won't mind *me* pointing out, but you live on the first storey. I live on the second. Frankly, is it any of your business?' She follows this with the steely-eyes, head-thrust-forward stance which has brow-beaten many a lesser mortal into silence. Even if they've been in the right.

Isabella Thomson gives her the smile reserved for badly behaved children. 'Aye, Ah thocht ye might come oot wi' that one.' She leans forward onto the table, maintains eye contact. 'Over the years, with me being the auldest resident in the close, Ah'm the yin folk come tae see if any problems develop. Try tae nip them in the bud. Irene Stuart, who lives next door tae ye, tells me she's twice pointed oot tae ye that it's your turn. They still haven'y been done.'

'Must have slipped my mind. There's a lot going on in my life at the moment.'

'Och, aye. It's easy done. Especially if you're no' used tae tenement life. But as Ah hope you'll appreciate, it's unfair on the other two households on your landing. They faithfully take their turn. You don't.' Granny gives a smile that Peter Lorre would envy. Ruby's mind races as she tries to think of a reply. Trouble is, this is a perfectly reasonable request.

The old woman continues, 'If ye don't want tae do them yourself, have a word wi' Irene Stuart. She'll put ye on tae Mrs Geoghan. That's the wumman who comes and does her turn for her. Irene's bothered wi' the athritis. Ah think she pays her half-a-croon each time. So there ye are, Mrs Baxter. Jist a few shillings every third week, and you'll no' have tae dae the stairs yerself. Your neebours will be happy. And civilisation will continue, as Mr Churchill once said, "on to broad, sunlit uplands".' Granny suppresses a smile as this unexpected quote – culled from the *Reader's Digest* – causes Ruby B's mouth to open, then close.

'Yes. Well.' Ruby clears her throat, prays some barbed response will come to her. It doesn't. Damn! She swallows hard. 'Right, Mrs Thomson. Just in case it slips my mind again, I think I'd best go straight up and have a word with Mrs Stuart. Ask her to tell, eh, Mrs Geoghan to come and see me.' She manages a fair imitation of a 'sorry for all this bother' smile. She knows it won't be fooling this old biddy for one minute. 'Right, Mrs Thomson. If that's all . . .'

'Aye. That's grand. Ah'm awfy pleased that's settled.' The matriarch pauses. Ruby assumes her 'hearing' is over. She turns towards the door . . . Granny continues, 'It would huv been *so* embarrassing for ye when your neebours took the next step: applying tae the factor for yin o' they Inspector Of Nuisances forms.'

Ruby stiffens, turns, 'A *whit*?' Fuck! She just manages to stop herself stamping her foot. This old bizzum has just made her forget the sophisticated persona she's been cultivating for years. Maybe she never noticed. I doubt it. 'What is an Inspector Of Nuisances form?'

'It's something that's been in force since the days o' the auld Queen. Back in the middle o' the last century, the housing in Glasgow was said tae be the worst in Europe. Overun wi' vermin, nae sanitation or running watter. When they began tae build these tenements, they were determined tae make folk look efter them. If there wiz a burst pipe or a blocked sewer,' Granny gives her a smile, 'or if folk were'ny keepin' the place clean, the neebours, or the factor, would report it tae the Corporation Health Department. A few days later the Inspector Of Nuisances would arrive at yer door, complaint form in hand, tae see whit the problem wiz. He'd find oot who wiz responsible for that pipe or this drain – or who has'nae been taking their turn. A few days later they'd get a letter telling them to get it done – or they'll lose their tenancy.' She sighs. 'Very embarrassing when word got roon' the close somebody had been subject tae yin.'

'Yes, I'm sure.'

'It's still in force, but very few o' them issued nooadays, thank goodness. Maist folk who live up a close take their turn. Efter aw', it's in everybody's interest.'

'Yes. Well, as I've said, while it's in my mind I'll go straight up and see Mrs Stuart.'

'That's good.' Granny watches her leave, listens to the clip-clops ascending the stairs.

As she climbs up to her landing, Ruby Baxter re-runs the events of the last few minutes. Face up to it, kid, you've been hung out to dry. A smile plays on the corners of her bright red mouth. She's a formidable old bugger, that yin. She places a finger on Irene's bell, doesn't yet press it. Ha! That auld yin has no need tae attend evening classes for grannies on 'how to suck eggs'.

It's later the same day. Twenty past four in the afternoon. A breathless Ella Cameron steps onto the top landing, opens her door, 'Are ye in, Katherine?'

'Aye, Mammy.'

Ella smiles, hangs her coat up, lugs her message bag through to the kitchen. As expected, Katherine sits at the table, pen poised over a school jotter. A couple of books lie open in front of her.

'Mair homework, hen?'

'Aye.'

'It's no' half an awfy school for homework that North Kelvinside.' Ella crosses over to the sink, lays the bag on the scrubbed-white draining board. 'Huv ye seen anything o' yer brother?'

'*Huh*! Aye, Ah saw him aw'right. On the Maryhill Road. He'd jist come oot yon snooker hall near the Star picture hoose.'

'Johnny May's. He's spending too much of his time in therr lately. Aw' the bloody hooks and crooks in Maryhill get in yon place!'

'Dae ye know whit he did, Ma? Tried tae tap two bob off me. And when Ah telt him Ah was skint, he did'nae believe me. Tried tae go through ma pockets in the street! Ah wid'nae let him.'

'He tried tae *whit*! Ah'll huv a word wi' that bugger when he comes in.'

'Ah told him Ah'd tell Daddy if he did'nae stop.'

'Oh, God! Don't tell yer Daddy, hen. He'll blow his top. Jist leave it tae me.'

Twenty minutes later. Ella sits on a fireside chair with a cigarette in one hand, this week's *People's Friend* opened on her knees, and a cup of tea standing on the tiled mantelpiece. Katherine is still absorbed in her homework. In the silence, the alarm clock ticks extra loud. A fly, trapped between curtain and window, buzzes angrily now and again. The sound of weans playing in the back courts drifts up. They hear footsteps on the stairs, growing louder as they near the top storey. Mother and daughter look at one another.

Katherine screws her face up. 'Ah know who *this* will be.'

The outside door is opened, there are heavy footsteps in the lobby, Archie junior makes his appearance. 'Hi yah!'

Ella folds her magazine, 'C'mere, you! Whit are you daeing bothering yer sister fur money in the middle o' the street?'

Archie turns to Katherine. 'Whit a wee clipe you are!'

'Never mind "wee clipe". Huv you nae shame? You're her big brother. You're supposed tae look *efter* yer wee sister, no' rake through her poakets in the middle o' the Maryhill Road.'

'It wiz'nae like that.'

'Oh, wiz it no'. Right, we're listening. Tell us whit it *wiz* like?'

'Och, Ah'm no' gonny waste ma time. Ye wid'nae believe me, anywye.'

Ella sits up, half turns in her chair to face her son. She has turned pale. 'You listen tae whit Ah'm about tae tell you, boy. And Ah'm gonny tell ye it straight. You are turnin' intae a bloody layabout. Dae ye know that? You'll neither work nor want. Jist look at Billy McClaren doon the stairs. Youse huv been pals since ye were boys. Like two peas in a pod so ye were. Look at the two of ye now. Baith twenty-wan. Billy's jist joined the polis. Drena's that proud of him—'

'Huh! Who'd want tae join the polis? No' me!'

'Naw. You're right therr. You are rapidly heading in the other direction, especially if the company ye keep is anything tae go by. A load of –'

'Och, Ah'm away through the room fur a read.' He turns on his heel.

'Jist you wait until Ah'm finished with what—' He continues toward the door *'Hey you! You fuckin' stand there until Ah'm finished tellin' you whit Ah want tae say tae ye!'* The vehemence of her outburst stops him in his tracks. 'You either stay therr till Ah'm finished – or else Ah'll follow ye intae that room. Either wye you're gonny listen. *Got that?'* He stops, his eyes fixed firmly on the floor, unable to look his mother or sister in the eye. 'Ah don't tell your faither *half* the things you get up tae, or how nasty ye are tae me and your sister oan a regular basis. But that incident in the street wi' your sister . . . *that* is the straw that huz jist broke the camel's back. As far as Ah'm concerned, if you're no' gonny take a telling fae me, Ah've nae option but tae get yer faither involved in future. And wan last thing. You need'nae think Ah've no' noticed money has been going missing fae ma purse noo and again.' Katherine looks from her mother to her brother. 'That's why Ah don't leave it oan the mantelpiece anymair.' She's gratified to see him blush. 'So think yerself lucky Ah hav'nae telt him aboot that – or aboot yer latest stunt, trying tae go through yer sister's poakets oan the Maryhill Road. Eh? Can you imagine whit he'd dae tae you? Don't you *ever* bother your sister again, yah bloody toerag. Go on, fuck off oot o' ma sight!'

They watch him, face and neck red to the tips of his ears, exit from the kitchen. Then listen as he strides along the short lobby to the bedroom. When they hear its door shut, Ella walks over to close the kitchen door quietly.

Katherine leans over the table, speaks in a low voice. 'Oh, Mammy. Ah did'nae know he's been taking money oot yer purse.'

'Aye, for this last wee while, hen.'

'But you'll really have tae mean what you've jist said. If he diz something bad and you *don't* tell Daddy, well, he'll know you're jist gonny keep covering up for him. He'll get worse and worse so he will.'

'Don't you worry, hen. It cannae go oan like this. That wiz his last warning. Next time he steps oot o' line Ah'm tellin' yer da.'

CHAPTER TWELVE

Good for the Soul

The number 29 tram, travelling north up the Maryhill Road, slows as it approaches the junction with Dalbeattie Street. Frank Galloway stands on the bottom step of its rear platform, his right hand gripping the short, curved handrail. He gives the conductress a smile. 'Cheerio, hen.'

'Good night, Frank. See ye the morra.'

With a skill inherent in all Glasgow-born males over the age of fourteen, he lets go the rail, falls back off the platform, and at the moment it becomes obvious he's doomed, pushes hard with his feet. His rearward momentum cancels out the fifteen miles per hour the tram is doing and he effortlessly 'hits the ground walking'. This skill is rated essential for anyone wishing to be classed as 'dead gallus'. He waves a hand in thanks, knows the driver will see it in his wing mirror. The tram accelerates up the last half-mile then turns left into Maryhill Depot.

Frank glances at his watch. Ten past eleven. He turns the collar of his gaberdine mac up as a few spits of rain start to fall on his back. As he makes his solitary way along a deserted Dalbeattie Street, the tall lamp standards cast circles of light onto the pavement. A row of spotlit stages and all for him. The segs on the heels of his shoes sound extra loud in the stillness. He glances at the tenement block opposite. There are only three houses where folk are not yet abed, their lights shining out through curtains and blinds. The rest, the great majority, are dark and silent. As he nears his close he glances up. Granny's window is lit, though not with the orange-tinted glare of electric. For her it's the pale glow of gaslight. Should he give her a knock? She's told him many a time, 'If ma lights are burnin', Ah'm up, and ye can guarantee the kettle will be singing.' He's not in the least tired. Feels restless. The last thing he wants is to go up to that empty room. I'm day off tomorrow. Can have a long-lie in the morning. That's the clincher.

As he climbs the short flight leading to her landing, he looks up. Granny's door, the middle of three, stands directly under the stairhead light. The single bulb glares down. Stark illumination for a dark door in a grey close. He's appearing in a black and white movie. Is her door locked? He tries the handle, it opens easily. Stepping into the lobby he raises his knuckles . . .

'Jist come in, Frank!'

He pauses in the darkness between doors for a moment, smiles, opens the inner. 'Is your cup of tea still on offer?'

'Aye, of course. In ye come, son.'

He quietly closes both doors. 'You knew it was me, then?'

'Ye dinnae need tae be Sherlock Holmes tae recognise the sound o' *your* tackety shoes. Spotted ye as soon as ye turned in aff the Maryhill Road.' She rises. 'Ah'll get the tea masket. So whit's brocht ye in the night?'

Frank takes his mac off, lays it over the back of a kitchen chair, pulls another one out to sit on. He's wearing a double-breasted jacket. 'Ach, Ah'm in one o' yon funny moods, Granny. Not quite ready tae go tae bed yet.'

'Humph! That's me every nicht. So where huv ye been, aw' dressed up?'

'Jist at the pictures. Went doon tae the Paramount tae see a film called *The Hustler*. Paul Newman's in it. It wiz good.' He thinks for a moment, 'Do ye know Paul Newman?'

'Ah ken Paul Muni.' They laugh. 'Ah've seen his name in magazines noo and again, but Ah cannae bring his face tae mind.' She turns. 'Huv ye ever thocht how funny it is, that folk above a certain age still call that picture hoose the Paramount? It huz'nae been the Paramount for many a year. In fact Ah could'nae tell ye whit its name is nooadays.'

'It's the Odeon now. But Ah'm like you, it's still the Paramount as far as Ah'm concerned. Over the years, Ah've often said tae some o' the younger staff at the depot, "There's a rerr picture oan at the Paramount this week" and maist o' them say, "Where?"'

'Dae ye remember it in its heyday, Frank? Afore the war.' She doesn't wait for an answer. 'Your feet used tae sink intae them carpets. And the staff, aw' smart in their uniforms. Beautiful it wiz.' She sighs.

'Aye. When Ah was courting Josie – my late wife – we used tae go, very near on a weekly basis. She loved walking intae it. "Sooo luxurious," she'd say. Poor Josie.' He reaches inside his jacket for the ever-present cigarettes; pats himself down until he finds his lighter. 'Ah'll use your ashtray, Granny.' He lifts it over, places it on top of an *Evening Citizen*. He smiles. 'Don't want tae be burning a hole in the chenille.' She watches him go through his 'preparing a cigarette' routine. Satisfied, he sparks the lighter into life. The smoke exhaled after his first deep draw seems to have lost its blueness. He leans back in the chair. 'It's lovely being back in a room that's lit by gas. I grew up with it.' The old woman watches the smoke roll from his mouth in time to the words, somehow part of his speech. He takes another draw. 'If Ah remember right, Granny, the day Ah flitted intae the close – and you asked me in for a cuppa . . .' He flicks the cigarette into the ashtray. 'Ah think Ah said to you, Ah'll eventually get round tae telling you how my wife died.'

'Ye did. But that's only if ye want tae, Frank. And as Ah said tae you, it'll no' go any further.'

'Ach!' He sits up straight. 'Ah think this is as good a time as any. Is there plenty of tea in the pot?'

She reaches for the strainer. Fills his cup. A big draw is taken on the cigarette, as though his life depended on it. He follows it with a good mouthful of tea. 'Well. Where tae start. It was a year past on June the eighth, since Josie died. This is, aye, August. Be a year and two months in a few days' time. She was knocked doon by a lorry. Ah was jist yards away when it happened.' He touches the tip of his cigarette on the bottom of the ashtray, dislodges more ash.

'My God! That must huv been an awfy shock for ye, Frank.'

'In more ways than one. Ah heard the screech of brakes. Ran ower tae see if Ah could help. And find it's my ain wife under the lorry. Can ye imagine? She wasn't killed outright. Was still conscious. Then, as Ah'm kneeling doon beside the wee soul, trying to comfort her until the ambulance comes . . .' He rubs his face with a hand. 'She suddenly tells me she knows Ah've been cheating on her! And it's *my* fault she ran oot ontae the road!'

'Your fault?'

'Aye. You have no idea, Granny. One minute it's just an ordinary day. The next, Ah'm in the middle of my worst nightmare. Ah can see she's badly hurt. Yet, Ah can't help thinking – where did she get that from? What if she dies, believing that's true? Then Ah'm saying tae myself, "This is'nae the time tae try and explain anything tae her. Get her tae the hospital!" But all the time Ah can't help praying "God? Don't let her die thinking Ah've cheated on her. You *must* gie me time tae talk tae her."'

'Would ye like a wee drap o' whisky in yer tea?'

'That would be grand.' While the old woman goes to the sideboard, he lights another cigarette from the first. She pours a generous measure into his cup, tops it up with tea. He takes a mouthful, 'Ahhh, Bisto!' They both laugh.

'So whitever made her think you'd been cheating on her?'

'That's what Ah'm about tae tell ye, Granny. Josie and I got married in '35. Oor son Daniel was born in '37. It wiz a happy marriage, except for one thing. Josie had this jealous streak. It was in her nature. No control over it. She thought women found me attractive, and she also believed that auld nonsense aboot drivers and conductresses. You know, they spend so much time thegither they're *bound* to finish up havin' an affair. Ah'm over twenty years wi' the Corporation, Granny. Had umpteen conductresses working wi' me in that time. It never happened. Wasn't even tempted. Ah was more than happy wi' my wee wife. But Josie never quite believed it, nor could I convince her. Now what there *has* been over the years, has been some great friendships noo and again wi'

me and some of my clippies. But purely friendship. Ah like
women's company. Always have. Truth told, I prefer it tae
men's. And that's how it was wi' ma last conductress at
Dalmarnock. Rosemary Fleming. A great kid. She was twenty-
one when she wiz allocated tae me and we worked thegither
for four years.' Frank stubs his cigarette out. 'In fact, she was
maybe the best I ever had. Hard-working, frightened of
naebody on a Saturday night, *and* the bonniest wee lassie.
Now remember, Granny. Ah've got a son. Ah'd have loved a
daughter as well. Rosemary is a year aulder than my Daniel.
She didn't have a dad – he wiz killed in Italy during the war.
So, Ah used to get aw' her worries. Always asking me for
advice.' He sighs. 'It was a lovely relationship.'

The matriarch cuts in. 'Ah'll jist make a fresh pot o' tay.'

Frank looks at his watch. 'My God! Granny. It's gone half
past midnight. Do ye want me tae finish this another time?'

'Indeed Ah do not, Frank Galloway. Ah'm beginning tae
get an idea what mibbe happened, but Ah'd rather hear the
full story fae you, son. Right tae the bitter end.'

Fresh tea steams in their cups, smoke from another cigarette
rises into the air. Some thirty-five minutes ago the last tram,
unnoticed, echoed its way down the Maryhill Road. Granny's
windows are now the only ones in Dalbeattie Street to show
a light. Frank leans his elbows on the table, 'My wee conductress had been with me just a year when she got married.
Josie and I were at the wedding – though it made nae difference tae her suspicious mind. Ah would come hame fae work
and say to her, 'What a laugh the day, Rosemary did this or
she said that.' And Josie, she could'nae help herself, she'd
go quiet, sort of stiffen. Stupid really, but that's the way she

was. And Rosemary's man, Andy, him and I got on great. He'd often come by Dalmarnock Depot in his van, meet her and me in the local cafe at break-time. We'd huv a good laugh. Ah'd come hame that night and tell Josie and Daniel all about it when we were having oor dinner.' Frank sips his tea. 'Still jealous. Could not help herself. So eventually, Ah just stopped saying anything aboot Rosemary,' he shakes his head, 'but that jist made her worse.'

Granny reaches for the teapot and strainer. Fills his cup.' Jayz! It's a bit stewed. Will Ah mask a fresh pot?'

'Naw, that's fine.' He doesn't object when she unscrews the half-bottle of whisky, tops him up. 'Thanks, Granny.' He takes an appreciative sip. 'Anyway, during the last two years Ah was at Dalmarnock, Rosemary and her man had been trying tae have a bairn. With nae luck.' He pauses, takes another sip of fortified tea. 'Well. Now we come tae the eighth o' June last year.' He reaches for his cigarettes, again. 'Rosemary and Andy had taken the day off. She had an appointment doon at the Royal tae see this consultant.' Granny watches as he picks a real, or imagined, shred of tobacco from inside his lower lip. He clears his throat. 'On that same day, the eighth, Josie had been doon the toon shopping, seen something she wanted tae buy – sheets, if Ah remember – and as she often did, had come tae the depot tae get some money from me.'

Granny feels the tension rise in her stomach.

'A lovely sunny day it was. Ah'm walking oot the depot heading for the cafe. Andy had taken Rosemary doon tae the hospital in the firm's van and now, unknown tae me, they're sitting on the other side of the road waiting for me to appear. She was aw' excited 'cause they'd had good news and she just could'nae wait until the next day tae tell me. When she sees me leaving the depot she lets herself oot the van and comes running across to me. "Frank! Frank!" Right away, it's obvious she's got good news. So Ah stop on the pavement, open ma arms wide, gie her a big hug and a kiss, then she's telling me, "Oh, Frank, Ah'm expecting! In't it great?" Andy, her man, is on the other side o' the road, sitting in the van. He gives me a big thumbs-up and he's smiling like a pooch. It was a wonderful moment, Granny.'

She can hear a tremor in his voice. He swallows hard. Looks at her. 'Naebody in this world would have forecast that within seconds it was gonny turn tae tragedy. At the exact instant that Rosemary runs over tae me, unknown tae us, Josie is walking along the pavement, coming tae see me at the cafe tae get some money. She's just a few yards away, and what does she see – Rosemary running intae my arms! She's not in uniform. It looks like she's come tae meet me and Ah'm giving her a kiss and a hug! Oh, Granny! If only Josie had just come along and confronted us, said, "What the hell is going on here?" She'd have found out *why* Rosemary was there. We'd have pointed across the road to Andy sitting in his van. It could aw' have been explained in two minutes flat. But no. Not Josie. Seeing Rosemary and me must have been a shock. Put her intae a panic. She must have decided she did'nae want us to know she'd seen us. Withoot thinking, withoot looking, she turns and tries to run across the road before we spot her.' Frank tries to keep his voice steady. 'Dashes straight out ontae the road from between two parked vans – right in front of a lorry.'

'Oh, my Jesus-God!' Granny puts a hand to her mouth. In her mind's eye she has seen it happen. 'And all for nuthin', Frank. For nae reason at all.'

'Ah know. But do ye know what's always on ma mind, Granny? The timing. It's so cruel. If Josie had been one minute earlier, or one minute later, everything would have been all right. It would never have happened. At this very moment, Josie and I would be lying in oor bed in oor room and kitchen in Dalmarnock.'

'Oh, Frank. How horrible. But did ye get the chance tae explain tae Josie that it was aw' quite innocent?'

Frank rubs his face with both hands. He looks worn-out. An hour ago he wasn't in the least tired. Now, he looks as if he might fall asleep where he sits. Yet another cigarette is lit. He wants to finish the whole, tragic tale. Get it off his chest again. Maybe *this* time it'll ease the pain. Without asking, he reaches for the whisky, pours some into his empty cup.

'When we get tae the Western, Josie is taken straight intae Casualty, then tae the theatre. By six in the evening she's in a ward, unconscious. Daniel, arrives. Ah've been wi' Josie since about half past one. Ah say tae Daniel, "You sit wi' your mother, son. Ah'll go hame and get changed, grab something tae eat on the way back, then we'll both sit wi' her." Ah'm away about forty minutes. During that time Josie comes round. She tells Daniel that she caught me blatantly kissing ma conductress in the middle o' the street, and that's what caused her tae run across the road. When Ah come back tae the hospital he comes oot intae the corridor and gets tore intae me aboot cheating on his mother! Doesn't give me the lickings of a dog! Ah try tae explain, but he's not interested. Believes everything his mother told him. Of course, ye cannae blame the laddie for that. She's told him what she seen. Anyway, Daniel says he's not going to sit wi' me at his mother's bedside. Says he'll come back at nine o'clock and he doesn't want tae see me still there. So away he goes, storms oot the hospital.

'When Ah go back intae the ward, thank God, Josie's still conscious. Ah at least got the chance tae sit wi' her and explain what *really* happened – Rosemary had come tae tell me her good news. Andy's sitting across the road in his van. There's nothing going on. It did'nae take long tae get her to believe me. We finish up holding hands. She says that when Daniel comes in at nine she'll tell him how stupid she's been. It was all quite innocent.' Frank looks at Granny. Shrugs his shoulders. 'What happens? Some time after eight o'clock she takes a fit, goes unconscious. They rush her into surgery, suspect she's bleeding round her brain.' There's a long pause, the tremor is back in his voice, 'She died on the operating table . . .'

'Oh, my God! So she never got the chance tae tell your laddie?'

'No. From that night tae this, he's had nuthin' tae do wi' me. Won't talk to me.' He looks at Granny. 'Ah did nothing tae deserve all this – yet it's endless.'

'Couldn't Rosemary and her man tell him what happened?'

'They could. But Ah don't want tae involve them. Ah've never told Rosemary that Josie had seen us kiss. She just thinks she was knocked down while coming tae meet me. But also, just weeks after Josie's accident, Rosemary had to pack the job in on doctor's orders. Problems wi' blood pressure affecting her pregnancy. Ah felt it would be very upsetting for her if Ah told her the truth, asked her tae speak tae Daniel. Ah decided it was best tae leave it.' Frank rises. 'Gone one o' clock, Granny. So there it is, hen. That's the whole sorry saga.'

The old woman pushes herself to her feet. 'Jeez! It's nae

wonder you're so sad aboot it all, Frank. You've lost your wife *and* your son – for nae reason at all. You're no' tae blame. And it has tae be said, it wiz aw' caused by Josie's jealous nature. Though if ye try and tell that tae yer laddie, he would'nae believe ye. He's never gonny listen tae a bad word said against his mother.'

She walks him to the inner door. Frank bends forward, gives her a kiss on the cheek. 'Anyway. All that is jist between you and me, Granny. Okay?'

'Aye, of course, Frank. Ah hope it's mibbe done ye a wee bit o' good tae get it off yer chest again. But, oh! It really is a tragedy, son. There's nae other word for it.'

He steps into the small lobby, then turns. Bends his head round the kitchen door so his voice won't carry out onto the landing. 'Ah nearly forgot, Granny. The manager called me intae his office this morning. He had a mixture of bad news and good news. The last trams will run from Maryhill on the twenty-second of October. That's now definite.'

'Aw, Frank! That's jist two months away. That's no' as long as ye expected.'

'No, it's not. But the good news is, they're letting me have a temporary transfer tae Partick. Drive the number twenty-six route out of there until it finishes next year – June '62.'

'Ah hope you're no' gonny be flitting ower tae Partick tae live?'

'No, no. Ah'll jist travel over there every day. Ach! Ah'm only putting off the inevitable.' He gives a deep sigh. 'Anyway, it gives me nearly nine months more oan the trams. It's the best Ah can hope for.' He turns, about to leave, pauses yet again. 'And my wee conductress, Wilma. She's gonny transfer tae Partick with me for the duration. Then June next year we'll come back tae Maryhill, and whether we like it or not, go on tae the busses.'

'Och, well that's nice, Frank. The wee lassie must like working with ye.'

'Aye, even though we've only been teamed up for a few months, we seem tae work well together. Anywye, Ah'm away this time, Granny. Goodnight, hen.'

She stands at her door, looks out onto the silent, middle-of-the-night stairway, until Frank climbs out of sight. She remains there, hears him step onto the top landing, listens to the faint noises as he searches through his pockets. There comes the smooth metallic sound of a Yale key being inserted into its lock. She tries to remember where she read recently that men can't manage living on their own as well as women can. Poor laddie. Moments later she turns, comes back into her room. He has closed his door so softly she never heard it.

CHAPTER THIRTEEN

Three Generations

A Sunday morning in September. Robert Stewart is halfway through *The Sunday Times*, about to turn a page, when he glimpses Rhea furtively dab her eyes with one of her minuscule hankies. He laughs. 'Ah bet you're reading Francis Gay's *Seven Days Hard*.'

She gives another dab, followed by a sniff. 'Nane o' your beeswax, Robert Stewart!' Louise sits at the table with the Fun Section. She looks up. 'Is it a sad bit, Mammy?'

'Aye, hen. Ah'll read it tae ye when your Daddy goes fur his walk – which Ah hope wull be *soon*! He'll jist laugh if Ah read it the noo. He's dead heartless, him.'

Robert stretches his legs out and up, tries for the thousandth time to discover a niche for his heels on their modern tiled fireplace. 'Ah sometimes wish we hud'nae got rid o' the auld range. Ye could put your feet up and always find a nice wee cranny tae rest them on.' As evidence, his stockinged feet slide remorselessly down the smooth tiles and thump onto the hearth.

Rhea tuts. 'Aww! Whit a shame. It's a pity fur ye.' She returns to her paper. Louise gets back to her puzzles. The Sunday morning quietness descends once more. In the distance the song of a tram can be heard. Robert concentrates on its tone, tries to work out whether it's going up or down the Maryhill Road. Decides it's in the lower key. Heading north, away from the city. Jeez, Ah'll no' be hearing that for much longer. The eighteen went a couple of months ago. Just the twenty-nine left. It's a goner next month. He sighs. Ah cannot picture Glasgow without cars everywhere. Rhea turns a page. Louise sucks the end of her pencil. The clock on the mantelpiece fills the kitchen with its extra-loud Sunday 'tick'. He turns his head as, with the regularity of a metronome, the brass tap 'bloops' another drop of water into the sink. 'That drip's getting oan ma nerves!' mutters Rhea. There's more silence.

Robert breaks it. 'Fancy the pictures the night? There's a good Western oan at the Blythsie. James Stewart.'

She lowers the paper. 'No' oan a Sunday, Robert. Telly's too good the night. *Danger Man* and *Hawaiian Eye* are baith oan. We can go during the week if ye want.'

It's Robert's turn to tut. 'Oh, excuse me for offering tae take ye oot. Ah did'nae mean tae come between you and . . . whit's their names? Aye, Tom Lopaka and Cricket Blake. Where dae they get them names fae? Oot a lucky bag?'

'You're taking me away fae ma paper, never mind the telly. Away doon the stairs an' visit your Ma and Da, wull ye. Then you and yer faither can go for a walk. A *long* wan!'

'Aye, Ah think Ah will.' He continues to sit. 'Where's young Sam? Is he at your Ma and Da's, or mine?'

'Fur jumpin' sufferin'! Are ye gonny gie me peace tae read this paper?'

Louise speaks. 'He's doon at Granny Stewart's.'

Robert rises. 'Right! Ah'll get oot o' your hair, darling.'

'Ah'd rether ye got oot o' ma kitchen, then Ah might get this paper finished.'

'Okayyyy. A nod's as good as a wink – tae a blind man.' He pauses, rubs his chin. 'Better make a quick visit tae the lavvy first Ah think.' Rhea gazes heavenwards. Shakes her head.

Key in hand, Robert makes his way down the short flight of stairs to the half-landing. Two minutes later he returns to the house, quietly enters the long, narrow lobby. The sound of the cistern refilling drifts up the stairs. He tries not to laugh in anticipation as he adopts the position Tom and Jerry do when they're about to tiptoe somewhere; arms held up in front of his chest, hands hanging limp like a praying mantis. He pushes the door open, bursts into the kitchen with cartoon-like, bouncy short steps, while managing to keep his face straight. 'Oh, *Gawd*!' Rhea and daughter go into peals of laughter as he circles the table, stops to give Louise a peck, then his wife, then exits in the same manner, hanging the lavvy key up en route. All in silence.

'It's just me!' He opens his parents' kitchen door. Mary Stewart, as he could have forecast, is silhouetted against a window as she prepares veg at the sink. Samuel Stewart sits in his chair, reading the *Sunday Pictorial*, feet up on the low mantelpiece of his tiled grate. Sam Junior sits opposite, absorbed in the latest edition of *Commando Comics*. Robert is greeted with a chorus of 'Hello, Son!' and 'Hi-yah, Dad!' With long-familiar ease he pulls out a kitchen chair, sits down at the table he's known all his life. He looks at his father. 'Are ye for a walk, Da?'

Samuel Stewart lowers his paper. 'Och, aye. Ah think sae. Ah'll jist finish this article. It's all aboot the reasons why the East Germans are building this wall in Berlin. Whit a carry-oan!' As his father absorbs himself in the paper once more, Robert glances at his son. The gung-ho illustration on the front cover of the comic book takes his eye. 'Sam? Do ye know what type of plane that is on the front of your book?'

Sam junior gives a last burst of 20mm cannon fire at the Junkers 88 he's pursuing. As he banks away he's pleased to see black smoke coming from its port engine. He turns the comic round. 'Dae ye mean the British one, Da?'

'Yeah.'

'It's a Spitfire. Everybody knows that. The German wan is a Junkers eighty-eight.'

'Good lad. But Ah'll tell you something ye *don't* know. Your Granda sitting there, he built Spitfires during the war. Thousands of them!' He watches the boy's eyes widen.

'Geee, Granda! Did ye? And did ye get tae sit inside them sometimes?'

Samuel Stewart laughs. 'Ah used tae sit inside them every day, son. One of my main jobs was fitting the instruments intae them. So Ah had tae sit in the cockpit.'

'Aw, Granda! You're dead lucky. Imagine gettin' tae sit inside a Spitfire *every* day. Geee!'

'Just you sit there, Sammy. Ah'm gonny get something fae the room tae show ye.' As he walks along the lobby towards the bedroom, Samuel listens to his grandson's excited chatter. At almost eleven years old, this is as good a time as any to tell him about 'Granda's War'.

* * *

Minutes later, Samuel returns to the kitchen carrying a large brown envelope. Mary, still busy at the sink, turns her head for a moment to confirm what she expected to see. 'Oh, this will interest you, Sammy,' she says. 'I bet you'll like these.'

The boy looks at the well-worn envelope lying in front of him. Excitement is building inside him as Granda Stewart pulls a kitchen chair round. Sammy now sits between his father and grandfather. 'Right, pal.' Granda nudges him. 'Early in 1941, jist a few months after we'd won the Battle of Britain, the Air Ministry sent up a couple of photographers tae take photies of oor factory oot at Paisley, while we were in full production. We were allowed tae buy copies if we wanted.' He looks at his grandson. 'So I bought a set.' He reaches into the envelope, brings out a dozen 10" by 8" black and white prints, places the top one in front of his grandson. The boy looks intently at the glossy photograph. It has been taken inside a large factory. Overhead, the criss-cross tracery of girders supporting the roof goes off into the distance. Powerful electric lamps hang from them, shine down onto two long production lines of Spitfires which are in various stages of completion. Each plane has one, or more, fitters and mechanics working on it. Men and women.

'Aw, Granda!'

Robert Stewart feels his eyes grow moist as he watches grandfather and grandson become totally absorbed in this record of wartime Scotland. Only twenty years into the recent past. He remembers well the day he was first shown them.

Samuel Stewart places another print in front of his namesake. It has been taken in the machine shop. Lathes and milling machines line up, all confined to areas marked by painted white lines. A couple of fork-lift trucks go past. 'Dae ye see anybody ye know in this photie, Sammy?'

The youngster pores over each face until . . . 'Aww! That's you, Granda!' Two men, arms folded, stand at the far side of a lathe. They smile as they look up at the photographer who, judging by the high angle of the shot, is either standing on a ladder or sitting in an overhead crane.

'Got me first time!' says Samuel, pleased his grandson has picked him out. Robert looks up. His mother has temporarily suspended the preparation of Sunday's dinner. Wearing her usual wrap-around peenie, she has her back to the windows and sits, arms folded, on the lid of the coal bunker as she takes pleasure in the rapport between her man and their grandson. Robert catches his mother's eye. He grins, nods his head in the direction of the two poring over the photos. She gives a contented smile.

Samuel senior leans back in his chair. 'They're smashing photies, pal, aren't they?'

'They're great, Granda. Ah wish Ah'd been auld enough tae work in the factory in them days.'

'Would ye no' rather have been flying them?'

'Naw. Ah'd have loved building them. Being in amongst loads of Spitfires every day.' He pauses, eyes sparkling. 'It would huv been great. Getting tae sit inside them, climbing all over them. And anywye, Granda. If you build stacks of Spits you would kill mair Germans than jist being a pilot!'

Robert looks at his father. 'You cannae fault his logic.' The two men laugh.

Mary walks over to the table. 'But there's something you must remember, Sammy. Don't be saying anything like that when Auntie Irma is around. She's German, don't forget. And she had two or three relations killed during the war. So you might hurt her feelings if she heard you say something like that. Will you remember, son?'

'Oh, Ah know Auntie Irma's German, so Ah would'nae say something like that if she was in, Granny.'

'Good lad.'

'Right!' Samuel Stewart stands up, puts the photos back in their envelope. He points a finger at his grandson. 'Don't move! I've got one mair surprise for ye.' He leans forward. 'Even better!'

Sam junior almost seems to vibrate with anticipation. he looks at his father. 'Dae you know what it is, Dad?'

'Ah've a good idea – but Ah'm no' telling ye!'

'Aw, *Dad*!'

'Here he's coming!' They hear Samuel's returning footsteps in the lobby.

When he re-enters the kitchen Samuel Stewart has one hand tucked up under his pullover. This time he sits opposite his grandson. 'Right, put your two hands out in front of you, together. Palms up so as I can place something on them. Now, close your eyes. Don't open them till Ah say so.' The boy complies. He hears and feels movement. Then something cold, metallic, yet light in weight, is placed across his palms. With a major effort of will he manages to keep his eyes shut.

'You can open them now.'

A thin brass plate lies on his outstretched palms. Five inches long, three inches wide, it has words and numbers embossed into it. Lots of them.

'Turn it round and read what it says.'

The boy looks at it. At the top it states: Rolls-Royce Ltd.

England. Underneath that is the legend Merlin 3, followed by a long number. Next, comes a list of Operational Limitations and yet more numbers, showing maximum engine revs, oil temperatures, oil pressures etc.

'Dae ye know what a Merlin is, Sammy?'

'Aye. It's the engine that was in the Spitfire.' He pauses. 'And the Hurricane and the Lancaster and lots of other fighters and bombers.' He pauses again. 'And also the American Mustang.'

'Good lad! Ye know your stuff. This is the manufacturer's plate that was fixed tae every Merlin engine when it came oot the factory. This yin was on the engine of a Spitfire that crash-landed up on the Pentlands in 1943. We thought we might be able tae repair the engine, but it was too badly damaged. So, when Ah heard they were gonny scrap it, Ah screwed off the engine plate as a souvenir. Ah worked on this plane when it was first assembled.'

'Awww! That's great, Granda.' Sam junior holds the plate in both hands, mesmerised by it.

Samuel taps his grandson on the arm. 'Now what Ah'm gonny do, is give you this tae keep—'

'*Oh*! *Granda*! Ah'll look efter it. Ah really will!'

'Well, Ah want tae make sure that ye do. And your Daddy is a witness. These engine plates, especially the ones from Spitfires, are as rare as hen's teeth—'

'Whit, Granda?'

'Your Dad will explain later. Now, you must promise me you'll never, *ever* take this out of the house. You don't take it tae school, or oot intae the street tae show your pals. And your must promise me you'll never sell it, or swop it for anything. Have Ah got your word?'

'Oh aye, Granda. This is the best thing Ah've ever had. Off a *real* Spitfire!'

'Right, it's yours, son.'

'Gee! Thanks very much, Granda. But this is extra special, because you worked on the plane. Ah promise, Ah'll always, always keep it.'

'Good lad.'

Half an hour later, father and son slowly climb the stairs up to the first storey. Robert, his walk forgotten, puts his hand on Sam's shoulder. 'There you are now, you did'nae know Granda Stewart did such important work during the war, did ye?'

'Naw. That was really great finding oot all that stuff, the day.' They pause on the half-landing for a moment, look into the back court. 'You remember the war, Dad. Dain't ye?'

'Oh, aye. Ah was eleven when it started. Ah remember a lot of it. Specially the air raids.'

'And when you had tae go intae the army, you were in the war in Korea, weren't ye? Did anything exciting happen tae you, Dad?'

'Naaa! It was aw' nice and quiet where Ah was.'

'But you've got yon two medals, haven't ye?'

'Everybody who got sent tae Korea during that war got them two. They aren't bravery medals. They're what's called campaign medals. The goldie coloured one, wi' the blue and white ribbon. The United Nations gave us all that one. And the other one, wi' the Queen's head on it, all the British soldiers got that. You just got them because you were there. All Ah did was drive a lorry. Never even got tae see an angry Korean.'

Sam laughs. Looks again at the engine plate. 'Ah'm gonny keep this for ever, Dad.'

'Good. Ah hope so. That's part of British history, you know. Anyway, Ah'm ready for a cup of tea, pal. Let's go up and show your mammy and Louise what Granda Stewart gave ye. Though mind, don't be disappointed if they don't get aw' excited about it.'

'Ah know, Dad. Lassies. Huh! They haven'y got a clue aboot whit's interesting, huv they?'

'Naw. That's the difference between us and them, son. It's sort of, well, "horses for courses".

'It's whit?'

'It's jist a saying, pal. Ah'll explain it tae ye later.'

'Aye. Oh, and there's that other thing that Granda said . . . something aboot "hen's teeth"?'

'Aye, later on. Your faither will need tae have a cup o' tea first, son. Ah'm running oan empty.'

'Eh?'

'Oh, Gawd!' Robert shakes his head. 'Ah'll never get a paper read, the day.'

CHAPTER FOURTEEN

The Sound of Silence

Saturday 21 October, 1961. The tram, a number 29, makes its slow, shoogly way over the multi-point crossing of St George's Cross then, once free, resumes its song as it gains the straightway of Maryhill Road. As she hadn't the energy to climb to the top deck for a smoke, Ella Cameron sits in the lower saloon, looking out the window at nothing in particular. She glances at her watch. Twenty to six. Seconds after the tram pulls away from a stop Ella becomes aware someone stands in the aisle, close by her.

'Are ye wanting the whole seat ta yersel'?'

She looks up. 'Aw, Agnes. Sorry. Ah'm miles away.' She slides along, her neighbour eases in beside her. 'Huv ye been busy at the City Bakeries the day?'

'Oh, aye. It alwiz is on a Saturday. From the minute we open that door, till we shut it, it's non-stop. Ah wish Ah hud shares in the place.' She turns to Ella. 'Ah'd imagine you'll be the same at Cakeland?'

'Exactly. Of course, Ah'm not on the counter. Ah'm in the

bakehoose. But as the two of us know, Agnes, ye cannae go wrong if ye open a baker's shop in Glesga—'

Agnes cuts in. 'Aye, no' half! Glesga folk love thurr cakes and tea bread, dain't they?'

'Could eat them tae a band playing!' says Ella.

At the end of a busy day, the tram sways them into silence for a while. Agnes breaks it. 'Ah'll tell ye. I can *not* believe this is the last time Ah'll ever sit oan a tramcaur going up the Maryhill Road. Can you?'

'Is it today they finish?' says Ella.

Agnes leans back, looks at her in surprise. 'Aye, this is the last day. Did ye no' know?'

'Ah knew it wiz shortly, but for some reason Ah thought we hud another week or so.'

'Nawww! It's the day. Look at the notice oan the windae!' She points.

Ella peers at it. 'Jeez-oh! You're right.' She reads aloud . . . '"Saturday twenty-first October. Last day in service of route number twenty-nine . . ."' She skips some of it. '". . . replaced by number sixty-one bus."' She half turns towards her neighbour. 'Diz that mean we'll be gawn tae work oan Monday by bus?'

'If ye don't, you'll be hoofing it! There's nae mair caurs on the Maryhill Road efter the night.'

'Jesus-johnny! That'll be strange, win't it?' Ella shakes her head.

'Ah jist cannot imagine the Maryhill Road without trams.' Agnes has said this as much to herself as anyone else. 'There huz *alwiz* been trams.' She sits, lost in thought, then. 'Do ye know whit, Ella? Ah think folk will find they'll miss *hearing* them every bit as much as seeing them. Ah know Ah will.

Wi' me sleeping tae the front, Ah can hear them as clear as a bell, going up and doon the Maryhill Road every night.'

'Aye. We sleep in the recess bed in the kitchen, so Ah'll no' hear them as well as you. But when Ah'm working at the sink, noo that ye mention it, Agnes, Ah can hear them nae bother through the windae. Especially oan a Sunday. With it being sae quiet, they're in the background aw' day long. Ah suppose they're a part of ma Sundays.'

'That's gonny be the biggest miss for me, Ella. The sound. Every night that God sends, Ah lie in bed reading till it's time fur the last tram. When it's nearly midnight and there's nae traffic on the Maryhill Road. Always, Ah listen for the first faint sound of it in the distance.'

Ella glances at her from the corner of her eye. She's never heard Agnes speak with so much . . . what? It's more than feeling. That's passion. Her eyes are glistening . . .

'As soon as Ah hear it, Ah put ma book doon, switch the bedlight aff and jist lie in the dark. If ye *really* listen tae it, like Ah do, it's a most beautiful sound, Ella. The wheels sing louder and louder as it comes near. And when it passes the end of oor street, that's the best of it. For a few seconds it fills the whole street. The whole night, really. Then it's past, and it goes back tae singing and echoing aff the buildings, fainter and fainter as it goes doon the Maryhill Road. And Ah'll tell ye something else. The sound it makes coming *towards* the street, is different from the one it makes when it's going *away*.' She looks at Ella, gives an embarrassed laugh. Yet she is undaunted. 'Dae ye know what Ah dae every night, Ella? As Ah'm lying in the dark listening tae it going intae the distance, Ah hardly breathe, so's Ah can hear it for as long as possible. And alwiz, every time, Ah fall asleep before it fades away.' She turns, looks shyly at Ella. 'Ah bet ye think Ah'm daft.'

Ella has a lump in her throat. She places a hand on top of Agnes's. 'Not a bit of it. In fact, that's one advantage of living on your own, hen. You get tae appreciate things like that. Wi' a man and two kids, it's never quiet for two minutes in oor hoose. There is alwiz noise. Ah can hardly hear maself think sometimes.'

An elderly man, sitting directly in front of them, turns round. He speaks low, not wishing to be overheard. 'Excuse me coming into your conversation, ladies.' He looks at Agnes. 'That was quite beautiful, my dear. In fact, lyrical! I know *exactly* what you mean. My room windows look out onto the Maryhill Road. Just like you, I also lie in bed every night listening for the last tram.' He raises a hand, finger extended. 'But isn't it strange that it's only the *last* tram which has this magical effect on us? They are going up and down the road all day. I love every one of them. Ahhh! But once it gets near midnight and it's quiet outside, I suddenly find I can't concentrate on my book.' He shrugs his shoulders. 'Because, just like you, I'm half-listening for the first sound of it. What makes it so special?' He smiles. 'Anyway, ladies. It's nice to know I'm not the only one who is going to miss our lullaby.' He again looks at Agnes. 'And tonight, we'll be listening to the *last*, last tram on the Maryhill Road.' He shakes his head mournfully. 'It doesn't bear thinking about. What will we do? What will happen to us?'

Agnes sighs. 'Ah really don't know. Probably turn intae insomniacs!'

'Hah! You may be right.' He rises from his seat. 'The next stop is mine. Anyway, good evening, ladies.' He touches his cap, makes his way to the platform. Moments later they watch him cross the road then walk along the pavement. Before they can see which close he enters, the tram pulls away from the stop and he is lost to sight.

CHAPTER FIFTEEN

Money is . . .

A rchie Cameron junior steps out of Johnny May's billiard hall onto the Maryhill road. Behind him he can hear subdued laughter. Aimed at him. Bastards! That fuckin' Elky McCann. Thinks he huz the edge on me. Ah hate losing. But Ah double-hate losing tae that prick. Christ! Ah came in that bloody door less than an hour ago wi' a ten-bob note in ma pocket. Gone. Four straight games. If Ah'd jist had another few bob. Every game he won, he wiz winnin' by less and less. Another game, two at the maist, and Ah'd huv started tae take *him*. And he fuckin' knew it.

Archie glances at his watch. Twenty tae four. Where am Ah, gonny get some money? He strides up an increasingly misty Maryhill Road, past heaps of cobbled setts, stacked rows of newly lifted tramlines. It all seems to make the road untidy, cluttered. Somehow abandoned. A number 61 Corporation bus rolls past, its headlights making the fog seem denser, its exhaust fumes adding to it.

As he climbs the stairs at 18 Dalbeattie Street he is in a

bad mood. Should Ah try and tap Ma for a few bob? Ach! Be a waste o' time. He noisily opens the outside door. 'It's me, Ma!'

'*Aye!*' Her voice, unwelcoming, comes from the bedroom. She's still no' talking tae me since that row aboot going through Katherine's pockets, he thinks. He walks into the kitchen. A grand fire chuckles away to itself in the grate. From the radio, Dickie Valentine is serenading the empty room with 'The Finger of Suspicion'. Katherine's no' in fae school yet. He stands for a moment. Should Ah go through the room and ask her? She carries her purse wi' her aw' the time noo; never leaves it on the mantelpiece anymair . . . As he has this thought he casually glances in that direction. Fuck me! It *is* on the mantelpiece. Force o' habit. He can't take his eyes off it. Whit's she daeing through that room? He steps over to the kitchen door, looks along the lobby, listens. The bedroom door is ajar. A chair's leg scrapes along the linoleum. A grunt as she climbs up onto it. There's the sound of a springy wire being withdrawn from a curtain. Once free, it stoats off wall and window in celebration. Aye! She telt ma faither this morning, she was gonny change the curtains. He strides over to the mantelpiece, reaches up.

The fact there's nae noise from the kitchen gives him away. For no obvious reason, Ella stops what she's doing. Listens. The silence grasses him up. She's still for a moment – then her hand goes to her apron pocket. Holding the back of the chair with both hands she quietly reaches a slippered foot down to the floor, stifles a grunt. Knowing the hinges of the half-open door will squeak if she opens it wide, she turns sideways to slip through. A few quiet steps along the runner on the lobby floor bring her to the kitchen, '*Yah bad bastard!*'

A startled Archie junior is on the point of closing her purse. He quickly puts his right hand into his pocket. 'Whit?'

'Gie me ma purse – and the money you've took oot it!'

'Ah huv'nae taken anything. Never hud a chance.'

As she walks towards him he takes his right hand out of his pocket. There's no arguing with the clink of the coins he's just let go. He puts her purse back on the mantelpiece.

'Gie me whitever you've taken. This is your last chance, Archie Cameron!'

'Ah never took anything.' She watches him blush. He's never been a good liar.

'*Right*!' She steps closer to him, reaches for his pocket. He turns away.

'You're no' goin' through ma pockets.' He deflects her hand.

'Oh! Ye mean jist like you went through your sister's pockets no' sae long ago?'

He shoves his right hand back into his pocket; the coins chink together again, aggravate his mother. Ella grabs him by the wrist, attempts to wrest it out. He gives her a shove with his left hand. She staggers back, immediately returns, grapples with him. 'Hand ower whitever you've taken, *now*!' She takes hold of his wrist with both hands this time, pulls as hard as she can. It's not enough.

'Get fuckin' aff!' He takes his hand out of the pocket, the coins inflame the situation some more. He windmills his arm a couple of times until he breaks her grip, then steps back. Ella advances towards him yet again. This time he pushes her with both hands. 'Fuckin' quit it, Ma!' He watches her go off balance and fall back, hard, against the kitchen table.

'*Ohhh*!' The square corner of the table catches her on her right side just below the ribs. Not only is it painful, it has winded her. She leans on the table for support, tries to get her breath.

Archie junior pauses for a moment, then makes for the door. 'Ye should'nae huv tried tae go through ma pockets!' He stops at the door, looks at his mother. She's staring at him, unable to speak. Her eyes say more than enough.

He steps out onto the landing, starts down the stairs. The quietness is welcome after the rammy of the last few minutes. The fog has seeped into the close, makes a halo round every stairhead light. As he passes each window on the half-landings he glances outside. Already he can't see the back of the tenement on nearby Rothesay Street; can barely make out some of the lit windows. Oh, God! Ah wish Ah had'nae shoved her. If she tells ma faither he'll fuckin' kill me. Should Ah go back up and tell her Ah'm really sorry, Ah did'nae mean it? He stops at the close-mouth, leans against the wall, looks out into the increasingly fogbound, November street. It must be aboot four o'clock. Ah've got two half-croons. Ah'll go back tae Johnny May's, take a few games aff Elky, gie her her money back. Mibbe a few bob extra. Aye. *Then* tell her Ah'm really sorry. Ma faither diz'nae get hame until efter six. There's jist enough time . . .

A figure emerges from the swirling fog.

'Hello, son!'

He feels a shaft of fear in his stomach. 'Oh, hello, Da. Whit urr you daeing hame at this time?'

'Got an early lowse the day. No' often that happens. Ma bloody lathe huz broken doon. We could'nae fix it oorselves so they've hud tae send for the maker's men.' He shrugs, smiles. 'The foreman said Ah might as well go hame early.' He taps the newspaper sticking out of his old mac, 'Ah'll away up and surprise yer ma. Huv a cup o' tea and a good read at the *Citizen*. Where are you off tae?'

'Aw, jist goin' tae see a pal o' mine.'

'Don't be too late back. Your ma will probably make the dinner earlier the night.'

'Right. See ye later, Da.'

As he sets off towards the Maryhill Road, Archie junior shakes his head. Ah don't fuckin' believe it! Ma faither is *never* hame early. Never fuckin' ever!. Not wance has it happened. Another shaft of fear stabs deep inside him. He begins to get a bad feeling. Jeez! Ah hope she diz'nae tell him. Up tae now she's never telt on me. She knows he'd go mad. If Ah can jist win a few bob Ah'll make it up tae her the morra. He turns the corner into the Maryhill Road, almost bumps into his young sister. Katherine is carrying her school satchel. She stops. Smiles.

'Hullo, Erchie. Where are *you* gawn in such a hurry?' He doesn't reply, walks past her without looking. She watches the fog swallow him up. 'Miserable bugger,' she murmurs.

Archie Cameron opens his front door, steps into the lobby, anticipates the surprise he's about to give Ella when he walks into the kitchen.

'You need'nae think you've come back tae apologise and that'll make everything awright, yah nasty wee get that ye are! You've hurt ma side. Ah'm tellin' yer faither this time. This is the end of the line for . . . *huh*!' She raises a hand to her mouth as the door opens and her husband appears.

'Whit urr you daeing hame sae—'

'Whit's he done tae ye?'

She jerks her hand away from her side, straightens up. 'It wiz jist a wee argument betwee—'

'Never mind jist a wee argument, Ella. Whit huz he done?'

'It's nuthin'. Him and me are alwiz fawin'-oot.'

'Let me see yer side.' She makes no move. 'Ella, ye either let me see it, or Ah'll lift up yer blouse and look maself.'

She knows he means it. Sighs. 'Awright.' She takes her apron off, lifts up her blouse and the cotton vest under it. Shows him her left side. 'See! There's nuthin' tae see, Erchie.'

'Uhuh. Show me yer *other* side noo.' Her lip trembles. He steps nearer to her. 'Ella, hen. You show me it or Ah'll look maself.' He spreads his arms wide. 'Whit's it gonny be?'

The normally self-assertive Ella crumples. She turns round, slowly pulls up her blouse and vest, starts to sob. 'He did'nae really mean it, Erchie, it wiz jist an accident. He did'nae mean it, honest.'

She has only half-pulled up her clothing. Archie reaches over, gently pulls her cream blouse higher, reveals a large red weal the size of a dinner plate. She watches his face turn white, the blood draining from his lips. He looks at her. 'Ah want no more lies, no more fuckin' covering up for him.' He points a finger at her. 'NO! MORE! LIES!' He turns his head as the kitchen door opens, Katherine enters. She stands still, a little frightened, heard the shouting.

Archie speaks. 'Jist a minute, hen. Ah'm trying tae get oot o' yer mother what your brother's been up tae. Your Mammy's got a big mark oan her side. *He's* done it!'

'Oh, Mammy! Whit's he done?' She runs to her mother's side. Looks at her father. 'He's alwiz daeing things, Daddy!'

'*Katherine!*' Her mother looks hard at her.

'Ah don't care!' She turns back to her father. 'He steals oot her purse, swears at her and everything. She alwiz says she's gonny tell you, but she never diz. Ah telt her he'd jist get worse and worse if she diz'nae tell ye. He even stopped me on the Maryhill Road wan day and went through ma pockets lookin' fur money.'

As these revelations are unfolded, Archie Cameron can hardly contain his anger. He turns to Ella. 'Why huv ye been letting him bully the two of you, eh?' He shakes his head. 'Are ye fuckin' stupid? Noo tell me *exactly* whit happened in this hoose jist before Ah came in.'

Through sobs Ella tells him the full story. When she finishes, Katherine speaks. 'Ah telt Mammy this would happen. Ah jist passed him on the Maryhill Road aboot ten minutes ago. He walked right by, did'nae speak. *Huh*! Nae wonder!'

'Dae ye huv any idea where he'd be going, hen?'

'Ah *know* where he'd be going. Johnny May's. He's never oot o' there.'

'Oh, Katherine!' Ella is tucking her blouse back into her skirt.

'Mammy, you've been lettin' him get away wi' murder.' She sniffs, tosses her head. 'It's time he wiz put in his place, so it is.'

'Right!' Archie takes his worn gaberdine mac off, leaves his jacket on. 'Ah'll see youse later.'

'Erchie, please. Leave it till he comes in. Erchie, you're too het up!' Ella bursts into tears again, has to sit down. Archie walks over to the kitchen door, opens it, turns.

'The wee bully-boy is gonny find oot that it's no' nice being bullied. This'll no' take long.'

As Archie Cameron turns the corner at the end of the street he has already worked out what he intends to do. All senses on the alert, he chooses the right moment to cross the fog-bound Maryhill Road. With his anger making the adrenaline flow, his instinct is to run all the way to the billiards hall, grab hold of the young bastard . . . *No!* Even now, forty-four years old and sixteen years after the war, the para training is ingrained. You don't *run* to the scene of the action, arrive out of breath. He strides out at just the right pace to keep the blood flowing, stay warm, loose. Years of working in heavy engineering have kept him fit, muscular. If it wasn't foggy I'd be taking deep breaths. Get oxygen intae ma blood. With visibility down to less than ten feet, all of a sudden he finds himself under the sign. He gazes up. The red, white and blue neon tubes, spelling out 'Johnny May's Billiard Parlour', are wreathed in a haze as they are increasingly overwhelmed by the fog. Just as he reaches for the door, it opens. The guy who is leaving smiles, holds it for him. Archie nods, steps inside, stands still. The door sighs shut. The hall is almost dark, except for one isolated pool of light above a table. An oasis, way over on the far right, on the other side of the hut-like office. No one has seen him come in. All they know is that one of their number just left. Archie is pleased at how good he feels. Now he's out of the acrid fog he takes slow, deep breaths, feels the oxygen and adrenaline flow. He moves silently to his right, deeper into the shadows. Stops, counts the number round the table. Two playing, three watching – two of whom hold cues. Five. He detects a movement inside the office. Six. There are regular outbursts of laughter or conversation. Whenever the noise swells he moves further into their territory. Soon, shrouded by his friend, darkness, he has crossed to the right-hand wall of the large hall. Stands at the other end of the office from the group.

From here he can only see the two men who are playing,

one of them his son. He knows the three spectators sit on a high bench running along the wall, watching the play. For the moment they are hidden. It doesn't matter. He knows where *all* six of them are. They are unaware of him. The guy in the office sits watching the game through the windows, his back to the intruder. Archie moves along the wall until he stands just behind the office, can observe the players through the windows. Wait for the right moment. Pleased at how calm he feels, he continues to take deep, measured breaths. Time to make the adrenaline peak. He feels a couple of twinges in his stomach. Anticipation, not nerves. Ah fuckin' love it! That same high as in the Dakota ower Arnhem. At last, his son moves to the end of the table nearest Archie, his back is to his father as he watches his opponent play. *Now*! Strike hard! In his rubber-soled 'Tuf' boots, Archie Cameron steps swiftly, silently from the shadows. He is three paces from his son when two of the three young men sitting on the bench spot him. Their mouths fall open, one drops the cue he holds. The guy about to take his shot straightens up, starts to remonstrate with the spectator. 'Fur fuck sake will ye . . .' Archie comes quickly up behind his son, grabs his right arm just above its elbow, the boy drops his cue, reaches down with his left to take firm hold of his left wrist, whips that arm up his back to where it is immediately painful. Even though it's years since his demob, the old skills kick in. Next step – unnerve the rest! Archie starts screaming like a banshee . . .

'RIGHT YAH FUCKING WEE BASTARD! BEEN BULLYING YER MOTHER AND SISTER, HUV YE? STEALING OOT YER MA'S PURSE, HUV YE?' He propels his son forward the length of the table, runs him face-first into the end wall, holds him there while he looks round, checks what the rest are doing. Is anyone thinking of interfering? The three spectators and the other player have come together, as though for protection. Two of them at last find their tongues, start talking earnestly. From the corner of his eye he sees the man in the office rise from his chair. He pushes Archie junior's arm up to painful again. 'Tell yer pals where ye got the money tae come and gamble.' There is no response. 'TELL THEM!' The arm is moved up a notch.

'*Ahh*! Ah stole it oot ma ma's purse,' he mumbles.

'THEY CANNAE HEAR YE!' The arm is ratcheted up further.

'AHHHH! FUCK! AH STOLE IT OOT MY MA'S PURSE.'

The two young men are now having an animated conversation. Thinking of intervening? They move away from the other two. One puts a hand into his inside pocket. Probably a weapon. Archie looks at them. 'Urr you two fancying some o' the action, eh?' If they try to rush him he will trip his son, let him fall to the ground, then turn to face them. The tall figure of the manager steps out from the office.

'*Joe*! *Wullie*! C'mere a minute!' His voice is rasping, but authoritative. Archie watches the pair turn away for the moment, walk over to the manager. He cannot hear their conversation. If he could, it would be of interest to him.

'Ye don't want tae fuck wi' that man. He's an ex-Para,' says the manager.

'But Billy, we cannae huv that fucker jist walking in here an daeing whit he likes.'

'That's Archie's faither. Ye heard him. He's been stealing fae his mother. Needs sorting oot.'

'Aye. But he should'nae come in here and dae it, Billy. This is oor place. That's no' right. He's oot of order!'

'Anywye,' says the second young man, 'there's two of us. Ex-Para or no', Ah think Joe an' me could take him.' He rolls his shoulders in the prescribed manner of a Glasgow hard man. The manager shakes his head, sighs as though saddened by such foolishness.

Archie senior keeps his son pressed firmly against the wall while this meeting takes place. He looks at the tall man with the rasping voice. Something familiar about him. He glances at his son's recent opponent; he has sat himself on the bench seat. Archie turns his attention back to the other two. Feels sure he can handle them if needs be. He half smiles. Huh, when ma dander's up Ah don't give a fuck! Ah'd take on Rocky Marciano!

The manager puts a hand on each of the young men's shoulders, bends his head down, pulls them in nearer to him. 'Listen tae whit Ah'm gonny tell youse,' he rasps. 'Ah take it youse know there wiz a time when Ah wiz supposed tae be the hardest man in Merryhill. And nae doot youse huv also heard how, ten year ago, a guy done me in the 419 Bar – in jig-time! Took him less than a minute!' He gives the rattling cough needed to clear his throat when he's been talking for too long, dips his head lower, pulls the two young men closer. 'Split ma fuckin' Adam's apple. Squeezed ma balls that tight Ah wiz pishing blood fur a month! Took me years tae get ma reputation back.' He nods his head in Archie's direction. 'Yur lookin' at him! Take ma warning, boys!' he croaks. 'That's fuckin' Audie Murphy!'

'Oh, well. Right,' says the spokesman of the two, 'If you think so, Billy. We'll take yer advice. Let it go.'

The other one continues to stare intently at Archie. 'Urr you *sure*, Billy? Ah've seen nearly aw' his fillums. Ah don't think that's him. In fact, Ah'm sure Audie Murphy's American!'

'Fuck me!' The manager looks heavenwards, shakes his head.

'It's awright, Billy, Ah'll explain it tae him later.' The youth turns to his pal, 'C'mon, Joe. We'll sit back up oan the bench, then the guy will know there is'nae gonny be any bother.'

'Right, Mr Cameron,' says the manager. 'If you'd like tae take yer boy hame.'

'C'mon you.' Archie lets go his son, gives him a hard push in the direction of the door, follows on behind. The tall man stands with his hands in his pockets, watching.

'Dae ye still get intae the 419 Bar, Mr Cameron?'

'Aye. Still consider it ma pub.' He looks at the guy. That must be where Ah've seen him. 'You get in there, dae ye?'

The guy gives a gravelly laugh. 'Huvnae been in fur years. Ah'm sort of, barred, ye could say.'

'Mmm, then it cannae be the 419 Ah know ye from,' says Archie, 'but Ah definitely know ye.'

'Aye, that's fur certain,' rasps the manager. 'Name's Billy Webster.'

Archie walks on. Stops. Turns. 'Ah! You wur the guy in the 419 that Setterday efterninn.' He points a finger at his own throat, then back towards the tall man, 'Did Ah dae that?'

Billy Webster nods deferentially. 'Ye certainly did.'

Archie screws his face up. 'Trouble is, when Ah start, Ah never know when tae fuckin' stop.' He shrugs his shoulders. 'Learned it in the Paras. Ye go in at full throttle.'

'Hah! Tell me aboot it!' croaks the manager. He looks at the man who did him so much damage in such a short time.

'Well, it's aw' watter under the bridge, noo.' He watches Archie reach the door, on the point of leaving the premises. 'Ah'll tell ye whit,' he coughs to clear his throat. 'You're some fuckin' machine when ye start. Never seen anybody like ye.'

Archie feels himself blush. He stops. 'If ye really mean that, it's, eh, good of ye tae say so.'

'Oh, Ah mean it, aw'right. Ah've hud plenty time tae think aboot it ower the years.'

'Right!' Archie pulls the door open, pushes Archie junior out. He looks back. The manager still stands, hands in pockets, watching him. 'Cheerio,' says Archie.

The tall man takes a hand out of his pocket, raises it and touches his temple in a kind of salute.

'So long!'

The door swings shut behind them. They walk out into thicker than ever, now freezing, fog. Visibilty is, maybe, eight feet, 'Jeez-oh! We'll be lucky if we can *find* Dalbeattie Street the night.' They stop at the edge of the pavement, listen carefully. All is silent. Archie takes his son by the elbow. 'C'mon, there's nuthin' coming.' They safely negotiate the Maryhill Road. Five minutes later, in silence, they enter Dalbeattie Street. Walking quickly to keep warm.

'Da? Wiz it really you that did Billy Webster?'

'Ye heard whit the man said.'

'He's *still* got a reputation as somebody ye should'nae mess wi'.'

'Huz he? Anywye, never mind Billy Webster. You think aw' that bunch in Johnny May's are the sort o' guys you want tae run aboot wi', dain't ye? Well they're no'. They're aw' lazy bastards. A good day's work wid kill them.' He looks hard at his son. 'But then again, that describes you, dizn't it?'

There is no reply.

A minute later they walk into their close. 'Ah'd think the only difference between you and them, is that they wid'nae stoop sae low as tae steal fae their mother – or rake through their wee sister's pockets in the middle o' the street.'

Yet again there is no reply.

They reach the final half-landing, just before the top storey. Archie Cameron stops, turns. He reaches a hand up, grabs his son by his shirt front, pulls him close, looks into his eyes. 'If you *ever* dae anything like that again tae your mother and sister, Ah'll no' jist show ye up in front o' yer mates. Ah'll gie ye a fuckin' good hiding in front o' them. Be warned!' He lets him go. 'And now that Ah know whit you've been up tae, listen tae whit Ah'm gonny tell ye. Ah'm no' yer mother. You will *not* be getting a string of empty threats from me. Step oot o' line one mair time and Ah'm throwing ye oot the hoose. And don't think your mother will save ye. You'll be oot intae that street, permanent!' He leans closer to his son. 'Take fuckin' warning! Now get intae this hoose and apologise tae both yer mother *and* yer sister.' He opens his front door. 'We're back!'

CHAPTER SIXTEEN

. . . the Root of All Evil

Ruby Baxter reaches for the poker, starts breaking through the dross used to bank up the fire last night. Two minutes and some energetic poking later, her only reward is lots of smoke and the occasional flame. Opening up a double page of the *Evening Citizen* she covers the front of the fireplace. The up draught soon gets to work. A minute later there's a 'whoosh' and a lovely orange glow behind the newsprint. That's better. The paper is folded up, she moves her chair nearer to the hearth. 'Oh-oh! Don't want to get fireside tartan on the legs. She stretches her nightdress down to cover her shins.

A letter from Bernard's lawyer lies on the table. She reaches for the long envelope, takes a mouthful of tea then, cup in hand, starts rereading it. This time it becomes *bo-ring* as early as the third line. She skips through the rest . . . 'behalf of our client, Mr Bernard Baxter . . . we advise . . . no need to support you . . . your long-running adulterous . . . our evidence . . . photographs . . . witnessess . . . hotel bills'. 'Bastards!' She throws the letter in the direction of the table. It doesn't make it. She watches as, in slow-motion, it wafts back a few inches and gently floats down to the linoleum. 'Bloody bastards!' She wishes there was something expensive at hand which she could smash. Instead, she scoops the letter up, half crushes it and its envelope, throws them both onto the fire, finds pleasure at the sight of them flaring up.

Sitting back, she reaches for her purse. 'Jesus wept!' Just short of four shillings. She sits for the next couple of minutes deep in thought. An unusual noise begins to distract her. A deep, roaring sound. She turns her head. '*Ahh*!' The bastard chimney's on fire! Him and that bastarding letter! What can I . . . what was it me da used to do? Aye.

She dashes to the sink, half fills the enamel basin, rushes back with shiveringly cold water slopping out over her hands, splashing her feet. Grabbing a couple of newspapers she separates them into sheets, crunches them into balls, soaks them in the basin, piles them on top of the fire until it can't be seen any more. Great gouts of steam and smoke rise up to fill the chimney, cut off the air supply. She keeps still, listens. The frightening roar lessens, soon stops. 'Phewww!' Don't want them bloody joists going up. She pauses. Sits back in her chair. What the hell *are* joists anyway? Since childhood, whenever there was a chimney fire in the street – one with flames shooting out – spectators would gather. Two or three of them – always men – would nod wisely and forecast that 'The joists will go up any minute!'

Five minutes later she sits down with a fresh cup of tea. I have *got* to get some money. The rent's due next week. Need to get some messages in. She glances at the dead fire. And get some coal. It's almost December, so it's not gonny get any warmer. And now that bloody chimney will have to be swept! All essentials. She sits back. Right, take stock, Ruby. Remember that article in the *Reader's Digest*? Be logical. '*Huh*!' That's gonny be easy. There's nuthin' left to pawn. What about the chinchilla? She shakes her head. No way is that going the journey. Not my pride and joy. That coat *is* me! Well, you'll have to get a job. You've *got* to earn a living. Okay. What skills have you got? Is there anything you're good at, Ruby . . .

It's almost nine p.m. as Ruby Baxter ambles down West Nile Street. The heavy, green swagger coat is living up to its name as she saunters along, high heels clicking. She's well made-up; the extra lipstick applied makes her lips look fuller. Lusher than normal. The luxuriant red hair sways gently as she walks. She stops on the junction with St Vincent Street. Slips into the shadows of an office doorway. Looks across the road towards St Vincent Place. The permanent coffee stall is already open, its shutter propped up, light streaming out onto the broad pavement. She looks at the green, wooden construction. Everybody in Glasgow knows this is where the Ladies of the . . . Cut the bullshit, Ruby! Call a whore a whore! This is where most of Glasgow's *whores* come to pick up customers. She leans back against the office door, deeper into the shadows. I'll just watch. See what goes on. Yeah, do a recce. Suppose it ain't a bad night for it. Three women stand together to the left of the coffee stall, away from its lights. I don't think they'll see forty again. Or maybe they've had a hard life.

Two men come along, one of them a little tipsy. Dutch courage? The pair stand away from the women for a few minutes, then saunter past, blatantly having a good look. They order drinks at the stall, then walk over, engage the women in conversation. It develops into a bit of badinage, laughter. Then, it's down to business. The tipsy man goes off with one of the women. Ruby watches them disappear up an unlit lane between two, closed for the night, office blocks. Less than ten minutes later they return. Very few words are spoken now. The man walks off with his pal. As the woman rejoins her friends, Ruby sets her jaw. I'm damned sure I won't be standing up an alley with my back to the wall. That's for bloody certain!

A solitary woman approaches the coffee stall, has a light-hearted conversation with the stallholder while he makes her drink. She then wanders off to the right. Stands on her own, also away from the brightness. She makes no acknowledge-ment of the trio on the other side. While she was at the stall, Ruby has taken a good look at her. Probably about my age, mid-thirties. Better dressed than the other women. Long dark hair. Quite attractive.

Ruby makes her mind up. C'mon! No good standing here all bloody night. Do it while it's quiet. Butterflies stir in her stomach. She takes a deep breath, strides out across the road, straight for the coffee stall. Minutes later, mug of tea in hand, she walks over to the solitary woman. Close up, she's not at all bad-looking. 'Hello! May I speak to you? This is my first time down here. I'd appreciate some advice.'

The woman looks hard at her, then gives a sympathetic smile. 'Advice? Turn round and bugger off home!' It's not said unkindly.

Ruby continues to look at her, shrugs her shoulders. 'That's not an option, I'm afraid. I've got to raise the rent money by next week. And I won't be eating after tomorrow!'

'Fair enough. Well, first of all, sweetheart. You're too smart for this part of town. Too good-looking. It's only "short times" round here. That's up an alley for a quick knock-off, or any other service that's done standing up. Or kneeling. Have you brought some French letters with you?'

'Eh, no. Don't the customers bring them?'

The woman shakes her head, 'We supply them – *and* put them on. You can't trust the Johns to do it. You'll finish up with a dose of the wee men if you don't make sure they wear them. You know what I mean?'

'I can guess.'

'You should be doing hotels, sweetheart. Cocktail bars. You know, businessmen, reps, tourists. You're a classy-looking girl. You'll easily get a fiver for all night. And, if they like your company, quite often they'll take you for a meal beforehand. Cash in on your looks while they last, honey. Got a cigarette?'

'Yes.' Ruby takes her cigarette case from her bag, clicks it open, proffers it to the woman. She reaches into her bag again, supplies a light. As she puts the lighter away she looks at her. 'My name's Ruby Baxter.'

'Helen.' She blows a mouthful of smoke straight up in the air.

'Could I point out something?' Ruby doesn't wait for a reply. 'You're an attractive woman. Why aren't you taking your own advice, about working hotels?'

'I normally do. But tonight's different. Did you know the US fleet is in at the Tail o' the Bank out at Greenock?'

'Ah! Now you mention it, I did notice quite a few American sailors about as I got off the subway. I walked down the back streets to come here tonight. Must have missed most of them. Even so, is it not a bit quiet for a Friday night?'

'Won't be for long. Pubs will be emptying soon, then you'll see the Yanks drifting down here. These boys have been at sea for months. When they're on shore leave, or liberty as they call it, they don't half enjoy themselves.' She takes a draw on the cigarette. 'There's money to be made, kid. We'll all be smoking Lucky Strikes tomorrow.'

Ten minutes later, as Ruby's education continues, she notices Helen's eyes straying, looking somewhere over her shoulder. 'Don't turn round. There are two Yanks heading our way.' Helen pauses, narrows her eyes. 'Both officers!' She lays a hand on Ruby's forearm. 'I need a quick answer. If they ask us, are you up for it?'

Ruby feels a tingle of excitement, hardly pauses. 'Ah, yes. Why not!'

'Don't worry about going with a Yank. They get French letters issued to them before they come ashore. They're never without . . .'

'Good evening, ladies. How'd y'all like to do your bit for Anglo-American relations?' Ruby turns to face two young, US Navy officers. Probably mid-twenties.

'My friend and I were just discussing where we should go for a meal,' says Helen.

'Well, Ma'am, when y'all arrive at a decision, it would be our pleasure to treat you fine-lookin' ladies to that meal. Yes indeed! Oh, Ah'm forgettin' mah manners. I'm Ensign Mercer. May I introduce my friend?' He gestures towards the other young officer. 'Lieutenant Grunwald.'

'At your service, ladies.' The Lieutenant gives a half-bow, followed by an exaggerated salute.

Helen looks from one to the other. 'Well, if we can arrange a price here and now, boys, my friend Ruby and I – my name is Helen – will be at *your* service.' She smiles. 'We always give satisfaction – and *then* some! Now, I find it's best to get the business details out of the way first. Then the rest of the evening can be devoted to just three things. Fun! Fun! And *fun!*'

'*Mercy*! Ah do like the cut of your jib, Miss Helen,' says Grunwald. 'What's the deal?'

'We go for a nice meal. I know the very place,' says Helen. 'En-route, may I suggest you book two double rooms in a hotel for later tonight, then—'

Ensign Mercer interrupts. 'As soon as we docked in Greenock this a.m. I phoned the Central Hotel and did just that, Ma'am.' He smiles. 'This is mah third trip to these heah parts!'

Helen pinches his cheek, 'Isn't he a darling boy? Shouldn't be long till they give you your own ship, honey. Anyway,' she continues, 'let's get to basics. To spend a night with Ruby or me it's five pounds each. We'd like this to be paid on arrival in the room, *before* we start giving you su'then boys a reason to always remember Glasgow!' She smiles. 'Is that acceptable?'

Ensign Mercer looks at his shipmate. 'Isn't she a dahlin'? Ah *do* love a woman who talks dirty!' They all laugh. 'It most surely is acceptable, Ma'am. Yes indeed. C'mon, folks. No time tuh waste. Let's hit this heah town!'

Mercer holds an arm akimbo, offers it to Ruby. She links her's through his. Helen takes the proffered arm of Lieutenant Grunwald. 'You know something, Miss Helen,' he says. 'Ah do declare! Y'all have *got* to be the classiest ladies in this heah city! Can't remember when I last seen such good-lookin' gals.' They set off along the street. They've barely gone twenty yards when Ensign Mercer turns his head, speaks to both

Helen and Ruby. 'Did I mention, sweet ladies. We've booked these rooms for *two* nights. Fleet doan' sail till Sunday!'

Their laughter peals up into the cool night air of St Vincent Street, echoes briefly off staid Victorian sandstone, then vanishes for ever, somewhere above the ornate lamp standards.

CHAPTER SEVENTEEN

Up and Doon and In and Oot

'*G*ranny! GRANNY! It's me!' Without benefit of a knock Jane Marshall comes running into Isabella Thomson's. The old woman had heard the door opening on the landing above followed by Jane's footsteps as she'd come galloping down the stairs. She lays the *Reader's Digest* face down on the table as her visitor bursts in. 'Eeeh! Whit a lovely surprise. Ma wee pal from two-up.'

Jane halts just inside the room, keeps her right hand behind her back. 'Granny, I've to stay with you until Mummy and Daddy come back from doon the toon. Isn't that good?'

'It is'nae half, darling. But what about the kaleidoscope? Have ye forgot it? You said you'd bring it doon wi' ye.'

She watches the child put on a serious face, shake her head. 'Could'nae find it, Granny.' Jack and Marjorie walk into the room. As Jane turns to look up at her parents, Granny glimpses the kaleidoscope behind her back. 'We searched everywhere, didn't we, Daddy?'

'Don't know where it can be,' says Jack. He pulls a face,

nods his head in Jane's direction. For a second, he reminds the old woman of Chic Murray pulling faces behind Maidie's back.

'Awww, whit a shame. It's ages since Ah last had a wee look through it. Ah was fair looking forward tae you and me sitting at the table, seeing who can make the most beautiful picture inside it.' She gives an exaggerated sigh.

Marjorie leans forward. Speaks in a stage whisper. 'Do ye think that maybe you should put poor Granny out of her misery. Tell her the truth?'

'*Yes*!' The child swings her right hand from behind her, holds her magical toy high in the air. 'I've got it, Granny! I was playing a trick on you.' She goes into peals of laughter.

'Well, whit a wee imp! Ah really believed ye could'nae find it. Och, but never mind. That's grand, hen. We can now have a lovely time while Mammy and Daddy are away, can't we?'

'Yes.' She wriggles with excitement, her mop of blonde curls bouncing like springs.

'We shouldn't be *too* long, Bella. We're only going for some new bedding for Miss Marshall.' She doesn't sleep in the cot any more, you know. She now has the double-bed through the room all to herself. We've put a postcard in Ken's window, to sell the cot.'

'Goodness me,' says Granny, 'so you've not jist got a *big* bed all tae yourself, but a *room* as well! You really are getting tae be a big girl.'

'Aye,' says Jack. 'She might be small, but the cot is now far too wee for her nowadays.'

'And Mammy and Daddy are baith taking a day off work – jist tae go looking for bedding for you! Ah'll tell ye, whit a wee lucky-bag you are.' The child beams with pleasure. 'Oh!

And that reminds me. There's something else Ah've been wanting to ask you, Jane Marshall. Ah think you might know.' Granny glances round the room as though not wanting to be overheard. She leans forward, drops her voice. 'Can you tell me,' she pauses again, looks to left and right, 'is *this* the month that, eh, what's his name comes?' It's said in a whisper, 'Santa Claus?'

Adopting the same conspiratorial manner, Jane reaches up to Granny's ear, whispers, 'Yes. At Christmas time, Granny.' Marjorie and Jack stifle a laugh, not wanting to break the spell.

'Aye, Ah thocht it was.' The matriarch sits back. Rubs her chin. 'Mmmm. But wait a meenit. Ah'm sure there was another thing Ah wanted tae ask you. Noo whit was it?' Jane looks on as her friend appears to be deep in thought. Suddenly, 'Ah remember whit it wiz.' She points at the little girl. 'Have you got a birthday this month?'

'Uhuh'

'And how auld will ye be?'

'Six.'

'Noo jist hang on. Ah'll huv tae work this oot.' Granny holds up a hand. Using her fingers, she ticks off the forthcoming events for December. 'You're gettin' new bedding the day. You're having a birthday this month. And this is *also* the month that Santa comes.' She sits back, keeps the three fingers up in the air, looks at Marjorie. 'Are folk alloo'ed tae huv *three* good things aw' in the same month?'

'Not always. But seeing as she's been a very good girl, Daddy and I think it will be all right.'

'Oh well, if ye think sae. Anyway, Jane. Ah think it's time Mammy and Daddy were away, so we can start looking intae the kaleidoscope. But first,' she leans on the table, 'whit aboot some tea for Granny and a big drink o' ginger for Jane? American Cream Soda?'

'Oh, yes please, Granny.'

'Och, whit a well-mannered girl ye are.' The old woman half turns, reaches for one of the tins sitting on the sideboard. 'And mibbe a couple o'them new biscuits – Jammie Dodgers!'

'Oooo-Hoooo!' Jane claps her hands together. 'I like them, Granny.'

'Put oor magic machine on the table, hen. Eee! Granny has'nae seen inside it for ages and ages. Ah'm fair excited so Ah am.' The child places the long, triangular instrument on the multi-coloured cover. The matriarch picks it up, gazes at it, runs a hand along the varnished wooden case. 'When Ah see it, Jane, Ah always wonder how many boys and girls – right back tae the days of the auld Queen – have played wi' this and looked inside it, like we do.'

Jane's hand emerges from the tin clutching a Jammie Dodger. 'Lots and lots of them, Granny.'

'Now, whit we have tae decide next is, do ye want Granny to switch the electric light on for the kaleidoscope? Or do ye jist want tae keep—'

Jane interrupts. Points to the twin gas lamps singing softly to themselves above the mantelpiece. 'These ones, Granny, 'cause your light makes the colours different from my house, so it does.' She shakes her head vehemently, 'Don't switch the lectric on, Granny.'

'Okay, darlin'.' With an effort, Isabella Thomson rises to her feet. 'Ah'll jist get a dish o' tay on the go, but first . . .' She reaches up to the nearest gaslight, 'Ah'll turn this up a wee bit.'

* * *

For the last few minutes Marjorie and Jack have stood, as though eavesdropping, quite forgotten by the two at the table. Marjorie holds her fingers to her lips, motions with her eyes to Jack. They step backwards into the small lobby, close the kitchen door. Once out on the landing they push the front door to. Only then do they breathe normally. Jack turns, 'Ah'll tell ye. When them two get thegither they go intae a wee world of their own, dain't they?'

Seconds later, they walk out the close into Dalbeattie Street. Marjorie takes Jack's arm. As they set off, she glances up at Granny's. She can picture the scene behind those double windows . . . Jane sitting at the table, occasionally circling her palms on the chenille. Granny pouring tea, or maybe American Cream Soda, as the two of them chatter non-stop. The coals in the grate glowing red; Granny is now the last one at number 18 who still has her original kitchen range. From above the mantelpiece the gas lamps – also the last of their kind in the close – illuminate this tableau with light from a bygone era. And on the table another relic from the Victorian age awaits their pleasure. The kaleidoscope. When they are ready, it will delight them with wonders never before seen. Time after time after time . . .

It has just gone four o'clock in the afternoon of that same Monday in December. Jack and Marjorie Marshall make their way along the aisle of a number 61 bus. As they approach the platform the conductress rings her bell. At this precise moment Ella Cameron descends from the top deck, steps onto the platform. 'Eh, hello you two.' She inclines her head towards the large, brown paper parcels the Marshalls carry. 'Looks like a bit o' money huz been gettin' spent the day.'

Marjorie answers. 'Yes. We've finally persuaded Jane tae give up her cot and sleep ben the room –' Jack cuts in, finishes Marjorie's sentence, '. . . but it's cost us new bedding tae entice her intae it.'

Ella smiles. 'Och well, it'll be worth it.'

The three of them step off the bus, walk companionably along the Maryhill Road towards Dalbeattie Street. Although it's just after four, it's already a dark, dank December evening. Light from the shops straggles out onto pavement and road, fails to alleviate the gloom. Ella looks around. 'God! Is this weather no' enough tae gie ye the boke!'

Jack agrees. 'Dead miserable, in't it.'

'Mind,' says Marjorie, 'the state the Maryhill Road is in at the minute is nae help. Lifting tramlines and causies, putting doon Tarmac. What a damn mess!'

'Don't mention it,' says Ella. 'Ah'm no' kidding. Ah did'nae think Ah would miss the caurs so much. Ah was recently laughing at Agnes when she wiz going on aboot them finishing. But now? Nae caurs, nae tramlines, nae cobbled setts.' She tuts. 'It's jist no' Glesga anymair.'

'And there's aw' the upheaval it's causing the tram staff,' says Jack. 'Did ye know that Frank up the stairs huz transferred ower tae Partick for a few months? Jist so he can drive caurs fur a wee while longer.'

'Aye, he wiz tellin' Erchie. Ah think it's only until the middle o' next year, then he huz tae come back tae Maryhill and start driving a bus – whether he likes it or no'. Whit a shame!'

'No' half!'

As they enter Dalbeattie Street, Marjorie tunes out of the conversation. She looks along the front of their tenement. Behind drawn curtains and blinds a large number of flats have their lights on. Electric lights, their windows all reflecting the same palette of orange, yellow and beige. Granny Thomson's pale, gas-lit blinds seem isolated. Under siege by a brash twentieth century.

'Ah'll love ye and leave ye,' says Ella, as they enter the close. 'Ah'm away intae Drena's fur a cuppa. If Ah don't report in every night, she phones the polis and reports me missing! See yah!' As Jack and Marjorie set foot on the stairs, behind them they hear Ella open the door. 'It's me, Drena!'

'Aye. In ye come! The kettle's oan.'

Ella enters the kitchen. Drena sits by the fire, a magazine on her lap. She turns her head, smiles. 'Zat you jist in fae yer work, Ella?'

'Ah'm refusing tae answer that, oan the grounds Ah might lose the heid an' stoat ye wan!'

'Och! Ye know Ah keep forgetting. Anywye, Ah'll make the tea.'

Ella sighs, raises her eyes ceiling-ward. Placing her Rexine shopping bag on a kitchen chair, she delves into it. 'A couple of custard tarts each – courtesy of Cakeland.'

Five minutes later, Ella reaches into her bag again, produces a ten Woodbine. 'Ye want wan?'

'Naw. Ah'll jist huv a couple o' draws o' yours.'

She lights the cigarette, inhales the first, the best, draw. Exhales in obvious enjoyment. Sits back in her chair. 'Wiz you oot yesterday, Drena?'

'Aye. Seeing as William's away at the polis college at the minute, Billy and me took Charles doon tae Kelvingrove Art Gallery fur the efterninn. We fair enjoyed oorselves. As usual, Charles made a bee-line fur yon room that has aw' the big model ships in it. He'd spend the whole day in there if ye let him.' She reaches for Ella's cigarette, 'Ah wonder who made aw' them? Jeez! Must huv been a full-time job. Take years and years tae make aw' them.'

Ella looks at her. As usual her pal is serious, completely without guile. 'Drena. They were'nae aw' made by the same guy.'

'Wur they no'? Ah thought that. The poor sowel wid never get a day aff if he made aw' them.' Yet again, she reaches for the Woodbine. 'Wiz there two or three of them making them?'

Ella sighs. 'Drena, at one time there wiz lots o' shipyards alang the Clyde. Whenever they got an order fur a new ship, while it wiz gettin' built, they used tae *also* make a scale model of it.' Ella can see Drena's brows are knitted – 'darned' would be more accurate – in concentration. 'When the ship wiz launched they used tae present the owners wi' the model. The shipping companies used tae display them in their heid office.'

The penny drops. 'Awww! Is *that* why there wiz so many made.' Drena pauses, thinks about it. 'How come they've aw' finished up doon at the Kelvingrove?'

'Because ower the years a lot o' the shipping lines huv gone oot o' business. So they presented the models tae the museum. So slowly but surely the collection huz grew and grew – jist like Topsy.' Instantly, Ella wishes she hadn't said that.

'Topsy who?'

Fuck me! She thinks quickly. 'Ahhh, you don't know her. She wiz in ma class at the school.'

'Oh! Anywye, you alwiz seem tae know aw' that stuff, Ella. How dae ye get tae know that?'

Ella takes a thoughtful draw on her Woodbine. 'Because Ah read the fuckin' notices hingin' up in the room where the ships urr!' As the two of them start to laugh, Ella chokes on unexhaled smoke. There now follow five minutes of laughing, coughing, choking and back-slapping until she's brought back from the brink. 'You'll be the bloody death o' me, Drena McClaren!'

They sit in silence to give Ella more time to convalesce, frightened to look at one another in case it sets them off again. They hear voices, footsteps from one-up . . . 'Cheerio, Granny. I'll come to see you again soon.' Ella smiles. 'Ah got Jack and Marjorie hame on the caur, eh, the bus. They'd been doon the toon and had left the wean wi' Granny. That's them away up the stairs.'

'Oh, that wee yin diz'nae half love being doon at Granny's, dizn't she.'

A fresh pot of tea is placed on the table. 'Whit day urr ye going tae the bagwash, Ella?'

'Thursday, when Ah come hame fae work. Anywye, ye should be giving it its proper name, Drena. The *Citizen* says that's an awfy name. They don't call it the Bagwash ower in Hillheid.'

'Oh, excuuuse me!' Drena attempts to talk 'pan loaf'. 'So, Eleanor, H'ahm I correct in saying that on Thursday we shall be proceeding tae, eh, Ah mean *to* the Maryhill Laundrette. How naice!' She lifts her cup, little finger sticking out. 'Oh! Do ye know whit else Billy and me did at the Kelvingrove. We went tae huv another look at yon painting by Salvatory Dally. Dae ye remember aw' the fuss there wiz when Glesga Corporation bought that?'

'Aye, no' half. If Ah remember right, that was roon aboot 'forty-nine. Or wiz it 'fifty? Jeez-oh!! Because it cost seven or eight thousand quid, there wiz a right auld stushie aboot it.'

'Well, Billy and me wur standing in front of it yesterday when, honestly, absolutely oot o' the blue it came to me *why* the Corporation bought it.' She shrugs her shoulders. 'It's a Glesga painting! Dally did it wi' us in mind. Salvatory's no' daft.'

'Mmmm. If Ah remember right, *that* wiz a matter of opinion.' Ella reaches for a Woodbine, pauses. Should Ah ask? Ah'll probably regret it. 'Whit makes ye think it's a Glesga painting?'

'The title! *Christ of St George's Cross*. Whit other city wid it be meant fur?'

Ella sighs. Ah knew Ah should'nae huv asked. Wishing to avoid another bout of terminal coughing, she delays lighting the cigarette. Should Ah tell her it's actually called *Christ of St John of the Cross*? Jeez! Drena *always* gets the wrang end o' the stick. Ella finds she can't resist taking the next step. 'Oh! Ah did'nae know it wiz called *Christ of St George's Cross*.'

'Aye. Billy and me stood looking at it fur ages, trying tae work oot *why* he gave it that title. As ye know, he's got Jesus floating in the sky above some watter. So, if it's called *Christ of St George's Cross*, you'd think he would huv hud Him floating above Massey's, widn't ye?'

Ella decides to temporarily give up smoking. She returns the Woodbine to the packet.

Drena continues. 'Billy and me stood fur a long time yesterday. Jist looking at it and talking aboot it. Then suddenly it hit me!'

'The attendants?'

'Nawww! The solution.'

'Oh, right. Let's hear it.'

'It wid'nae be such a grand picture if Jesus wiz floating up above a grocer's shop, noo wid it?'

Unfortunately, this opinion is expressed as Ella takes a mouthful of tea – most of which is returned to the cup via her nose.

'My God! Whit *is* the matter wi' you the day, Ella?'

'Ah'm fine,' splutters Ella, 'jist get oan wi' the reasons why Dali gave it its name.'

'Well, Billy and me think Dally took artistic . . . whit is it they call it, Ella, when artists take liberties? It's artistic something?'

'Licence!'

'That's it. Now, if Dally had painted Him floating above a grocer's shoap it wid huv offended a lot o' folk. Also, St George's Cross is a busy junction, so he would huv had tae put wan or two trams and buses intae the scene, widn't he? And that's gonny spoil it.' Drena leans forward. 'Even Dally would'nae huv got away wi' that! So he found a solution, Ella. We think he must huv looked aroon' fur the nearest place tae St George's Cross that *wiz* paintable. There is only wan place, in't there? Jist a toaty wee bit further alang Great Western Road – the Boating Pond! Full marks tae Dally, eh? Wizn't that clever?' She pauses. 'Though mind,' Drena draws herself up, 'Billy did notice his deliberate mistake . . .'

Ella comes in, 'And what wiz that?'

Drena smiles. 'He forgot tae paint the numbers oan the skiffs!'

Ella has her cup halfway to her lips. 'Jesus wept!' She places it back in the saucer.

Drena is now in full flow. 'But he still calls it *Christ of St George's Cross*. Eh? Is that, or is that no' artistic licence? Salvatory knew, that wi' a title like that, Glesga's bound tae buy it!'

Ella feels a distinct weariness come over her. She takes a last sip of tea, rises, lifts her bag. 'Ah'll tell ye whit, Drena. They cannae pull the wool ower your eyes. Ah'll see ye the morra.'

'Aye, cheerio, Ella.' As her best pal leaves, Drena starts clearing the table, putting the dishes into the sink, humming to herself all the while. She straightens up for a moment, smiles. 'Uhuh!' It's no' often Ah'm able tae tell Ella something *she* diz'nae know. But today wiz the day. That's wan up tae you, Drena!

CHAPTER EIGHTEEN

Absent Friends

It's twenty minutes to four, Tuesday afternoon, late December 1961. A raw, damp day with a blustery wind blowing. Perfect for a funeral. Two taxis follow one another into Dalbeattie Street and pull up at number eighteen. Normally, such an arrival is enough to bring Granny Thomson to her window. But not today. She is in one of the taxis.

'Can ye manage, Granny?' Drena McClaren stands at the kerb, holds the cab door wide open. Dennis O'Malley hovers nearby. Inside the cab Teresa O'Malley sits beside the old woman, ready to shove, slide or supply whatever else is needed to get her out of the back seat. Passengers from the other taxi – Mary Stewart, Irma Armstrong and Irene Stuart – have already decanted themselves onto the pavement. At the moment they're doing their sums; trying to see if thirty-eight shillings plus three more for a tip is divisible by three. 'If we make the tip *four* shillings it'll make it easier,' says Irene. 'It'll be fourteen shillings each.' This is agreed. Moments later their transport drives off. The trio join the others to see if they can come up with any further suggestions which might be a help in extracting Granny from the rear of the hackney cab.

'Teresa, pull doon that wee foldy-up seat and move Granny on tae it. It's nearer the door. Wance she's on it, she jist has tae swing herself roond and she can step oot ontae the road.'

'Good idea, Drena.' Teresa weighs up the situation. Granny is sitting so low and so far back in the well-worn, bench seat it looks like she is sinking into it. She is.

'Jayz! I'll tell ye what. I t'ink I'll move to the foldy seat *next* to the one we want Granny on. Then I'll be pulling her straight toward me and out o' that back seat.'

'Aye, that might be best,' says Drena. 'And Ah'll reach in from the pavement and pull her by her left hand, while you're pullin' oan the right.'

'Eeeh, is this no' a carry-oan?' says Granny. 'Noo' mind, the pair o' ye, divn't be pullin' me arms oot their sockets!'

'Right! Wan, two, three. Heeeave!'

The two of them manage to get the old woman halfway out of the back seat, but haven't the strength to pull her up onto its front edge. Despite all the groans and grunts coming from Drena and Teresa, they are unable to drag their elderly neighbour from this leather trap.

'Youse are jist gonny huv tae leave me,' she squeaks. 'A'h'm fated tae spend whitever time's left tae me, going roon' and roon' Glesga in the back o' a ta—' She is unable to finish as she takes a fit of the giggles. It proves to be infectious.

Teresa O'Malley is first to succumb. 'Aw, Grannyyyy!' The spectators watch her shake with silent laughter, weaken and let go her friend's right hand. Granny slips back a little, but Drena continues to pull her left hand. Alas, this causes her to keel over to her right, execute a forward one-and-a-half pike, with tuck, and come to rest at a bad angle, peering out of the cab's right rear window.

When Drena sees where Granny has finished up, this causes her to lose control. 'Ah cannae hing oan any longer!' She lets go her left hand. The matriarch now does a slow, reverse roll and finishes up in her original position – sunk deep into the back seat. She lies there, quivering, unable to get her laugh out.

The failure of this major attempt to retrieve Granny proves too much for the three from the other cab. Mary, Irma and Irene stand close together, arms linked, helpless . . .

'Huv ye ever seen the like?' gasps Mary.

'Can Ah huv a lend of your lavvy key?' whispers Irene.

'Help ma Boab!' says Irma.

'If this goes on any longer,' mutters the driver, 'Ah'll huv tae set the meter away again.'

Dennis O'Malley goes round to the other side of the cab, opens the door. 'Oi'll swop yer places, Teresa.'

'Jayz, ye'd better.' She climbs out, her husband replaces her, sits facing Granny. He looks at Drena. 'To be on the safe side, do ye t'ink ye should maybe let the driver take yer place?'

'Aye. Might be fur the best.'

Minutes later Granny Thomson is free, stands once more on terra firma. As Drena puts it, 'Saved from a fate worse than fate!'

'Right, c'mon. All of yez up t' our house,' says Dennis. 'We could do wit' a small refreshment Oi'm t'inking.'

Fifteen minutes later finds the seven mourners spread round the O'Malleys' kitchen. A spare chair has been brought through from the room and five of them sit at the dining table. Mary Stewart and Teresa sit on fireside chairs. Granny Thomson has wisely opted to sit on a wooden kitchen chair at the table. Drinks have been poured: a whisky for Dennis and Drena, sherry for the rest. Dennis chaps the table loudly with his knuckles to interrupt the various conversations. 'Best of order please, folks. Before we relax and talk of other t'ings, I t'ink a final toast should be drunk to the memory of our friend and former neighbour.' He raises his glass, the assembled company follow suit, 'To the memory of Lena McDermot. May God rest her soul, and I hope she's reunited at last wit' Andrew.'

There's a mixed chorus of 'To Lena!', 'God rest her!', 'She's gone tae a better place!'

'Though mind ye,' says Granny, 'she'll not know who this Andrew is. It wiz alwiz Andra!'

'Aye, that's whit Ah wiz thinkin',' says Drena. 'Even oan a Sunday he never got his Sunday Name. Seven days a week, it wiz Andra.'

'How long is it since he went?' asks Granny. 'Bound tae be aboot ten year.'

'Yes, Ah'm certain it was 1951,' says Mary Stewart. She looks at Teresa. 'Because oor Robert and your Rhea got the vacant flat when they married in '52. Lena had just moved oot.'

'Yer right,' says Teresa. 'Lena didna' stay on for long after Andra died. Too many memories in that house. She flitted over t' Clarkston to live wit' Maisie.'

'Oh, jings, yah. I remember how very sad she is when her man dies,' says Irma. 'They were not just man and wife. They were best of pals also.'

'She never got ower losing Andra,' says Granny. 'A light went oot in her life when he—'

'It definitely did,' interrupts Drena. 'Dae ye remember, if ye ever called in oan a Saturday morning, withoot fail Andra wid be sitting up in the recess bed, cup o' tea and a roll-up on the go, studying the horses. And oor William. He used tae love goin' in tae play draughts wi' him.'

'He loved weans, didn't he?' says Irene Stuart. 'Used to torment the life oot o' them. Especially his grandweans.'

'Yah, and I always remember, Drena, the days when we all go to the Steamie. You, Ella and Lena. You all teach me what to do at . . .' there's a catch in Irma's voice, 'We all have such rerr laughs . . .' She stops as her voice fails her.

Drena reaches out, puts an arm round her shoulder. 'We did'nae half. Except fur that day ye scalded yerself. Wiz'nae any laughs yon day, hen.'

'Oh, crivvens! Don't remind me, Drena. That was so very sore!'

Ella is the first of the late arrivals. Just after four-thirty. There's a short rap on the O'Malleys' kitchen door, then it's opened. 'Is this where ye's aw' are!'

All heads turn. '*Ella*!' says Drena.

'Get yerself in here,' says Dennis. 'You'll take a glass o' sherry?'

'Ah wid'nae say naw.' Ella looks round the assembled company. 'So how did it go ower at Clarkston?'

'T'was very nice,' says Teresa. 'A grand service so it was. I t'ink Lena's family were very pleased to see so many old neighbours from Dalbeattie Street.'

'Oh, that's good.'

Dennis leaves the kitchen, returns with another chair. 'Squeeze yerself onto the table, Ella. You'll have had a hard day. Sit yerself down.'

Ten minutes later, conversations are going at full throttle. Mary Stewart is the first to become aware that Granny Thomson is not 'with them' at the moment. She is staring intently, somewhere behind those who sit facing her at the table. Mary catches Teresa's eye, inclines her head in Granny's direction. At that same moment, Ella also picks up on it.

'Bella?' says Teresa, softly. The old woman 'comes back'. 'What could ye see, Bella? What were ye looking at?' asks Teresa. The room grows still. Electric.

'Och,' Granny has to clear her throat. 'It was mibbe jist the light in—'

'C'mon, Bella. Ah've known ye for far too long.' Teresa pauses. 'Was it herself? Was it Lena?' Two or three of the company draw in sharp breaths.

Granny nods. 'Standing ower there, between the fireplace and the press door, leaning against the wa'. Fair enjoying the craic she was. Smiling tae herself. She had her auld broon coat on.' She sighs. 'That's her awa' noo. She'll no' be back. Jist wanted tae see us yin last time.'

'Ah could tell there was something goin' on,' says Mary. 'Soon as Ah looked at you.'

Teresa turns toward Dennis. 'There ye are now. Haven't Oi told ye Granny has the Gift.'

Dennis nods. 'Indeed ye have . . .' He's about to continue, but at this moment the hinges on the kitchen door creak, then slowly, very slowly, it begins to open. Conversation stops. Heads turn. A hand, gloved in black, appears round its edge . . .

'Jings!' exclaims Irma.

'Fuck me!' says Ella.

A head peeps round.

'*Agnes*! Jesus Christ! Urr ye trying tae gie us aw' a heart attack?'

The newcomer blushes. 'Youse were that quiet, Ah thought ye were huvin' a wake.'

'Get yerself in here. Sure and you've just missed Lena.'

Agnes Dalrymple has taken a few steps into the room. She stops, '*Eh*?'

'Oi'll tell ye later.'

Drena leans over to Ella, says in a stage whisper, 'Ah think Ah'm needin' tae change maself!'

'Join the queue!'

'Will ye take a glass o' sherry, Agnes?'

Teresa gives Dennis a look.

'Oh, ah, or maybe a dish o' tay seeing as yer just in from yer work?'

'Tea would be lovely, Dennis.' She looks around for somewhere to put herself.

'Oi'll bring yer a chair through. Oi'm sure there's one left.'

'Ye can have this yin,' says Granny. 'It's time Ah—' She's interrupted by three or four voices expressing the same sentiment in various ways, 'Surely you're no' going, Granny?'

She struggles up onto her feet. 'Youse are aw' forgettin' Ah'm eighty-six. It's been a long day. *And* Ah wiz snatched frae the jaws o' death in yon taxi! Ah've normally had three or fower wee dozes tae maself by noo'. Ah'm fair tired. Ah might wander in later oan.'

'Well, make sure you do, Granny.' They watch as she takes her leave. Agnes tentatively fills the vacant place.

Bert Armstrong is next to appear. All of a sudden he's there, framed in the doorway.

'Oh, here is *mein* man,' says Irma. Her face lights up.

'It's big Geordie,' says Dennis. 'Will ye manage a glass o' whisky, Bert?'

'Divn't mind if Ah do, Dennis.'

'Oi'll fetch you a chair . . .'

'No, don't bother. Honest. Ah've been sitting ahll day driving me lorry. I'll just stand ower here and lean on the sideboard. Cheers, everybody!'

'Is Arthur in the haus, Bert?'

'Divn't worry aboot him, pet. He's watching *Ivanhoe*. Nowt's a bother.'

By early evening a spontaneous party is in full swing. Archie Cameron and Billy McClaren look in as they come home from work, make quick visits to their respective houses for a wash, reappear twenty minutes later with shiny faces and wet hair combed back. Drena and Ella look up as their men re-enter the premises. Ella nudges Drena, says sotto voce, 'Here they urr – the Scout's Double!' Their menfolk ignore this, sit themselves down on either side of Irma. '*Liebchen!*' says Archie. '*Wir hat uns nicht unterhalten fur viel so lange.*'

Ella purses her lips. 'Here we buggerin' go. At a theatre near you – "The Sound of Berchtesgaden!"'

Drena splutters into her sherry. The assembled company laugh and nudge one another.

It's twenty to eight when Bert Armstrong stands up and calls for order. 'Ah divn't kna' aboot yee folks, but Ah huvn't had me denner. And neether huv any of yee as far as Ah kna. What aboot getting up a kitty and Ah'll gan for some fish and chips.'

'Best idea Ah've heard aw' night, Bert,' says Archie. 'Ma stomach thinks ma throat's cut. And, eh, whit aboot going tae the licensed grocer's for a few bottles o' beer and some lemonade. Make shandies for the ladies.'

'Bert, take the lorry and go down to Bundoni's in Trossachs Street,' says Irma. 'They are the *best* fish and chips.'

'Would ye get me a black pudden supper,' requests Agnes.

'Could Ah have pie and chips, please,' asks Mary Stewart.

'Hang on, pet. Somebody gie's a pencil and paper,' says Bert. 'Ah'm nivver ganning tae remember ahll this. It's a good job Ah've got a lorry – this will finish up a shipping order!'

'Oh, whit aboot a couple o' jars o' mixed pickles?' suggests Drena.

'Will Ah ask for scrunchings?' enquires Bert.

A silence falls. Heads turn. 'Whit the buggerin' hell is scrunchings?' asks Ella.

Irma supplies the answer. 'You know, the little bits of batter that are falling off the fish and becoming well-done in the hot fat? In Newcastle they keep them on one side in the fryer and you can ask for some. They call them scrunchings.'

'Well we dae the same here,' says Drena, 'but we jist call them well-done bits.'

'Bugger me,' says Archie Cameron. 'Them Geordies will eat anything.'

'Hey! Now mind, lad.' Bert finishes his list. 'Is one o' yee coming wi' me. Gie's a bit hand?'

'Ah'll come wit' ye, Bert. Get a bit o' fresh air.' Dennis rises from the table.

'Don't be long, *Liebe*. Keep them hot.'

'Divn't worry. We'll get the fish suppers last. Get them wrapped in plenty o' newspapers.'

It's nine p.m. The O'Malleys' kitchen smells strongly of tobacco smoke, beer and a soupçon of recently demolished fish suppers. Archie rises unsteadily to his feet. 'Best of order, *bitte*. Ah think it's *zeit* for a wee sing-song. Finish the night wi' a song, eh?'

Ella sniffs. 'As long as it's no' the *Horst Wessel*.'

Archie looks at Irma, then Bert. 'Zat no' terrible? Ah'm no' kidding, Ah knew guards in the camp that were mair civil than Ella.' He goes into a kink of laughing. Ella tries to keep her face straight. Archie continues, 'You see, Bert, you wur lucky. You married a German who wiz'nae a Nahzee.' He points to himself. 'Ah wiz dead *un*-lucky, Ah married a Nahzee who wiz'nae a German!' He goes into another kink, until he notices none of the women are laughing. He points at Ella. 'Naw. Only kiddin', hen.'

Ella gives him a smile that could freeze the Forth and Clyde canal. 'Ah'll gie ye "kidding", pal, if Ah start.'

Irma tugs Archie's sleeve. 'Archie, that is not a nice thing to say. *Schrecklich*!'

'It's jist a wee joke, Irma. *Nur eine witze*.' He tuts, sighs. 'Naebody huz a sense o' humour nooadays. Anywye.' He looks through the haze of cigarette smoke. 'Whit aboot this wee sing-song afore we go hame? The auld favourites, eh? "White Cliffs o' Dover", "Roll Oot the Barre" . . .'

Ella turns. 'Ah'd imagine, wi' you and Billy, it'll probably be "Roll Oot the Barbed Wire"! She and Drena go into fits, along with the rest of the company. Archie looks at Billy. 'Huv ye ever noticed, the mair Ah drink – the funnier she gets!'

'Erchie, *mein alte freund*,' Billy looks up at him. 'Ah've telt ye afore, you never know when yer beat. You should tackle somebody your ain size. Ella's too big for ye!'

Archie shakes his head, like a boxer who's just been trapped in a corner. The tiredness of the day is rapidly creeping over him. 'You are dead right, Billy, and Ah'll tell ye whit else . . .' He pauses, sways, forgets what he wanted to say. 'Ach, Ah think it's aboot time *Ich schlafen gehen*, Billy. *Ich bin* dead *mude*. Ready for *mein bett*.'

'Aye, and don't forget, it's only a week tae Ne'erday. Ye don't want tae peak too soon.' Archie taps the side of his nose with a finger. Winks. 'Ah think *Du hat recht mein auld pal*.'

Billy laughs. 'Ah alwiz know when you're tired, Erchie. Ye start coming oot wi' sentences that are *halbe Deutsch*, half English. It's definitely time ye were in yer scratcher.'

'Ella! Ah think it's time for up the stairs, hen. Baw-baw time. Eh?'

Ella breaks off the conversation she's having with Drena. 'Aye, cheerio. Ah'll be up later.'

'Awww, are you no' coming up wi' me, Ella?' He sounds aggrieved.

She shakes her head. 'Naw. You're the wan that's tired. No' me. Ah'm still enjoying maself.'

'Now dae ye see whit she's like?' Archie addresses the entire company. 'In fact, Ah'll tell ye something else. During that last bit o' bother wi' Germany, Ah met SS men who wur mair sociable than Ella!' He stands for a moment. Swaying. Ella and Drena sit facing one another, their shoulders shaking. Everyone else tries not to laugh.

'Right! Ah'm away. Good night, Irma. *Gute nacht*, Billy.' He pushes his chair back. Waves a hand in the direction of the rest of the company. 'Cheerio, everybody. Ah'm away tae ma bed. Fawing asleep oan ma feet so Ah am.' Midst various 'Goodnights' and 'All the bests!' Archie Cameron makes his way to the door. He turns. 'Thanks for a nice evening, Teresa, Dennis. Fair enjoyed masel'.' A final wave of his hand and he's gone. They listen to his footsteps fading as he climbs the dimly lit stairs, then, after a long period, a door is closed.

Ella and Drena are the last to leave the O'Malleys'. They stand for a moment on the first storey landing. 'Jeez!' says Ella. 'Ah bet ye Ah'll huv trouble gettin' oot ma bed in the morning. Whit time is it, Drena? Did ye notice?'

'It's aboot ten past wan.'

'Oh, my God! Ah'd better get masel' up them dancers. Probably find Erchie's fell asleep in the chair.' Ella turns, about to step onto the first stair. 'It's aw'right fur you, Drena. You don't work. Can lie in yer bed in the morning if ye feel like it.'

'Oh, Ella?' Drena touches her forearm. 'Could ye lend me thirty bob till Friday, hen?'

Ella sighs. 'Ah don't think Ah can manage thirty bob. Can lend ye a pound. That's the best Ah can dae.'

Drena tuts. 'Well, Ah suppose it'll huv tae dae. Can ye let me huv it in the morning?'

Ella looks at her. 'You know whit it is, Drena. You say that as if Ah'm no' being very helpful. Three weeks oot o' four you tap me for a pound or thirty bob. It's got tae the stage where that money is'nae ma own. Every week, Ah huv tae make sure Ah don't spend all ma money, because Ah huv tae keep some of it back tae lend tae you! One of these days Ah'm gonny huv tae say naw, sorry, Drena, Ah need it masel' this week.'

There's a pause. 'Well? Are ye gonny lend me a pound – or no'?' Drena looks at her.

With an effort of will, Ella bites her tongue. 'Ah'll hand it in in the morning when Ah'm going tae ma work. Good night.' She turns, starts up the stairs. No answering 'Good night' comes from Drena. Instead, she hears a distinct 'Humpf!' followed by footsteps as her friend descends to the close. There comes a loud bang as Drena slams her door shut. Ella, halfway to the top storey, feels the hairs stand on the nape of her neck. 'Ah'm gettin' fuckin' sick o' this!' she murmurs.

CHAPTER NINETEEN

Home Truths

The lone Coronation tram, a survivor of Glasgow's romance with Art Deco, stands at Clydebank terminus. Water streams down its sides as the blustery wind hurls a mix of rain and sleet against it. A man, his mac starting to drip onto his trouser legs, looks enviously through the windows at the driver and conductress as they sit, snug and dry, inside the brightly lit vehicle. Frank Galloway and Wilma Ballantyne share a bench seat at one end of the lower saloon. Wilma turns her head as another sheet of rain bids for her attention by dashing itself against the windows. 'Jeez-oh! Whit a night, Frank. Good job we're no' on an auld caur. The platforms alwiz get soaked when it's like this, dain't they?'

'Ah know. There's nothing tae stop the rain driving in. The doors on these Coronations are a blessing.' He peers past rivulets of rain racing one another down a window. 'Ah'll tell ye whit. Even Gene Kelly would refuse point-blank tae go oot the night!' As he's sitting half-facing Wilma, he watches her take a delicate bite of sandwich. While she unscrews her flask and fills its cap he looks, yet again, at her delicate shell-like ears. She's wearing tiny gold earrings. Like the ones lassies wear when they first get their ears pierced. Aye! Sleepers they call them. Her hair curls down from under her hat. The nearer it gets to her ears the fairer it becomes. She has hardly any make-up on. Doesn't need it, really. Pale smooth skin with the merest blush on her cheeks. It's funny how you can work with a lassie, and start off by thinking she's a bit plain. Then, as months go by, you begin to notice things about her. Nice things. I bet if I saw her made-up for a night out . . . Wilma has become aware Frank is staring at her. She turns her head, looks straight at him. Suddenly self-conscious at being caught, he tries to think of something to say. Finds himself blurting out what he's been trying to say for days.

'Wilma I, eh, hope I'm not out of order. But I've took it on maself to, ah . . .' My God! It's like being fifteen again, like when it took me three months tae ask Marie Fildes to go tae the pictures . . . Wilma is still looking. Be the first time she's seen me tongue-tied. He reaches into his pockets for cigarettes and lighter. Goes into his 'preparing a cigarette for smoking' routine. As usual it helps, gives him time to think, slows him down. 'Sorry Wilma,' he clears his throat, 'Ah think Ah'm a bit concerned in case you look on what I'm about to ask you, as if I'm, eh, asking you out on a date.' He feels he's recovered his poise. 'We've been working thegither aboot six months now. We get on well. And I was really pleased you came ower tae Partrick with me for this few months . . .' He lights the cigarette. Wilma watches the smoke tumble out of his mouth. 'So, as it's nearly Christmas and I'm gonny be on my own and, eh, as far as Ah know you're no' winching at the moment, Ah was wondering if . . .'

There comes a loud 'Ding-Ding!'

'*Bullocks*!' says Frank. They both laugh, look through what will be the front of the tram for the return trip, confirm what they expect to see. Another Coronation, a beacon in the bleak night, sits a few yards away. 'Time we were off. Will ye shove my piece stuff intae my bag for me?'

'Aye, nae bother.'

Frank stands up. 'Wilma, it'll probably be a few stops before we find anybody waiting for a caur on a night like this. Will ye come through the front once we're away and Ah might finish what Ah'm trying tae say?' He finds he's blushing. Starts to make his way along the aisle. God! This is *worse* than when Ah asked Marie to go tae the Ascot at Anniesland! It's funny. We pass that cinema every day on this route. Call it the Gaumont now. Without fail, every time I go by I think of that date. Only took her out once. He smiles. Ahhh, but it was my *first* date.

He slots himself into his seat, releases the brake. As he ratchets up the power he listens to the electrical riffs from the cupboard just inside the saloon. Like somebody practising their scales. The tram moves off. He's two hundred yards along the road when . . .

'Ah'm here, Frank.'

Sitting midst the moving shadows of the driver's cubicle, he already knew that. The perfume from the soap she uses preceded her. Josie used the same brand. He checks his side mirrors. The wintry road is empty behind and no figure stands at the stop ahead. He brings the tram to a halt. The small wiper continues its battle with the driving rain. He half turns, smiles. At least it should be easier in the dark. 'Right, Wilma Ballantyne. Ah should have asked you this at *least* a week ago.

I've took it on myself tae book us a table at a restaurant on the evening of the twenty-seventh. Now, this is simply a wee "thank-you" for being such a good conductress. That's the main reason. But as Ah was saying, Ah was on ma own last Christmas and it was, well . . . miserable. So it would be nice tae have company on at least *one* night during the so-called festive season. Is that all right? Would you let me take you out tae dinner?'

'Oh, goodness! That would be nice. But, tae be honest, Frank. Ah'm no' used tae eating in posh restaurants.' As she says this, she is thinking, Ah'd rather not go. Ah wish he hud'nae asked me. But Ah don't want tae hurt his feelings. 'Eh, is it awfy posh?'

'No, not at all. It's a nice wee family-run place. Italian. Have ye ever eaten in an Italian restaurant?'

'Well . . .' She laughs. He can tell she's almost certainly blushing. 'If having sit-doon fish and chips in an Italian cafe counts – I have!'

'This is really homely. Stromboli it's called. Ah guarantee you'll enjoy yourself, Wilma. It's on the Byres Road.'

'Oh, my God! It'll be full o' toffs, Frank. Can ye no' pick somewhere—'

'Wilma, it's doon the bottom end of the Byres Road, near Dumbarton Road. It's no' the Ritz, honest. And anyway, even if it *was* full o' toffs – are you no' as good as them? I think you are. In fact, probably better than some! Ah can promise you we'll have a nice evening.'

'Mmmm, well, okay then. Ah'll believe ye.'

'Good.' He turns his head, looks through the windscreen. 'We'd better go in case some poor souls are waiting for a caur.' He turns back to her. 'Do you use Knights Castile soap, Wilma?'

'Aye.'

'Thought so.' The tram glides off into the stormy night.

'*Buona sera, Signor, Signorina*. Please to come in.'

'*Buona sera*,' says Frank. 'I have a table for two booked. Galloway is the name.'

Wilma stands behind Frank. She looks around. It is nice. Red and white check tablecloths; a fat green wine bottle trailing candle grease stands on every table. Dean Martin is crooning 'Volare' in the background. It's quiet, only three tables occupied. She feels herself relax . . .

It has been a lovely evening. Frank knows it has been a success. Yet, as he escorts Wilma home he notices she is becoming quieter. Conversation is faltering. As they approach Crombie Street she appears to be on edge. She stops on the corner with Saracen Street. 'We can just say good night here, Frank. Ah live along the far end o' the street. Save you a walk.'

'Now, you know I'm an old-fashioned boy, Wilma. I'll see you safely to the close-mouth.'

'Honestly, there's nae need.'

'It's gone eleven o'clock. I'll be happier seeing ye to your close.'

She gives a big sigh. 'Aw'right, then. We'll walk on that side.' She crosses the street. As they make their way along the pavement she walks close to the building, almost brushing her shoulder against the wall now and again. Her nervousness is now palpable.

Frank begins to feel uncomfortable. 'Wilma. I'm not walking you to your close because I'm expecting a couple of goodnight kisses. It's just good manners to see you home.'

'Oh, no, it's no' that, Frank.' She stops outside number 27. 'This is me.' It's almost a whisper.

'Right. Well, I'd better get myself away. Don't want you sleeping in—' He's interrupted by the sound of a window being thrown up. Hears Wilma say, 'Oh, my God!' He looks up in time to see a head, complete with curlers, appear from a first-storey window.

'THAT'S WHERE YE ARE! It's gone eleven o'clock. Get yersel' up these stairs NOW! THIS MINUTE!'

'Ma! This is ma driver. He just took me for a meal because it's Christmas—'

'Get up these stairs now or Ah'm lockin' the door. You've got two minutes yah wee hoor! Of course, it wid probably suit you tae be oot aw' night. That's the time o' night hoors like best! TWO MINUTES or you'll be—'

Frank has stepped back a couple of paces to get a better look, '*Hey*! Who dae you think you're talkin' tae, yah nasty piece o' work?'

The woman pauses, slightly taken aback. But not for long. 'Ah've got nuthin' tae say tae you. It's nane o' your business—'

'Ah! But it *is* my business. Wilma's my friend *and* my work colleague. And we've just been for a meal. Nothing more, nothing less.'

'*Huh*! So ye say. Ah suppose you're a married man as well?'

'*Ma*! Frank's a widower.'

'Is that so? Well Ah'm no' interested in hearing any mair o' yer nonsense. Get yourself up these stairs this minute.' She turns her head towards Frank. 'And you can fuck off!' The window is slammed shut.

Frank looks at Wilma. Sees tears illuminated by the street-lights. 'Ah'm SO sorry, Frank. That's why Ah did'nae want ye tae bring me tae the close. She hates me going oot. Ah'm jist supposed tae come hame fae ma work and stay in the hoose wi' her. If Ah don't, well, ye heard for yerself.'

He takes one of her hands. 'Don't worry, Wilma. Ah'll see ye the morra and you can tell me all about it. You're a grown woman, hen. You should *not* have tae put up wi' that.' He pauses for a second, then gives her a quick kiss on the cheek. 'You don't deserve any of that nonsense. You're a good lassie. Keep your chin up, pal! Goodnight.'

'Aye.' She turns and makes her way into the close. He looks up at the first-storey window. The curtains have been drawn, the light still burns behind them. Ah've a bloody good mind tae go up and knock on her door. He thinks about it. Better not. Would'nae be doing Wilma any favours. He sets off along Crombie Street towards Saracen Street, the evening now spoiled.

Wilma turns the handle on the outside door, steps into the lobby. As she closes the front door and turns the big key, the kitchen door is thrown wide open. Her mother switches the lobby light on, takes two steps towards her. 'Who wiz that cheeky bastard?'

'Ma, he's not. He's a lov—' The blow is delivered with a clenched fist. It catches Wilma just to the side of her left eye. 'He's a cheeky bastard. And you're jist like yer faither. He wiz a hoor-maister – and you've got it in ye tae be a hoor. It's in the blood. Runnin' aboot wi' a married man proves it!'

'*Ma*! His wife got ran ower and killed a year or so—'

'Don't fuckin' argue wi' me! Get tae your bed NOW! Not another word or Ah'll throw ye oot ontae them stairs and you'll no' get back intae this hoose again! That's yer last warning.' She turns and walks back into the kitchen. Wilma watches her go. God! How I hate you! Her mother has gone out of sight but she can hear her moving around, making herself a cup of tea by the sound of it. Wilma continues to stand facing the kitchen door, touching her cheek. Nae wonder Daddy left you. She gives a shuddering sigh. Daddy! Why did ye no' take me with ye?

'Whit are you daeing in therr?'

'Ah'm jist taking ma coat aff. Ah'll need tae go tae the lavvy before Ah go tae ma bed.'

'Well be bloody quick aboot it. And when ye come back, jist go straight through tae that room and get tae bed. Don't bother coming intae this kitchen. Ah've seen enough o' ye for wan night!'

Wilma reaches up, takes the key off its hook, makes her way down the draughty stairs to the half-landing. She sits inside the small WC, glad of the dark. Stares at the pale grey slat of light underlining the bottom of the door; the best the stairhead light can offer. It's cold sitting here. Not as cold as it is up there wi' her. Anyway, it's a chance to let the tears come. Ah'm no' gonny cry in front of her. Bad bitch loves tae see me greetin'. She reaches up, touches her cheek again. 'Oh-yah!' That'll be a big bruise the morra. Have tae put make-up oan tae camouflage it. Oh God! Ah cannae live like this anymair. It's nae life. She's getting worse. Takes pleasure in getting on tae me, bullying me. She gives it some more thought. Wilma! It's nae good sitting here greetin' like a bairn. You're gonny have tae find a way out of all this. Get away from her. C'mon, get yer thinking-cap oan. There's bound tae be something ye can do. And when it eventually comes to ye, Wilma Ballantyne. *Do it*!

CHAPTER TWENTY

And Many O' Them!

It's ideal weather for first-footing. Dry and cold, with a slight breeze.

George Lockerbie leans forward. 'This'll do fine, driver. Just drop us on the corner, please. We want to slip along to our friends' close without them spotting us.' The cab pulls up, George climbs out, offers a hand to Ruth. He leans into the taxi's front alcove. The man slides his window open. 'How much do I owe you?' He has raised his voice to compete with the throbbing of the diesel engine. The cabbie looks at his meter. 'Four shillings and sixpence, gaffer.'

He extracts a red, Bank of England ten-shilling note from his wallet, presses it into the driver's hand. 'Don't bother wi' the change – and a Happy New Year to you!'

'Oh! Thanks very much, sir. And aw' the best tae you. And yer lady wife!' He engages gear; the rhythmic idling of the motor is lost as the cab moves off, slowly at first, to let another taxi overtake. The driver still has his window open, George hears him begin to whistle a jaunty version of the pipe tune, 'The Black Bear'.

'I guess I've just paid the piper.' He looks sideways at Ruth.

She links her arm through his, presses it to her side. As they set off, he again turns his head. 'Ah thought that deserved better!'

She tries to keep her face straight. 'Yes. It was *very* clever, darling.'

They round the corner into Dalbeattie Street. Light streams out from the tenements on both sides. Nine out of ten houses getting ready to let another year in. George leads her off the pavement so as to saunter along the middle of the road. He stops opposite his former close. Looks the length of the street. 'I love it, you know. There's nowhere better to be on a Hogmanay than in the middle of a Glasgow street.' They stand in silence, let the atmosphere seep into them, listen to the last of the old year. From all airts and pairts, outbursts of laughter, singing and music drift out of windows, hang in the air. The volume fluctuates, until it seems a giant radio is being tuned. Now and again brief snatches can be identified . . . a few bars of 'See You Later, Alligator' . . .

'Mmmm, I guess somebody still likes their Bill Haley,' says Ruth. Seconds later Jimmy Shand and his Band make themselves heard – accompanied by much Hooching! and Hawing! from folk in the house where it's being played.

During the last few minutes four men, like sentries, have taken up post outside four closes. George nods in their direction. 'It's surprising how many fellas like tae be their own first foot. Ah guess that's a sign that it's just about time for the Bells.' He turns to Ruth. 'I'm not going to look at my watch. There's no need to. The noise will announce when the New Year's arrived.'

They stand close together, heads slightly on the side, trying to identify individual sounds. The overall crescendo increases slightly. 'That's folk turning their televisions up,' says George. From most windows, filling the night air, there now comes an instantly recognisable voice. 'Ahah! There ye are. That's Andy Stewart getting ready tae welcome in the New Year.' George laughs. 'In Scotland it's no' officially New Year until Andy says so.' A sudden roar, of football crowd proportions, drowns out the music. Cries of, 'Aw' the best!' 'Happy New Year!' 'Same tae you!' 'An' many o' them!' now flood out of windows, fill the street, the night. As one, the men who were outside their closes have vanished. For a moment George and Ruth stand alone, but not lonely, in the middle of Dalbeattie Street. He disentangles his arm, turns to face her, they put their arms round one another. 'Well that's it sweetheart. Happy New '62!'

'And the same to you, my darling.' They kiss, long and tender. He finishes by pressing his lips against her cheek. 'Mmmm, I love to kiss your cheek when it's cold.'

'Do you?' she whispers.

'Aye. Nae germs!'

'Beast!'

'Ah! Listen,' he says. 'Now isn't that lovely. Can you hear it?'

Ruth listens intently. In the distance, sometimes faint, waxing and waning with the breeze, comes a new sound. She looks at him. 'Sounds like a ship's horn?'

'That's exactly what it is. More than one. All the ships tied up in the docks always welcome the New Year in like that. Whoever's on watch gives a few blasts. It'll be happening in every port in the country.'

She listens again, sighs. 'It's a lovely, melancholy sound, isn't it?'

'Sure is. When I hear it, I always wonder – what ports were they in last year? And where will they be twelve months from now?' He pauses. 'Right! Just one last thing before we go up to Robert and Rhea's. Wait and see what's going to happen next,' says George. They stand at a slight angle to one another so as to look along the street. The music, laughter and shouting increases in volume as New Year parties warm up, folk start to dance and sing. It's not yet five past midnight when the first two couples appear; coats and scarves on, carrying message bags that clink, they seem to be in a hurry. George nudges Ruth. 'Keep watching.' Within the next few minutes, individuals and various-sized groups, all warmly clad and similarly weighed-down, emerge from their closes, their paths often criss-crossing as they make haste to nearby closes, or further afield. Many of the men have the traditional 'Bottle' sticking out of their coat pockets. Often, they barely cover a few yards before someone hails them. Groups stop, inter-mingle, kisses and greetings are exchanged. 'You'll huv tae huv a drink oot ma boattle, John.' 'Aye, and you'll huv tae huv wan oot o' mine, Andy.'

'They've all brought the New Year in, in their own house,' says George. 'Now they're off tae first-foot family and friends. This is when the fun really starts.' As he speaks, as if to prove his point, he is twice interrupted as some of these 'New Year missionaries' – complete strangers – shout. 'Happy New Year, folks!' to him and Ruth, then head off to wherever they are going.

Ten minutes later, for just a moment, they once more have the street to themselves. They look up a noisy, yet deserted,

Dalbeattie Street. Along the edge of the pavements, the lamp standards shine down, lighting the way to another New Year. George laughs. 'When I was a kid, I used to wonder why the adults didn't arrange to have fun like this *every* week. With the logic of a child, it seemed common sense to me.' He looks at Ruth. 'And also, I've always felt that Hogmanay really belongs to us Scots. There might be other cities make a big night of it. New York, Rio, places like that. But I don't think they put their hearts intae it like the Scots. Especially the Glesga working man. He looks forward tae it aw' year.' George takes a last look along the street. 'I love being a part of it. Watch folk having such pleasure. Anyway, beloved. Shall we go and first-foot Robert and Rhea – and anybody else who gets in our way?'

As they approach number 18, George points to the bedroom windows of his former flat. 'It seems no time at all since I was living in that room and kitchen with Joan.' He pauses, 'Jeez! You've no idea how depressing that last year was.' They enter the close. He kisses Ruth on the cheek as they pass what had been his front door. He looks at her. 'Then I got that job in the Bar Deco,' he stops, turns to face her, 'and met you.' This time she's kissed on the temple. 'And for the last ten years I've been the *happiest* guy in Glasgow.' Ruth squeezes his hand.

As they climb the two flights of stairs to the first storey, they can hear someone, in high heels; descending from above. They slow as the woman steps onto the landing, turns towards them, ready to descend further. She suddenly falters, almost goes off balance.

Ruth looks up. '*Ruby*! Goodness me! You're the last person I'd expect to meet up a close!'

For a moment, Ruby Baxter has lost more than her timing. She steps back onto the landing, 'Oh, goodness! Well, Ruth and George. I suppose I could say the same about you two.'

All three now stand on the first-storey landing. Kisses on the cheek are exchanged, 'So whatever brings you here?' Ruth smiles, genuinely pleased to see her.

'Oh, just been visiting a friend who lives up the stairs.' Ruby forces a smile that she hopes will look natural. It doesn't. 'And what about the pair of you, what are you doing here?'

'When I first met George, he was living here. In the close. Nowadays we're good friends with a young couple, the Stewarts, who live here.' Ruth points to the half-open door. 'We're about to surprise them. They're not expecting us.' She lays a hand on Ruby's forearm, 'But how *are* you, darling? We did hear that you and Bernard are . . . estranged?'

'Oh, yes. That's all over, I'm afraid. Time to move on and all the rest of it.'

'Well, there's nothing to stop you having the occasional night at the Bar Rendezvous, dear. Bernard never comes any more. So you won't bump into him. We haven't seen you for an absolute age.' As she looks at her, Ruth can't help but notice, Ruby seems very much 'on edge'.

'Anyway,' Ruby makes a move. 'How nice to bump into the two of you. I'd better get on my way. You know how hard it is to get a cab on Hogmanay,' she looks at her watch, 'or as I should say now, Ne'erday.'

'Where are you living now, darling?' enquires Ruth.

'Oh, haven't got anywhere permanent yet. Staying with a friend at the moment, over in, ah, Hyndland.' Ruby leans forwards, kisses are exchanged once more. 'I really must get on, Ruth. But I will try and have a night at the club. That's a promise. You know I always loved it. Bye for now.' She begins to descend the stairs. Ruth and George watch for a moment, then turn to face the Stewarts' door. Ruth puts a hand on George's arm.

'Wait a minute,' she whispers. Although Ruby's now out of earshot, Ruth continues to speak low. 'That was a funny encounter, wasn't it?'

'Not half. Never known Ruby to be so . . . what would you call it? Rattled?' That's *not* the Ruby Baxter we know.' George shakes his head. 'There's something not right somewhere.'

'Yeah, she wasn't at all pleased at bumping into us. We really caught her on the hop there.'

George pushes the Stewarts' door wide open. A hubbub of voices and music comes from the kitchen. He remains in the lobby, calls out, 'Is their anybody in? You've got visitors! HELLO! Anybody at hame?'

While the Lockerbies make their noisy entrance into the Stewarts', Ruby Baxter stands on the pavement, just a step away from the close-mouth, listening. When she feels certain Ruth and George have gone into the flat, she re-enters the close, walks along to where she can look up the stairwell. She peers through the bannister rails, towards the first landing. Right! They're in the flat. Do it *now*! Taking her shoes off, she softly pads her way back up the cold stairs. As she approaches the first storey, nerves a-jangle, the Stewarts' door opens . . . Fuck! Oh, thank God! It's Robert's dad.

'Hello, hen.' Samuel Stewart's face lights up. 'Ah'll huv a wee kiss for ma New Year. Aw the best tae ye!'

Ruby offers a cheek. 'Aye, all the best, Mr Stewart.' She keeps an eye on the door.

'So how are ye doing, hen?'

'Fine. You'll have tae excuse me. Ah'm in a wee bit of a hurry.' She starts up the stairs again.

'Aye, Ah know whit ye mean.' He holds up a hand bearing the lavatory key. 'That's where Ah'm going maself. Cheerio, Ruby. Come doon tae ma son's later oan if ye have the time . . .'

'Will you shut up!' she mutters, as Samuel Stewart's good wishes persist in following her up the stairs. At last he stops. She risks a look through the bannisters. He's making his way down to the half-landing. 'Thank Christ!' She slips her feet back into her shoes.

Yale key in hand, ready to let herself in if needs be, Ruby Baxter stands outside her door on the second storey. She weighs up her options. It's too bloody early to stay locked in the house all night. But I dare not bump into Ruth and George again. I'll never be able to explain why I'm in the close for the second time. She looks up to the top storey. Might be fun to first foot Frank Galloway. Should be safe in there. The sounds of good times being had are all around her. C'mon! It's only twelve-thirty. I'll just nip in and get a bottle . . .

Ten minutes later finds Ruby, a half-bottle of White Horse in hand, standing outside Frank's door praying for an answer to her knock. She hears voices and movement from below, people stepping out onto the landing. Reaching a hand out, she rattles Frank's letterbox as loud as she dare. 'Come *onnnn*!' She sneaks a look through the rails, past the second storey down to the first. Robert Stewart stands outside his door. She hears Rhea's voice . . .

'Where urr ye goin'?

'Up tae see if Archie and Ella are coming doon.'

Ruby gives the letterbox another rattle, reaches into her pocket for her door key, walks over and stands at the top of the stairs. If any of the Lockerbies appear, I'll have to dive down them stairs tae the second storey and into my hoose faster than Stirling Moss!

'Gie Agnes a wee knock, tae,' says Rhea.

'Okay.' Robert turns, about to start up the stairs.

Ruby hears movement behind Frank's door. Thank God! It opens. 'Happy New Year, Frank!' It's little more than a whisper. She can hear Robert climbing the stairs.

'Oh, aye. And a Happy New Year to you.' Frank stands back, gestures with a hand. 'Eh, just come—' He's knocked to the side as Ruby speeds past. He swivels his head as she vanishes into the room. 'Oh, you're in! Jist make yerself at hame, Ruby.' He closes the outside door.

Rhea Stewart comes back into her kitchen, sits down beside her mother and mother-in-law. Those two, Teresa O'Malley and Mary Stewart, sit companionably together at the kitchen table. Ruth Lockerbie sits beside them. 'Ah hope Ella and Archie come doon,' says Rhea. 'You'll like her, Ruth. Ah'm no' kidding. Ella's a scream when she starts. And Ah'll get Robert tae go doon and invite Drena and Billy, tae. They stay in George's auld house. Oh! *and* we'll ask the wee German lassie, Irma, and her man. Ah'm telling ye, when ye get them aw' thegither in the same company, it's a laugh a minute.' Rhea takes a sip of sherry. 'So whit's been happening since we last seen ye, Ruth?'

Ruth purses her lips. 'Can't think of anything special. Nothing out of the ordinary.' She smiles. 'Well, I'm saying that. Actually, we had a surprise meeting right outside your door, tonight. Ran into someone we would never, in a month of Sundays, expect to see up a close in Maryhill.'

'Ootside oor door? On the landing? Wiz'nae Frank Sinatra, wiz it? He usually first-foots us.'

Ruth laughs, reaches for the box of Sobranie. 'Have you heard of Baxter's furniture stores?'

'Oh, aye. Mind, we've never, ever bought anything aff them. Too dear.'

'Jaysus! Too rich for our blood,' says Teresa. 'We have a look in their windows now and again when we're down the town.'

'The chap who owns the chain, Bernard Baxter, he and his wife used to be regulars at the club until they split up. George and I ran slap bang into her on your landing, tonight!'

'Oh, you mean Ruby?'

For the second time in half an hour, Ruth Lockerbie is surprised. 'Do you know her?'

'Of course Ah dae. She lives two-up, in the single-end. Been here aboot six months Ah think.'

'George! Come and hear this.' She watches her husband disentangle himself from the one-sided conversation he's having with Samuel Stewart. He walks over to the kitchen table. 'Yes, dearly beloved?'

'Rhea's just been telling me. Ruby Baxter has been living up this close for about six months!'

'Has she really.' He gives a wry smile. Thinks about it. 'So much for "Just visiting a friend". Poor soul! She must have been too embarrassed to admit this is where she's living.'

'Yes.' Ruth thinks about it. 'She told us she was staying with a friend in Hyndland!'

*　　*　　*

Ruby Baxter looks at the clock on the mantelpiece. 'That twenty past two, Frank?'

'Sure is.' He hopes the next thing he's going to hear is 'Time I was going.'

She picks up the almost empty half-bottle of whisky. 'Are ye for another wee drop?'

'Thanks aw' the same, Ruby, but I'm late shift tomorrow, well, *this* afternoon. So I'll have to get some shut-eye.' He hopes she'll take the hint. She doesn't. Drunk folk never do.

'Ah'll just finish it, maself.' She stretches over from the fireside chair, decants it into her glass. 'A wee drop watt watt— . . . eh, water.' She rises, walks unsteadily to the sink, lets the cold water run a while before putting some into the glass. Returning to the chair, she drops into it, crosses her legs. The floral dress she wears has buttons up the front. The bottom two are unbuttoned, there is plenty of leg on show. Not that the drink is to blame – they were undone when she arrived. 'You got a smoke, Frank?'

He opens the twenty-pack, holds it out to her. She leans forward. His eyes take in the generous amount of cleavage on show. He supplies a light. Sitting back, she slowly re-crosses her legs. As he's in the fireside chair opposite, he gets more than a fleeting glimpse up between her thighs. He feels himself stir. She certainly is fuckable. Why don't I fancy her?

Five past three. It's obvious she intends to sit a while yet. 'Ah, Ruby. I'm afraid I'm going to have to be rather ungentlemanly. I really am ready for my bed. I've got to go to work today, remember?' He takes a draw. Jeez, I'm fed-up smoking. Throws most of the cigarette into the fire. He stands up. 'So

I'm afraid, my dear, I'm gonny have tae give you the bum's rush. I am *so* tired. Can hardly keep my eyes open.'

She looks up. 'Aw, that's a shame. Pity you're working, Frank.' She starts to rise. He offers both hands, which she takes, and pulls her to her feet. 'Oh, goodness. Ah've definitely had too much.' She staggers forward and he moves his hands to her upper arms to steady her. She slips her arms under his, wraps them round his waist, presses herself against him. Her face is just inches away. The red lips are now an out-of-focus blur, yet somehow the sexier for it. There is the scent of good perfume, a hint of fresh perspiration. He's always found that sexier than Chanel No.5. She does smell good. All woman. He begins to get really hard, moves back from the waist so it won't press against her. She smiles. 'Well, I guess I'll just have to settle for a couple of *good*, goodnight kisses.' The red lips, moist from the last mouthful of whisky, are full and luscious. They open slightly, her tongue tries to part his lips. He resists the tempting offer. She is now breathing heavily. He feels himself weakening. Jeez! She is aching for it. He tries *not* to picture the body that will be under that dress. She sways back, looks him in the eye. 'How much of an invitation do you want, Frank?' She is so turned on there's a breathless catch in her voice. 'Would you like me to go down on you? Will that help?'

'No, no. It's not that, Ruby. Ah'm just not ready for another relationship at the moment.'

Instantly, he sees that 'Hell hath no fury' glint in her eyes. 'Huv you any idea how many guys would think aw' their birthdays had come at wance if they got the chance wi' me?' She is now completely forgetting to talk 'proper'.

'Ruby, it's not you – it's me. You are absolutely gorgeous.

Ah cannae believe Ah'm turning down a looker like you. It's just I don't want to get involved with *anybody* at the moment.'

'Think yerself too fucking good for me, dae ye?' She's about to turn into an unreasonable drunk. Her arms are pulled away from round his waist. Her face is now a scowl.

'Of course not. Couldn't be further from the truth.' She's obviously going to lose her temper. Fuck! It's bloody impossible to reason with someone who's drunk too much. He looks at the way she's standing. Wouldn't be surprised if she takes a swing at me.

'Well I want tae know *why* you aren'y interested. Let's fucking hear yer reasons.'

'Okay. If that's the way you want it.' He looks her straight in the eye. 'Ah've seen ye a time or two hanging aboot the coffee stall doon at St Vincent Place, Ruby.'

Her mouth opens, no sound comes out. It closes.

Frank lifts her green, cloth coat from the back of the chair. Hands it to her. She doesn't meet his eyes. 'Sorry, Ruby. You did ask.'

CHAPTER TWENTY-ONE

A Problem Solved?

F rank Galloway, in uniform, stands on the corner of Hayburn Street and Dumbarton Road. Tramways staff pass at intervals as they go in and out of Partick Depot.

'Ahh!' He catches a first glimpse of Wilma coming from the expected direction. She always takes the subway to Merkland Street. He takes a last draw on the cigarette, walks to the edge of the pavement, drops the stub down a sewer.

He watches her approach. Smart in her uniform, she wears the small hat at a slight angle, held by a couple of kirby grips. A woollen tartan scarf is wrapped round her neck then crisscrossed at the front so barely an inch of it shows above her lapels. 'Hi yah!' She stops, stands facing him.

'Hello, Wilma.' He takes an extra second to look at her. Reaches a finger out, uses the scarf as an excuse to touch her, 'What clan is that?'

She tucks her chin in, squints downward. 'Corn beef tartan, Ah think.'

'Yeah. It looks like Fray Bentos. Shall we go and have a bite tae eat afore our shift?'

'Good idea. Ah'm quite hungry.'

'Huh! Tell me news, no' history. Fur the size of ye, ye cannae half put the grub away.'

She tuts loudly. 'Whit a cheek.' As they set off along the Dumbarton Road they fall into step.

'It's true,' says Frank. 'Do you know what you'd have been called in The Andrew?'

'Whit's The Andrew when it's at hame?'

'Have ye no' heard me say that afore?'

'Ah don't think so.'

'That's what matelots, sailors, call the navy. The Andrew.'

'Naw, Ah don't remember that. And what was that other wan, mattylows?'

'That's the French word for sailors. For some reason, we used that often.'

'Oh! So ye wur in the French Navy wur ye. Anywye, what would they huv called me?'

'Oh, aye. They'd have called ye a right wee gannet!'

'Seeing as Ah don't know whit a gannet is, Ah don't know whether tae be insulted or no'.'

'You should definitely feel insulted. It's a sea bird, a bit like a gull, that's known for . . .' he stops as he begins to laugh. It takes two attempts, by which time they are both helpless, before he manages to say, 'It's known for gobbling its food at a great rate of knots. Jist like yerself – it hardly touches the sides!' Passers-by on the Dumbarton Road smile, as they see this driver and conductress having such a good laugh to themselves.

When they eventually stop, it's followed by a silence. Frank breaks it. 'How did it go with your mother? Did you work yourself up to having it out wi' her?' He looks closely at Wilma.

'Ah'll tell ye in the cafe. Ah take it we're going tae Alfie's?'

'Aye. It's as good as anywhere.' He takes another glance at her. 'Anyway, it's the best place tae take you. He's the only cafe that does large portions – in a galvanised bucket!'

'You'd better watch yersel', son!'

They cross Dumbarton Road towards the cafe. As usual its windows are steamed up. This, in turn, diffuses the lights burning inside and gives a welcoming, golden glow to the passer-by. The hand-written menu on the outside of the window is barely legible. 'It's aboot time Alfie was getting tae work wi' the whitewash brush and touching-up that me-an-u.'

'Och, Ah think by noo everybody knows whit's available. That's why he dis'nae bother.'

Frank swings the door open. 'Phew!' A wall of humidity greets them.

'Jeez-oh! It's like the hothoose in the Kibble Palace,' says Wilma. They find an empty table. Tram staff, already eating, nod and smile. Frank picks up two menus, offers one to Wilma.

'It's aw'right, Frank. Ah know what Ah'm gonny have. A sandwich will dae me.'

'Is it the usual – an elephant between two bread vans?' He tries to keep his face straight.

'You're dicing wi' death so ye are!'

'Sorry. Ah'm just trying to put off the inevitable. Ah cannae wait any longer. What happened at the weekend, Wilma? Did ye manage to face up tae her?'

She leans forward. 'Ah did.'

'And? Will you stop dragging it oot!'

'Well. Ah gave it a lot of thought after we had oor talk. You know, worked oot whit Ah was gonny say. Then, Ah had a brain wave! Don't know why Ah had'nae thought of it before. Oan Sunday efterninn Ah went ower tae see ma Auntie Margaret, that's Ma's older sister. Auntie Margaret never takes any nonsense off her. She's eight years older. So Ah told her aboot aw' the bother she's been giving me. And how she's getting worse. Auntie Maggie was fair annoyed because Ah had'nae told her earlier.'

'What happened? Did she come over with you?'

'She did. Ah'm no' kidding, Frank, she got laced intae her. Reminded ma Ma whit she wiz like when she wiz young. Alwiz wanting tae go oot. Causing rows wi' *her* ma and da if they tried tae restrict her. Pointed oot whit a two-faced bugger she's turned intae, trying tae stop me having any pleasure. And reminded her, that Ah'm no' a teenager. Ah'm a grown wumman *and* Ah'm the breadwinner. It wiz great!'

Frank sits back. 'Three cheers for Auntie Maggie. Good for her. So how have things been in the house since then?'

'Well, she's been very subdued. We haven't spoke aboot it. Then again, she's no' in the habit of talking things over wi' me, anywye.'

'I would think, what you have to do now, Wilma, is test her. Have an evening out. Don't come back *too* late – that would be pushing it. You'll have tae break her in to this new routine slowly. What about me taking you to the pictures?'

'That should be okay. Ah should be back hame by eleven if Ah'm jist at the flicks.'

'And if we're not oot the cinema till after half-ten, Ah'll

put ye in a taxi tae make sure you're definitely in by eleven.' He pauses. 'Of course, that's if you'll let me take you tae the pictures?'

Wilma blushes. They both know that, really, this is a date. 'Oh, that would be good, Frank. Sort of test her oot. Is there anything oan worth seeing?'

'Yon musical, *West Side Story*, is still running doon the toon—'

She interrupts. 'Ah've always fancied seeing that. It's been oan for months, huzn't it?'

'Yeah. It's on at the Regal. Will we, ah, go on Wednesday? It'll not be so busy then. But mind, we'll have tae meet at seven. It's an extra long picture. That okay?'

Frank Galloway stands under the Regal's bright canopy. He's wearing a mac and a scarf. He looks along Sauchiehall Street. Sure is a January evening. He's been here since five to seven, in case Wilma arrived early. He'd like to look at his watch. But if Wilma sees him, she might think he's becoming impatient. Och, it's probably only about five past. Jeez! Forty-eight years old and got a date for the pictures. You're needing your heid examined so ye are! He gives a sigh. Ah wouldn't be here if Josie hadn't . . . C'mon, Frank! Don't go doon that road . . .

'Hi yah!'

He turns, she's smiling. The beginnings of the dark mood vanish like snow in a puddle. 'My! Don't you look smart. Not half!' She's wearing a dark blue coat. 'That looks as if it's new.'

'Thank you, kind sir. It is new. With me no' going out very often, ma wardrobe's a bit behind the times. So Ah've lashed oot on one or two new things.'

'What about your mother? Any aggravation?'

'No. Ah told her Ah was going tae see this musical. Didn't say Ah was going with someone—'

Frank cuts in. 'That's probably wise. Ah don't think she'll be quite ready for that.'

'Anywye. Ah would'nae say she wiz overjoyed. But she never gave me any argument. Just stomped aboot the hoose huffing and sighing an' aw' the rest of it.'

'Well, that sounds good, Wilma. We'll definitely make sure you're home before eleven.' He pauses. 'I keep meaning to ask you. What *is* your mother's first name?'

'Myra.' She watches the corners of his mouth turn down. She smiles. 'Suits her, dizn't it.'

It's twenty past ten when, moving slowly amongst the departing audience, they step out of the Regal into a cold, damp Sauchiehall Street. Wilma dabs her eyes. Frank shakes his head. 'Ah guess Ah don't need tae ask if ye enjoyed yourself, kid?'

She looks up at him, 'Oh! That was smashing, Frank. It's a long time since Ah've had such a good greet. Anywye, *you* cannae talk. Ah glanced at you when he wiz singing that last song – your eyes were brimming, tae. So don't you kid yerself!'

He laughs. 'Aye, Ah must be honest. It was gettin' to me as well. It was really sad.'

She spontaneously links her arm through his, presses it to her side. 'Ah knew it wiz. *Hah*! Big tough guy.' Suddenly embarrassed, she lets go. He can still feel the touch of her.

'Well, Wilma, it would be so nice if we could finish the evening by going somewhere for a nightcap. But we both know, at the moment anyway, that's out o' the question. More's the pity. So, I'll put you into a taxi and we'll get you home before eleven. Keep Myra happy.'

'Och, Ah should be aw'right on public transport, Frank. Even if Ah get in jist after ele—'

'No.' Frank shakes his head. 'No way, kid. If we can grab a cab fairly quickly, it'll easily get you home before eleven. Here's one coming!' He steps to the edge of the pavement, waves vigorously. The driver indicates, slows. 'Great!' Frank reaches for his wallet, extracts a pound note. 'Here you are, pal.'

'Ah can get it maself, Frank.'

'You will not. You're out with me.'

'It'll no' be as much as that.'

'Well, that'll be okay. You can give me the change tomorrow.' He opens the cab's door, 'I suggest you get off at the end of your street – not at the close. Oh, and give the driver a two-bob tip. See you tomorrow.' He looks at her. 'I've really enjoyed myself. Goodnight, Wilma.'

'Me too. Goodnight, Frank.'

He bends his head, kisses her on the cheek. Once she's safely on board he closes the door. He leans into the front alcove, the driver's window is open. 'The lady will give you the address.' Frank steps back towards the door, looks into the back of the cab. She sits there, so petite. He wishes he was next to her, taking her home to Possilpark. Spend a few extra minutes with her. No. Mustn't take a chance on her mother seeing me. As the engine revs he gives a wave. Wilma smiles. The cab slips into the traffic.

He stands at the pavement's edge, looks at the rear window. He can see the back of her head. He watches until the taxi gets lost amidst the traffic and he loses sight of her. Out of nowhere, the thought of Ruby Baxter being in the house with him last week comes into his mind. Jeez, I'm *so* glad I never went to bed with her. He sets off towards Charing Cross. A few paces later he stops in his tracks. Suddenly it's as clear as day – it was because of Wilma I turned her down. He sets off again into the cold, dreich night. Whistling, as though it were a summer's evening.

CHAPTER TWENTY-TWO

Why?

As she hears another 'swish' from the direction of her windows, Granny Thomson turns her head, watches the wind dash regular handfuls of snow against them. Each pane is hazed with moisture inside; clear trails wriggle through it, showing where water droplets have made a run for the sill. Outside on the pavement, a tall lamp standard shines down, diffusing the condensation into a silvery glow. This makes it seem extra wintry outside – but all the cosier in.

She looks round her room. Ah love it when the weather's like this. Teresa O'Malley's forever saying tae me, 'Snug as a bug in a rug, so ye are.' She reaches a hand out, selects a few choice lumps of coal, places them on the fire where they're most needed, rubs her fingers on her peenie. The electric hasn't been switched on for days. The faithful gas lamps provide all the light she needs. The light she's used to. The radio is on. Sandy Macpherson is giving it laldy on the theatre organ at the minute. There's a play oan at nine. She turns her head again. 'Ah'll pu' them curtains. A lot o' cauld air hangs aboot them windaes when it's like this. Still, it's the end o' buggerin' January. Whit mair can ye expect? You're talkin' tae yerself again, Bella.' She gets to her feet.

By twenty past nine the play is getting into its stride. The old woman has been dozing for the last ten minutes. She doesn't hear Marjorie Marshall's first knock. Nor the inside door being opened and Marjorie's tentative 'Granny?' A second *'Granny!'* does the trick.

'Oh! Aye! It's yerself, hen. Don't usually see you at this time o'—'

'Granny, Ah know it's a bother for ye tae go up the stairs. But Jane's not very well. Ah'm getting a wee bit worried. I'd bring her down, but I think it's best if she's no' disturbed. If I give ye a hand up the stairs, would ye mind having a look at her?'

She gives a loud tut. 'Of course, Marjorie! It's nae bother if my wee pal's no' weel.'

Minutes later, a shawl round her shoulders, her arm linked through Marjorie's, a puffing Granny Thomson makes it up the chilled, grey stairs to the second storey. Jack Marshall steps out onto the landing as they climb the last flight. 'Thanks, Granny. Sorry tae be dragging ye . . .'

The old woman waves a hand at him. 'If ma wee darlin's no weel,' she pauses to take a breath, 'Ah can assure ye, you're no' draggin' me anywhere.'

'In ye come.' They enter the flat. Stop just inside, between kitchen and bedroom.

'So whit symptoms has she got?' The heads and shoulders of all three are starkly lit by the overhead bulb in the cold lobby. It's an image that will remain in their memories.

Marjorie speaks. 'It's come on gradually during the day. Round about twelve or so, she said she wasn't feeling very well. Just wanted to lie on the settee and watch the telly. As the day has gone on she's steadily got all the more hangy. Doesn't want tae be bothered, just wants tae sleep.' The old woman mutters the occasional 'Uh huh.' Majorie finishes listing Jane's symptoms. 'But this last hour, maybe less, she's just out of it. Unresponsive. Moans if you bother her. Oh, and boiling hot. So warm.' As she speaks, she is near to tears.

'Right, Ah'll have a wee look at her.' The instant Granny turns, faces the bedroom, a mood of bleakness, like a cape, envelops her. As she lays a hand on the doorknob she senses a presence. Knows who is already there. Laying claim. Oh, my God! Ah'll jist have tae go through the motions. Try no' tae frighten them. She walks to the bedside, looks down on the child, places the back of her hand on her forehead. 'Aye, she's hot right enough.' She bends forward. 'Jane? It's Granny, hen. *Jane!*' No response. She puts a hand behind the bairn's neck, gently lifts. There's a moan. She lets go. Jane's head flops back onto the pillow. Her parents watch anxiously. The matriarch now lifts her arm a couple of inches, releases it. It also flops. She does it once more. Same result. 'Ah'll have to have a wee look under her nightie.'

'Aye, of course.' Marjorie lifts the covers back.

Granny reaches for the hem of the nightdress. With a terrible certainty she knows what she's about to find. Easing the nightie up as far as the child's chest, she bends down to see better. Her eyes focus and there comes an instant cold chill, deep in her stomach. It takes a conscious effort not to blurt out Oh, my God! With a heavy heart, she is looking at what she didn't want to see. An outbreak of very small, bright red spots that runs the length of Jane's right side – then spread out towards her stomach. Meningitis! Everything has become urgent. Now she can't help but frighten them. She pulls the nightie back down. Takes a second to herself to look at this beautiful child. As she straightens up, she catches a glimpse of the kaleidoscope lying on a chair. An almost irresistible wave of sadness comes over her. She is on the brink of breaking down in front of them.

'What do ye think, Granny?' The apprehension on both their faces is terrible to see.

She swallows hard. 'Mmm, she's, eh, no' very well—'

Marjorie interrupts her. 'Will we get the doctor in? Or do ye think she maybe needs an ambulance?'

There's no easy way now. Granny looks at her. 'There isnae time for an ambulance, Marjorie. Get her wrapped up in a blanket.' She turns. 'Jack, go straight doonstairs tae Robert Stewart and ask him if he'll run ye all tae Oakbank Hospital right away. Tell him Ah said it's urgent.' A terrible fear comes into their eyes. She hates being the one who's caused it. 'Jack, son. Hurry!'

'Aye! Right!' He comes out of his paralysis, runs out of the room, along the lobby then they listen to him clattering down the stairs two at a time.

'Oh, Granny! What do ye think it is?' With Jack gone, Marjorie is instantly lost.

Once again, the old woman thinks before she speaks. There's nae point saying, Ah wish ye had sent for me hours ago, or, Ye should have had the doctor in earlier. If they lose that wean, Ah don't want them blaming themselves the rest o' their lives. 'Well, Ah'm no' really that sure, hen. All Ah do know is, she's no' very well. She needs tae be seen at a hospital. Oakbank's a grand place. They'll find oot whit's wrong.'

Barely five minutes after Jack had been sent down to Robert Stewart's, the three Marshalls are in the old Riley being driven to Oakbank Children's Hospital. Rhea Stewart has come up to see if she can do anything. While her man drives off into the night, she helps Granny back down the stairs. As they step onto the landing, Teresa O' Malley opens her door. 'Is there sumt'ing the matter?'

'They've hud tae rush wee Jane away tae the hospital, Ma,' says Rhea.

'Jayzus, Mary and Joseph!' Teresa blesses herself.

'Come intae the hoose wi' me, the pair o' ye,' commands Granny. 'Teresa, will ye mask a dish o' tay. Ah'm choking. Rhea, will ye get the whisky bottle oot o' the sideboard.'

Rhea walks Granny over to her chair, then brings an almost full bottle of Grant's Standfast from the sideboard. As she places it on the table, she can't wait any longer. 'Whit dae ye think's up wi' the wee yin, Granny?'

The old woman stares into the fire, the despair heavy on her. 'Ah'm almost . . .' She bursts into tears. Her neighbours move to stand either side of her. Teresa strokes her back, Rhea places a hand on her shoulder. They now know the answer will be bad. Tears stream down Teresa's face, Rhea tries to blink her's back.

'Oh, Jayz,' says Teresa. 'Is it sum'ting terrible, Bella? If Marjorie and Jack lose that . . .' she cannot continue. She pulls the nearest chair out from under the table, sits herself next to her old friend. Reaching for the whisky, she pours some into a cup.

Rhea also takes a measure. 'If anything happens tae that wean. Oh, my God! It diz'nae bear thinking aboot. That wee yin is their whole life . . .' She breaks off to look at Granny, who still cannot speak. Rhea watches the tears stream over the broken veins on the old woman's red cheeks. It's the saddest sight she's ever seen.

Robert Stewart returns home around ten-thirty. He is unable to tell them anything about Jane's condition. Only that, after a brief examination on arrival, she'd been rushed through to the emergency treatment room. When he'd left the hospital there hadn't yet been a report on her. Jack and Marjorie were at her bedside. Rhea tells him what Granny thinks it is.

Until just short of midnight a regular procession of neighbours, mostly womenfolk, call into Granny Thomson's for any news as word of the Marshalls' crisis spreads through the close.

After a sleepless night, the darkness filled with much foreboding, Granny Thomson rises just after six, lights the fire, then sits at it with a cup of tea. At twenty to seven there's a knock on the door. 'It's just me, Bella.' Teresa enters. 'Oi' take it Marjorie and Jack aren't back yet?'

'No.' Granny stares into the flames. 'They'll be back some time this morning.'

Teresa doesn't enquire as to how she knows. 'Anyways, Oi'm away t' do me offices. On me way back, Oi'll take a walk up to Saint Columba's on Hopehill Road. Say a prayer for that mite.'

'Aye.'

'Cheerio the now.' Teresa departs.

Granny Thomson builds the fire up, places a kitchen chair at the window with a pillow on it, then wraps a shawl round her shoulders to keep the cold air at bay. Just before eight a.m. she takes up her vigil. As it's too cold to open the window, she tucks the net curtain up behind its wire, then sits herself at an angle so as to see part-way along the street. Now and again she wipes away the ever-forming condensation from inside the panes. She sometimes tries to comfort herself – maybe Ah'll be wrong this time. Then she recalls what was waiting in that bedroom last night.

She hasn't long to wait. It's not quite ten a.m. when a taxi turns into Dalbeattie Street, pulls up below her window. The matriarch lets her curtain fall, watches through the nets. Jack Marshall emerges, pays the driver, then helps Marjorie out. Just to look at them is to know the worst. Jack puts an arm round his wife to support her as they enter the close.

With the shawl still round her shoulders Granny Thomson goes to her front door, takes a step out onto the landing. She can hear Jack. 'Weesh, hen. We'll soon be hame. Weesh, now.' As she listens, her own tears begin.

As they come onto the half-landing, turn, and start up the next flight, Jack is first to see the old woman. He looks at her, shakes his head slightly from side to side. It says more than a thousand words. Two steps later Marjorie looks up. Their eyes meet. She falters, stops just short of the landing. 'Granny, we haven'y got our wee lassie anymair. She's . . .' The wail, the howl that comes from somewhere inside her isn't human. If Jack wasn't holding her she would fall. All three stand, unable to move, overcome.

'C'mon, Marjorie. Just a bit further.' Jack gets her moving again. Almost carries her. As they come onto the landing Granny steps forward, opens her arms. Marjorie buries her face into her shoulder, tries again to get some of her grief out. It won't come. She gulps, gasps for breath. Only painful, dry sobs emerge. The old woman strokes her back, sways them both gently from side to side as tears stream down her own face.

'Ah know, hen. Ah know. Jist try and get your greet oot. It'll have tae come oot.' She knows she cannot help. Nobody can. Nothing can. Only having her daughter back. She nods to Jack to take her. 'Get the doctor tae gie her something, Jack. She'll have tae have sleep.' She reaches up, lays a hand on his shoulder, gently rubs it, looks him in the eye. 'Ah know you're sufferin' tae, son. Every bit as much.'

It's four days later. A bitter cold, January day. Yet the sun shines. Marjorie Marshall makes her way down to the first storey. 'It's me, Granny.'

'Aye, in ye come, hen.' The old woman looks up as her visitor enters. 'How are ye doing? Dae ye think you'll be aw'right the day?'

Marjorie sits down on the fireside chair opposite. She carries the kaleidoscope. 'I'll have to be. I really don't want tae go, Bella. Now and again I think I'll refuse! Nobody can make me.' She shrugs. 'But I'll have tae face it, Granny. I have tae go tae her funeral. I'm her mammy.'

'Has the doctor given ye something?'

'Aye, thank God. Whatever it is, it works. Ah feel sort of detached. Emotionless. Don't know what I'll be like when it wears off. But long may it last.'

'Whit time are ye leaving the hoose?'

'The cars are coming at one. Only the hearse and one car. We're no' having anybody in the house beforehand – or after. I'll no' be in any state tae make small talk. Jack and I are going tae the cemetery in the car by oorselves. Anybody who wants to go will have tae make their own way. Meet at the cemetery. After the service, folk can go straight tae Hubbards tearoom on Great Western Road. That's all been laid on.' She gives a heavy sigh.

Granny looks at the clock. 'It's jist five past eleven. Will ye take a dish o' tay with me?'

'Aye. That'll be nice. Just you and me.'

As the old woman makes the tea, Marjorie sits looking into the fire, the kaleidoscope on her knees. 'We decided to put the lid on the coffin, yesterday. Jack and I could'nae bear it any longer.' She gently strokes the kaleidoscope.

'That's why Ah've never came up, Marjorie. Ah jist do *not* want tae see ma wee pal in her coffin. It's no' right. It should'nae be.' As she speaks, she blinks back tears. 'And that's why Ah'm no' coming tae the funeral. It would be too much for me. Ah cannae face the thought Ah'll never see that bairn again. Ah hope that has'nae offended ye?'

'Bella, the idea never entered my head. We *know* you loved Jane as much as we do. Ah don't blame you for not wanting to go. It'll be an ordeal.' She puts a hand on top of Granny's, squeezes it gently. 'Just you stay here till it's all over.'

Granny pours the tea. Puts the strainer back on its stand. 'Dae ye want a wee drop o' something in that, hen?'

'Better not. The doctor said Ah cannae touch any alcohol while Ah'm taking these tablets.'

The matriarch sits back in her chair, takes a sip of tea. 'Ahhh! That's grand.'

'Oh! Before I forget,' says Marjorie. She shakes her head. 'These tablets have got me wandered.' She reaches forward with the kaleidoscope, places it on Granny's lap. 'Jack and I thought it would be nice if you had this. Jane and you had such fun with it.'

'Awww! That's awfy nice of the two o' ye, Marjorie.' She looks down at her and Jane's magical instrument. 'Oh! Ah really am touched. The pair of us had such wonderfu—' She stops. Stares at it for a moment. With a hand at either end she raises it to her face, then holds it vertical, presses it to her right cheek. She closes her eyes. Marjorie watches, her cup poised halfway to her mouth.

'No!' Granny opens her eyes, looks at Marjorie. She smiles. 'Ah'd love tae have it, hen, but Ah cannae. It's no' meant for me. You and Jack have tae keep this. Don't *ever* give it away.' She looks down at the varnished wooden case one last time, then leans forward, returns it. As Marjorie takes it into her hand, the old woman holds onto the other end for a moment longer. 'And mind, it's not to be put away in a drawer or a cupboard, Marjorie. It must always be in sight. Out in the light.' She lets go the end she's been holding, sits back, smiles. 'As long as you have that,' she almost touches it again, 'she's never far away.'

As Isabella Thomson speaks, Marjorie feels a peace, a calmness come over her. She presses the kaleidoscope to her breast, eyes brimming with tears. 'Thanks, Granny.'

When Marjorie returns to their flat, Jack notices she still carries the kaleidoscope, 'Did ye forget tae gie Granny . . .'

'No. Ah'll tell ye later, Jack. We'd better get ready.' She looks at the small, white coffin, standing on the trestles by the wall. How can Jane be in there? I'm longing to see the kitchen without it. It seems to have been there forever.

Jack comes over to her, wraps her in his strong arms. She turns her head to the side, rests it against his chest. 'Are ye gonny be okay, hen?'

She looks up at him. 'As long as I've got you, Jack Marshall, I'll survive. What about you, my love? Are *you* going to be all right?'

'Aye. Ah think so.' He gives a great, juddering sigh.

'Ah couldn't have got through these last few days without you, Jack. I love you *so* much.'

He lifts his coat from the back of the chair. 'They should be here in a few minutes.'

'Yes. I'll go and get my coat and scarf.' As she walks along the lobby she realises she's still carrying the kaleidoscope. She swings the door open and enters the quiet bedroom. The low winter sun streams in through the net curtains, falls across the bottom corner of the double bed. Jane's bed. For such a short time. Recalling what Granny has just told her, Marjorie walks over, places the kaleidoscope on the bottom corner of the bed nearest the window. Fully in the sun. She turns it so that the eyepiece faces directly into it. Some of the light finds its way in, reflects all the way through the instrument – and the coloured pieces of glass – and spills out onto the candle-wick spread as a delicate, oval splash of colour. She slowly runs her fingers through this pale rainbow, finds herself smiling. This would have tickled Jane.

As the undertaker's men descend the stairs the coffin bobs in time to their step. Marjorie and Jack follow behind, unable to take their eyes from it, so white and pure in the dim stairway. At last they reach the bottom. Marjorie looks past the coffin and its bearers, along the last few yards of shadowy close to where the winter sunlight floods the street. She can see the rear of the hearse, its back already open. Ah don't want my wee lassie tae go in that. She's only six. She should *not* have tae go inside that. It's no' right. Jack senses her turmoil, looks at her, squeezes her hand tight. Gives her strength.

They emerge from the dark close into the brightness. Marjorie narrows her eyes, hardly able to see in the low, winter sun. The lone funeral car should be behind the hearse. As her eyes begin to adjust she becomes aware there are a lot of folk, silent folk, standing on the pavement either side of the close mouth. Two Alexander's Bluebird single-decker buses are parked behind the funeral car! Somewhere between fifty to sixty neighbours stand quietly on the pavement. Jack and Marjorie stop. Look. Try to take in this bewilderment of faces . . . Ella and Archie Cameron, Drena and Billy McLaren, Irma and Bert, Agnes Dalrymple, Irene Stuart, even Frank Galloway and Ruby Baxter, whom they hardly know, all the children of the close, big and small. Everybody from number 18, all in their best clothes. There are others. Folk from adjoining closes and nearby streets. Many from the Maryhill Road. People whose faces they know, whom they say 'Hello' to in passing, who work in the local shops. All have taken a walk round to show sympathy. To be there. Drena points upward, behind them. Jack and Marjorie turn. Granny Thomson, her heavy shawl over her shoulders, leans on a cushion on her window sill, her shock of white hair so bright in the sun.

'The Manageress cannae make it,' says Drena. Granny manages a smile.

'Aye. I know. Granny and I had a cuppa this morning.' Marjorie smiles, then instantly feels guilty for smiling on the day she's burying her wee lassie.

As they take the last few steps to the car, Marjorie sees other faces. Ken from the paper shop. The ladies who serve in the Scotia Bakery. Mary from Dalbeattie Street's dairy.

They climb into the funeral car, the driver clicks the door shut, gets behind the wheel. The smell of the leather uphol-stery, the silence, envelops them. They cannot hear the engine. It feels good to be isolated for a moment. Try to take it all in. Jack looks at her. When he speaks there's a tremor in his voice. 'Wasn't that something? Did you know about that?'

Marjorie shakes her head. 'Ah knew there were a few from the close going, but nothing like that. I imagine Ella and Drena, and probably Rhea, organised everything. But all those other folk who don't belong to our close . . .' she has to stop. Tries again. 'Just walking round . . .' She stops again. Can't say any more.

*   *   *

The hearse turns onto the Maryhill Road, the funeral car in close attendance. Robert Stewart and family follow in the Riley, then the Bluebird single-deckers. All the way to Lambhill, Marjorie and Jack never take their eyes off the small white coffin in the back of the hearse.

It has just gone four o'clock when, drained after their ordeal, Marjorie and Jack return to 18 Dalbeattie Street. At this moment, more than anything, they just want to be by themselves. Much to their surprise, they had managed to stay thirty minutes at Hubbards. Before leaving, Jack had taken the chance, in an impromptu, emotional few words, to thank their friends and neighbours for their support and kindness. And to tell them how touched they had been to step into the street and find so many folk gathered. Marjorie and he would never forget it. Or them.

Jack opens the door and they step into their silent house. Walk into the kitchen. 'Oh, Jack. Thank God the coffin has gone. Put the kettle on. I'll take my coat through the room.'

The bedroom is as quiet and still as it had been a few hours ago. The sun has moved across the sky, now shines through the window at a different angle, no longer falls on the bed. Marjorie starts to take her coat off . . . The kaleidoscope has gone! She knows she left it on the bottom corner of the bed. Placed it so as to catch the rays of the sun. 'Jack! Did you move the kaleidoscope?' She can hear him filling the kettle.

'Naw. Never seen it. You had it, hen.'

She thinks back. Jack had already brought his coat through to the kitchen. Had it hanging on the back of a chair. I was the only one who came in here. She looks around. There it is! It's lying on the window sill on the *other* side of the net curtain. Jack calls from the kitchen. 'Have ye found it? Will Ah gie ye a hand tae look . . .'

'No, no, it's all right. I've got it. It's okay.' She's relieved to hear him walk away. She crosses over to the window. Looks down through the net curtain. The kaleidoscope lies in the last of the day's sun. Pale colours spill out onto the sill. She reaches a hand under the curtain. Runs her fingers along the varnished wooden case. It's warm to the touch. She lifts it, presses it against her cheek. Closes her eyes.

CHAPTER TWENTY-THREE

Some Enchanted Evening

F red Dickinson isn't used to being out on a Saturday evening. But, business is business. He lifts the tumbler to his lips. The peaty smell of the single-malt rises up, gives his nostrils a treat. He looks at the man sitting opposite him in the bar of the Central Hotel. At the moment all he can see is the top of Sammy Wilding's head as he signs their contract. In triplicate. The last signature is done with a flourish. Sammy looks up, screws the cap onto his fountain pen, clips it into his inside pocket. He offers his hand. 'All done, Fred. Our solicitors have completed their side of things. We've now done ours.'

'Yes, indeed.' Fred gives him a firm handshake. 'I'm rather pleased to be going a bit upmarket. Hillhead has always been considered desirable. I'm surprised you're selling such a good quality building. Chester Crescent has a lot of potential.'

'As I said. There's no catch, Fred. I live in Edinburgh. My properties are all there – with the exception of Chester Crescent. It's consolidation. With all my interests now in the capital, it cuts out regular trips to Glasgow. Common sense.'

'Will you take another glass afore ye go?'

'No. Thanks all the same, Fred. There's an Edinburgh train at eight-fifteen, which I'll just about make.' He rises. 'Nice to do business with you. Sorry to drag you out on a Saturday night.' He glances round the bar. 'Not the usual time or place, where I exchange contracts.'

'It was no trouble. Anyway, as you're off on holiday on Monday, it could have been weeks before we got together to finalise things. The major effort has been on your part, Sammy, travelling from Edinburgh. I'm just a fifteen-minute taxi ride away.'

'Okay! I'm going to have to put a spurt on to get my train. See you around, Fred. Bye.'

Fred Dickinson looks at his watch. Quarter to nine. 'Mmmm.' *Candid Camera*'s on at half-past. He purses his lips. *The Avengers* at ten. Could catch both of them if I leave now – *and* I've still got the *Telegraph* crossword to finish. Gee whiz! The pace is relentless. Too much for one man to handle. He sips his whisky, sits back in the leather chair, looks slowly round the Central's lounge bar. He feels himself relax as the ambience – and the Laphroaig – gets to him. Soft lights on woodwork and rows of bottles, ice chinking in glasses, muted conversations. Can't remember when I last went out of an evening. Seems to be all business lunches nowadays. I'm really pleased about that deal. Couple of times I thought we might have to abort. He stares into space. Abort. Funny how those wartime words stay in the vocabulary. Whenever a raid on Berlin was aborted, we were always bloody delighted. Flak Alley! A chance to live for another day. As usual, he goes with this train of thought. Five minutes later this middle-aged man, sitting alone in a busy Saturday night bar, is twenty years back in time. Images flash into his mind one after the other: Ops Room, large map of Western Europe, synchronised groan when Berlin is revealed as tonights's target. Dimly lit instruments, flares, searchlights, flak. Tracer rising lazily into the sky, eyes peeled for night fighters. As always happens, remembered faces start to appear. So many. Some forever young. God! That line gets to me every Armistice Day . . . 'as we that are left grow old' . . . Those boyish faces. I love them all. Every man jack of them. The best of the best . . .

She's halfway across the floor when some part of his brain recognises 'the walk'. The memories of the 23-year-old bomber pilot are instantly returned to storage. The 43-year-old businessman looks up – in time to watch Ruby Baxter sashay the last few yards to the bar. His heart skips God knows how many beats. The almost-forgotten tingle returns. Man-oh-man! The merest glimpse of that woman is enough. Must be months since we crossed paths. As he looks at her, other memories are brought forth; more recent ones . . . The Rotary Club dances. I'd keep an eye on the door until, at last, she'd walk in with . . . What was his name? Bernard. Aye, Bernard Baxter. Then she'd dominate the rest of my evening. Wouldn't be able to take my eyes off her. Watch her dance by, work out when they were due to glide back into view, down by the bandstand. A half-smile plays on his lips. This is your chance, Fred. She's separated from Baxter. You've been hoping you might bump into her. There she is, boy! Just twenty feet away, sitting on a bar stool. Och, maybe she's waiting for someone. *So?* Don't start finding excuses. At the very least you have a chance to talk to her. What did they call it on that business course? Yeah, register your interest. Six years. And you haven't said one bloody word to her. What *can* I say? Go for the jugular! He almost laughs . . . I just wanted to let you know, Ruby Baxter, that for the last six years I've been besotted with you. He looks at her. So near. You'll never get a better chance. He gulps the rest of the single malt, Oh, great God of the Islay peat bogs – give me strength! Fred Dickinson rises to his feet.

The barman is mixing her drink; he stops to light her cigarette. Fred walks over, stands at the bar. Not too near. 'Good evening.'

She turns her head, eyes aware, sharp. He doesn't notice. He passes muster, so they soften. 'Good evening.' She turns her head to blow smoke away from him.

'May I buy you that drink?'

'That would be nice. Thank you.'

'Allow me to introduce myself. My name is Fred Dickinson.'

'Ruby Baxter.'

'Hello, Ruby Baxter.' Jeez, it's a good job I've had a couple of shorts. Wish I could play the man about town the way Cary Grant does. No chance. What about attempting an easy-going James Stewart? He sighs. Probably be more like Jimmy Durante! At the moment I'm not calm enough to play it cool. He looks at her. Smiles. I'm having enough bloody trouble playing me! Can't believe I'm two feet away from Ruby Baxter. She's sitting on a bar stool looking up at me. I can smell her perfume. He looks at the red hair flowing down to the white shoulders. In the soft lights of the bar she is utterly gorgeous.

God, she overawes me! Please don't let me make a mess of it. He gives what he hopes sounds like a discreet cough. It's really an attempt to clear the giant toad – it's too big to be a frog – that's stuck in his throat. 'Ah, I'm sitting at a table over there. I'd be very pleased if you'd join me.' I bet she can hear how nervous I am.

Ruby braces herself. I hate this next bit, especially when it's a nice guy, but they have to be put in the picture straight away. Probably shatter his illusions. 'I'd be delighted to join you, Fred. However,' she draws on her cigarette, 'I think it's best if I let you know right away – I'm a working girl. I come in here to do business, if you know what I mean?' She looks at him. What will his reaction be? Will he make an excuse and turn on his heel? Become embarrassed? Screw his face up in disgust, then come out with some cutting remark . . .

Fred looks at her. He wonders if his mouth has fallen open. Jesus Christ! She's on the game! He hears somebody say, 'Oh, that's quite all right.' It sounds like him.

Ruby instantly relaxes. 'Good. In that case I will join you.' She likes the look of him. Seems to be a nice guy. This could finish up a pleasant evening. She looks at him again. Smiles. I feel sure I know that face.

'I'll have another couple of drinks brought to the table. What would you like, Ruby?'

'Campari and soda, please. With ice.'

Their conversation is light, inconsequential, until the barman places the fresh drinks on the table and heads back to his bar. Ruby leans forward, speaks low. 'Would you like to get the business details out of the way first? Then, we can enjoy one another's company.'

'Yes, that's a good idea.' Fred is still bewildered. Feels he's flown into turbulence. Yet, he is also very much aware that, at long last, he's in company with Ruby Baxter. A dream come true. But she's on the game! These two extremes are too much. They've been chasing one another round and round in his head since she told him.

Ruby leans over. 'Are you thinking of all night? Or just a couple of hours? In either case, we'll need a hotel room. And whatever option you choose, the price is the same. Five pounds.'

Yet again, he feels caught on the hop. He tries to regain control – get a grip – of his whirling mind. 'Ahhh, probably all night. And, eh, if it's any help, I live alone out at Langside. If you're quite happy to come to my place, I think you'll find it much more, well, relaxing and comfortable. Oh! And of course, I'll send you home in a taxi in the morning.'

She sits back. 'Now please don't take offence – but sometimes it can finish up being a rather unpleasant experience for a girl, when she goes to a guy's place.' She looks at him.

Fred holds his hands up, palms forward. 'Oh! I am sorry. I'm afraid I'm not used to this, eh, sort of thing. I'm forgetting that you don't know me from Adam. Okay then. What about this? Let me take you to dinner. Is it all right for me to do that? I really would like to make an evening of it. Enjoy your company for a few hours.'

'Now that would be nice.' She gives him a smile. 'I'd like to have dinner with you.'

As she speaks and he looks at her, he at last begins to calm down. Take it all in. He looks into her eyes. Smiles. 'There's a nice place on West Regent Street. The Excelsior. Do you know it? It's quiet. I like to be able to talk over dinner.'

'I know *of* it, but I've never eaten there.'

'I think you'll like it.'

Ruby suddenly gets a good feeling about this man. She lowers her voice. 'I haven't been very long in this line of work, Fred, but I'm a pretty good judge of people. I think I'll enjoy spending the rest of the evening with you.'

He looks at her face. Really looks at her. So what if she's on the game? This is Ruby Baxter. I've dreamed of this. He gently places a hand on top of hers. 'Good. That makes two of us.'

It has gone eleven o'clock. That time of night when waiters gather together, start willing their customers to fancy an early night. Fred and Ruby have a corner table. Well away from the remaining diners. The food has been good, as has the conversation. Coffee cups have been refilled, Fred is savouring another Laphroaig. Ruby is enjoying herself, sometimes forgetting she's 'doing business'. Fred is what she calls a toucher. As the evening has slipped by he's regularly reached over to stroke her hand or forearm, sometimes merely touch her with a finger while he makes a point. It's not lascivious. Just gentle, friendly. She has also decided, that if he asks her again, she will go home with him.

She sips her coffee, puts the cup on its saucer. 'Fred, all evening I've been thinking I know you from somewhere. But I can't recall where.'

He thinks it over for a moment. 'Shall I tell you?'

'Yes, please.'

'Over the last few years we've now and again been at the same events. Rotary Club dances, Chamber of Commerce functions. You were always there with your husband.'

'Oh!' She feels herself blush. Her good mood evaporates. She has just been reminded that, no matter how nice all of this is, she *is* with a customer. Fred is a punter.

He senses the mood change, leans forward. 'Ruby, there's no need to feel in the least put out. It doesn't matter.'

'You know Bernard, do you?'

'Knew him to see. Only in passing.' He can't resist. 'Never liked him!'

In spite of her change of key she manages a smile. She watches Fred push his plate and cutlery to the side, rest his elbows in the cleared space. 'I'd like to ask you something, Ruby. And *please* believe me, there's a good reason for my question. Would you mind telling me how many nights a week you come down town to, as you call it, be a "working girl"?'

She looks him in the eye. 'I don't mind telling you. Two. Friday and Saturday evenings.'

It's obvious from her manner that she *does* mind. Very much. Until a few minutes ago she'd been enjoying herself. It's now clear to him that the evening is on the brink of turning sour. God! What if she suddenly decides to walk out? I couldn't stand it. Not after getting so near. He watches her lean back in her chair. Away from him. Fred, you're going to have to tell her. He leans further forward, closes this gap between them. He takes both her hands in his, feels the tenseness in hers. 'Ruby, don't take offence, I've asked you that question for the very *best* of reasons.'

'Oh, and what would they be?' At least, she's still letting him hold her hands. For the moment.

'Because, from now on, I want to be the only fellow you see on Fridays and Saturdays. Just me.' He tries to read her face. Surprise? Curiosity might be nearer the mark. No matter. As long as I hold her interest and she doesn't walk out.

'Why would you want to do that, Fred?'

'The answer to that is very simple. I want to have your company on those two nights. I'll be very happy to pay you five pounds on each of those evenings, for the privilege of taking Ruby Baxter out. That way, you won't lose any money, and I get to see you twice a week. We'll go for dinner. If there's a show on in town you'd like to see, I'll get tickets. Maybe go to the cinema some nights. Anything you wish. You only have to ask. The most important thing that I hope will happen is that both of us – not just me – *both* of us, will get used to the idea that you and I go out on a date two nights a week. Every week.' He's relieved to see she isn't so edgy any more. 'Oh! And may I say, I, eh, don't expect to take you to bed *every* time.'

'That sounds very nice, Fred. In fact, almost too good to be true. You still haven't answered my question. Why would you want to do that?' She lifts her head, thrusts her chin forward.

He gives a heavy sigh. 'Okay, Ruby. You're obviously determined to get the reason out of me. The short answer is, I can't *bear* the thought of you being with any other guy except me!' He's glad to see she is, quite literally, taken aback. 'The long answer?' He shrugs. Gives an embarrassed smile. 'I would have got round to telling you all this eventually. Bare my soul when I thought the time was right.' He looks at his empty glass. 'But before I confess all, because that's what I'm about to do, I'm going to need a bit of Dutch courage.' He raises his tumbler, catches a waiter's eye, mouths the word 'another'. He turns to her, 'Would you like something?'

'No, thanks.'

'Have you heard the Latin saying, *In Vino Veritas*, Ruby?'

'I have. Roughly translated, it means, when folk are drunk they're liable to tell the truth!'

He laughs out loud. 'Correct! Well, Ruby Baxter. You're about to see it in action.'

Fred Dickinson sips his fresh drink, leans forward onto his elbows again. Closer to her, so he won't have to speak too loud. He thinks for a moment. Obviously choosing his words . . .

'What I'm about to tell you, Ruby, I hope you will take it at full value. I'd hate to think you'd look on it as something you can take advantage of, use it to make a fool of me. If you do, I'll be very upset. It will also be the end of things between us. I'm not the type of guy who'd stick around to be used. Or misused.' He clears his throat. Takes a deep breath. 'First time I ever saw you, Ruby Baxter, was six years ago at a wedding reception in the Assembly Rooms. March 1956. You came in late, on Bernard's arm, and strode straight across the middle of that floor like a film star. Every guy in the place was watching you. I don't know what number that commandment is, the one about, covet thy neighbour's wife.' He takes another sip from his tumbler, the ice chinking. 'But I can tell you, before you got to your table, I was coveting you.' She can hear the emotion in his voice. He looks into her face. 'And you'll have to brace yourself once again, I'm about to say the stupidest thing you've ever heard in your life. I've loved you from that very moment to this!' She hears the quaver in his voice; sees his eyes brim with tears. He swallows hard. 'Six years. Wanted you all to myself. Yet never dreamed

I'd ever get near you. I really have loved you from afar. Oh! And let me say, it's not *just* a sexual attraction.' As she looks at him she sees him blush. 'It was a textbook case of love at first sight!' Once more he places his hands on top of hers. 'So there you are. For better or worse – I've declared myself. Probably sounded too silly for words from where you're sitting.'

She looks at this middle-aged man sitting in front of her. She feels a surge of . . . just about everything. Surprise. Hope. And from when he was halfway through, tenderness. Tenderness for this man who has just opened his heart to her. She reaches for his glass. Takes more than a sip of his whisky. 'But surely, Fred, knowing how I'm earning my living, that has got to change things? I'm not the Ruby Baxter you thought I was.' She feels herself becoming emotional. 'If only we'd met a few months ago, before I started doing this. Let's face it, you can only think of me now as soiled goods.'

'Nonsense! When I first spoke to you in the bar at the Central tonight, when you told me you were "doing business", that certainly was a shock. But I quickly got over it. That's not the real you. I believe you're better than that. Now, I know you were foolish the way you buggered up your marriage, lost a nice lifestyle. And you're most certainly going through a bad patch at the moment. But what can you do? I can't see you taking a job in a factory, or a grocer's shop. You have to make ends meet. So,' he shrugs his shoulders, 'you're cashing in on your assets.'

'Huh! That's a polite way of putting it, Fred. Let's face it, I've gone as low as—'

He interrupts. 'Ruby, the way I feel about you, none of that matters in the least. I want to be the only guy you go out with. That way I know you'll be safe. Anyway, I take it you only go out two nights a week because that earns you enough to pay your bills?'

'God, yes. If I could get by on one night, I would. But I need ten pounds. So it has to be two. After Bernard put me out of the house I had a little bit of money.' She sighs. 'But once it ran out . . .'

'Where are you living, now?'

'I've got a single-end in Maryhill. Cheapest accommodation I could find . . .' She falters. He sees tears brim in her eyes. 'Fred. With the best will in the world, you can't still look on me the way you did before tonight. Be realistic.'

'Will you stop trying to play devil's advocate, Ruby. You keep telling me what I *should* be thinking. Do you know what's been the one recurring thought in my mind the entire evening?'

'No.'

He leans forward. 'At regular intervals I look at you and think, Ruby Baxter is sitting opposite me. It's really happening.' He spreads his hands wide. 'So why don't you give me the chance to prove how I feel about you? Instead of you telling me it won't work – and me telling you it *will*. Why don't we let time tell. That's the finest test of all. Please. Let me be the only guy you meet on those two nights. Think about it. For a start, you won't be getting picked up by strangers. Now that has got to be an improvement. What have you got to lose? Let's try it for a few weeks. I really don't want you to . . . In fact, Ruby, now that I know what you've been doing to get by, I can't *stand* the thought of it. But also – I want you to be *my* girl. It's as simple as that. I've waited six years for you.' He pauses. 'I'll tell you what. If you want, I'll pay you for the two nights, but you only have to go out with me one night. You can stay at home the other evening. How is that?'

'All right. You've convinced me you mean it. From now on, I only go out with you, Fred.'

Ten minutes later, they step out of the Excelsior into a blustery West Regent Street. They shelter in the portico for a moment. Ruby smiles. 'I'll tell you what, Fred. It's a bit late to start finding a hotel room. If you want, I'll go back to Langside with you tonight.'

'Ah! That will be the perfect end to a perfect evening.' He looks at her upturned face. 'I'd like it if you took my arm, Ruby.' She does, snuggles in close. He bends his head, kisses her on the cheek. 'Now, after me opening my heart to you, Ruby Baxter. To prove to you that it's not just about sex, I will *not* be taking you to bed tonight. You can sleep in the guest bedroom.'

She kisses him on the cheek. 'What a funny guy you are, Fred Dickinson.'

CHAPTER TWENTY-FOUR

A Man's Gotta Do . . .

'Ah think Ah quite like the night-shift, Sarge.' Billy McClaren junior, PC 330, turns his head to look at Sergeant Joe Garland.

'You do, do ye.' The sergeant pauses, takes hold of both handles on the doors of the Commercial Bank of Scotland. A couple of turns and a good push and pull satisfies him they are securely locked. 'And whit dae ye like aboot it?'

Billy pauses before answering, allowing Garland time to do his next check. He watches the older man peer through a clear slit in the bank's etched glass windows. Over in a corner, illuminated by a bulb which burns all night, the large safe squats, unmolested. His superior officer straightens up. They resume their patrol.

'It's the idea of having the streets tae oorselves.' He takes a sideways glance at the sergeant. 'Ah sort of feel that we're, well, looking after things while everybody sleeps.' He feels himself blush.

Garland keeps his face straight. 'Did you fall aff a recruiting poster?'

'Ah know that sounds awfy idealistic, Sarge,' Billy laughs, 'but we're the only two oot and aboot in the district. If somebody was looking doon from the top of a tenement, we'd be the only sign o' life in the empty streets and dark buildings. Until Ah joined the polis Ah'd never been oot in the early hours. It's a different world, in't it? A bit like yon film, *The Third Man.*'

'Mmmm, it's maybe a bit like that from Sunday tae Thursday. But whit aboot Friday and Saturday nights when the pubs come oot? It's *another* kind of world then – the land of the gubby bastards who'll no' take a tellin'!' They both laugh, their voices echoing along a quiet Maryhill Road. Garland looks at his watch. 'Right! We'll nip along tae VC Pies on Firhill Road, huv a quick cup o' tea wi' the night-shift lads. And Ah mean quick.'

They set off at a brisk pace, their tackety boots and steel-shod heels sending up such a rhythmic ring from the pavement, that folk lying half-asleep in their beds could be forgiven for thinking Fred Astaire and Gene Kelly are stoating up the Firhill Road.

They stop at the metal gate which leads into the bakehouse. The inner wooden door lies open, allowing cool air in to the premises. Light spills out onto the pavement. Garland presses his face against the bars. 'ANYBODY HAME?' He turns to his partner. 'Betwen the heat coming through these bars and the smell of whit they're baking at the minute, Ah could quite happily spend the rest o' the shift right here.'

They hear footsteps, a figure in baker's whites appears. 'Hello, Joe. You oan the bloody mooch, again?' As he speaks, the man reaches for the key to the gate.

The sergeant looks at Billy. 'Zat no' terrible? Defend these people wi' oor lives – and therr's the thanks we get!'

'It's jist the wan sugar in your tea, in't it?' The baker opens the gate wide.

'Yes please, Albert.' They step into the warmth.

He smiles at Billy. 'How are you the night, son?'

'Fine, Albert.' PC McClaren follows the two older men into the humid bakehouse. His sergeant turns. 'Noo' mind, Billy. Don't be sitting doon. Everything's covered in flooer. If the duty inspector sees the arse o' yer troosers are aw' white, he'll have oor guts for garters!'

'Aye, Ah know. Last time we were here, Ah finished up looking like a snawman.'

As he pours their mugs of tea, the baker turns his head. 'Ah don't suppose youse could manage a mutton pie and a rhubarb tart?'

'The very two things that VC Pies are famous fur! How could we resist?' Garland rubs his hands briskly together in anticipation. 'Bring on the dancing girls!'

'It's only a couple o' pies.' Albert winks at Billy. 'He's easily pleased, in't he?'

Ten minutes later they are back on the beat. They round the corner at Queens Cross, resume their patrol down the Maryhill Road. The sarge burps onto the back of his hand. 'Pardon me, I cannae lie. It wiz'nae me – it wiz ma pie!' Billy groans, looks heavenward.

'Oh, ho! The sergeant dramatically flings his arm out across Billy's chest, stops him in his tracks. 'The blue light's flashing on the polis box doon at Raeberry Street. The game's afoot! The inspector huz mibbe hud a treble up on the dugs at

Firhill, the night. Step oot a bit, son. It's a good job we've hud a pie!'

Three minutes later, Billy leans against the open door of the police box. His sergeant stands inside, brightly lit by the overhead bulb, his medal ribbons more colourful than ever. Billy can only hear one side of the conversation. It's enough . . . 'Aye, the Maryhill Road back courts between Braeside Street and Kelvinside Avenue. Right! On oor way, Inspector.'

As they set off, yet again, up the main road, Joe Garland fills in the details. 'It's straightforward, son. Somebody's rang Maryhill polis office tae say they've heard a noise oot the back. A lot o' the premises along that stretch are shops. So when we—' He breaks off as they hear a vehicle in the distance. The sergeant turns. 'Great! It's a midden motor. He'll be going back tae the depot in Oran Street. We'll cadge a lift.'

'No' in the back, Ah hope.'

The Sarge screws his face up. 'Watch it! When you've three stripes up, then ye can make the jokes.' He stands at the edge of the pavement, flashes his torch at the oncoming vehicle. 'Whit we'll dae, young 'un. We'll jist stand on the running boards. You drop aff at Braeside, Ah'll come aff at Kelvinside.' The Corporation Sanitation Department lorry pulls up. Garland continues, 'We'll check oot the rear entrances, back yards and back courts. Work towards yin another.' He breaks off. 'Ah'll be with ye in a minute, driver.' He turns back to Billy. 'Now, when you're checking them oot, huv PC Wood ready in yer hand, right? Ye don't take any chances. If ye come across somebody and he shows the *least* sign of resisting – split the bastard wide open! No hesitation. Got it?'

'Okay, Sarge.'

'Can we bum a lift, pal? Drap ma lad aff at Braeside Street, me at Kelvinside Avenue?'

Billy McLaren junior is climbing the steep stairs from Braeside Street up to Agnes Street. He makes his way into the dark lane which gives access to the backs of the Maryhill Road tenements. Torch in hand, systematically he begins to check the long stretch of back yards belonging to shops and other premises. Most gates are locked, but he easily gains access by climbing the walls. Quite a few have broken glass embedded along the top. He leaves them. He smiles as he wonders how his sarge is coping.

He comes to the fifth back gate on his stretch. It's unlocked. On the alert, he enters. The rear door of the shop is secure, as are the bars on the windows. As he turns to leave he becomes conscious of . . . something? Movement rather than noise – from the direction of the midden. He walks over, stands at the open end, shines his torch in. Gets ready to kick out if a rat makes a run for it. Three galvanished bins are illuminated. Leaning over, he shines his torch into the space where a fourth should be. In the distance, he can faintly hear the noise of his sergeant.

'Hah!' Billy catches his breath as the beam falls on the back of a crouching figure. 'Right, come tae fuck oot of it! Ah've got ma truncheon in ma hand. If ye try anything Ah'll split ye wide o—'

Archie Cameron junior, Ella's son, slowly stands up in the space behind the bins. Billy looks at him. 'Trust it tae be you yah dozy fucker! Ah might have known.'

'Wan o' them things, Billy.' He squints, face screwed up against the brightness of the torch.

221

'ARE YOU AW'RIGHT, BILLY?' The sarge sounds a lot nearer.

Billy looks at his boyhood pal. Ah'll have tae answer quick. The premises haven't been breached. Auntie Ella will be upset if Ah nick him. He turns his head. 'AYE! FINE, SARGE.'

'THOUGHT AH HEARD YE TALKING TAE SOME-BODY?'

Fuck! 'IT WAS WAN O' THE RESIDENTS. WONDERING WHIT THE NOISE WAS.'

'AH! RIGHT.'

Billy leans into the midden, speaks in a whisper. 'Ah don't know why Ah did that. You've jist had the *only* break you'll ever get from me. Fuckin' remember it! Get doon behind them bins.'

'Thanks, Billy. You're a pal.'

Minutes later the sergeant joins him in the lane. 'All right, son?'

'Aye. Everything was fine. Premises all locked up.' He feels guilty lying to his sarge. Ah should have nicked that git. Bloody gas meter bandit! Ah'll no' let him aff next time.

'If there wiz an intruder, Billy. They must huv slipped away when they heard us arrive.'

'Aye, must huv.'

Side-by-side they descend the stairs at Braeside Street, regain the Maryhill Road. 'Och well, never mind,' says Joe Garland. 'That's killed nearly an hour. Soon be lowsed.'

CHAPTER TWENTY-FIVE

Carousel

Outside the steamed-up window of the Maryhill Laundrette, the month of March is trying to live up to its reputation for 'coming in like a lion'. Inside, the shop is its usual warm, humid self, i.e. on a par with the Belgian Congo. At the moment, there also seems to be somebody having a fly smoke in the jungle. Drena McClaren draws on her cigarette as she watches her washing circling interminably behind the glass. She nudges Irma, points to the porthole. 'Ah'll tell ye whit. This is better than whit wiz oan the telly last night.'

'Oh, yah. No' half.'

'Billy wanted tae watch some discussion programme. Auld whit's his name wiz in it,' she concentrates. 'You know. Carnaptious auld bugger. Muggeridge! Malcolm Muggeridge. Ah'm no' kiddin'. Jist aboot bored the tits aff me. Ah've spent a better night wi' the toothache.'

The door opens. Frank Galloway, impelled by a gust of wind, makes his entrance. He carries a bolster, bulging with dirty laundry.

'Hello, Frank. First time Ah've seen you in here.' Drena nips her cigarette onto the concrete floor, grinds the sole of her shoe on the glowing tip.

'Hello, girls! Oh, I come in fairly regular. Usually early evening. Most folk are having their dinner then, so it's normally quiet. Often have the place tae maself.'

'Aye, Ah suppose being on yer own, ye can pick and choose whitever time suits ye.'

'I come here tae wash big items. Ah do most of my gear myself, in the sink. It's an auld habit from my navy days. If you served on small ships, you'd nae option but tae do your own dhobi.'

Irma leans forward. 'Bert uses this "dhobi" word sometimes. But he cannot tell me where it comes from. Do you know, Frank?'

'Aye,' says Drena. 'Billy uses it if he's gonny gie something a rinse-through in the sink. Ah know whit it *means* – but Ah don't know where it comes fae, either.'

Frank is in the middle of lighting a cigarette. He offers the packet to the two women.

'Oh! Cannae remember the last time Ah hud a Senior Service,' says Drena. Little finger extended, she delicately takes one. Frank supplies a light.

'No, thank you. I don't smoke, Frank.' Irma smiles at him.

'Ah! How I wish I could say the same, Irma. Right, girls! Let me get ma washing underway then I'll tell you where the word dhobi comes from.'

Drena and Irma watch as he efficiently transfers his laundry from the bolster to the machine, then takes a small box of soap powder from the bottom of the large pillowcase.

'Still using Tide Ah see, Frank.'

'Aye. I'm a great believer in the Blue Whitener!' He laughs. 'I hope youse two did'nae catch a glimpse of ma underwear. I'm no' wanting tae inflame yer senses.'

'You're safe enough, sunshine.' Drena draws luxuriously on the cigarette.

Frank drops onto the bench beside Irma, turns so as to speak to them both. 'Right. The reason you've often heard your men use the word dhobi is because they've picked it up in the forces. It's been used by British servicemen for, I would imagine, a hundred years or more. It comes from the early days when India was part o' the British Empire. In Victorian times labour was cheap oot there. Even a private could afford to pay to have his laundry done. Every barracks had two or three regular Dhobi wallahs who, for jist a few rupees, would take your dirty laundry – your dhobi – and wash and iron it for you. So that's what Dhobi whallah means. The laundry man. I think it's Hindi. All the thousands of soldiers and sailors who passed through India picked up the words and they became forces slang. It's still used by servicemen to this day – even if they've never seen India. Your dirty washing is – your dhobi.'

'Cricky-jings, that is so interesting, Frank. When Bert comes home tonight I will tell him where it comes from.'

'Ah'll ask Billy if he knew that. Ah've known the word for long enough, Ah picked it up from him. But Ah've never gave any thought as to where it came fae.' Another draw is taken on the cigarette. The smoke struggles to rise in the moist air. 'Jist shows ye, you can learn something new every day.' She watches her washing tumble round behind the glass, then, almost to herself. 'Mmm, Ah wonder if Ella knows that.'

Their heads turn as the street door is opened. '*Agnes*! In the name o' the wee man,' says Drena. 'Ah did'nae know the Bagwash wiz reserved oan Tuesdays, fur folk fae oor close!'

Unexpectedly faced with three of her neighbours, Agnes Dalrymple blushes and gives a shy smile at the same time. 'Well, Tuesdays are half-day closing at the City Bakeries so, eh, it's ideal for me tae get ma wee bit washing done before Ah go hame. Ah take it tae work wi' me, then come straight here when Ah finish.' She extracts the dirty washing from her large bag.

'Oh, my God! Agnes Dalrymple! You're alwiz bringing we snasters hame wi' ye in that bag. The times Ah've eaten a pineapple cake or a strawberry tart . . . oh! It diz'nae bear thinking aboot. If Ah hud known it has mibbe spent half the morning snuggled up against a perr o' your – Oh, Jeez! Can ye imag—' She looks in mock horror at Irma. 'You tae! How often huv you sampled the delights o' that bag?'

Irma turns towards the accused. 'Don't pay any attention to her, Agnes. You know she is a big troublemaker.'

Agnes, red in the face because of Frank's presence, tries to defend herself. 'Ah always huv ma laundry inside a carrier bag, *then* inside the big bag.' As if to prove it, she reaches into her message bag, extracts a brown paper carrier and, without thinking, empties it onto the floor in front of a washer. Prominent are two pairs of oft-washed, faded red knickers. 'Huh!' Agnes scrabbles on the floor, hurriedly crams all her laundry into the machine, out of Frank's sight. Slamming the door shut she turns, dramatically blocks his view of the glass panel.

Drena looks at Irma and Frank. 'Did youse see whit Ah

seen? Two perr o' passion-killers. Ohhh! Ah've jist went right aff pineapple cakes. Fur life!'

'Don't you listen to her, Agnes,' says Frank.

Irma shakes her head. 'Well, I tell you. Drena would not have this problem if she is carrying cakes with her laundry. She never has knickers to wash – she does not *wear* any!'

'Eeee! Ya cheeky wee bizzum!' They all, Agnes included, dissolve into laughter.

When order has been restored, Agnes reaches into her bag, pulls out a small box of Daz.

Drena points. 'Huv ye forgot, Agnes? When you got yerself intae a bit of a stramash a couple o' minutes ago, you went and shoved *all* yer washing intae the machine. If there's any woollens or nylons amongst it, ye don't want tae be doing them on the hot wash, mind.'

'Oh, aye, so Ah did.' They watch in amusement as Agnes, for the second time, strategically places herself to stop Frank getting further sightings of her nether garments. The load re-sorted, she starts the machine, sits down rather primly. 'See the trouble you caused me, Drena McClaren.'

Drena looks to left and right, tuts. 'Ah'm gettin' aw' the blame. Well, can Ah point oot, it wiz'nae me that wiz lettin' everybody see ma knickers!'

'Always with the knickers!' says Irma. She places a hand on Agnes's arm. 'How are you getting on with that wee job, Agnes. Visiting folk who are in the hospital?'

'Aw, it's really smashing. Ah'm no' half pleased youse suggested it tae me—'

Frank interrupts. 'Aye, that's a good thing to do, Agnes. I had an auntie used tae do that, back in the late forties.'

Agnes leans forward. 'It's supposed to be me that's doing

them a favour. You know, visiting folk who have'nae got anybody. But Ah must be honest. Ah get as much out of it as they do. Some o' the very old ones, they've been all over the world, had some wonderful experiences. And it does them such a lot o' good tae tell you their tales. Ah often sit doon at somebody's bedside, and they can hardly keep their eyes open . . .' Frank looks at his next door neighbour. He's never seen her so animated . . . 'but see when they start telling you some story, oh, they become so lively. The years jist drap away fae them. Diz them the world o' good.'

'That's made tae measure for you,' says Drena.

'Yah, that is a perfect job for you,' Irma agrees.

'Aye,' Drena keeps her face straight, 'Ah wiz wondering why you were goin' through so many perrs o' drawers in a week, Agnes. But Ah suppose your mammy used tae say the same as mine. "Alwiz put clean knickers oan, whenever ye visit the hospital."'

It's later that afternoon. Drena sits reading a story in the *People's Friend*. Ella always passes it on to her when she's finished with it. The gas is set on a wee peep under the kettle, it's just starting to sing. Minutes later, she hears the expected footsteps enter the close. Her door is opened, the feet now pitter-patter as they step onto the linoleum in the lobby.

'It's jist me!'

'Aye, in ye come.' Drena finishes a paragraph, lets the magazine fall onto the floral-patterned oilcloth on the table. She rises from the chair as the kitchen door is opened. 'Zat you jist in fae yer work, Ella?'

'Naw, Ah've jist docked doon at the Broomielaw. Been fur a cruise wi' Jacques Cousteau.'

Drena ignores this. 'You wanting a biscuit?'

'Naw, thanks. It'll put me aff ma dinner.' Ella places her faithful red Rexine bag against a leg of the table, drops onto the kitchen chair just vacated by Drena.

'You stopped eating between meals, again?'

'Aye. Gonny try and get at least a stone aff fur the holidays.'

'You and Archie decided where yer going, yet?'

'He wants tae go back tae Blackpool. Ah fancy Torquay.'

'Archie loves his Blackpool, dizn't he?'

'He'd go *every* year if Ah'd let him. It's the shows he loves. You get aw' the big stars at Blackpool. Mind, we huv seen some great turns ower the years: Frankie Howerd, Ronnie Hilton, Frankie Vaughan, Vera Lynn, Jimmy Edwards. They aw' come tae Blackpool. But och, Ah fancy a change.'

Drena starts pouring the tea. 'Ah think Billy and me are jist gonny huv a week doon at Ayr. Huv'nae decided whether tae take a cottage or go bed and breakfast.'

'Why don't ye get a wee job? You could go further afield wi' a bit extra money in yer pocket.'

'Och! Ah'm no' gonny knock ma pan in aw' year jist tae huv a fortnight's holiday.'

'It would'nae be *just* for a holiday, Drena. The extra money would come in handy for lots o' things. Archie and me could'nae dae withoot ma wage coming in.'

'Aye, but you've got a trade, Ella. Ah'd finish up wi' a skivvie's job.'

'You would not. Christ! There's plenty o' good wee jobs tae be had. Shop assistant, stuff like that.'

'Nahhh! Ah'll jist stay as Ah am.'

*   *   *

It's half an hour later. Ella reaches out, accurately throws her cigarette end into the fire, sips the last of her tea. The conversation has faltered since the discussion about Drena perhaps taking a job. Ella rises. 'Well, Ah'd better get away up the stairs. Start getting the dinner ready.' She lifts her bag, drops the packet of Woodbines and the box of matches inside it. 'Ah'll see ye the morra, Drena.' As she turns towards the door she knows, absolutely *knows*, what will come next.

'Aye, see ye the morra. Oh! Ella, dae ye think ye could lend me thirty bob till Friday?' It sounds like a bad actress saying her lines. Ella can hear the nervousness, a dryness in Drena's throat that tells her she is aware this might be 'the moment'. The limit has been reached. Ella has just opened the kitchen door. She stops, turns. 'Ah'm afraid not, Drena. Ah'm a bit short maself this week.'

Drena tries to shift the frog from her throat. 'Hrrumph! Can ye manage a pound, then?'

The pause seems to go on for ages. Ella gives a heavy sigh, returns to the table, extracts her purse from her bag. Taking a pound note from it, she places it on the table. 'Right, therr's a pound, Drena.' She looks straight at her. 'Noo, ye can keep it. Ah don't want it back. Okay? So that means that you've got a pound start. You're a pound up. But Ah don't want ye tae tap me for money again. Aw'right?'

For a moment, Drena is taken aback, then, 'Whit dae ye mean Ah can keep it? Ah don't want tae keep it. It's jist a lend. Ah'll gie ye it back.'

'Yer gettin' a pound fur nuthing. It's a gift. Ah'm fed up wi' having tae keep money back every week in case you tap me. It's like my money's not ma own. So make this the last. Okay?'

'Ah'll tell ye whit.' Drena, face flushed, rises from her chair. She reaches forward with her hand, skites the note back towards Ella using her fingertips. They watch it fly to the end of the table, lose momentum, flutter down to the floor. 'You can keep it! Ah don't want it. In fact, ye can stick it up yer arse!'

Ella, red in the face, lifts her bag, bites her tongue, and walks out of Drena's house.

Ella, choking for a cup of tea, stands at her cooker as the kettle seems to take ages to boil. Unbidden, the events of a few minutes ago run over and over in her mind. She shakes her head. Naw, it had tae happen. Ah'm sick of it. It could'nae go on. She hears a noise from the lobby, her heart rises for a moment. But it's not a knock. She opens the kitchen door, looks down. An already used, roughly opened envelope lies on the threadbare runner. She picks it up, looks at the front. As expected, it has originally been addressed to Mr W. McClaren. Opening it, she takes out a half-sheet of writing paper, sighs when she finds the pound note inside it, recognises Drena's handwriting . . . You can keep your pound. Don't bother calling in when you come home from your work in future. And don't waste your time speaking to me if we pass one another. I don't consider you a friend any longer. D. McClaren.'

She re-reads it a few times. Ah'll have tae have a drink o' tea. She sits at the table, sips from her cup, stares at the note. It had tae come. Ella takes a last look at the piece of paper, crunches it and the envelope up, throws them at the fire.

They bounce off the coals, land on the hearth. 'Fuck!' She rises, places them carefully in a gap between two lumps of coal. There's a brief pause, then they flare up, quickly burn away to nothing. 'Well, Drena. You're gonny huv a long wait if ye expect me tae speak first.'

CHAPTER TWENTY-SIX

You Never Know
the Minute!

With a damp, rolled-up towel under his arm and a soap dish containing a bar of Lifebuoy inside that, Frank Galloway exits the Maryhill Public Baths and Wash-house in Burnhouse Street. He pauses for a moment to light a cigarette, before stepping out in the direction of the main road. He takes a few deep breaths. 'Ahhhh!' Whit a nice fresh April morning. Right, a good brisk walk hame is in order. Then a big fry-up and a read at the paper. He increases his pace. 'Mmm.' Followed by an hour's kip. He smiles, then looks to see if any passers-by have noticed.

He's meeting Wilma that night. He feels a glow. *And* Ah'm off the morra. Can have a long lie. He starts whistling. Then stops. What is that tune? Ah whistle it often. It's from a movie. Romantic. But which one? He tries to recall a scene from it. It was definitely in colour. William Holden in a leather jerkin flashes into his mind. Right! There was a blonde. Aye. Kim Novak! William thinks he's too auld for her, but she's no' bothered, she's nuts about him. But he leaves town. Frank shakes his head at such folly. Naebody in their right mind would walk away from Kim Novak. He strides on down the Maryhill Road. There's yon dance scene in the open air. Sultry night. A floating dance floor wi' fairy lights strung up. Kim's waiting for him. Aye! And this wee combo is playing *that* tune. Jeez-oh! Whit's the name of it? William walks slowly doon this gangway thing towards her, snapping his fingers tae the rhythm. Wiz dead romantic. They start dancing. It's the town's annual fair that day. They've had a big picnic and now . . . *That's it*! *picnic*, that's the buggering name o' the picture, and that music is the film's theme tune. It's got a long title. Ah'm sure 'picnic' is in it, tae. His mind races; it's oan the tip of . . . 'Yessss!' It comes out like a sigh. Got yah! 'Moonglow and the Theme From Picnic', that's whit it's called. He walks on, whistling the tune again. This time in triumph. He stops at a junction. Jeez! It would'nae half be a bit of a blow if Wilma said I was too old for her. But then again, Kim wiz'nae worried aboot him being older. It wiz him caused the bother. Not her. This thought cheers him up as he turns the corner into Dalbeattie Street. He resumes whistling.

Late evening on the same day. Frank Galloway opens the door of the Stromboli restaurant amid calls of '*Grazie mille*' and '*Buona notte*'. He and Wilma step out onto the Byres Road. Frank looks at his watch. 'Just coming up for half-nine, Wilma. Bit early to go hame, don't you think?'

'Mmm, it is a bit.'

'And we're both day off the morra.' He looks at her. 'You know, when ye think about it, it's hard bloody lines that two adults cannae enjoy a night out together because of your mother.'

'Aye, Ah suppose it is.'

He holds an arm akimbo. Wilma takes it. 'Since your Auntie Maggie got onto her, she's been behaving herself tae a certain extent. But that's probably 'cause we make sure you're home by eleven. But even so, Wilma, you're a grown woman in your thirties. You work full time tae support her. It's bloody ridiculous that you cannae stay oot later than eleven o'clock, withoot her making your life a misery. Naebody would believe it if we told them.'

'Ah know you're right, Frank, but as Ah've said, even when Ah'm in for eleven she still stomps aboot the hoose in a bad mood. She knows Ah've been seeing you.'

Frank blows his cheeks out. 'You cannae go on living like this the rest o' your life. She has nae right tae treat ye like that. Ah know it's your mother. But you'll have tae face it. She's a nasty piece o' work who gets great pleasure out of dominating you. And as long as she gets away wi' it, she'll carry on doing it. What about you *and* me making a stand? Ah'll back you up. What do you think?'

'Well, Ah have been thinking of facing up tae her. Whit dae ye suggest? Whit can we do?'

'Slowly but surely we'll have tae push it. Get her used to ye coming hame whenever it suits *you* – not her! After all, you're no' a teenager.'

Wilma feels her hopes rise. Maybe with Frank behind her . . . 'When dae ye suggest we start?'

'Tonight!'

'*The night*!'

He looks at his watch again. 'We've just had a nice meal. It's only twenty to ten. At oor age, and especially as we're day off tomorrow, the night should just be *starting*, not finishing!' He turns to face her, puts his arms round her, kisses her on the forehead. 'Ah want tae take you dancing! There's a—'

'*Dancing*! At this time o' night? Ah'm, eh, no' really dressed for it, Frank.'

With his arms still round her waist, he sways her from side-to-side, leans forward and gives her a kiss which approaches lingering. 'Nonsense! Ah've been thinking all evening what a nice wee frock that is. And I really would like to take ma favourite conductress for a wee dance.' Her innocent face gazes up at him. 'Do ye realise we've never danced together, Wilma?'

She looks into his eyes, takes confidence from his familiar face. 'Where were ye thinking? The Locarno? Greens?'

'Nope! Ah nice classy, smoochy wee place. Ah've never been in it, but Ah've heard it's very nice. It's doon on Woodlands Road. Le Bar Rendezvous. A bit like a nightclub, Ah've been told.'

'Oh, Ah know the place ye mean. Ah've passed it many a time ower the years. In fact, Ah've often thought, Ah bet ye it's nice in there.'

Frank puts on his best Charles Boyer impression. 'Well tonight, *ma cherie*, you are going to find out. Toot sweet!'

'Ohhh! Foreign languages is it? Ah did'nae know ye wiz a linguini – or is that something on Stromboli's menu?'

'*Excusez-moi*, hen. I'll have you know that I am fluent in *three* languages. Yiddish, Polish – and rubbish!'

She tuts. 'You're oot o' luck, pal. It jist so happens Ah wiz also watching Ken Dodd oan the telly the other night – when he came oot wi' that wan.'

'*Sacré bleu!*' Frank pretends he's embarrassed. He suddenly sticks his arm out. 'Here's a taxi, Wilma. Get us there all the quicker.'

It's just gone eleven-thirty when, reluctantly, the two of them leave Le Bar Rendezvous. Frank looks to his right. 'Ah, good. There's a couple o' cabs sitting along there. Anyway, Wilma, have you enjoyed yourself?'

She reaches up, kisses him on the cheek. 'Frank, this is the best night out Ah've ever had. It really is.' As she says it, she feels a little shaft of fear. Ah've got tae go hame now. In twenty-five minutes. Less. Ah'll have tae face ma mother.

Frank looks at the alarm clock. Twenty to one. He turns down the corner of a page to mark his place. Reaches out from the bed, places the book on a corner of the table. Ah hope Wilma did'nae get too hard a time from that auld get. He turns onto his right side, glances at the book, reads the title on its spine. *Very Ordinary Seaman*. Aye. It's well seen Mallalieu wrote that during the war. Only a guy who's done sea-time on a destroyer could write a book like that. You can very near taste the salt spray. He raises a hand, finds the switch, puts the light out. Turning onto his back, he takes an indolent stretch, clasps his hands behind his head. Ah used tae love lying in ma hammock like this. That book always brings it back. This must be the third time Ah'm reading it. Might be the fourth. The comrade-ship, the banter. Shared danger. Often it wiz pure, solid fear. Somewhere in his brain the little door marked 'Royal Navy' opens. Faces, names, scenes, snatches of conversation, spill out. What did Dickens say? Something about 'It wiz the best of times, it wiz the worst of times.' Bloody sure an' it was. As he stares up into the blackness of the ceiling the precious memories come helter-skelter. His eyes begin to close.

He doesn't hear the first knock. It's the gentle, but insistent, rattle of the letterbox that drags him back from the shallows of sleep. His eyes snap open, he looks at the luminous clock. Five to one! Who the hell can it be at this time? Clad in vest and underpants, he rises, pads over to the door, steps into the lobby. 'Who is it?'

The letterbox is opened. 'It's Wilma!' she whispers.

'Jesusjohnny! Jist a minute, hen. Ah'll have tae put a pair o' troosers on.'

He opens the door. A forlorn figure stands on the chilly, dimly lit landing, a suitcase on one side of her, a duffel bag on the other. She holds a hanger with her tramways uniform on it.

'Oh, ma poor wee soul. Has Mad Myra thrown you oot?'

She nods her head, near to tears. 'Aye. Ah did'nae know where tae go, so Ah—'

'Well, you've come tae the right place, pal.' He steps out onto the landing, puts an arm round her shoulder. Speaks softly. 'Don't worry, Wilma. You're all right now. In ye come.'

He lifts her case and bag. 'We're no' working the morra. We'll have a cuppa and a good blether. You can tell me all about it. Hang your uniform up on one o' the hooks in the lobby.' He places her other luggage under the table for the moment.

'Oh, Frank. Ah don't know whit Ah'm gonny dae.' She fights back the tears.

'Wilma. Will you believe me when Ah tell ye, you've nothing tae be upset aboot. You've finally broken free from that terrible wumman. There's nothing tae greet aboot. In fact, you should be turning somersaults. You've escaped!'

'It's no' that. Ah have'nae a clue what tae do. Ah'm gonny have tae get digs. Ah've never had tae manage on ma own, look efter maself. And it's gonny be a big drain oan ma wages.'

Frank pulls a chair out from the table. 'Sit yerself doon there, hen.' He puts the kettle on the gas, plugs in his emergency electric fire. Last of all, he pulls a sweater on over his pyjama jacket. 'Right, Wilma Ballantyne. Let me brew the tea – in which we'll both have a wee dollop of dark rum – and in a few minutes I'll have convinced you this is the *best* thing that's ever happened to you!'

'You'll huv a job. Ah cannae believe whit's happened. Ah've just had the best night oot that Ah've ever had – and two hours later, it's turning intae the worst night o' ma life!'

'Naw it's no'! Ah'll make sure it is'nae. So what happened when you arrived hame?'

'Ah let maself in, went intae the kitchen tae tell her Ah'm back. She's got the case and bag already standin' in the middle o' the floor. My uniform lying on top o' them! As soon as Ah put ma nose through the door, she started her usual ranting and raving. Ye heard it yon night ye took me hame. Jist ordered me oot.' She begins to look tearful again. 'So Ah went.'

He reaches across the table, takes both her hands in his. 'Listen tae what Ah'm gonny tell you, Wilma. At long last you're free of your mother. Finally, your adult life is about tae begin.'

'Ah know that's good, Frank. But it's the rest. How will Ah manage being on ma own. Where Ah'm Ah gonny stay—'

Frank cuts in. 'Ah'll sort all those problems oot for ye, hen. Just let me pour the tea.'

*   *   *

Frank screws the top back onto the bottle of navy rum. He lifts his mug. 'Cheers!'

Wilma lifts hers. 'Huh! Cheers aw'right.' She takes a sip. 'Oh! That's nice wi' rum in it.'

'Right! To business. At last you've left your mother. Now that, nae matter what way ye look at it, is definitely good. No argument about it. Next problem? Where are ye gonny stay?' He taps the table with the point of a finger. 'Here! You can share this place wi' me until you find somewhere else.'

Wide-eyed, she looks at him. 'This is a single-end, Frank.'

'So? Not as big a problem as you might think. When is the *only* time two people need privacy?' He holds up his hand, ticks them off on his fingers. 'One: Getting ready for bed at night. Two: Getting up in the morning, washing at the sink, getting dressed. So. Only twice a day will we need tae be on oor own. When one of us is doing their ablutions, the other one can go into the wee lobby with the paper or a magazine, shut the door and have a read. When you've finished, got your jammies on ready for bed – or got dressed ready for work – you just give me a shout that it's all clear. You wait and see, it won't be a problem. Believe me, it'll work.'

'When you say it like that it sounds as if it might.'

'Wilma. You've known me for about a year now. You'll be safe here wi' me. I wouldn't dream of trying tae take advantage of the situation. In fact, I'm going to make a forecast. Within the next two weeks, maybe *less*, I bet you'll find you're enjoying sharing the house. We'll be into a routine and you'll be quite relaxed about it all. And there's one thing for sure, the company will be an improvement to what you've been used to. And remember, Wilma, don't feel you have to be in a hurry to move out. We'll take plenty of time and make sure we get you a room or a flat that you'll be happy with. And last, but not least. For whatever length of time you're here, if something annoys you, bothers you, just tell me. Don't hold back because you don't want to hurt my feelings. Okay?'

'Right, okay.' She looks at his strong, good face. Feels herself relax. 'Well, Ah'll give it a try, Frank. Ah hav'nae much option. But Ah'm gonny find it awfy strange at first.'

'Huh! Don't talk tae me aboot strange. It was the same for me when I got called-up for the navy. I remember thinking, there is no way I will *ever* get used to this. Living in barracks, or in the cramped conditions you get on board ship. Yet, when I got demobbed in 1945 and walked out of a naval barracks for the last time – I burst into tears.'

She looks at him. 'Ah've already got one question, Frank. Ah don't want tae worry ye, but can Ah point oot – there's only wan bed!'

He gives an exaggerated sigh. 'Oh, ye of little faith. In fact, ye of toaty faith.' He walks over to the recess bed, reaches a hand under the valance. He reverts back to the Charles Boyer persona of last evening. 'Voila! Mam'selle. Zee trundle-bed!' He pulls out what looks like a camp bed – on wheels. 'I shall sleep in zis, you will sleep in zee bed of the recess!'

'Aw naw, Frank. Ah'm not putting ye oot o' your bed. Ah'm wee. That's jist a nice size for me.'

He leans his hands on the table. 'Wilma, Ah'm partly responsible for your mother giving you your marching orders. You are now *my* guest and I want you to be comfortable.' He points to the makeshift bed. 'I spent years sleeping in a hammock. Getting my head down in that will be no bother at all.' He places a hand on top of hers. 'And I must level with you. I really don't like living on my own. So, I'm going to enjoy having you here. No way will you be an inconvenience or a trouble. Oh, and to save you asking,' he points, 'the lavvy key hangs behind that door.'

It's forty minutes later. '*Right*! Ah'm in bed, Frank.'

The kitchen door opens, a pyjama-clad Frank emerges from the lobby. 'Ready or not, here Ah come!' Wilma looks on as, with some difficulty, he climbs into the low, narrow bed. 'Lovely!' He forces a smile while lying through his teeth. 'Isn't this a turn-up for the books? You and me sharing digs. You can put the light out if you're ready, hen.' She reaches up, there's a click. All is dark. There's movement as both get comfortable. Silence falls. Then, 'Wilma?'

'Aye?'

'Do you realise, from now on we can stay out as late as we like? Good, eh?'

'Aye, terrific!'

'You'll be all right here, Wilma. Don't worry. Ah'll look after you. Goodnight, hen.'

There's the briefest of pauses. 'That's nice tae know, Frank. Good night.'

As her voice comes out of the blackness, Frank smiles. He no longer feels lonely.

CHAPTER TWENTY-SEVEN

Much Ado About Nothing

The Rover 90 glides up to the pavement outside 18 Dalbeattie Street. As requested, Fred Dickinson gives a brief 'pip' on the horn. Two storeys up, Ruby Baxter feels a surge of pleasure. That's Fred! Yet this is immediately followed by a feeling of apprehension. What am I going to do? Should I chance it? He'll marry me in a minute if I say 'yes'. But what if he . . . 'Oh, to hell with it!' She shrugs her coat on, flicks her hair back free of her coat collar, grabs her bag. Takes a last glance in the mirror.

Fred sounds the horn again. He knows it's mainly for the benefit of her neighbours. Ruby would be pleased to know it's having the desired effect. One storey up, Granny Thomson looks through her net curtains, sniffs. 'Hmm! He's getting tae be a regular, that yin.'

Agnes Dalrymple, lays her cup back in its saucer. 'Whit yin?'

'Him that calls for Lady Muck, up above.' Granny's halfway back to her chair when the distinctive clip-clop of Ruby's high-heels make themselves heard. 'Might as well hang oan and see whit it's wearing the night. Wan thing fur certain – it'll no' include drawers!'

'Eeee, Granny! The things you say.' Agnes rises and joins her friend at the windows. They stand a foot or so back, peer through the nets.

The engine of the black automobile is barely audible as it purrs outside the close. Fred keeps his head turned, wants to catch that first sight of her. Moments later his heart lifts as Ruby lopes out of the shadows. The open chinchilla coats swings, the long red hair follows suit. His heart gives a double-thump when he notices she's carrying her large bag. That usually means she's going to stay the night. This is only Thursday. Am I getting *three* nights this week? He stretches over to his left, pushes the passenger door wide open. Then gives himself up to the performance . . . Act One; Scene One: *Action*! Midst an invisible, but potent, cloud of Chanel No. 5, backed up by a delectable show of leg, she swishes into the front seat of the Rover.

'Hello, Fred.' She leans to the side and he is kissed. As happens every time, he tingles. He leans back so as to look at her, take pleasure in the fact he is dating Ruby Baxter. At least, that is how he looks at it. The fact that money changes hands is immaterial to him.

'That seemed to be a genuine, pleased to see you, kiss, Ruby.'

'It is, darling. And you do realise this is Thursday? Not just our usual Friday and Saturday.'

'I do indeed. Why an extra night? Not that I'm complaining.'

She smiles. 'You're always fishing, Fred Dickinson. Okay, I'll tell you. I couldn't wait until tomorrow night to see you.

I thought, to pot. I'll give Fred a ring. I hope you didn't mind?'

'Mind? I was reading the paper when you rang. Barely two minutes earlier I'd been thinking, thank goodness tomorrow's Friday, I'll be seeing Ruby.'

'It's almost three months since we started going out, Fred, and as you forecast, I really am getting to like your company. You're becoming part of my life, darling.'

'I did warn you.' He gives an embarrassed laugh. 'Also, I've been meaning to ask you, Ruby. Are you still, eh, quite happy with our, ahmm, fiscal arrangement? Hopefully, you now have enough to pay your way. As long as there is, eh, no need for you to have to, well, you know—'

She cuts in. 'No need for me to go on the game any more! Is that what you mean, darling?'

'Ruby! Do you *always* have to call a spade a spade?'

She sighs. 'For such a positive person – successful businessman, decorated bomber pilot – when it comes to talking about what I was doing that night in the Central Bar, you always go all round the houses, don't you?' She laughs out loud. Perhaps *too* loud, he thinks.

He turns further in his seat, leans back against the door. 'That's because I adore you, Ruby buggering Baxter! I won't hear a word said against you – not even by yourself! I don't consider you were "on the game". You had rent to pay, food to put on the table. As far as I'm concerned, you'd barely dipped a toe in the water.' He gives her a stern look. 'So would you mind *not* running yourself down in front of me!'

She feels her eyes brim with tears. She reaches out, places a hand on top of his. 'In a funny, convoluted way, Fred Dickinson, that is probably one of the sweetest declarations of love ever made.' She gives him the tenderest of kisses, then draws back, looks at him. 'You really are getting to be my darling, you know.'

'Ahhh. That's a wonderful thing for me to hear, Ruby. But, when are you going to take the next step?' He takes both her hands into his. 'Come live with me and be my love.'

'Just give me a little more time, Fred. There are things I've got to, well, sort of get straight in my mind.' She touches his cheek. 'I will tell you one thing. I already love you more than I ever loved Bernard Baxter. That's for certain.' She leans forward, kisses him again. 'Anyway, come on, darling. Are we going out?'

He engages gear and the Rover moves smoothly away from the pavement. One storey up, Granny Thomson and Agnes Dalrymple turn away from the windows. The matriarch gives a wry smile, shakes her head. 'Aye, he's been calling on her for quite a while noo, that fella. Ah think the bold Ruby has fell oan her feet.' She stops for a moment, rests a hand on the table. 'Ach! Good luck tae her. Ah'm jist jealous, that's ma trouble.'

Ruby sits back in her chair, sighs. 'Mmmm! I do *love* Rogano's, Fred.'

He folds the linen napkin, places it beside his empty plate. 'We're getting to be such regulars, the girl in the cloakroom was asking me if we'll be at the staff Christmas party this year!'

She gives a loud *tut!* 'So you grudge me the odd visit to Rogano's, do you?'

He lifts his wine glass. 'Ruby Baxter. Most delicious woman in Glasgow. You know I couldn't deny you anything. You only have to ask, give the merest hint. And whatever it is – it's yours!'

She looks at him with eyes aglisten. 'You do make me feel wanted, Fred.'

'And so I should. For six long years I wanted you. And you never knew I existed.'

'Oh, don't remind me. Do you know what, Fred? Since you first told me that, you have no idea how often it comes into my mind.' She reaches out, takes his hand. 'It always makes me sad to think of you, literally, loving me from afar. I wish I'd known.'

'Good! So if you really want to make it up to me. That's easy. Marry me, Ruby Baxter!'

She smiles. 'I am getting round to it, darling. It's just that I want to be two hundred per cent certain. This time it has to be for keeps. I'm not getting any younger, you know.'

'Maybe so. But you *are* growing more beautiful as you get older. You don't have a problem.'

Fred turns back his shirt cuff with a finger. 'Just gone eleven, sweet lady. You want to finish the night at the Bar Rendezvous?'

She puts her head on one side, suddenly coquettish. 'Mmmm, maybe tomorrow night. Or Saturday. Let's go home to Langside.'

As usual, when Ruby 'turns it on' she has the desired effect on him. He purses his lips. 'You're doing it to me again, Miss Baxter.'

'I'm intending to, Mr Dickinson. You don't want things to become boring, do you?'

'That's the last thing I'd want. Anyway. I can't see that happening with you and me.'

'Good! Pay the bill, Fred. Let's go.'

When he has attracted the attention of their waiter, he leans over towards Ruby. 'By the way, do you realise you just said, "Let's go *home* to Langside?"'

She raises a hand to her mouth, 'Did I? Goodness! Is that one of those Freudian slips?'

'Oooyah!' Fred pretends to shudder. 'I do *love* it when you talk dirty.'

As the waiter approaches this couple, who are helpless with laughter, he decides he'd happily give up half of tonight's tips to be in on the joke.

Ruby is curled up in the corner of the sofa. 'That's that lovely, romantic music again, Fred. Who did you say it was?'

'It's the Jackie Gleason Orchestra.'

She listens for a moment longer. 'I didn't think there was anybody better than Nelson Riddle at this sort of thing.' She inclines her head. 'Just listen to this version of "Tangerine". Absolutely lush. How come I hadn't heard this guy's stuff, until you introduced me to it?'

Fred sips his Laphroaig. 'He was very popular in the States in the early fifties. Then, when rock 'n' roll came on the scene, like many others, he just sort of faded. I find him so classy.'

'Not half. Yet, somehow I feel I do know the name, Jackie Gleason.'

'He's a comedian. Also does a bit of acting. Did you see the film, *The Hustler*?'

'Yeah. Paul Newman. It was doing the rounds a year or so ago.'

'Remember the big guy who played his main opponent, Minnesota Fats?' Fred doesn't wait for an answer. 'That was Jackie Gleason.'

'Ah! Now I know who you mean.' She sits for a while, listening to the music. Thinking. 'Fred?'

'Yeah?' He is also listening to the music.

'I know you were married to Dorothy. Got married during the war. Can I ask you? Why didn't it last?'

'Because the war ended too soon!'

She laughs. 'Don't be silly! I don't think that's grounds for divorce, darling.'

He sips his whisky. 'Well, of course that's too simplistic, but it actually pretty much covers it. We were crazy about one another during the war. You know. Both on the same bomber station. She's in the radio room, I'm a dashing pilot. Stolen moments, crazy weekends in York or London. By 1947 we're civilians, married, going to work. Two years later, it's as stale as last week's bread. No big rows or anything. So we decided, amicably, to get a divorce. To speed things up in the divorce courts, we got our heads together – and pleaded non-consummation!'

'*Hah*!' Ruby almost chokes on her Campari. 'Well I definitely know that wouldn't be true.'

'Thank you for that vote of confidence, dear.' He takes another sip of Laphroaig. 'It was all quite civilised. We both realised we weren't set for the long haul.' He half turns on the sofa to face her. 'Do you know, I've loved you longer than I loved Dorothy. Trouble was, I was the only one who knew! So why don't you make it up to me, by marrying me, Ruby Baxter?'

She sips her Campari. 'It will happen, Fred, but exactly when, I'm still not sure. I need time to be really certain.'

'Okay. Well can I at least ask – do you mean certain of me? Or of yourself?' He leans towards her. 'Ruby, why don't you tell me straight out what's bothering you? I might be able to see off all your fears in one fell swoop. Now wouldn't that be great? I have no problems whatsoever about us. I'd marry you tomorrow if you'd say "yes". So let's try. Tell me what's troubling you, Ruby?'

She takes another sip from her glass. 'You're right. I'll have to tell you eventually, Fred. I suppose the sooner I face up to it, the better. Right. What's worrying me, might seem simple enough to you, but you must believe me when I tell you, it's *always* on my mind. And spoils my pleasure in our relationship . . .' She stops as she becomes upset.

'Let's see if I can make it easier for you, Ruby. I think I might know what you're frightened of.' He lays his hand on her arm. 'If we were to get married, are you concerned that, the first time we have a row, I'll bring up your past? Remind you what you were doing that night in the Central Hotel bar? Is that what's always on your mind?'

'It is. All the time. One day you'll tell me I'm nothing but a whore!' She looks at him, sobbing, tears running down her cheeks. 'If you ever said that to me, Fred, it would break my heart.'

He sighs. 'It's all in your mind, honey.' He moves closer to her. 'Ruby! Look at me. I often think of that night in the Central Hotel. You know why? Because *that* was the night all those years of waiting came to an end. The night that led to Ruby Baxter becoming *my* girl! It only has *good* memories for me. Because I bumped into you that night, you're now looking at the happiest man in Glasgow! Don't spoil it for the two of us, Ruby. We could be as happy as the day is long.'

'Oh, Fred. I know we should, but I can't get this stupid thing out of my head.'

'You'll have to. Because it's not going to happen. This fear is all in *your* mind, not mine.

'I have thought of all that, Fred. I know it's unfair on you. And I *do* want to beat it.'

He takes both her hands in his. 'Shall I tell you what will happen if you won't marry me or come and live with me? Nothing! That's what. I won't give up on you. We'll just carry on seeing one another like we do at the moment. We'll go out together. I'll always take care of you. Then one day, years from now, it'll suddenly hit you. You'll think, this guy really loves me! And that's when you'll realise how stupid you've been. All those lost years when we could have been living together.' He rises from the sofa. 'Give me your glass, darling. I'm going to go and make the two of us a cup of real coffee.'

Holding both glasses in one hand, he stands in front of her, reaches out and puts a finger under her chin, tilts her head up. He kisses her on the lips. 'I'm going to come back with two deluxe cups of coffee, snuggle up to you on the sofa, then I'm going to tell you a story. It's almost one o'clock. The perfect time of night for a *true* bedtime story.'

He places the mugs of coffee on the small table. 'There you are, woman who doesn't believe how much she's loved.'

'I do, Fred. I know it's stupid of me.'

He sits down next to her. 'As Max Bygrave says, "I'm gonna tell you a stoh-ryyyy!" But first of all . . .' He takes a sip of coffee. 'Ahh! Lovely.' He moves closer to her. 'Right, darling. Once upon a time – the middle of 1945 to be exact – the war in Europe hadn't long finished and we, my squadron that is, were billeted in these former Luftwaffe barracks near Hamburg. Just outside the camp was a *gasthof*, which we soon adopted as our local. Every weekend, without fail, in the middle of the evening, in would come this very attractive woman. Be in her thirties. She wasn't German. She was there to offer her services. Yet, she somehow remained aloof. Reserved. Men had to approach her. She never touted for customers. In fact, she'd often decline a guy if she didn't like the look of him. She'd now and again go off with a customer, for anything from ten minutes to half an hour, then return to the bar, to her table, to wait for the next one. It soon became quite clear, that once she'd made enough for her needs, she'd finish for the night. Go home. Most nights, well before ten, I'd glance over at her table and find she'd gone. As time went on, we got to know her story. Oh! Not from her I hasten to add. She was a Polish countess, no less! Alicia was her name. Her husband had gone off to war in September '39 and was never heard of again. The Germans took over her estate for the next five years until, at last, the advancing Russians pushed them back. She and her children, and a million others who didn't fancy living under the Russians, joined the retreating Wehrmacht and trekked all the way to Germany. Finished up near Hamburg, just outside our airfield.' He sips his coffee. 'I wish I could find the words to describe her, Ruby. The best I can do is – think Ingrid Bergman in *Casablanca*. But she was more than that. Oh! Such presence. At weekends, after I'd had a few drinks, I could never resist glancing at her. Sometimes finish up staring!' He laughs, 'Wellll! I was just twenty-six. I was newly married. But nevertheless, she fascinated me. The bar would be crowded, noisy, smoky. She'd sit at her table, somehow apart from it all. And always, so tranquil.'

Ruby interrupts. 'The way you're describing her, Fred. I can almost see her.'

'As time went on she'd often catch me looking at her. She'd incline her head, give me a half-smile. Obviously knew I found her fascinating. But also, she knew I understood. This part of our lives would not last for ever. A sort of rapport grew between us. And I knew it was fragile.' He looks at Ruby. 'I never wanted to take her to bed. That would have spoiled it. This was a beautiful, cultured woman. Spoke four or five languages. Had moved in high society before the war. And now she's penniless – with two children to feed. So, she did what had to be done.' He looks at Ruby again. 'There was no blame attached to it. Through this terrible time in her life she still remained what she was. A lady. Nothing could change that. And everybody *knew* that and treated her as one. Even her regular customers!'

Fred drains the last of his coffee. 'I often wish I'd got to know her a little better. Had some conversation with her. But I was young. And I was so worried I'd shatter this delicate "thing" that existed between us. When I first found out her nationality, I got one of our Polish pilots to teach me to say, phonetically, "Good evening" in Polish.' He laughs. 'I still remember it to this day, "Dobray veerchoor". I only learned it as a courtesy to her. A gesture. As I only ever saw her in the evenings, there was no point learning anything else. She spoke fluent English, anyway.' Fred's eyes are far away as he continues. 'I remember the night I came into the bar. Ready with my two words of Polish. I'd been rehearsing for days!' He laughs. 'As I passed her table I said, so casual, "Dobray veerchoor!" And blushed to the tips of my toes. She raised her eyebrows, smiled. "Dobray veerchoor," she said. "So you are learning Polish?" And I went even redder and said, "Oh, just a little bit for you, Madame."' He sighs. 'That was the longest conversation we ever had.' He sits, holding the empty mug, lost in reverie.

'You really are an old romantic, Fred.' Ruby nudges him. 'Well? What happened to her?'

'Oh! Yes. Well, a few months later we had some Americans posted to the base. Anyway, this American colonel, boy did he fall for her! Told us he'd never known a woman like her. "Class with a capital K," he said. She stopped coming to the bar, of course. But what impressed me with this colonel was his single-mindedness. As soon as he met her, he knew she was "the one"! Wasn't bothered about her past. Or people's opinions. When his time was up, he married her. That was in '46.' Fred places the mug on a side table. 'Last I heard, they were living in fine style in Boston!'

Ruby claps her hands together. 'Oh, that's good! I am glad.'

'I'm happy to hear that, Ruby.' He looks into her eyes. 'Will you please be *my* countess?'

CHAPTER TWENTY-EIGHT

Chamberlain Strikes Again!

———

As Ella Cameron approaches 18 Dalbeattie Street the sun beats down relentlessly from a clear sky, bouncing off pavements and walls. She blows her cheeks out. 'Pheww!' At just that moment Teresa O'Malley emerges from the close. She has her pinny on, a turban, fashioned from a head scarf, covers her hair. She carries her purse in her hand.

'Tis yerself, Ella. That'll be you just back from your work.'

'Right first time, Teresa.' Jeez! Never knew she wiz kin tae Drena.

'I'm nipping t' Mary's for a quarter of the Brooke Bond. There are times that wee dairy's a blessing, so t'is.'

'Aye, no' half.'

Teresa draws herself up. Without being aware of it, she makes an upward adjustment of her right bosom. Ella reads the signs, waits for the leading question that's about to follow. 'Are you and herself,' Teresa nods in the direction of Drena's downstairs windows, 'any nearer to mending railings? Oh! Or is it fences?'

'Naw. And we're no' likely tae be either. Ah'm no' interested in talkin' tae her.'

The corners of Teresa's mouth droop in disappointment. 'Och, but 'tis a shame, Ella. Best o' pals for all these years, and not to be talking now.'

'Aye. Well that's the wye it is.'

'I can tell ye, yer neighbours wish you were talking, so we do.'

'Now don't be trying tae put oot any peace feelers, Teresa. Ah'm no' interested in making it up. You'd be wasting yer time. Anywye, Ah'm dying tae get oot o' this heat. Ah put ma coat oan this morning 'cause it wiz cool first thing. Ah'm jist about melted noo.'

Teresa looks along the street. 'Turned into a scorcher so it has. I'll let ye go, Ella.'

'Aye, cheerio.' Eyes narrowed against the glare, Ella takes the last few paces needed to enter number 18. After the brightness outside, the close seems extra dark. A warm breeze funnels through from the back courts. As she walks towards the stairs she passes Drena's front door. It's ajar as usual. Be nice if it wiz like normal times . . . jist push it open. 'It's me, Drena!' 'Aye, in ye come. Is that you hame fae . . .' Ach! Well, it is'nae normal times.

She climbs the first flight of stairs, stops on the half-landing. Looks out the window for a moment, watches the weans playing in the sizzling back court. Her thoughts go back to the conversation with Teresa a few minutes ago. Irma tried the same thing a couple o' weeks ago. They're aw' dying tae get me and Drena back thegither. It's upsetting the in and oot o' wan another's hooses. They cannae ask the baith of us. But they're feart tae ask wan – in case the other wan takes the huff. It cannae be helped. With a heavy heart she starts climbing the stairs.

Drena McClaren sits at her kitchen table. The house is quiet. The kitchen seems dark. Its windows never get the sun. The fact she has the light off and no fire burns adds to the gloom. It all suits her mood. She sips her tea, draws on a Woodbine. Ella's familiar footsteps have just gone past. Didn't even falter. Ah still expect them to stop. How long is it now? She tries to work it out. Got tae be two, mibbe three, months since we fell oot. Jeez-oh! She shakes her head imperceptibly. Gives a heavy sigh. Ah cannae see us making it up noo. It's gone oan for too long. Nane of us will give in and make the first move. She reaches for another Woodbine. Ah don't half miss her.

Archie Cameron pushes open the door of the 419 Bar. Mmm! The smell of a busy pub. You cannae beat it. He breathes in again; beer, cigarette smoke, damp sawdust. Heaven should smell like this. Well, the men's section anywye. Whit wiz that article Ah read? Aboot yon French fella. He was the first wan tae write aboot smells bringing back memories, triggering them. Proost? Something like that. If Proost caught a whiff o' the 419, he probably would'nae make heid nor tail of it. Ah, therr he is! Billy McClaren has both elbows on the bar. Stands four square in front of his pint. Archie approaches without being seen.

'Herr McClaren. *Wie gehts du?*'

Billy turns. 'Ach! Herr Cameron. *Es gehts ganz gut. Du auch?*'

'*Ja, immer gut.*' Archie looks past Billy. The man standing behind him has his pint poised halfway to his mouth – which hangs open. Archie leans forward. 'Don't pay any attention tae us, pal. We're jist two auld POWs trying tae keep oor German sharp.'

'Ahhh, is that whit it is. Ah thought, fuck me! Urr these a couple o' East German spies – trying tae strip the 419 of its secrets?' The man gets back to his beer.

A freshly drawn pint of heavy is placed in front of Archie. 'Aw' the best!' He contemplates it.

'Ah see the big fight's fixed up for September. Who dae ye fancy, Archie?'

'Ye cannae go past Sonny Liston. He's the best heavy Ah've seen since Marciano. He's already beaten five oot o' the top ten contenders. The man's unstoppable.'

'Even so, Ah still huv a wee fancy fur Floyd Patterson. He's really fast. And he *is* the champ.'

'Huh!' Archie has lifted his pint, about to take that first mouthful. He places it back on the bar, untouched. 'Billy, he's still champ 'cause he's dodged Liston fur the last two years. Come September he'll get spifflicated. Be like a man against a boy!'

'Well, we'll see what we see.' Billy sips his beer. 'Anywye, has Ella still no' said anything yet aboot the big "no talkies"?'

'Not a word. Whit aboot Drena?'

'Same.' Billy folds his arms, leans on the bar.

Archie takes the chance to savour his pint. 'Ahhh, Bisto! That first moothfy is alwiz like nectar, in't it?'

'It is. But huv ye ever wondered: why diz that first taste no' last aw' the way tae the end?'

'Aye, you're right, mind. Strange in't it?' Archie regards his glass. 'Dae ye think we should try and get the government tae launch an enquiry intae that?'

Billy turns his head. 'Naw!'

'Okay, fair enuffski! Jist a suggestion. Anywye, talkin' aboot enquiries. Tae get back tae yon two. Whit are we gonny dae aboot them?' Archie lifts his glass.

Billy looks at him. 'Nuthin'. It's mair than oor lives are worth tae interfere wi' yon two.'

'Well, Ah think we should. They must huv fell oot ower something serious, Billy. It's months since they stopped talking. That's never happened before, huz it?'

'Exactly! And that's why Ah'm keeping oot o' it, Erchie. They've obviously had a big barney. They're in nae hurry tae make up. If ye try and interfere you'll only get the nose bitten aff ye.'

'But dae ye no' think if the *two* of us spoke tae them. You know, a sort of joint deputation. That might impress them, that we think it's time they buried the hatchet before—'

'Hah! And Ah know where they'll fuckin' bury it,' splutters Billy. 'In the back o' your heid!'

'Okay, that's mibbe no' the right choice o' words. But something will huv tae be done. If your Drena is behaving anything like ma Ella, they are definitely missing wan another. They've always been sich great pals . . .'

'Erchie, Ah quite agree wi' ye. But there is *no* chance of me saying anything tae Drena. Jist leave them tae sort it oot themselves. You'll regret it if ye interfere. Ah'll tell ye, even the United Nations would gie them two a body-swerve!'

'Well Ah disagree. Ah think it's worth the risk, Billy. It's jist like auld Chamberlain, when he made a last-ditch attempt tae stoap the war by sending Hitler yon note – "A last appeal tae reason". That's whit we should dae wi' the pair o' them. Send them a note.'

Billy McClaren's mouth falls open. 'It wiz'nae Chamberlain

that sent it. It wiz *Hitler* that sent it tae Chamberlain. He wiz trying tae con him intae letting the Germans hing oan tae territory they'd already conquered. You've got it arse aboot elbow!'

'Aw!' Archie looks thoughtful as he takes a mouthful of beer. 'Anywye, Ah suppose Adolf and Neville are'nae a very good pair to use as an example. Because then, we'd huv tae decide between Ella and Drena. Who's gonny be Hitler? And who's gonny be Chamberlain?'

Billy leans companionably on the bar beside his pal. 'Och! It wid'nae be that difficult – they could baith be Hitler!'

CHAPTER TWENTY-NINE

Tea and Empathy

Agnes Dalrymple is chopping sticks on the landing. She kneels on a cushion placed on the front door mat, her feet stretch back into the lobby. She hears footsteps pattering on the lino behind Frank Galloway's door. It opens, his 'lady friend' steps out onto the landing. So far they haven't yet gone beyond nodding and saying Hello to one another. Agnes doesn't want the lassie to think she disapproves of her staying with Frank. C'mon, Agnes. This is a golden chance tae huv a wee blether. 'Oh, hello. Ye hav'nae got your uniform on the day. Are ye on holiday?'

Wilma also sees this as a chance to get to know one of her neighbours. The 'spinster', as Frank calls her. He says she's nice. Wilma has the passing thought . . . at thirty-five years old, there's many a one would class *you* as a spinster, Wilma Ballantyne. She gives Agnes a smile. 'No, Ah'm only off this morning. Frank and me are on late shift this efterninn.'

'Oh. Of course, the two of you are back at Maryhill again, aren't youse?'

'Aye. The trams were withdrawn fae Partick Depot last month. So Frank is learning tae drive a bus at the minute. Once he gets his licence, they call it a PSV, him and me will have oor ain bus. Until Frank passes his test, Ah'm jist going oot wi' anybody that's short of a conductress.'

'Och! Them and their buses. Ah fair miss the caurs, so it must be worse for you two.'

'No' half. At least it'll be a bit better when we get oor ain bus. Anywye, Frank's away doon the toon at the minute. Ah'm jist gonny nip roon tae the shops for a few messages.'

Agnes sits back on her heels. 'Ah'll leave the door open. When ye come back, jist give a wee knock and come in for a cup o' tea and a blether for half an hour. Ah work at the City Bakeries, so Ah'm never withoot a wee snaster tae go wi' a cup o' tea – and it's all freshly pilfered! This is ma day aff, so Ah alwiz pinch extra the day before!'

Wilma smiles. 'Sounds good tae me. Ah'll no' be long – thirty, forty minutes. See ye shortly, eh, it's Agnes, isn't it?'

Agnes puts her hands on her hips. 'Here! If ye know ma name, diz that mean that yon Frank Galloway huz been talkin' aboot me behind ma back?'

'Oh, ye don't need tae worry, Agnes. Frank likes ye. So anything he's said has alwiz been good.'

'Ohhh! Ah'm flattered.' She sniffs. 'Jist wish Ah wiz twenty years younger!' They both laugh.

'Right, Ah'll skip away tae the shops. Oh, and by the way, Ah'm Wilma. Wilma Ballantyne.'

'Okay, Wilma. Ah'll put the kettle on at a wee peep. See ye shortly, hen.'

As Wilma descends the stairs she hears Agnes resume chopping her sticks.

Ten minutes after Wilma has exited the close, Ruby Baxter, shopping bag in hand, enters it. Granny Thomson is leaning against the wall at the foot of the first flight of stairs.

Ruby stops. 'You all right?'

'Aye, Ah'm fine. Jist waiting a wee minute till Ah've raised enough pech tae get me up the stairs.'

Ruby reaches down for the old woman's shopping bag, 'I'll take your—'

'Naw, ye don't have tae. Ah'll manage.'

Ruby regards her with a stern eye. 'Now don't start, Independent Annie! I'm going up the stairs. I've got a free hand – Oh, my God! What have you got in this bag? House bricks?'

'Ah know. It's some wecht, in't it? This last wee while Ah've been buying an awfy lot o' tinned stuff. The aulder Ah get, Ah find Ah cannae be bothered cooking. It's easier jist tae open a tin.'

They step onto the first storey landing. Granny pushes her door open.

'Don't you lock it?'

'Whit fur? Naebody's gonny rob me.' She reaches a hand out. 'Ah'll manage ma bag from here, Mrs Baxter.'

'I'll take it through, put it on the table for you.'

'You could put it on top o' the bunker if ye dinnae mind. Handier for putting the stuff away in the press.'

'No bother.' Ruby rests her own bag against a table leg,

totes Granny's over to the wooden coal bunker next to the sink. 'Hup!' She swings it up onto the brown-painted lid. 'There you are.'

'That's grand, Mrs Baxter. If ye have the time, will ye take a drink o' tea? Go on, huv a blaw.'

Ruby pauses. 'Yes, I was just fancying one.' She sits herself down on the chair against which her bag rests. Without being conscious of it, Ruby lays her palms flat on the well-worn chenille cover, finds a couple of areas where there is still some pile, gently digs her fingertips into the rich, lushness. As the old woman busies herself at the range, Ruby looks round the room. This is only the second time she's been in. The previous time she hadn't time to look around. She takes in all the Victoriana. The coals in the range have burnt down while the matriarch has been for her messages, but the kettle still sings. As she looks at all the bric-a-brac, Ruby half listens to the tea-making procedure . . . the lid removed from the teapot, 'chinked' down onto the cast iron range. Hot water poured into the pot to heat it, then thrown down the sink. The heavily embossed tin caddy is brought down from the mantelpiece, its lid removed, and three times the caddy spoon delves into the loose tea with a 'sheee' sound. There's a change of note as each spoonful of dry tea is thrown into the warmed teapot – like the pitter-patter of dry rain! With a grunt, Granny lifts the heavy kettle and there comes the sound of simmering water swishing onto waiting tea. Infusion is about to take place; we have lift off! The final sound is of the brewing tea being stirred, the metallic note as the teaspoon hits the inside of the aluminium teapot, the lid being put back on. The Japanese have nothing to teach Granny Thomson when it comes to tea ceremonies.

'We'll jist leave that a wee minute.' She places the pot on its stand in the middle of the table. 'Will ye take a biscuit?'

'No thanks, eh, Mrs Thomson. Tea will be fine.'

'Ah weesh you'd stop wi' the "Mrs Thomson". It's Granny. Anywye, Ah'll have tae have a bit biscuit maself. Tea's too wet on its own.' Ruby watches her open one of her tins, return to the table with two tea biscuits on a plate. 'Right!' She lets herself drop onto a kitchen chair.

The visitor sighs. 'For the last few minutes I've been back in my own Granny's kitchen. If I shut my eyes and just went along with the sounds and smells, that's where I'd be.'

'Ohh! Are ye trying tae say ma hoose smells, Ruby Baxter?'

Ruby sighs again. 'It does – it smells *wonderful!*'

'You have nae idea how many folk say exactly those words tae me.' The old woman presses one of the tea biscuits on the surface of her plate until it neatly snaps in half. She dips it into her tea. 'And whereaboots wiz your Granny's hoose?'

The elegant Ruby pauses for an instant. 'Brig'ton.'

'Mmm, Brig'ton. Even Dalbeattie Street is a step-up fae there.'

'Yes. The trouble is, until recently my address was Hyndland. A step-up from everywhere!'

'Aye, Ah would think sae. The nearest Ah've ever been tae Hyndland, is when noo' and again Ah've passed through it oan a bus or a tram.' She takes a sip of tea, looks wistful. 'Big hooses standing in their ain gardens. It would be like living in the park-keeper's hoose! It must huv been grand.'

'It was. And all the more so when you started life in a room and kitchen in Abercromby Street. Seven of us. I shared a bed with my three sisters. My father would neither work nor want. My mother worked herself to death before she was fifty.'

Ruby gives a humourless laugh. 'Until I was six, I thought knives and forks were jewellery!'

'Hah!' Granny looks at her. 'Careful, Ruby. Ah can see me gettin' tae like you!'

'Heaven forfend! We might juuust manage Christmas cards this year. But don't rush things.'

'Ah'm surprised you're still living in the close. Ah would huv thocht that fella that calls for ye in the big black car would have whisked ye away by noo. He's been taking ye oot for months.'

'Fred. He's actually a lovely man, Granny. He'd marry me tomorrow if I'd say the word—'

Granny cuts in. 'So why huvn't ye? Whit's the matter wi' ye?'

'Nothing. Not a thing. I think I love him. But I want to be one hundred per cent sure. I married my first man for his money. If there *is* a next time, I want it to be for love. And if he also happens to have money, well, that's a bonus!' Ruby sits thinking for a moment, then . . . 'Do you know what it is, Granny? I've got nobody to talk to about it. Just this couple of minutes sitting here, telling you about him, it seems to have brought it all into focus. Made it clear.' She sits back in her chair. 'You know what? I think, maybe I will marry him!' As she talks to the matriarch, Ruby still has her open palms placed flat on the chenille cover.

The old woman reaches out, takes Ruby's left hand between both of hers, 'It sounds tae me as if you're—' she suddenly stops. Ruby looks at her. She has closed her eyes. She opens them again, lifts one of her hands, points to the large dress ring Ruby wears. 'He bought you that, didn't he?'

'He did.'

'Uh huh!' It's as if the old woman has taken on a different

persona. Even her voice is stronger. Once more she takes Ruby's left hand between both of hers, holds it firmly, raises their joined hands so they no longer rest on the cover, are suspended a few inches above it. Granny's face is quite relaxed. She opens her eyes, continues to hold Ruby's hand, looks directly at her. 'This man is'nae bothered aboot your past, yah silly lassie!' Ruby feels a shiver run up her spine. 'It's your future he's concerned aboot. He's more interested in that than you seem tae be. This is a good man. He adores ye, dae ye know that?'

Ruby's eyes brim with tears. One spills down her cheek. 'Yes.' She can't stop her voice trembling. Granny Thomson lets go her hand. 'Away and put the poor soul oot o' his misery. Tell him!'

Ruby looks at her, tries to think of something to say.

'*Now!*' The old woman leans forward onto the table. 'Right this minute, wumman!'

Ruby feels energised. She laughs, excited, 'Right! I will.' She stands up, thinks for a moment. 'I've heard a phone ring somewhere now and again. Who has it?'

'The Stewarts, next door tae me.'

'Oh, they'll be at work. I'll have to go to—'

Granny interrupts. 'Naw, Rhea's on holiday this week. She's in.'

'Great!' Ruby almost turns full circle in her excitement. 'Right, I'll leave my bag there for the minute.' She dashes out of the flat, takes the few steps over to Rhea's half-open door. She knocks. 'Mrs Stewart, are you in?' Granny Thomson continues to sit at her table, listening.

'Aye, come in. Oh, hello! Eh, Mrs . . . it's Baxter, in't it?'

'Hello! Ruby, will do fine. Could I be a nuisance and use your phone? I'll pay for it of course.'

'Nae bother. Is it an emergency?'

'Well,' she laughs. 'According to Granny it is!' She feels quite light-headed.

Rhea stands at the sink peeling potatoes, half-turned towards her visitor. 'It's oan the top o' the sideboard, there. Dae ye want some privacy?'

'No, no,' she giggles. 'I don't care who hears.'

'As long as you're sure.' Rhea turns back to the sink, resumes peeling. Wonders what on earth is going on.

Ruby has dialled the number, there's a slight pause. 'Fred?' Rhea can barely hear the tinny-sounding reply. She stops peeling so as to make less noise. The tap still runs, water splashing into the basin. If she turns it off it'll be obvious she's listening. She puts her arm under the tap, lets the cold water run quietly down her arm into the sink. That's better. If she keeps still she can hear both sides of the conversation . . .

'Ruby! What a nice surprise.'

'I have an even nicer one for you, darling!'

'Do you? Sounds good. I hope you're letting me take you out an extra night this week.'

'Oh, it's even better than that, Fred.'

'Better than another evening out? Goodness. It must be something special.'

'I'll marry you, darling Fred!' Rhea drops the potato peeler into the sink.

There's a pause. 'I hope I heard you right, Ruby.'

'You did – and I will.'

There's a longer pause, then . . . 'Oh, Ruby. That is simply wonderful. What's made you make your mind up all of a sudden?'

'Because I've finally come to my senses.'

'God! I was beginning to think I'd never find the words to persuade you. I knew you should – but it was getting you to believe me.'

'Well, it's all over. I've just realised you're the man for me. So I thought you'd want to know right away. Put you out of your misery. I've kept you waiting long enough. If you take me to Rogano's tonight, I'll tell you the whole story about how it all came about.'

'Hah! I'll take you to New York sweetheart, never mind Rogano's!'

She pretends to think for a moment. 'Mmmm, no. Rogano's will be fine. New York will have to wait – I've got a machine booked at the bagwash tomorrow.' When they finish laughing, Ruby continues, 'Will you be coming by to pick me up at the usual seven-thirty tonight?'

'But of course. Can't wait. Oh, Ruby, I'm *so* looking forward to seeing you.'

'Bye, darling Fred.' The 'click' can be heard as he hangs up. Ruby holds the phone to her ear a moment longer, then gently replaces it in the cradle. She sighs, turns to Rhea, 'Did you get any of that?'

'No' really.'

'I'm going to be married!' She has the proverbial dreamy look on her face.

Rhea hurriedly dries her hands on a towel hanging from a brass hook, runs the few steps over to Ruby, kisses her on the cheek. 'Aw! Ah'm awfy glad for ye. Congratulations, Ruby.' An impish twinkle comes into her eyes. 'Ye can alwiz dae New York another time!' The two of them dissolve into laughter.

*　　*　　*

Ruby retraces the few steps to Granny Thomson's, re-enters the single-end, walks over, stands beside the old woman, who still sits in her chair. She looks up at Ruby.

'Well?'

'I've just told him. I am *so* grateful to you, Granny. I don't quite know how you did it, but you made me see things so clearly. Of *course* I should marry him. Anyway, thanks a million.' Ruby bends forward, kisses her on one of her ruddy cheeks. 'You'll be receiving an invitation to the wedding. Well, I'd better get away up the stairs.' She lifts her bag, makes for the door.

'Aye, Ah'll look forward tae that.' The matriarch waits until Ruby reaches the door. 'Oh! Dinnae forget your appointment at the bagwash the morra!'

CHAPTER THIRTY

Just the Ticket

As Frank Galloway enters the staff canteen in Maryhill Depot, Wilma Ballantyne looks up. He smiles at her, then makes his way to the counter. She gives an audible 'tut!' Could'nae tell anything from that smile. Jeez! Have tae wait another couple o' minutes. She hasn't much else to do but watch him as the queue moves along. Tall, slim, he looks smart in the bottle-green uniform and peaked hat. He's forever pressing that uniform of his. The double-breasted jacket suits him. Ah, here he is!

Frank sets his mug of tea on the table, 'Do you want tae get something tae eat here, or make something at hame?'

'Ah'll make something at hame. Anywye, never mind that.' She moves up as he slips onto the bench seat beside her. 'How long urr ye gonny keep me waiting? How did ye get on?'

He decides to keep her on tenterhooks. Looks at her. 'How did Ah get on wi' what?'

'Yah big scunner that ye are!' she hisses. 'Wi' yer driving test oan the bus, whit else?'

'Awww, that.' He reaches for his tea, takes a sip, puts the mug down on the Formica. From the corner of his eye he can see she's simmering, vibrating with impatience. 'Ah passed! That's me got ma PSV. Come Monday morning the two of us will be driving oot o' here in our own Leyland Titan double-decker. A team once again!'

'Aw, Frank. That's great!' She sways towards him for a moment, leans her shoulder against his. 'Ah know it's only a few weeks since we left Partick, but Ah've fair missed ma driver. No' the same going oot wi' drivers Ah don't know.'

He turns his head, he can see her eyes are full. 'Same for me, hen. It'll be nice tae look in my rear-view mirror and see my wee conductress standing on the platform, or going up and doon the aisle collecting fares – and giving me a wee smile noo and again.'

'Aye, it will.' She blushes. 'Dae ye know whit else Ah've been missing?'

'No, what?'

'Having oor break at the terminus. When there's jist the two of us sitting oan a bench seat, huving oor sannie and a flask o' tea. It wiz always nice on the caurs.'

'Wasn't it. Ah hope it'll be just as good when we're having oor break on a bus. Anyway, I'll still enjoy it if I'm sitting wi' you.' He's silent for a moment . . . 'But, och, I always thought I'd be driving trams till I retired.' He gives a big sigh. 'Never dreamt I'd finish up driving a bus.'

'Mibbe so, Frank. But jist think whit would have happened if ye had'nae got your PSV. You'd have tae finish the rest o' yer service as a conductor running up and—'

'*Huh*! Wash your mooth oot, Wilma Ballantyne! Can you see me doing *lassie's* work!'

'Eeee!' She leans back so as to slap him on the shoulder. 'Yah cheeky big bugger! Ah'll gie ye "lassie's" work. There's plenty o' male conductors. And let me tell you, boy, the majority are'ny a patch oan us lassies when it comes tae efficiency.' She sits upright. 'And you know it!'

He laughs. 'I'll tell you one thing. That's the last time I ever bring up that subject.' He gives a low whistle. 'For a minute I thought it was Mad Myra sitting there.'

'Oh, my God! Was that who Ah sounded like?' She joins him in laughter.

It's thirty minutes later. As he enters his close, Frank is whistling a spirited version of 'Stranger in Paradise' which Tony Bennett would be hard-put to keep up with. As he steps onto the first-storey landing he doesn't hear his name being called. A second, louder, '*Frank*!' is needed.

'Aye, Granny?' He pushes her front door open, steps into the lobby. 'What can Ah do for you?'

'Wi' aw' that whistling, Ah wiz'nae sure whether it wiz you – or Ronnie Ronalde! Huv ye time tae come in? Ah want tae ask ye a wee favour.'

'I've always got time for you, darling.' He walks into the small room. His first breath, as usual, whisks him straight back to childhood visits to his own granny. He sits himself at the table. Granny is in her chair.

'Will Ah mask a drink o' tay?'

'No, it's okay. Wilma's at the shops getting something tae eat, so I'll no' bother at the minute . . .'

'That reminds me, Frank Galloway. Ah've been meaning tae say tae you. That wiz'nae half a surprise when Ah heard a lady friend had moved in with ye!'

He shakes his head, 'Naebody will believe me. She's actually lodging wi' me at the minute.'

The old woman raises her eyebrows, cocks her head to one side. 'In a single-end?'

'Granny. Let me say right away, I would be as happy as the day is long if we *were* living – as the French would say – *a-deux*!'

'A doo! Like a perr o' pigeons?'

'And I'll tell you the *main* reason why I wish we were a couple. Since she moved in, I've been letting Wilma have the recess bed and I'm using the trundle one – and it's killing ma back! But I'm not letting on. I like her company, so I'm just putting up wi' it.'

She looks at him. 'Dae ye know what? Ah actually believe ye. Thousands wid'nae!'

Frank produces the statutory twenty-pack of cigarettes and a box of Swan Vestas.

'Whit's the matter wi' your lighter?'

'Something wrong wi' it. Ah'll have tae take it doon tae the Ronson dealer's. Anyway, is that all you've dragged me in here for, Isabella Thomson. Tae cross-question me aboot my non-existent sex life?'

'Not at all. But if it ever diz perk up, remember tae let me know! No. Whit it is, Frank, Ah've been reading that there's gonny be a big celebration, the night the trams finish. Is that right?'

'Aye, not half!' As he speaks, she watches him strike a match, then enjoys the aroma as the smoke drifts lazily around her. She always finds it pleasurable when a man smokes a cigarette in the house.

He attempts to remove the usual, real or imagined, shred

of tobacco from inside his lip. 'As you probably know, Wilma and I returned tae Maryhill Depot last month after the number twenty-six trams were withdrawn at Partick. Since then I've been learning tae drive a bus. The only tram route left in the city now is the number nine oot of Dalmarnock. They're due tae be withdrawn in September. That's when the Corporation are putting on this big Last Tram Ceremony.'

'Aye. According tae this article,' says Granny, 'because we're the last city tae have the trams, the Corporation intends tae make it a night tae remember.'

'Yeah, it's gonny be pretty special. For this last wee while they've been withdrawing certain trams and restoring them, back tae whit they used tae be: horse-drawn, open-top ones, painting them in the different colours and liveries that were used ower the years. It should be quite spectacular, Bella.'

'Good. So Ah'd like ye tae do me a favour, Frank. Ah'll be eighty-seven in September,' she looks at him, 'the month the trams finish. Now, Ah've never known Glesga withoot trams. Ah came up frae Girvan and went intae service when Ah wiz twenty-seven. That wiz 1902. There were still a few horse-drawn ones, but maist o' them were already running oan electric. Glesga Corporation wiz determined tae have the whole fleet bang up tae date.'

Frank comes in, 'Boy! I'll bet that was something, the change from horses to electric traction.'

She laughs. 'Oh! Ah'll tell ye. Me and the lassies Ah worked with, we thocht it was wonderful. Sunday was oor day off, so we used tae go for a run on the tram. They were lots of them still open-top and part open-top. Eeeeh! The speed o' them. Fair took your breath away so it did!'

'Ah'd imagine they'd be like the Eighth Wonder o' the World, back then.'

'No' half. We were aw' country lassies. We thocht Glesga was *so* modern.' She lays a hand on his forearm. 'Now, what Ah'd like ye to do for me, if ye can, is buy me a ticket for this last tram thingummy, the minute they go on sale . . .'

'Of course I will, I'll—'

She squeezes his arm. Interrupts him. 'Ah! But no' jist that, Frank. Ah want ye tae buy the dearest ticket that can be had. Ah've set ma heart on going for a hurl once again on an open-top tram.' She sits back, a determined look on her face. 'Ah saw them in – and Ah want tae see them oot!'

'*Right!*' Frank is moved by her enthusiasm. 'I'll see to all that, Granny. Now let me tell you. It's not that the tickets will be dear. It's the fact that the numbers are limited for the last run. The main thing will be tae get you an upstairs seat booked in advance. It's going to be run on a first come, first served basis. That means I'll have to make sure I'm at the front o' the queue, to get you the seat you want. So, even if I have tae pull a few strings, by hook or by crook, Isabella Thomson, you'll ride in an open-top tram on that last night. How's that?'

'Oh! That'll be grand. Even if Ah have tae take a taxi tae get there early. But Ah really want tae be in that last parade. That'll be ma birthday present tae maself.'

'Leave it tae me,' says Frank. He gives her a conspiratorial wink. 'As soon as I go into the depot tomorrow, I'll start making enquiries. Now, this is the first week in July. The big farewell is the first week in September. We've got two full months tae work . . .' He thinks for a moment. 'I've just had an idea. On the actual night, I'm sure Robert Stewart next door would be happy tae run you over tae Dalmarnock in that old Riley of his. Arrive in style!'

She claps her hands together. 'Hah! Now that would be grand.'

He throws his cigarette end into the fire, stands up. 'I'll organise it all for you, Granny. The day the tickets go on sale I'll be outside that office door – champing at the bit! Guaranteed!'

CHAPTER THIRTY-ONE

Visits

It's a warm July evening as Marjorie Marshall steps into her lobby. As she reaches for the door handle she calls through to the kitchen, 'I'll not be long, Jack. I might as well go and see Granny now. It'll have to be done some time.'

'Aye, right enough, hen. There's nae hurry if you want tae stay for a blether. Ah'll get the dishes done while you're away.' She hears the rustle of the newspaper as he gets back to the *Citizen*.

As she descends to the first storey, she wonders why she's always liked Jack calling her 'hen'. No other man does. Suppose most of them wouldn't think of me as the homely type. Now Drena and Ella, she smiles, they are definitely 'hens'. She's avoided adding 'motherly' to her attributes. You're not a mother, are you? Not any more. There are voices from below, folk climbing the stairs. Thank God! Stop me thinking of the bairn, slipping into melancholy. Again. She pauses, so as to let them climb onto the half-landing before she reaches it. The couple turn towards her. Oh, it's Irene's brother James and his wife. The man speaks.

'Hello, Mrs Marshall. And how are you?'

'Fine thank you . . .' Ohhh, what's his surname? Now that Irene's married and is Mrs Stuart, and he's moved away. Can't remember, have to use his first name . . . 'eh, James. And how are you?' She feels herself blush. That's the first time I've ever called him James.

'Och, not sae bad. It's a nice summer's evening.'

Marjorie smiles at his wife. 'It's lovely.' She turns again to him. 'Ah'm just on my way to see Granny. Keep her up to date with what's going on – otherwise I'll be in trouble.'

'Humph! You do right. Isabella's got to be kept in the picture. Anyway, nice tae see you again, Mrs Marshall.' He pauses a moment, then, to her surprise, gently cups her elbow with his hand. 'I hope things are easing for you, ah, Marjorie. Cheerio.'

Instantly her eyes fill with tears, she swallows hard. 'Thank you. That's very kind of you.' She nods her head, smiles. Can't trust herself to say any more. As she descends to the first storey, she feels comforted by his kind words. That would be an effort for a man as reserved as . . . Pentland! That's his surname. Damn! James Pentland. This train of thought is abandoned as she approaches Granny's half-open door. 'Are ye in, Granny?'

She hears the old woman clear her throat. Probably been dozing. 'In ye come, Marjorie. Ah hope you've time for a blether. We huv'nae had a good chinwag for – Ah dinnae ken how long.'

'I've actually come down for a wee blether.'

'That's good. Ah'll mask some tay.' She pushes herself up from her chair. 'So, how are ye, hen?'

I forgot about Granny. She regularly calls me 'hen'. Then again, I think she calls most women 'hen'. Even Ruby Baxter. Marjorie forces a smile. 'Oh, I'm not so bad. As good as I'll ever get, I would think.'

Granny half turns as she busies herself at the range. 'Och, remember, it's still only six months or so, Marjorie. You don't get ower a loss like you've had in jist a few months. Ah wish you could.' She stops pouring the hot water. 'Ah miss that bairn. Still shed a wee tear for her noo and again. So Ah can magnify that a hundred times for you an' Jack.' She begins pouring again. 'You'll huv tae face it, you'll never really get ower it.' She puts the lid on the teapot, carries it the few steps to the table, places it on its stand. Reaching out, she touches Marjorie's hand. 'But it will ease. Whoever said, "Time is the great healer" knew whit they were talking aboot.' She drops onto a kitchen chair, puts a hand on top of Marjorie's once more. 'The pain will get less and less as the years go by. Diz'nae mean ye don't love the wean as much, or ye don't still miss her. But take it as a blessing, hen. That terrible ache will lessen wi' each year. Anywye! A dish o' tay for the pair of us.'

The tears have been running down Marjorie's face. As the tea is being poured, she dabs her cheeks dry.

'A wee greet diz ye the world o' good, hen. If ye could'nae greet, you'd be in trouble. Biscuit?'

'No thanks. We've just had our dinner.'

'Who wiz that going up the stairs? James Pentland?'

Marjorie nods her head in affirmation, then . . . 'Are you any kin to Sherlock Holmes?'

The matriarch dips half a tea biscuit into her cup. 'Ah'm

sworn tae secrecy!' She looks into her visitor's face. 'You're doon for a reason, unless Ah'm mistaken.'

Marjorie shakes her head again. 'In fact, never mind *just* Sherlock Holmes. I wouldn't mind a wee look at your birth certificate. I'd take a bet that under "parents" it's got, Sherlock Holmes *and* Gypsy Petulengro!'

When they stop laughing, Marjorie looks at her friend. 'Aye, I have come down to tell you something. Jack and I have decided we're going to flit. The house just isn't the same any more. Too many memories of Jane. She's everywhere.'

Granny gives a heavy sigh. 'Well, Ah cannae argue with ye. Ah can believe that.'

'Especially the place where her coffin stood. I don't know how many times I walk past it, or my eyes are simply drawn to it, and I think – that's where her coffin was. Then I see that white box in my mind's eye. I'm never going to lose that memory while we live there.'

'Ah know what you mean. That's the only way you'll get rid of it, Marjorie. Moving oot o' the hoose is the only answer.'

'She's everywhere in that room and kitchen, but that's the worst memory. The coffin. It's the same for Jack.'

'The best thing is tae flit oot o' the place. Dae ye have an idea where you'll go?'

'We're going to Wilton Street. Along the far end, past Wilton Crescent.'

'Oh, they're braw hooses along there. Red sandstone wi' bay windows. Lovely!'

'Yes, that's them. They're all self-contained flats.'

'Aye. You're moving intae "wally close" territory along there, hen. Good for you.'

'We just got a letter from the factor this morning, confirming it's ours. That's why I thought I'd come and tell you. All being well, we should be away the week after next.' Marjorie drains her tea and rises. 'Between then and now I'll be telling any of the neighbours I bump into. You can tell those who come in to see you, Granny. Spread the word.' She slides her chair back under the table, 'I'd better get away up. Jack said he'd wash the dishes, but I think there's a fair chance I'll find him sound asleep under tonight's *Citizen*.'

'Ah'll let folk know, Marjorie. Ah think you're daeing the best thing. A change of hoose, especially tae a better hoose, it'll be good for the two of ye.'

It's a couple of hours later. Marjorie and Jack Marshall sit watching television. Now and again they'll talk of how they're looking forward to moving to Wilton Street. It never fails to cheer them up – as long as they don't think of *why* they're leaving Dalbeattie Street.

At this same moment, behind the door facing the Marshalls', James and Mary Pentland sit at the table with his sister and her husband. Conversation has faltered from the moment they arrived. Normally, Irene and Mary would have blethered away to one another whether the men joined in or not. Alec Stuart glances at his three dinner companions. James contemplates his glass of beer, turns it round now and again with his fingers. Seems to be intent on *not* looking up. Mary and Irene regularly start a conversation, only for it to peter out. Alec Stuart decides this has gone on long enough. It will have to be talked about. He takes a sip of beer. Here goes! He looks at his brother-in-law.

'That must have been a helluva shock for you, James, the loco works going bankrupt?' Three pairs of eyes are looking at James. In the silence, Alec wonders if he's done the right thing. Irene looks at her brother, turns to her husband.

'Oh, Ah don't think James will want tae talk about th—'

'Why ever not?' All three look at the big man. 'It might help me make sense of it. Get it off ma mind.'

'That's why I've brought it up, James. We all know it's happened. We know what NB Loco meant to ye. We cannae avoid it, might as well talk aboot the bugger!' Alec rises. Picks up the whisky bottle. 'Are ye for a wee half, James?'

'Aye, go on.' Mary Pentland draws a breath in, looks at her man. He only ever drinks beer. James turns to her.

'Special circumstances!'

They watch Alec pour a goodly measure into a tumbler. 'A drop o' The Grouse, James. Ah'll be joining ye, of course.' There is that beautiful squeaky sound, which whisky corks make when they're twisted out the neck of the bottle. As both men watch the drinks being poured, Irene looks at Mary, turns her lips downwards. Mary looks heavenwards.

'*Slainte mhath*!' says James.

'Mmm!' says Mary. 'Ah did'nae ken your brother had the Gaelic?' Irene avoids her eyes.

'Don't start!' says Alec. He turns to James. 'To somebody like me, reading about it in the papers, it all seemed to happen so quickly. Have you known it was coming for a while?'

'Ah'm afraid so. North British Locomotive Company was king o' the world – as long as the world needed steam engines. We really were second tae none,' James shakes his head, 'but these last few years the demand has risen for diesel or electric and, well, we just never made the transition.' He sighs. 'So we've paid the penalty.'

'Even tae a layman like me, James, I always knew NB Loco was *there*! Up in Springburn. Quietly building locomotives. Folk took it for granted. Then out of the blue, bankrupt! Closing doon! If it's a shock tae Joe Public, what must it be tae the workforce? Tae Springburn folk?'

'Aye. And it's no' just losing my job, Alec. Think of all that skill, expertise, tradition. All lost. It doesn't bear thinking aboot. Even the prestige of working for such a company. I took a pride in saying, "Ah'm a timekeeper at NB Loco." All the tradesmen were the same.'

'Aye, and from what Ah read in the papers, James, ship-building on the Clyde is going the same way. Some o' the smaller yards have already gone. Others are amalgamating. The writing's on the wall. They might be the best in the world – but that will'nae save them!'

James Pentland nods in agreement. 'You're right, Alec. Germany, Japan. They're overtaking us, stealing orders from under our noses.' He sips his whisky, leans his elbows on the table. 'Do you know one of the main reasons for their success?' He doesn't wait for an answer. 'It's because we bombed their industry to bits – then helped them rebuild it with brand new factories and the latest machinery. Meanwhile, we're trying to compete with them from Victorian buildings with out-of-date heavy plant!'

'Aye,' says Alec. 'And don't forget all these bloody com-munist union leaders. Forever deliberately bringing oor men oot on strike! The Germans don't put up wi' that.'

'*Huh!*' All three turn, look at Irene. 'The only industries that would have done well under them, would have been anything connected wi' concentration camps and ovens!' She sits, bristling.

Alec blows his cheeks out. 'There's nae answer tae that, folks. Say "Goodnight!", Irene.'

CHAPTER THIRTY-TWO

Blood's Thicker Than . . . What?

D rena McClaren glances up at the mantelpiece. Quarter past five. Then she remembers. Ah'm Ah ever gonny get oot o' the habit of looking at that clock every night? Ella diz'nae come in anymair. Time you got used tae it. She turns the pages of a month-old *Woman's Own*. Tries to find a story she hasn't read. Och! Ah'll jist read this wan again. It wiz quite good. She shakes her head as she finds herself looking at the clock again. Seventeen minutes past five. Ah'll have another cuppa and a fag, read the story, then start Billy's dinner. Young Billy will'nae want up yet. Too early. He needs aw' the sleep he can get when he's on nights.

Just gone half-five. She stubs the Woodbine out in the ashtray. Tuts as a determined spiral of smoke continues to rise from the dowt. She uses an old fag end to stub out the troublemaker. Tries to get back into the story. S'funny, Ah have'nae heard Ella go past yet. She's late the night. Mibbe went for a few messages. She hears her outside door being opened. For a moment her hopes rise. There's a barely audible knock on the kitchen door, a head appears. 'Hallooo. It is just me,' it whispers.

Drena lets the magazine fall onto the table. 'Irma! Jeez-oh. Could'nae hear that knock behind a caur ticket!' She thinks for a moment. 'Ah suppose nooadays Ah should say a bus ticket!'

'Billy junior is in bett, yes?'

'Aye. Ye want a drink o' tea?'

'Yes, please.'

As Drena rises she looks at her neighbour. When something good happens to Irma, you can tell. She always beams, gives the show away. 'You've come in tae tell me something good, huven't ye?'

'Oh, michty me, yah! How do you know? Did Granny tell you?'

Drena laughs. 'Naw, it's written all over your coupon.'

'Coupon? Oh, yah, my face. It is a long time since I heard you say that one, Drena.' Five minutes have gone by. Drena lifts her cup, sips the hot tea. 'Right, c'mon, oot wi' it.'

'Well, it is mostly very good news, but also a little bit of not good. You know that I have never met the ma and da of Bert. Because his brother, Arthur, is killed in Normandy. And Bert marries a German lassie.' Irma gives a very continental shrug. 'So they do not wish to meet me, and even Bert is not welcome to come to his house any more.' She breaks into a smile. 'But this Friday, Drena, we are going to Newcastle to visit their house for two or three nights.'

'Ohhh! That's good, hen. What's brought this on?'

'Ah! Well. That is the little bit of bad news. The father of Bert has to go into hospital next week, for a big operation on his heart. He has said he wants to see Bert and meet me *and*, of course, to meet his grandson, Arthur . . .'

'Aye, ye named the wean after Bert's brother, didn't ye?'

'Yes. We get a letter this morning. It is from Bert's sister. She works in an office and she put the phone number in the letter so he can ring her. Bert talks to her an hour ago. She and Bert's young brother, Alan, are so happy he is coming. His father is too. It is the mother really, who turns against him when we are married. The sister, she is called Annie, says his father insists he wants to see Bert before he goes into hospital. So the mother has to give in. Bert says he had a lovely blether with his sister.'

'Aww, that's really good, Irma. Ah hope his da's operation goes well. Wi' a bit o' luck that might mean youse will all start seeing one another now and again.'

'Yah, this is what we hope for. Bert is very excited, Drena. He always tells me they were a very close family until we got married in 1946. He has not seen them since that time.'

'It sounds like everybody is happy aboot it, except his mother. If you can coax her round that will be great.'

'Yah. We intend to be very careful with her.' Irma takes a drink of tea. 'Oh, have you heard how Archie is doing?'

Drena looks at her. 'Archie Cameron? Ella's man?'

'Yah. I was wondering if there is any more news how he is doing?'

'Ah did'nae know he wiz not well. Billy never said anything. Anywye, how would Ah get tae know? Ella and me huv'nae spoke for months. So whit's the matter with him?'

'You have not heard? Has nobody come in to tell you?

This morning in the factory, not long after he starts work, he is in a bad accident. A chain or something snaps on a crane and a piece of metal falls and Archie is hit on the head—'

'Oh, my God! Did naebody think tae come and tell me? So how is he?'

Irma bites her lip. 'It is, I think, very bad, Drena. This afternoon the hospital puts out . . . I always forget how it is called. You know, when the family are told they must come quick . . .'

Drena's hand goes to her mouth. She interrupts. 'The Report Line! Huv they put the Report Line oot on him?'

'Yah, Agnes Dalrymple tells me. I thought she will also tell you.'

'Oh, Jesus God! Oh! Ella will be demented so she will.' Drena rises, almost turns a full circle. Her hand is at her mouth, her mind in turmoil. 'Right, jist wait there a wee minute, Irma, in case Billy comes in. Ah'm gonny dive up the stairs and see Agnes. See if she knows anymair.'

Drena rushes out the door, patters up the stairs as fast as she can. As she approaches the second landing, Archie Cameron junior, wearing his best suit, is on his way down. 'Is that right, whit Ah've jist heard aboot yer faither?'

'Aboot him being in the hospital? Aye. He got hurt at work.'

'And the Report Line's oot for him?'

'Aye.'

'Where's your ma?'

'She's doon at the Royal. Been there aw' day. Went straight fae her work this morning.'

Drena looks at his suit. 'Why are you no' doon there?'

'Well, whit's the point, Aunty Drena? He's unconscious. Ah cannae dae anything.'

'Whit aboot jist being wi' your mother? By the looks of ye, you're off tae the dancin'.'

'Ma faither's unconscious. Whit can Ah dae? Whit's the point o' me sitting doon the Royal, or staying in the hoose for hours oan end? Anyway, oor Katherine's wi' he.'

'Whit a useless fucker you've turned oot tae be!' Drena watches his face flush. 'Whit ward is yer faither in?'

'Eh, Ah'm no' sure o' the number, but it's upstairs on the first floor. Mens' Surgical, Ah think.'

Drena stands to the side. 'Go on, on your fucking way Useless Eustace! Ah hope Ah huv'nae held ye up.' He takes off down the stairs two at a time. She also descends, comes back into her kitchen.

'Irma, Ah'm gonny go doon tae the Royal tae be wi' Ella and Katherine. Billy should be in any minute. Will ye tell him his dinner's in the oven.' She points. 'And there's a tin o' garden peas and a pan, lying ready.' She opens a drawer. 'Ah'd better put the opener beside them. He never can find anything.'

'Do you think it will be all right if you go, Drena? You know, with you and Ella not . . .'

Drena waves a hand, still distracted. 'Aw! That'll no' make any difference. Anywye, if it diz – she'll jist tell me tae fuck off! Wid'nae be the first time.'

Irma feels tears come into her eyes. 'Yah, but I think it will be okay.'

Drena manages a smile. 'Me tae!' A minute later she stands at the kitchen door, pats herself down. 'Keys, money, fags.

Ah've got everything. You can either sit in here, or in your ain hoose, Irma. You'll hear him coming a mile away in yon tackety boots. Right! Ah'm away.'

Drena is a few yards from the junction of Dalbeattie Street and the Maryhill Road, when Billy turns the corner. 'Where are yo go—'

'Ah huv'nae time! Archie Cameron's in the Royal. Gie me a pound in case Ah run short!' She gives him the briefest of brief details and finishes with 'Irma's sitting in oor kitchen, she'll tell ye all aboot it.'

'Right, okay, hen. Dae ye want me tae come doon later? Archie's ma pal, remember. And unlike you two *we* huv'nae fell oot!'

'Get fucked!' says his beloved. 'Ah'll ring Rhea Stewart later on and bring her up tae date. If Ah think ye should come doon, Ah'll get her tae tell ye. Okay? Ah'm away.'

He gives her a kiss. 'God, Ah hope he's no' too badly hurt.' He watches until she turns the corner and goes out of sight. Just before he heads for the close he hears her call, 'TAXI!'

Drena doesn't bother with Reception as she enters the Royal Infirmary. She heads for the stairs, makes her way up to the first floor. As she sets foot on the landing, she looks to the left. Coming towards her is sixteen-year-old Katherine Cameron. 'Awww, Aunty Drena!'

'Hello, hen.' She gives her a kiss and a hug. 'How's your daddy doing?'

'We don't really know yet. They're still daeing things tae him.'

'Where's your mammy?'

Katherine turns. 'Just go along tae the end and turn right. She's further along there, sitting ootside the ward.' She links her arm through Drena's for a moment. 'Ah'm awfy glad you've come, Aunty Drena.'

'Ah hope your mammy will think so tae, hen.'

Her arm is squeezed tighter. 'Ah think she will.'

'So, are ye going hame?'

'Naw. Ah'm starving. Ma mammy's gave me money tae go and huv sit-doon fish and chips. She says there's a good place along the High Street. Ah'll be back when Ah've had them.'

'Aye, a good feed o' fish and chips wi' bread and butter and a pot o' tea,' says Drena. 'Ye cannae beat it. The Queen huz that every Friday night in Buckingham Palace. She sends Philip oot fur them.' For the first time today, Katherine laughs. 'Anywye, away ye go, hen. Don't rush. Enjoy them. Ah'll keep yer mammy company.'

'See yah!' Katherine makes for the stairs.

As Katherine's footsteps fade they aren't replaced by silence. Drena is alone, there is no one to be seen, yet she is surrounded by the faint echo of voices, movement, footsteps, metallic clinks, distant laughter. From all directions it seems, sounds drift out of unseen wards, rooms and corridors; above, below and nearby. She glances up as someone steps smartly along the corridor above. Follows their progress for a moment. C'mon! Deep breath. She walks the few yards to the corner, looks to her right along an identical Victorian corridor. A tall window at the far end is the only source of natural light, and not much of that. Most of the long, narrow landing is unlit, shadowy. Forty yards along it, the solitary figure of Ella Cameron sits on a bench. Her hands clasped, she looks, unseeing, at the floor. Lost in her thoughts. She doesn't hear, or see, Drena approach. Folk have passed by at regular intervals all day. She stopped paying them any heed long ago. Only if they stand in front of her, speak her name, do they get her attention. Otherwise, they neither disturb nor distract her.

Drena walks to the bench, sits down. She slides along the last few inches until their shoulders touch. Reaching out with her right hand, she places it on top of Ella's, which are folded in her lap. She doesn't speak, only turns her head to look at her. It takes a second for Ella to come out of her torpor. She looks at the hand, turns her head to the left, finds she's looking into the eyes of her best pal.

'Drena. Oh, Ah hoped ye would come.' She lays her head on Drena's shoulder.

'Ah only found oot half an hour ago. Nane o' the stupid buggers hud the sense tae come and tell me, or Ah wid huv been here hours ago.'

'It's aw'right. You're here noo.'

'Whit's happening wi' him?' Drena lifts her hand from Ella's, raises her right arm and puts it along her shoulders, pulls her in close. 'Whit's the latest?'

'We were sitting at his bed aw' afternoon, after he'd first been treated. He was unconscious. Anywye, aboot an hour ago, the instruments he was connected up tae began tae show something was going on. So they've rushed him back intae the theatre. They must still be working on him. That's aw' we know.'

Drena squeezes her tight. 'Don't worry, hen. He'll be aw'right. Ye know whit him and Billy are like. They've got heids like fuckin' coconuts!'

Drena's prognosis, though not couched in medical terms, will prove surprisingly accurate. Ten days later, head shaved, a four-inch scar showing where a silver plate has been inserted into his skull, Archibald Cameron will be released into the bosom of his family.

CHAPTER THIRTY-THREE

Movements

Monday 6 August, 1962. Early morning. Robert Stewart switches on the radio. It's tuned to the Light Programme. It always is. As the valves warm up Carole King increasingly fills the kitchen with 'It Might As Well Rain Until September'. Rhea is through the room supervising Sammy and Louise as they dress. The schools are on holiday so they're not pleased at having to get up early. He smiles as he hears Rhea raise her voice now and again. Using a fish slice, he turns over the rashers of bacon he's frying. Once that irresistible smell drifts along to the bedroom, the kids will emerge like the Bisto twins – nose first. Well, maybe not. Sammy has been having Quaker Puffed Wheat every morning this last wee while. He'd have it three times a day if we let him. The seven-thirty news comes on. He's only half-listening until . . . 'Oh, my God!'

Rhea heards him. She calls from the room. 'Whit are you, "Oh, my Godding" at?'

'Ah'll tell ye when ye come through.' A wave of sadness floods through him. 'Ah'm brewing the tea. Don't be long!'

As he pours boiling water into the teapot his mind runs on . . . Aw' that fame and money. And what good has it done?

'Get a move on, you two. Your faither and me huv got tae get tae work.' Robert hears their footsteps in the lobby as Rhea does her Black Bob, shepherds them through to the kitchen. It's a wonder she diz'nae nip their ankles. He knows what will be first on her agenda. 'What wiz on the news that made ye say, "Oh, my God?"'

He turns. 'Marilyn Monroe's dead!'

'*Hah*! Are you serious? Ah hope this is'nae wan o' them daft jokes, Robert Stewart. Where Ah'm supposed tae say, "Whit happened?" And you say, "She wiz singing 'Pennies Fae Heaven' and the gas meter fell oan her!"' Sammy and Louise laugh.

'It's true.' He puts the lid on the teapot. 'Anywye, it's Bing Crosby the gas meter falls on.'

Louise looks at her father. 'Has she really, *really* died, Daddy?'

'Ah'm afraid so.'

Rhea opens the cutlery drawer. 'How did it happen?'

'She was found dead in her bed. They suspect it's an overdose. We'll catch the news on the telly when we come hame fae work the night. Bound tae be the first thing on.'

Rhea looks sad. 'Ah know this last wee while she's been huving a lot o' trouble in her private life.' She gives a big sigh. 'But even so. Jeez! She's nae age. And still gorgeous. And that's her away.' She stands still. 'Ah'll be thinking aboot the poor soul the rest o' the day. Ah really liked Marilyn so Ah did.'

'Yeah, me tae. Ah can still remember the first time we seen her. It was in that film, *Niagara*. It was in Technicolor.

Man! She was jist luminous. Ah've never forgot that scene where she walks intae view and she's wearing a dark-red, two-piece costume. She was absolutely stunning! Came right off the screen.'

'Oh, ye remember that dae ye. Can ye mind whit *Ah* wiz wearing that night?'

Her question doesn't register . . . 'It was the same in *The Seven Year Itch*. When she had yon white, pleated skirt on. And she walks ower yon grating—'

Rhea interrupts. 'Can ye remember yon time ye made a pot o' tea – which is probably stewed stupid by noo!'

'Oh, aye!' He starts to pour. Sammy and Louise laugh. The two of them have been sitting at the table, their heads swivelling from side to side as they listen first to their mother then to their father.

'Right, kids,' says Rhea, 'who are youse going to the day? Granny O' Malley or Granny Stewart?'

'Ah want tae go to Granny Stewart's,' says Sammy.

Rhea looks at her daughter. 'Granny O' Malley,' says Louise. 'And I know I'll have tae go tae Granny Stewart's first, till Granny O' Malley comes back from cleaning her offices.'

'Can we go tae the school-kids matinee at the Roxy this efterninn?' asks Sammy.

Rhea looks at Louise. 'Do you want tae go, hen?'

'Aye, Ah don't mind.'

Rhea points a finger at the two of them. 'Noo remember, you sit thegither. Sammy! You do *not* slip off and sit wi' your pals. Louise, if he leaves you on your own, Ah want tae know.'

Robert joins in. 'Now pay attention tae what your ma's telling ye. Ah know you are eleven and ten and the pair of you think you know everything in the world. But you don't! You're brother and sister, and we want you to go together and come home together and look out for one another. Okay?'

'Aye, okay.' They reply in unison.

Rhea turns to Robert. 'You'll huv tae gie them some money.'

'Aye.' He brings a handful of coins out of his pocket, selects two two-shilling pieces from this change. 'Right, that's more than enough tae get youse in and buy some sweeties.' He laughs. 'Ah'm miles away. Still thinking about poor Marilyn.'

'Ah'll bet ye are!'

'Yes, dear. Anyway, what's the Roxy putting on for the kids?'

'Yon auld Robin Hood picture, wi' Errol Flynn.' says Sammy.

'*Aw*! *Gee*! Ah wish Ah'd known *that*,' says his father. 'Ah'd have took a half-day aff work and went with ye. That's is my all-time, number one, favourite picture in the world, *ever*!'

Rhea tuts. 'Worse than the weans! Anywye, Ah thought it wiz *Snow White*?'

'Close second.' This elicits another tut. Sammy rises from the table. Robert pretends to draw an imaginary sword. 'Ahah! Varlet. You are one of the Sheriff of Nottingham's men. Defend yourself, knave!' He and Sammy begin to fence, laughing and giggling as they dual back and forth in front of the coal bunker. Robert allows Sammy to win. He collapses into the corner by the press door. 'Ah! I am undone!'

'You'll be late for yer work as well,' says Rhea. Louise sits at the table, holding her side. 'Don't laugh at them, hen.' Rhea shakes her head. 'You'll only make them worse.' As she speaks, she's struggling to keep her face straight. 'Right, c'mon. Time we wiz all away.'

* * *

As the Stewarts exit onto the landing and head downstairs, Granny Thomson sits at her table. As usual her door is ajar. She enjoys the noise and laughter that regularly drifts out of her next-door neighbours, at all hours of the day She hears the convoy stop outside Mary Stewart's house in the close. 'Right, in ye go. You can go up tae Granny O' Malley's when she comes hame, Louise. And mind whit we telt the two of ye, aboot the pictures.'

'Aye, we'll remember.'

The matriarch takes a sip of tea as she listens to the final instructions echoing up the stairs. There are various 'Cheerios' and pauses as kisses are exchanged. She hears Mary Stewart's door closing. Robert and Rhea's footsteps fade as they exit the close. As the couple go to the Riley snatches of their conversation drift up from the pavement. The doors on Robert's car open, then close. The engine starts. Seconds later it purrs away from the pavement. All is now silent inside and outside 18 Dalbeattie Street. For the moment. The old woman sits back. That wiz like listening to a play on the radio. Sound effects and everything. She smiles. It turns to a sigh. Aye, for the Stewarts that's jist an ordinary morning. One of a thousand. Be the same again tomorrow. Yet, in a few short years the kids will be up and away. She shakes her head. And if Robert and Rhea were offered the chance to live this morning all over again. They would pay gold.

It's a couple of hours later. Just after ten. Granny hears the engine noise from the street. Looks out to confirm it's the expected removal van. Uhuh. Marjorie said it would be aboot ten. For the next forty minutes or so there are heavy feet up and down the stairs, cries of 'Drop your end a wee bit,

299

John.' 'Carefy! Don't scrape it on the wall!' 'Mind ma bloody fingers!'

She hears footsteps in the lobby. 'Granny?' It's Marjorie's voice.

'Aye!' She clears her throat. 'In ye come, hen.'

Marjorie Marshall walks into the single-end. Sits on the fireside chair opposite Granny.

'We'll be away in about ten minutes. Doesn't take long tae clear a room and kitchen.'

'Naw. And it'll no' take many minutes tae drive tae your new hoose in Wilton Street.' She smiles at Marjorie. 'When ye think of it. It's so near, yet it's a different world. Tree-lined streets, lovely red sandstone buildings.' She laughs. 'And no' having tae share a lavvy in future.'

'Ah'll certainly not miss going down to the lavatory on a winter's night.'

'Aye. And this move will do you and Jack the world of good. Too many bad memories up them stairs.'

Marjorie nods. 'Yet, there was a time I thought I'd beaten my bad luck, Bella. When Richard went out of my life and Jack came into it. I truly wouldn't have swopped places wi' the Queen. And then, when I had Jane totally out of the blue. Never even dreamed of falling pregnant.' Her eyes glisten. 'You hear people say. "Happy as the day is long!" That was us. For over five years. Jack and I . . . well, we doted on her.' She clears the lump from her throat. 'Then to have her taken away like that. That was so cruel. If there is a God. I can tell you, Bella, I'll never forgive him for taking oor wee lassie. Never!'

'You're preaching tae the converted, Marjorie. Ah've had bad things happen tae me in ma life. And seen them happen tae other folk. Good folk. And all you ever get oot of a minister or a priest, is the same auld stuff. Aboot *him* being merciful. *Huh*! The next time Ah hear that God has been merciful – it'll be the *first* bloody time!' She looks at Marjorie. 'Ah dream aboot her, ye know. And every time Ah do, she comes through that door carrying oor kaleidoscope. "It's me, Granny!"' She shakes her head, unable to say any more. Marjorie also cannot trust herself to speak. They sit in silence. The inner door is opened, Jack Marshall comes in.

'Hello, Granny.' He turns to Marjorie. 'That's us aw' ready, hen. Place is cleared.'

The old woman gets to her feet. 'Let's make it short and sweet, Marjorie, or we'll be in floods.'

'Don't I know it.' Marjorie walks over, puts her arms round her long-time neighbour, kisses her on the cheek then looks into her face. 'Thanks for everything ower the years. Everybody up this close thinks . . . knows . . . you're the Eighth Wonder o' the World. Do ye know that? We aw' love . . .' She's unable to continue. Jack comes to the rescue. He gently moves Marjorie to the side, enfolds Granny in his arms. Kisses her. 'And Ah'll second everything she's jist said. And Ah'm no' gonny say any more, either. Or Ah'll finish up greeting like a bairn. Cheerio, hen.'

The matriarch stands at one of her windows, holds a curtain up. As the van pulls away, Marjorie Marshall, crammed into the cab with the removal men, manages a wave. The old woman smiles, waves in return. A few seconds later, before it gets to the junction with the Maryhill Road, it goes out of her sight. She lets the curtain fall, but continues to stand at the window. Stares, unseeing, into the street. Lost in memories.

*   *   *

It's coming up for six o' clock. Agnes Dalrymple doesn't bother knocking the outside door. She knows she'll be sleeping. Stepping into the lobby, she raps her knuckles on the partly open inside door. 'It's jist me, Bella.' She pushes the kitchen door wide, takes a step into the small room, sees exactly what she expected. One of the twin gaslights burns. In the soft shadows Granny sits in her fireside chair, legs stretched out, hands clasped in her lap. Once again she has succumbed to the Victorian cure for insomnia: softly hissing gaslight, aided and abetted by a coal fire, supported by a singing kettle. '*Granny!*'

'Hummfff, aye. Aw, is it you Agnes? Did I doze aff? Eeeh! You're hame fae your work? It's no' that time already, is it? The kettles biling. Are ye stopping for ten minutes?'

Agnes holds up a hand, fingers splayed. Points to each fingertip in turn, 'It is, ye have, I am, it is, and, eh, Ah will.' She pulls out a kitchen chair, sits at the table.

Granny, still only half-awake, looks at her. 'Is that you making a cod o' me?'

'Indeed Ah am not. You asked me half-a-dozen questions or so, straight aff the belt.' She shrugs. 'So Ah've answered every wan o' them. It's jist good manners.'

'Ma arse in parsley!'

'You're gettin' awfy rude in yer auld age, Bella Thomson. Anywye, did Marjorie get away?'

Granny eases herself up a bit in her chair . . . 'Ohhhh, yah bugger! Ma auld bahookey's sore wi' sitting. Choking for a dish o' tay so Ah am. Aye, she did. That's her and Jack away. Och, in her quiet way she'll be a miss. The poor sowel. She's never carried much luck.'

'Naw, she huz'nae. She'll never get ower losing that bairn,

Bella. Never in a hundred years.' Agnes watches her friend rise from her chair, about to make the tea. 'Oh! Got wan or two wee items fur ye, Granny.' She lifts her large message bag onto the table, looks into it. 'Two apple tarts, two rhubarb. Two cream cookies and a wee loaf of soda bread. That dae ye?'

'That's lovely, hen. You must save me a fortune ower the course o' a year.'

'Maist of it would be thrown oot the next day. Be a shame tae waste it.'

'Aye, don't forget that auld wartime saying: "Waste not, want not – gie it tae Granny!"'

It's ten minutes later. 'Boyz-a-boyz! says Granny. 'Ah was ready for that cuppa.'

'Me tae. Here! Huv ye seen these new teabag things in the shops? Are ye gonny try them?'

Granny draws herself up. This is followed by a reflex, bosom adjustment. 'Humff! They'll no' be coming intae this hoose, Ah'll tell ye that for nothing. Ah wiz talking tae a wumman in Guthrie's the butcher's the other day. She says she has it oan good authority that it's an idea somebody thought up tae get rid of all the sweepings and the dust! It used tae go intae the bins. Noo they've found a wye tae sell it! There's only yin way tae make tea. Using dry tea.'

'Aye. It sounds logical, whit that wumman telt ye. Uh-huh, Ah think Ah'll steer clear of them as well. Anywye, they'll never catch on, Bella.'

'A flash in the pan! Oh, and Ah'm sure you would hear at work, Agnes. Did ye know yon Marilyn Monroe has died?'

'Aye. Aw' the lassies were talkin' aboot it this morning. Everybody thought it wiz sad.'

'Jist a young wumman,' says Granny. 'Everything tae live for. Yet diz'nae have the will tae live. That's the one thing ye must have . . .' Her voice fades.

Agnes looks at her. Suddenly, the old woman is elsewhere. Looks the way she always does when she 'sees' something, gets a premonition. 'Och, well Bella. That's wan thing that cannae be said aboot you. You've alwiz had the will tae live, haven't ye?'

There is no response. She is well away. Agnes feels uneasy as she looks at her. At this moment she can clearly see just how frail the old woman is. The flame is burning low. At any other time granny looks quite well, but, with a sudden awareness, Agnes knows her friend is beginning to fail.

Granny comes back. At once, looks better, yet . . . 'You really seen me there, didn't ye?'

Agnes tries to laugh it off. 'It wiz jist that you seemed tae be going intae wan of yer turns, Bella. Ah thought you were gonny huv a premonition.'

'Oh, Ah can gie ye a premonition, hen.' For a moment Agnes is pleased. That's the old Granny Thomson sitting there. She's back. The matriarch looks straight at her. 'Ah'll be away before this year is oot!'

'Och! Don't talk nonsense, Bella. We aw' know you've got a bit of a wheezy chest. And your arthritis gives ye some gyp. But otherwise you're as fit as a flea. Stop your havering!'

'Ah'm certainly no' havering, ma friend.'

Agnes is annoyed. 'Well excuse me. But Ah've been doing ma hospital visiting for this last year or so. When folk die, it's usually because they've been ill. You are'nae ill. So whit are ye proposing tae die of? If ye don't mind me asking?'

'Because it's ma time!' This is said with such certainty, it brooks no argument.

Agnes looks at her, feels a chill run up her spine. 'You're beginning tae frighten me, Bella.'

Isabella Thomson reaches for the teapot, refills her cup, sits back. 'Whit huv you got tae be frightened aboot, Agnes Dalrymple? It's me who'll be going the journey. No' you!'

CHAPTER THIRTY-FOUR

Nothing Stays the Same

F rank Galloway drives into Maryhill Depot at the wheel of 'his' Leyland Titan bus. He glances into his side mirror. Wilma stands on the edge of the platform, her right hand gripping the rear, curved rail. She presses her left hand down on the flap of the money satchel slung in front of her. Stop any coins flying out. As the bus swings through the large doorway, its engine note changes from the low growl of driving outside, to the booming reverberations of indoors. With practised ease she leans back, lets go the handrail, pushes off with her feet. With a style which would earn her '10' from Cyd Charisse – maybe a '9' from Margot Fonteyn – Wilma 'hits the ground walking' and makes for the office to cash-up.

Frank does a half-circle, then reverses into an empty space. Slotting the gear lever into neutral, he puts the handbrake on and cuts the engine. Quiet descends. The smell of diesel fumes drift into the cab through his side window. He wrinkles his nose. That's all the depot smells of nooadays. Who ever thought the day would come when I'd long for the smell . . . *No*! It wasn't a smell. Scent? Nearly. Perfume? Mmm, too feminine. What about . . . the masculine musk of a tram depot! That'll do! Lubricating oil, engine grease, the pungent smell of welding torches. Paint. Turps. And the indefinable smell of the overhead, high voltage cables, when they 'arc' and send showers of solid sparks pattering onto the ground which lie for ages glowing defiantly. Diesel fumes catch his throat yet again when another two double-deckers swing through the main entrance. Forgive them Father. They know not what they do.

As he walks over to the office he looks down, his eyes follow the tram rails as they seem to multiply, drift apart and make for various bays. Ahhh! The last tramlines in Maryhill. He looks intently at them. Jist over a year ago you could have driven a tram from one of those bays, out onto the main road and away tae anywhere you fancied in the city. Now? He looks the other way, towards the entrance. The tramlines end half-way there. Severed. A terminus – before they've even left the depot! From there on it's Tarmac out to the street then all the way up and down the Maryhill Road. Soon, the whole city. Just one route left and its days are numbered.

He comes into the office with his paperwork. Wilma stands at the cashier's desk. She gives him a smile. He winks at her. Through the glass in the Inspectors office, he can see Bill Joss sitting at his desk. Joss spots him, waves for him to come over. 'How are ye doing, Frank?'

'As well as a tram-driver can – who's having tae drive a bus.'

Joss shakes his head in sympathy. 'Whit can Ah say?' He sits back. 'You've just put a thought intae ma head. Ah'll bet you if they canvassed all the depots, they would find somebody, somewhere, who would say, "Well, actually Ah've found Ah'd rather drive a bus than a tram!" Would ye think so?'

'There's bound tae be wan,' Frank nods in agreement, 'there *alwiz* is!' He reaches into his pocket for his cigarettes. 'That reminds me of the tale about a British businessman who was over in Russia. As ye know, things have eased a lot in the ten years since Stalin died. So this fella is on the Metro in Moscow and says tae a Russian guy sitting next tae him, "Can I ask you, what did you think of Stalin?" This fella looks around, puts a finger to his lips and whispers, "Not now! Stay on the subway." They ride all the way to the terminus, get off, then walk out of the station. The businessman tries to speak . . . "No!" says the Russian, "Not now." They walk into the countryside for about three miles. Finish up in the middle of an enormous, flat field. The Russian makes sure there is nobody to be seen. Leans close to the businessman's ear, whispers, "Actually, I quite liked him!"'

Wilma appears. 'That's me cashed-up.'

'We're off now for two days. See you on Monday, Bill.' They turn towards the door.

'Oh, Frank! Wait a minute. Ah nearly forgot.' They watch as he opens a drawer. 'Ah got that ticket for you.' He takes an envelope out, 'Reserved seat, upstairs, semi-open top. Your old granny will be delighted.' He taps the side of his nose. 'Hud tae pull a few strings!'

'That's great, Bill. That's exactly what she wanted me to get.' He puts the envelope in a breast pocket, fastens its button. 'She's about tae turn eighty-seven. That'll be a great present for her.'

'She'll be turning somersaults when ye tell her!' says the inspector.

'Not wi' her arthritis, she'll no'!' says Frank. 'She might just manage tae turn roon' in bed!'

'Ah've written aw' the details on the back o' the ticket. It's the fourth tram in the parade.'

'That's great, Bill. Thanks a lot. See ye on Monday.'

As they walk out of the office, Wilma speaks out the side of her mouth. 'It's for ma auld granny. Lying bugger!'

'Well it is for "Granny".'

'Aye, but no' yours.' She looks up at the sky as they exit the depot. 'The clouds are beginning to break up.' She points. 'Look! There's enough blue there to patch a Dutchman's trousers!'

Frank laughs. 'Where did you get that one from?'

'It was from a pal of mine when Ah was wee. Her mother was Irish. She always used to say that when she saw the sky wiz clearing.'

They walk a few steps more. Frank turns. 'It's a nice saying, that, isn't it? When you're a kid, that's the sort of thing you always remember.' She glances at him as they walk along. He's lost in thought. She links her arm through his, he presses it to his side. She looks at him again. It must be about four months now. He said Ah'd get used to sharing the single-end. Ah would'nae dream of looking for somewhere now. Wonder how long we'll go on like this?

'Okay, Wilma. Will we donner down to Jaconelli's at Queens Cross, have something to eat?'

'Smashing. But it's my turn to pay – don't argue!'

'Fair enough. Anyway, so you should. You eat twice as much as me, yah wee gannet! He squeezes her arm to his side again. 'How's this for a suggestion? We've got two lovely days off. What if your landlord takes his ludger along to Stromboli's tonight for a bit of the old Italiano nosh. Then after that, we saunter oot ontae el Byres Road and take a taxi to Le Bar Rendezvous for a couple o' drinks and a wee dance. And adding to our pleasure all evening will be the thought that we can have a long-lie in the morning!'

She leans her head on his shoulder for a moment. 'Ah wid'nae call the Queen ma aunty!'

It's an hour later when they get back to the close. 'You got your key with you, Wilma?'

'Ah have.' She brings it out of her pocket, dangles it in the air.

'I'll nip intae Granny's with the ticket. You go on up tae the house, hen. Make a start.' They part on the first storey. She hears him knock.

As he enters her flat, Granny sits at the table reading a magazine, 'Time for a drink o' tay?'

'Thanks aw' the same, Bella. Ah haven't. Wilma and me are going oot the night.' He reaches into his breast pocket, brings out the envelope. 'But first of all, before Ah go anywhere, here's the ticket that's gonny take a certain lassie for a ride – for the first time in fifty years – on the open-top of a tram!'

Her hand goes to her mouth. 'Eeee! Son. That's wonderful.' He watches as she delicately extracts it from the envelope, holds the pink ticket stretched between her fingers. 'Oh! From Dalmarnock Depot oot toward Brig'ton Cross, huh! Alang Dumbarton Road tae. And only sixpence! Eee! Worth every penny, son.'

*   *   *

It's sometime later. Just gone twenty to seven. Frank is shaved and ready. Just has to put his jacket on. He stands in the tiny lobby reading the *Evening Citizen*. Can feel the heat of the lobby light as it burns in its green plastic shade, can smell the Brylcreem on his hair in the confined space. He listens to what are now familiar noises and movement, as Wilma carries out her ablutions at the kitchen sink. The cold tap turned on now and again, hot water pouring from the kettle into the basin. The paper blurs as he thinks of other things and his eyes go out of focus. If folk up this close could see me now, they would'nae believe it. They aw' think we're a couple. Granny's the only one who believes me. Yet, if they seen us at the club later on tonight, they'd definitely think we're sleepin' thegither . . . Dancing cheek to cheek, kissing and canoodling. Then, when we get back to the house – he almost laughs out loud – it becomes 'Chastity Rules. OK'. We do all this smooching when we're out. But once we're back hame . . . He shakes his head. Draws on his cigarette. Wilma's in bed in her nightie and Ah'm in my pyjamas, ready for the trundle bed. Hah! We don't even kiss 'goodnight'. Because we're alone in the house, in our night things, we might get carried away! The smoke rises from his cigarette. Och! But in a way it's sort of nice. Old fashioned. Anywye, Ah could'nae force maself on a wee soul like Wilma. It would'nae be right. We're fond of one another. Attracted to each other, in fact. But God knows when anything will ever happen. He goes back to the paper, tries to find his place.

'Frank?' He hears her running the tap into the basin. 'Can Ah ask ye something?'

'Aye?' He lowers the *Citizen* again.

'Noo Ah know it's nane o' ma business, so don't be taking

the huff. But do ye ever think of making another attempt tae get your boy Daniel tae listen to ye and finally realise –'

He interrupts. 'Wilma. If I thought he would listen, there's nothing I'd like better. But It would be a waste of time.' She hears him rustle the paper, signalling he wants to get back to it.

She perseveres. 'Do ye no' think it wid still be worth a try even it—'

He cuts her short again. 'Ah never mentioned it, Wilma. But about three weeks ago – it was the day I went doon the toon tae get yon pillowcases – bumped into him right in the middle of Lewis's. I said, "Hello, Daniel!" and stopped. He sailed right past me like I did'nae exist!'

'Oh, that wiz'nae very nice, Frank.'

'Ah'd rather you don't bring it up again, Wilma. Okay?'

'Aye. If Ah'd known he'd done that tae ye, Frank, Ah wouldn't huv mentioned it. Sorry.'

'It's aw'right, hen. I know you mean well. Forget it. We're going oot the night tae enjoy ourselves – and nothing's gonny stop us.' He pauses. 'That's if you ever get yourself ready!'

'Oh! Ah have. Jist finished, Frank. Ye can come through.'

He puts the cigarette between his lips, folds the broadsheet while shutting one eye against the smoke. He opens the door into the room.

'Oh, my God! Frank Galloway. If Ah did'nae know better, Ah'd think that loabby wiz oan fire! Look at the reek! Ye should take a pair o' herring in wi' ye – you'd come oot wi' two kippers!'

Frank puts on his best 'serious' face. 'Is that you casting "aspidistras" on my smoking, Miss Ballantyne? Whit a cheeky wee ludger you're gettin' tae be.'

Wilma reaches for the lavvy key. 'Right, a quick visit, then Stromboli here we come!'

It's almost eleven when they enter Le Bar Rendezvous. They both have a lovely feeling of anticipation. As Frank walks to the bar, the couple who run the place, George and Ruth, smile and say, 'Good evening.' The connection they have in common, that George once lived at 18 Dalbeattie Street, hasn't yet been made. The times when the Lockerbies have visited Robert and Rhea Stewart at number 18 have, so far, not led to any chance meetings in either street or close.

'How nice to see you,' says Ruth. 'I'm glad you're becoming regular customers.'

'Yes, we really do like your place,' says Frank. 'Lovely ambience. Not as impersonal as the large dance halls in the city. Though I must say, when I was younger, I loved them.' Frank lifts the drinks he has just ordered, smiles. 'Tastes change when you get older. See you later on.'

'Enjoy your evening,' says George. Ruth extracts what's left of a Sobranie cigarette from her holder. She reaches a hand out, rests it on George's sleeve.

'We may be in for a quiet night, darling. Do you think?'

'Mmmm, looks that way at the moment. But after all these years, we should know by now that you can never forecast. Forty minutes from now we may have had an influx of folk, and the joint, as they say, is jumping!' As he likes to do, he leans forward, kisses her on the temple.

Another couple come in. Young, smartly dressed. The man accompanies his wife to a banquette, then strolls over to the bar. As he does, the eyes of quite a few of the customers follow him. Especially the ladies. If he's aware he's being watched, it doesn't seem to bother him. Ruth looks at him. Probably a football player. George will know him. As he nears the bar he smiles, offers his hand. 'Hello, George.'

'Hi yah, John. You're looking well. In training?'

'Aye. We're hoping tae get another go at the European title.'

'Mmm, it's that Hungarian, Laszlo Papp, at the minute, isn't it? Mind, I've got to say it, you'll have to be at the top o' your game to take the title off that fella.'

The young man laughs. 'Aye, he's whit they call a seasoned pro! He's a tough nut. Laszlo.' As they speak, Ruth looks at him. Dark curly hair, rather pale. Even wearing a suit, you can tell he's fit. Lithe. Rather handsome for a boxer. His drinks are placed on a tray. Before he can lift them, Ruth speaks.

'Well, I've managed to deduce this young man's called, John. And he's a boxer . . .'

'Oh, Ruth! I'm sorry, darling. You know what I'm like for my boxing. John, this is my wife, Ruth. May I introduce John "Cowboy" McCormack, former British Middleweight Champion.' They shake hands.

'Didn't you go to see John fight a year or two ago, George?'

'Indeed I did.' George turns back to him. 'I was at Paisley Ice Rink when you beat the English lad, George Aldridge. August '60. That was also a title fight if I remember.'

McCormack laughs. 'Aye, wan o' my better nights. Anywye.' He reaches for his wallet.

'No! On the house, John. Good luck when the time comes.'

'That's very nice of you, George. Thanks. Nice to meet you, Ruth.'

As they watch him wend his way over to his wife, Ruth

turns to George. 'I'd never have taken him for a boxer. Far too good looking. I'd have thought, perhaps a football player.'

He laughs. 'Well, if you're a good boxer, you should be able to protect your looks. John's just about twenty-five or so. He's a talented boy. Could still go places.' As he finishes speaking, he sees Ruth's head turn towards the entrance.

'Oh, my God! It's them! Look who's just come in. Johnny and Veronica!' Ruth half rises from her bar stool, sticks her arm as high in the air as she can, waves vigorously in welcome. George beams.

'How wonderful!' He hurries across the floor. The new arrivals smile, obviously as pleased as the Lockerbies are. Ruth watches as George kisses then hugs Veronica Shaw, shakes Johnny McKinnon's hand with both of his. As he brings them over to Ruth she climbs off her stool, opens her arms wide.

'Come to Mama my number two man in the world!'

'Oh, my darling Ruth! It's been *far* too long since we were all together!' He gives her a resounding kiss, followed by a bear hug.

'It's easily nine months since you were last here. Why so long?'

'Well, you know how it is. The older you get, time just slips away.'

'I hope you're coming to Agincourt Avenue for a night-cap, after we close?' says George.

'But of course. "Normal Service Has Been Resumed!" as they're always saying on the telly.'

It's just gone half-past one. Frank Galloway comes back up to the flat from the lavatory. He pauses between doors. 'Are you decent?'

'Aye. Ah'm in bed.'

He comes into the room, rinses his hands under the cold tap. 'Eh, look at the time, Wilma.'

'Ah know. It's a good job we're no' working the morra.' She snuggles down. 'That was a lovely night oot, wizn't it, Frank?'

'Yeah. Ah think we should do that *at least* once a month. Dinner at the Stromboli, then away tae the Bar Rendezvous for a wee dance – and hame in a taxi at the end o' the night. Huh! Ah'll bet ye the Queen diz'nae huv nights oot as good as that!' They both laugh. Frank struggles into the trundle bed. 'Okay, Wilma. Lights out, hen. G'night.' A moment later there's a click. All is darkness.

He gets comfortable, lets out a sigh. 'Mmmm!'

Wilma's voice, tremulous, comes out of the dark above his head. 'Ah, Frank . . .' Her voice fades, she seems nervous. She clears her throat, starts again. 'Eh, if ye want tae, you can come in here beside me.'

CHAPTER THIRTY-FIVE

Keeping up to Date

The last day of August, 1962. A Friday. It's mid-morning when the Ford Zephyr turns in to Dalbeattie Street and parks outside number 18. Ruby Baxter looks at her watch. Ten past ten. Ah don't think Granny will be away to the shops this early. She looks the length of the street. It's quiet. Opening the driver's door, she lifts her shoulder bag, turns, and, with a magnificent show of leg, steps out onto the pavement. Alas, there are no men around. This treat goes to waste.

Ruby has also slipped under Granny's radar as she makes her grand arrival. At this same moment the matriarch is standing on her landing, discussing matters of great import with Teresa O' Malley.

'I told our Siobhan, so I did, you'll have t' pick another night,' says Teresa. She breaks off for a moment to put a finger inside a yellow duster, place it over the hole in a tin of Brasso. Shakes vigorously. As she rubs the fresh polish onto her letterbox, she continues. 'She wasn't best pleased. Jayz!

Oi'm not going to be missing me *Dr Kildare*. Not for love nor money.'

'It must be good,' says Granny.

'Oh, 'tis. And Dennis is as bad as me. You could hear a pin drop in our house when it's on. And there's not only Richard Chamberlain,' she looks at her neighbour, 'that's the young fella that plays Dr Kildare. There's Raymond Massey as well. He's the head doctor. Dr Gillespie.' She turns towards Granny again. 'You'll know Raymond Massey surely, Bella?'

'Indeed Ah do. Ah think so. Wiz it him that played Abraham Lincoln in yon picture, ohhh, before the war it wiz. Back in the thirties—'

Teresa cuts in. 'T'was! The very one.' She stops polishing for the moment, clutches the tin to her breast. 'I'm not kiddin' to ye. The two of them in this programme, ye wouldn't t'ink t'was acting. 'Tis like one o' them docyourmentarys. You'd swear blind it's been made in a real hospital, Bella. I'd trust the pair o' them wit' me life so I would! You don't know what yer missing. 'Tis worth gettin' a telly, just for that.'

'Aye, it sounds like it. But Ah've—' The old woman breaks off as the clip-clop of high heels are heard entering the close. She holds a finger up in the air, cocks her head to one side. 'Ruby Baxter,' she whispers. The two women fall silent as they listen to the high heels begin climbing the stairs. Teresa's polishing finger barely moves on the brasses. Granny looks down through the bannister rails. A mane of shoulder-length red hair sways into view.

'Ah thocht you'd done a moonlight flit, Ruby Baxter?'

'Did you now.' She steps onto the half-landing, turns, looks up at the two figures. Both wear floral pinnies. Teresa has topped hers off with a turban fashioned from a headscarf. 'No, none the fears of it, Bella. You haven't got rid of me yet. Though it won't be long.' She continues her ascent, steps onto the first storey. 'And how are you, Mrs O' Malley?'

'Foine, me dear. Haven't seen ye for a week or two.'

'No.' She turns back to Granny. 'I've come over to pick up a few items, so I thought it would be good manners to come in for a cuppa. Let you know how things have gone since you gave me that good advice.'

'Well, Ah must say, by the looks of ye, it's worked!' Granny turns. 'C'mon, then. No' take long tae make a pot o' tay for the pair of us.' As Granny walks into her house, Ruby notices Teresa's face fall at not being invited. Before she steps through Granny's front door, she turns.

'Don't worry, Teresa. She has my full permission to bring you up to date with what's been happening.'

'Oh! Aye.' For a moment, Teresa wonders if she's being catty. As it has been said with a smile, she decides she wasn't. She smiles in return. 'Sure, and it'll be nice to know you've turned the corner.'

Before she goes out of sight, Ruby laughs. 'I think you'll find I've not only turned the corner – I'm halfway up the street!' She stops just inside the lobby, sways back to look at Teresa again. 'Or maybe that should be halfway *out* of the street!'

The tea has been sugared and milked. The teapot placed on its stand. Granny points to the biscuit tins.

'No, thanks.'

'It seems ages since yon day. I don't think Ah've seen ye, or heard ye, for a month or more.'

'You haven't, Bella. Would you believe, it's nearer to eight weeks. After you drummed some sense into me and I phoned Fred to say I'd marry him, well, we went out to dinner that night. And at the end of it, I went back to Langside with him. Been there ever since. He wouldn't even let me come back to pick up a change of underwear or clothes. "Just buy what you need. Charge it!" It's been wonderful. Hasn't taken me long to get back into that lifestyle, again.'

'So you've managed tae get away today, huv ye?'

'Fred's off on business for a couple of days. So while he's away, I said I'd drive over and pick up some personal stuff.'

'And Ah hope you've definitely put aw' that nonsense oot o' yer heid. Aboot whether ye should marry him or no'?'

'Oh! I am so glad I came in to see you that day. My head was just buzzing, full of a lot of nonsense. When I look back now, it's all so obvious. I love Fred. And I know you've only got my word for it, Bella, but I assure you I'm not being big-headed. He really adores me. It will break his heart if I don't marry him. I'm so glad you made me see sense.' She stops, as she finds she's becoming emotional.

'Aye. It's funny how ye sometimes cannae see the obvious. Anywye, enough o' that. Whit are ye gonny dae aboot the hoose upstairs?'

'We've got the decorators in at Fred's bungalow at the moment. You can imagine what it was like. A man living on his own!' She looks heavenwards. 'Hasn't been done for years. I've got two or three wee things upstairs that are quality, and will fit in at Langside. I've just been keeping the single-end on to use it for storage. Fred's place will be finished in a few days, then we'll get my bits and pieces brought over. I would think, by the second week in September we'll have removed the items I want to keep. The rest can be junked. Fred says he'll get somebody to clear it.'

'That's grand, Ruby. Ah do hope ye realise whit a lucky lassie ye are? You've no' only got a second chance, but it sounds like you've found a guid man.' She leans forward, lays a hand on top of Ruby's for a moment. 'Though mind, *if* ye make a mess o' it again, you'll get nae sympathy fae me. Or anybody else. Take heed!' She sits back.

Ruby pauses. Thinks. 'Bella, even if I didn't love Fred, I wouldn't be stupid enough to bugger up my life again.' Granny watches her eyes grow moist. 'But I love him. And the more I see of him, get to know him, well, he's a smashing guy. I couldn't hurt him. This is the first time in my life I've been in love. I've always put myself first. I didn't love Bernard Baxter. He knew it. Yet, if I hadn't cheated on him we would still be together. That's not how it is now. It's all about Fred. *He* comes first.' She stops, looks at this old woman whom she once thought of as her enemy. She starts to speak. Manages to say, 'You really don't know how much I owe you, Granny.'

Isabella Thomson gives a strange smile. 'Oh, but Ah do.'

It's just after midday. Granny comes trauchling along Dalbeattie Street. She has just been to the shops for the rations. As she nears the close, she hears someone walking fast behind her. Knows who it is. The voice confirms it. 'Oh, Granny, I do not seem to have seen you for ages.'

She stops, turns. Tries to hide a smile. 'Well, Irma Armstrong. You've *twice* promised tae come up for a drink o' tay, so as ye can tell me whit happened when you and Bert went tae Newcastle.' She gives a magisterial sniff. 'Ah'm still waiting, thank ye very much!'

'Oh, jings! I know. But now I have my little job at Campbell-Duff's ironmongers, I do not have the one minute to spare, Granny. When I come home I have to cook and iron and wash—'

The old woman interrupts. 'You're no' at work at the minute.'

Irma looks at her watch. 'I have to be back for half-one. Right! You go and make the tea while I go to the shop of the Scotia Bakery for a bridie and a wee snaster. See you in two minutes.' She dashes across the street and into the baker's shop.

Granny hears her run into the close. She begins pouring the tea, looks up when the inner door is opened and Irma's perspiring face is revealed. She comes in, pulls out a kitchen chair, flops down onto it. 'Help ma Boab! Granny, I am fair worn oot!'

The matriarch smiles. Like everybody up the close, she continues to be captivated by Irma's vocabulary of 'auld Scots' – culled from the adventures of The Broons and Oor Wullie in the *Sunday Post*. As Ella once put it, 'Irma thinks she speaks Scots like a native. She diz. Of Brigadoon!'

Irma places two paper bags on the table, tears them open. 'Right, a bridie and a custard cake for me. And for you, two pineapple cakes, Granny.'

'Oh, that's nice, hen. Wait a minute till Ah get twa plates for us. Then we can kid oorselves oan it's high tea we're huving.' Irma waits as two plates are brought from the sideboard. 'Right.' The old woman sits opposite her visitor. 'Drena wiz saying things went well doon in Newcastle.'

Irma puts her cup down, beams. 'Oh, yah. I was so nervous

when we arrived. You know the reason we have to go is because the father of Bert – he is called Jack – he was going into hospital for a big operation on his heart. Bert has not seen his family since 1946, Granny. And I never have met them. Sixteen years! This is a long time . . .'

Granny comes in, 'Noo, tae save ye time, so as ye can get back tae work – in case ye get your jotters! – Ah know Bert's brother Arthur wiz killed during the war. Because Bert marries a German lassie his ma and da take the huff. Even though ye named Arthur after the lad who was killed, it made nae difference. But aw' these years later, because Bert's faither is going intae the hospital, he wants tae see the three of you – jist in case he snuffs it! Is that right?'

Irma tries not to giggle. 'Yah, Granny. So the father of Bert wants to see—'

Granny cuts her short again. 'Jeezus! We aw' know the reason fur the visit, okay? You're forgettin' Ah turn eighty-seven next month. If ye don't get oan wi' the story, it'll finish up that Ah'll snuff it before Bert's faither – *and* you'll get your books fae Campbell Duff fur being late! So will ye jist get oan wi'—' She is unable to finish this tirade before the two of them go helpless with laughter. Granny manages to say, 'Jist buggerin' tell me whit went oan at Newcastle will ye!'

'Michty me!' says Irma. She composes herself. 'Okay. We get to their house. Bert's brother and sister are so pleased to see us, especially to see Arthur, but they tell us the mother is still not happy about this visit. We are all standing in the lobby. His mother is waiting inside the room called the living room. Oh, I am so nervous to go through the door. The brother and sister go first, then us three. The mother stands at the fireplace.' Irma falters, tears brim in her eyes, she swallows hard. 'Then we are in front of her. She has not seen Bert for so long. And this is the first time to see her grandson who is named after the son killed in Normandy. He is now eleven years old . . .' Irma struggles to keep her voice steady. 'She looks at us, Granny, very much at Bert and Arthur, and she bursts into tears and cannot speak. She just opens her arms. And Bert also, he is crying.' Irma dabs her eyes. 'And me. It is so wonderful, Granny!'

'Buggerin' sounds like it!' Granny reaches for the tea towel, dabs her eyes.

'Oh, and Granny. For the rest of the day she is forever looking at Arthur, and always she says, "He is his Uncle Arthur's double when he was eleven." She is very happy about that.'

'Whit aboot Bert's dad?'

'Yah, he has his big op and touch wood, he is back home now. He seems to be better a lot.'

'And Ah take it everything is fine between you and her, noo?'

'All forgotten. She wants us to come down for Christmas.'

Granny puts the towel down. 'Mind, Ah alwiz thought when Arthur wiz born, she would huv wanted tae see the wean. But she did'nae.' She thinks for a moment. 'And whit good huz it done? Aw' them years wasted, Irma.'

'*Oh*! Michty me! Look at the time. Nearly twenty past one! I have to go. I hope a bus is coming, I have no time to walk.' She grabs her bag, makes for the door. 'Now you know why I have no time to see you, Granny. *Wiedersehen* . . . Eh, see you later.' She exits onto the landing.

The old woman listens to the staccato sound of Irma's leather soles as she races down the stairs and out of the close. The next dozen or so footsteps are heard coming up from the street, but they quickly fade with no close to echo them. Granny rises. 'Ach, she's a good wee lassie, Irma.' She looks towards her doors. Both lie open. 'It might be the last day of August, but there's a cauldness coming in.' She closes the inner door. Stands for a moment. Looks round her palace. The kettle sings away to itself. 'Right, stir up that fire a bit. Another wee drink o' tea, then catch the weemins' programme on the wireless.' She crosses over towards the range. Stops to plump up the cushions on her chair. Yawns. 'Humph! No' that Ah'll hear much o' it.'

CHAPTER THIRTY-SIX

Back in the Auld Routine

A Saturday evening. Archie Cameron looks in the mirror that hangs between the kitchen windows. 'Dae ye think Ah'll get away withoot a bunnet, Ella?'

'Och, aye. Your hair huz grown quite a bit. Ye cannae see the scar, noo.'

He bends his head forward then to the side. 'Well. Ah'm no sae sure. Ah think it can still be seen. Whit dae you think, Billy?'

Billy McClaren walks over to his pal, carries out a close inspection. 'You'll definitely get away withoot it. It's because you know where it is, your eyes home in oan it. Anywye, stick the bunnet in yer pocket. If ye feel ye need it, you've got it. But honestly, it looks okay. Your hair's grown ower it. Folk will jist think you've got a crew cut.'

Barely convinced, Archie makes a decision. 'Okay. Ah'll go withoot it.' As he puts his jacket on, Ella looks at him. 'Noo mind, Erchie Cameron. You still cannae take a drink. You've got roon' aboot ten days' tablets left. The consultant warned ye. Mix alcohol wi' them tablets and you'll be in trouble. Content yersel'.'

'Don't worry. Ah'm no' gonny spoil things for the sake of a moothfy o' pale ale.'

'Well, make sure ye don't.'

As the two friends exit their close, Billy looks at Archie. 'Where dae ye want tae go?'

'Ach, we'll jist go roon' the corner tae the Thistle. If it happens tae rain, we have'nae got far tae walk hame.'

Ten minutes later finds them standing at one end of the long bar. The Thistle has all the essential ingredients of a Glasgow pub: strong smell of ale, stronger smell of tobacco – and even stronger language. Conversations are carried on at a volume that wouldn't be allowed at a Hard of Hearing Convention. A recent fall of sawdust covers the floor.

Billy leans forward until his head almost touches Archie's. He pitches his voice to just below shouting level. 'Ah'm awfy glad them two huv made it up.'

'Eh?'

Billy moves even nearer, repeats himself with an increase in volume.

'Aye, definitely. Though mind, it's a pity Ah huv tae get ma heid split open tae bring them back thegither.'

His mate laughs, nods in agreement. 'It wiz a bit much.'

'Ah must say, Billy, when Ah heard aboot Drena flying doon tae the Royal tae be wi' Ella . . . That wiz a nice gesture. Ah mean, they hud'nae spoke for months,' he shakes his head, 'yet it was aw' forgotten the minute she found oot her pal needed her.'

Billy takes a mouthful of pale ale. 'Well, ye know the auld saying – A friend in need—'

Archie interrupts. '. . . is a pain in the arse!' He lifts his glass of Vimto, looks at it, takes a sip, places it back on the bar. 'Ah'll tell ye whit, mind. If them Russians keep shipping aw' that stuff ower tae Cuba, there might be a lot mair folk finish up wi' a bandage oan their heid!'

'You are *dead* right, Archie. Them commie bastards put that wall up in Berlin last year. Now they're putting loads o' military gear intae Cuba. Jist getting at it, so they are! The Russkies are trying tae see how far they can go. If they get away wi' it in Cuba, next thing they'll be trying it oan wi' us. You wait and see. Britain will be next. Probably attempt tae ship rockets ower tae, ohhh, Ailsa Craig or somewhere like that.'

Unfortunately, Archie has just taken a large mouthful of Vimto. This leads to a choking fit. He recovers. 'The Russians are'ny gonny put stuff ontae Ailsa buggering Craig,' he splutters.

'How no'? It's an island jist aff oor coast, in't it? Jist like Cuba is tae America. If they can try it oan wi' the Yanks, they'll no' think twice of trying it oan wi' us.'

'It's far too wee fur fuck sake. It's jist toaty, Billy. Huv ye ever seen Ailsa Craig?'

'Ah huv. The school took us oan a trip tae Girvan efter we sat the Qualie. Ah seen it oot the bus windae. Seemed pretty big tae me. Sort of, a bit like the Isle o' Man . . .' his voice fades as Archie continues to look at him, shaking his head all the while.

They fall silent for a spell after their in-depth discussion on the Cuban Missile Crisis. Archie points at his friend's pint,

'Ah'm no' half looking forward tae coming aff these tablets. Choking for a proper drink so Ah am. Spitting feathers. It's taking aw' ma willpower tae resist lifting your pint and downing it in a wanner.'

'Ah'll bet ye it is.' Just then, Archie happens to look away. Billy slides his pint out of harm's way. They lean on the bar in companionable silence, Archie occasionally glancing at Billy's pint.

Half a mile away from where their fathers are enjoying a wee refreshment in the Thistle Bar, Billy McClaren junior (PC 330) and Archie Cameron junior (Criminal Record Office No. 371524) are about to meet in the less than salubrious, dimly lit premises known as the Garscube Vaults. The occasion could not be considered as social.

The Black Maria pulls up a few yards from the pub. Sergeant Garland and a PC Robinson step onto the pavement. Garland walks to the back of the vehicle, opens one of the doors and Billy McClaren junior emerges. 'Soon as we go intae the pub, if he's there, jist point him oot. We'll have him straight oot, intae the van and offski. Don't engage him in conversation or listen tae any shite aboot "It wiz'nae me, Sarge." Okay?' He looks at Billy. 'He lives up the same close as you, dizn't he?'

'Aye. We grew up thegither.'

PC Robinson turns towards Billy. 'Will ye no' get any hassle fae his family?'

'Naw. Oor mothers and faithers are the best o' pals.'

'Fuck me! Life's funny sometimes, in't it?'

As they head for the premises, Garland speaks to their driver. 'Jist keep the engine running.'

* * *

The trio of policemen open both swing doors, stride into the bar, then halt. Look slowly around. The few patrons present, as one, suddenly seem to take a keen interest in their pints, the grain of the wooden tables, even the ashtrays. Garland looks at Billy junior. 'Is he in?'

'The guy wi' the blue jacket, standing at the bar talking tae the fella wi' the gaberdine mac.'

They walk over, halt close by the designated suspect. 'You Archie Cameron?'

'Aye.' As he turns to face the sergeant he gives his childhood pal a sour glance.

'Like ye tae come up the road tae Maryhill Polis Station wi' us. Want tae ask ye a few questions, Archie.'

'Can Ah ask whit it's aboot?'

'Ah'll tell ye when we get there. So are ye coming voluntarily, son? Or dae Ah huv tae arrest ye?' Garland smiles. 'Either wye you're still coming.'

A handcuffed Archie Cameron sits in the back of the Black Maria with Billy McClaren. As the van pulls away he looks at him. 'Ah did'nae think you wid huv identified me!'

'Why would Ah no' I.D. ye?'

'Well, ye know. You and me go back Ah long wye, Billy.'

PC McClaren leans forward. Shakes his head. 'Archie! Don't waste ma fuckin' time wi' aw' this shite. We certainly dae go back a long wye. Great pals when we were boys. But nooadays Ah'm a full-time polis – and you're a full-time thief, so . . .' He spreads his hands wide.

'Aw' Billy, that's a bit strong.'

'Quit it, Archie! Ah told ye when Ah caught ye in the back

of yon midden, *and* let ye off the hook, that wiz the first –
and last – break you'd ever get fae me.'

Archie Cameron looks at his boyhood pal. Realises he's
wasting his time. In spite of the cuffs he manages to get a
cigarette from his pocket. 'Can ye gies a light, Billy?'

PC McClaren leans forward, supplies a light. They both
sit back. Archie draws on his cigarette, stares up at the roof
of the van. Billy McClaren stretches his legs out, looks without
seeing at his toecaps. At just this moment the Black Maria is
passing the Thistle Bar. Inside this popular pub their fathers,
completely unaware, are enjoying their Saturday night . . .

'Ah take it ye know the Last Tram thingummy is being held
this coming Tuesday, Erchie?'

'Oh, aye. So it is.' He pauses. 'Do you know what, when
they withdrew them from Maryhill last year. Well, for me *that*
wiz the end o' them. Since then, Ah've been going tae work
oan the bus. Ah've never clapped eyes on a tram since the
day Ah took ma last run up the Maryhill Road. Ah know
there's still one route left in the city somewhere, but as far
as Ah'm concerned, Billy, the caurs finished last year.' He
stares into space, lost in thought.

'Ah'm the same, Erchie. Ah had read in the paper it wiz
the number nine service that wiz still running. But that's miles
away. Oot by Dalmarnock, Ah think.' He takes a long draught
of pale ale. 'Like you, Ah had'nae seen a tram either since
the twenty-nine finished . . .' He looks at his pal. 'But wait
till ye hear this, Erchie. Happened aboot ten days ago.' He
reaches for his cigarettes, then suddenly points a warning
finger at his friend. 'Noo mind, nae laughing! Ah had been
subcontracting tae this company, that wiz decorating a school

ower on the sooth side. They picked me up in the van every morning, took me tae the job. Anywye. On the very first day, Ah'm sitting in their van. The driver and his pal are talkin' away tae wan another,' Billy draws on his cigarette, 'and Ah'm jist looking oot the windae tae pass the time. Trying tae figure oot where we are.' He looks at Archie. 'Just like you, Ah rarely venture oot o' ma ain bit. Ah know the city centre. But all the other districts?' He shakes his head. 'Hav'nae got a clue. Ninety-five per cent o' my decorating jobs are within a mile o' ma hoose. They huv tae be, as Ah don't drive. Ah jist use the handcart for moving ma gear.'

Archie interrupts. 'Ah'm exactly the same. Rarely huv any reason tae leave ma ain bit.'

Billy cuts back in, anxious to finish his story. 'But wait tae ye hear this, Erchie. The van stops at lights, at a crossroads. Ah'm half looking oot the windae, this main road. Suddenly, Ah realise it's still got cobbled setts and tramlines and over-head wires – and *trams* are running! They are aw' new caurs. Coronations. Aw' number nines. You've nae idea whit a shock it wiz. It's a year since they withdrew oor caurs, oor tramlines have gone, the Maryhill Road's covered in tarmac. Jist like you, as far as Ah'm concerned the trams are finished. Ah'm used tae it by noo. Then this van stops at a junction – and suddenly Ah'm back in *my* Glasgow. But it wiz even stranger than that, Erchie. The van wiz a diesel, a real noisy bugger. On top o' that, the two fellas in the cab are talking and laughing away tae wan another. So Ah'm sort of on ma own, isolated, looking oot the windae. Then Ah find Ah'm in amongst tramcars, *but*, because the van's noisy Ah cannae hear them. They're jist silently gliding by. Ah've been trans-ported back in time! The two guys in the van aren'y paying any attention tae them. It's as if Ah'm the only wan that can see them! No kidding, Erchie. The hair wiz standing on the back o' ma neck. Ah had it in my mind the caurs were all away. Then Ah find Ah've been taken tae this place where trams still run.' He shakes his head. 'The whole experience wiz really strange.' He lifts his glass from the bar, gives a deep sigh. 'Then the lights changed and we drove away.' He looks at his friend somewhat sheepishly.

Archie smiles. 'Well, aw' Ah can say is, lucky you! Ah wish that hud happened tae me. Did ye see them again?'

'Aye. The job lasted nearly a week, so Ah seen them twice a day. Ah really got tae look forward tae it. It wiz smashing tae see them. But no' as good as that first day, Erchie.'

There's the usual Saturday night queue, spilling out onto the pavement, at Pacitti's chip shop on the Maryhill Road. Archie and Billy are still a yard away from the shop door. 'Oh! Will ye jist smell them fish and chips, Billy. Don't half go roond yer heart, dain't they?'

'Pure torture. The smell o' fish and chips. Or bacon frying. Guaranteed tae put the auld saliva glands ontae full production.'

Ten minutes later their patience is rewarded; first in the queue. Tony Pacitti approaches.

'Archie, Billy, how are you thees even-ing?'

'Fine, Tony. How's the family?'

'A very good, thank you. What you like, boys?'

'Three fish suppers and a jar o' mixed pickles, please.'

'Two fish suppers and a bag o' chips, Tony.'

'Okaaay!'

He relays the order to his mother in Italian as he walks

past the fryer, makes his way to the shelf at the back of the shop for the pickles. The two friends lean their elbows on the marble-topped counter. 'Is there jist you, Drena and wee Charles the night, Billy?'

'Aye, William junior's oan back-shift. No' be in till midnight. He always goes for a pint at the polis club afore he comes hame.'

'Mmm. Oor Archie's at the dancing as far as Ah know.'

'Is that you getting Katherine a fish supper tae herself?'

'Oh, God aye. She sixteen noo. Huh! Can wolf doon a fish supper nae bother. It's like feeding Zube-Zubes tae an elephant! Ye wid'nae think it tae look at her – she's wan o' Pharaoh's lean cattle yon yin, but she can tuck the grub away . . . Ah! Here's the man o' the moment coming.'

'Extra paper round them, boys?'

'Yes please, Tony. Keep them nice and warm till we get hame.'

They turn the corner into Dalbeattie Street, fish suppers tucked under their jackets. Billy speaks. 'Do ye fancy going wi' the wives and the younger kids tae see that Last Tram thingmy on Tuesday?'

'Noo that might be a good idea, Billy. It'll be wan o' them things. If we *don't* go, in a year or two we'll probably wish we hud. Yeah, Ah'm game.'

'Right, we'll ask them the night. And if they don't want tae, will we jist go oorselves?'

'We will. But Ah would think they'll probably want tae go. Jeez! Ah mean, we've never known Glesga withoot caurs, huv we?'

'Oh, and Ah meant tae tell ye. Did ye know that big Frank

Galloway has got Granny a ticket for Tuesday night? She's got a seat *upstairs* on the open-top bit of wan o' them caurs that were jist partially covered-in. The front and back ends were open if ye remember?'

'Ah! So auld Bella's gonny see them oot in style, is she.' They stop in the close, outside Billy's door. 'Right, *gute nacht mein alte kamerad.*'

'*Ja, Wilhelm. Schlaft Du Gute.* Ah'll gie ye a knock in the morning, let ye know if Ella and Katherine are going oan Tuesday.'

'*Ja, klopfen mein tur. Aber*, don't *klopfen* too bloody early if ye don't mind. Ah fancy a long-lie.' He pauses for a moment, then, 'Here, Erchie. Whit's German for a long-lie?'

His friend blows his cheeks out. 'Fucked if Ah know!'

Just then the McClaren front door is thrown open. Billy pretends to take fright. '*Huh! Mein Gott! Es ist meine Liebchen*, Frau Drena . . .'

'Naw it's no', it's Frau von Starvin'! Any chance o' ye bringing them fish suppers intae the hoose while there's some heat left in them? Every time youse two go oot thegither, me and the wean finish up eating cauld fish and chips.' She gives the two of them withering looks. 'The perr of ye alwiz start wi' yer buggering German.' She turns to Archie, 'And you'd better get up them stairs wi' yours, or you'll get your heid in your hands tae play wi', Archie Cameron.' She points to the stairs. '*SCHNELL MACHEN!*'

Archie bends forward, reaches up to his forehead to tug an imaginary forelock. '*Du hat recht*, Frau McClaren. *Gute nacht!*'

Drena looks at his head. 'Jeez! That's no' half left ye wi' some scar, huzn't it!'

Archie looks at Billy. 'You and Ella telt me ye could'nae see it! Lying buggers!'

'Could'nae see it?' says Drena. 'Ye cannae miss it! It's like a map o' the Forth and Clyde canal.' She struggles to keep her face straight.

'Awwww, man! Ah *knew* people wid be able tae see it.' He starts up the stairs. 'Ah'll talk tae ye the morra, Billy.' He stops on the half-landing. 'And Ah'll be wearing ma bunnet on Tuesday.'

CHAPTER THIRTY-SEVEN

The Newcomers

---

*H*ousewives' Choice is just about finished. Granny Thomson sits at her kitchen table, lips moving as she reads a clue in yesterday's *Sunday Express* crossword. Her concentration is broken as the last record of the morning intrudes. She sits back on her chair. 'Whae the buggerin' hell is that singing? Ah've heard better roon' the back courts!' She reaches out to turn the radio off, then, 'Naw, Ah've got tae find oot who this is. This has got tae be the worst singer in the world. Bar none!' She folds her arms, leans on the cherille-covered table.

At last the record spins to a close, the presenter comes in. 'And that was Bob Dylan with "Blowing In The Wind".'

The old woman turns to face the radio. 'Blowin' oot his arse mair like! He's jist been putting that voice on. It's got tae be a joke, surely.' She shakes her head. 'Don't know whit the world's coming tae.' The signature tune comes on, playing out the programme. The matriarch joins in. 'Dahdee dah dah dahdee dah dah dahdee . . .' Rising from the table, she leaves the paper lying open. Ah'll huv another go at that later. She puts her dishes and cutlery into the sink, 'dahdee dahing' all the while. 'Noo that's *TEN* times better than Blowing Doon the Lavvy Pan. Could'nae sing fur toffee. Ah've hud mair enjoyment oot o' the toothache!'

As she clicks the music off, she can hear the engine of a large vehicle. She walks towards her windows. Through the net curtains the top of a large van can be seen rolling to a stop. 'Oh-hoh! Could it be?' She takes up post, leaning on the scrubbed-white draining board, looks down into the street. Ah wonder how many times Ah've done this ower the years? The removal men have already exited the cab and are opening the large, rear doors. An old Ford Prefect has parked a few yards behind the pantechnicon. She watches its doors open, a couple get out. Eeeh, yah boys! They're whit-ye-ma-call-them? Indian? Asian? Fancy that! She reads the side of the van. Central Removals, Smethwick, Birmingham. 'My! That's a long wye tae come.' She has a good look. They're jist young so they are. The man talks to one of the removal men, then produces a key. The couple head for the close, the workmen for the rear of the van.

'Right!' Granny pushes herself up from the draining board, hirples across the room towards her doors. As she opens the outer one, the smell of boiled cabbage fills her nostrils. Jeez! Ah wonder why cabbage diz that? Alwiz fills the close from top tae bottom. That's a grand welcome for them. She can hear the couple talking as they climb the stairs. Speaking in their own language. When they approach the first storey, the old woman steps onto the landing.

'Hello! Are the two of you moving intae the empty flat on the landing above?' Granny has the sense to point with her finger, in case the couple, coming from foreign parts, might conceivably have trouble with the Queen's English as spoken in Glasgow. She has taken them by surprise. They stop in front of her, smile.

'Eee! Whit bonny smiles,' she says. 'And the pair o' ye have the most beautiful teeth Ah've ever seen in ma life!' She sniffs. 'Maist folk roond here, huv teeth like a set o' burglar's tools!' This is greeted with further smiles. Granny suspects that perhaps they didn't quite get that – otherwise they'd be lying on the stairhead slapping their thighs. The young man speaks.

'Yes, we are moving into the empty flat on the next floor up above.'

The matriarch takes another step forward. 'For the last,' she pauses, 'God knows how long, every time somebody new moves intae the close Ah alwiz—' She breaks off, looks from one to the other. 'Can the two of ye understand whit Ah'm saying?'

The young man presses both hands together in front of him. As if about to pray. 'Oh, please, if you are speaking perhaps a little slower. Then I can understand everything you say. Maybe.'

She reaches out, rests a hand on each of their forearms. In a mixture of 'pan loaf' and broken English, she intones, 'As soon as the men have moved your furniture intae – *into* the flat. Jist – *just* lock the door and come down here and Ah'll make ye a dish, eh, I'll make a *pot* of tea and we can have a wee blether – *talk*, and get tae know yin, eh, *one* another. Can you under—'

The young woman speaks. 'That is very nice of you. We will be very pleased to have a cup of tea with you.'

'Good.' Granny looks from one to the other. 'Ye have a lovely, lilting way of speaking. Ah did'nae know English could sound sae good!' The three of them laugh. Suddenly they hear voices and bustling footsteps from the close.

'Oh, my goodness me,' the young man looks through the bannister rails, 'the men are coming with our belongings.'

'Aye, you'd better get up there wi' the key. Oh, and tell the men tae come in for a cuppa as well. It's long wye back tae Birmingham withoot a drink o' tea.'

The newcomer has got the gist of that. 'Yes, my wife and I will tell them. And we will see you very, very soon.' They set off up the stairs.

Granny walks back into her room. Imagine that. That'll be fun, having two *real* foreigners biding up the close. She has left both doors ajar, so as to listen once more to the sounds of removal men coming in and out 18 Dalbeattie Street. She shakes her head. Ah remember when folk used horses and cairts tae do their flittings. And no' sae long ago either. Noo when wiz the first time that somebody arrived in a motor? Probably early thirties. Aye. And there's been many a yin, right on intae the fifties, who if they were jist moving fae a couple o' streets away, they saved themselves money by jist using a handcart. Huh! Youngsters nooadays. Don't know whit hard times means! She fills the kettle from the brass tap. 'Mmm, Ah'd better put it oan the gas. It will'nae have time tae bile on the fire.'

As cups, saucers and plates are removed from the sideboard, her thoughts run on. Now, that's Marjorie and Jack's hoose let. Ruby Baxter says she should be giving up her single-end in a week or two. She gives a heavy sigh. Nothing stays the same. Sometimes there's been long periods, years, when naebody's moved. And naebody's died. She stops laying the table. Stands still, begins to stare. Her eyes go out of focus.

Her 'turn' lasts for less than a minute. If Teresa O'Malley was in, she'd be asking me, 'What did ye just see, Bella?' The matriarch speaks softly to herself. 'Ah know whit Ah've seen. And Ah dinnae think it's far removed.' She resumes setting the table, then pauses again. Stands upright for a moment. Holds her chin up. 'And Ah'm not in the least worried. No. Nor frichted, either!'

'Come in, come in!' Like most of the newcomers over the years, especially young ones, the couple are shy as they come through her door. 'Sit yerselves at the table. Dinnae . . . don't be shy. And mind and tell me if Ah speak too fast for ye. Would you baith . . . both, like tea?'

'Thank you very much. You are so kind.'

'Och, stop your havering. Ah'm no' kind at all. Ah'm just a nosey auld woman who wants tae find oot, eh, find out, all about you!' Slow Bella, slow. 'Are the removal men coming?'

The girl laughs. 'Oh, goodness, no. They are very anxious to get to the nearest pub. They have gone.'

'That's what usually happens. Och, well. That'll be nice, just the three of us.' She begins to pour the freshly brewed tea. Remembers to speak slowly. 'So where are youse from originally? Ah don't mean Birmingham. And even more important, what's your names?'

'I am Mohammed Khan and my wife is Ayesha. We are from Pakistan.'

'Ah'm Isabella Thomson,' she waves a finger, 'but Ah want you tae get intae the habit, right from this moment, of calling me Granny. Everybody calls me Granny. So don't forget.' She proffers her usual selection of biscuits. 'What's made ye leave Birmingham and come tae Glasgow?'

'There are many reasons. The most important one is because I have secured a place at Glasgow University to study engineering.'

'Have you had tae come aw' the way tae Glasgow, son? Was there no room at Birmingham?'

Mohammed smiles. 'Well, I tell people I cannot get a vacancy in Birmingham.' He looks at Ayesha. 'We are not a long time married. We want very much to be away from our parents for a while.' He holds up his hands, palms spread. 'Oh, we love our families. But everyone expects us to live with them. All in one house. We want to be together on our own, so . . .' He shrugs his shoulders.

'Ahhh! So you told a little white lie did ye?'

They both laugh. 'This is so,' says Mohammed.

'We are not one hundred per cent away from family,' says Ayesha. 'I have an uncle who has a big grocer store in Dennistoun. But this is good. He is giving me a job. So I will earn money—'

Mohammed interrupts. 'And on the days I am not at university, I will also work in the shop of Ayesha's uncle. We think this should be very good arrangement.'

Granny looks at their two eager faces. 'Well, here's hoping it goes tae plan. The main thing is, the two of you will have your own place. And if you make enough money tae pay aw' your bills that will—' She stops as she hears footsteps.

'It's just me, Bella!' The inner door is pushed open.

The old woman turns to her visitors. 'Here's trouble!'

Teresa O'Malley walks in, shopping bag in hand. 'Ah, Jayz! Now this has got t' be the new folk, I'm t'inking.'

'Ten oot o' ten. This is my long-time neighbour, Teresa O'Malley. Lives on this landing here.'

Mohammed introduces himself and Ayesha.

'She was an immigrant just like yourselves, ye know.' Granny nods towards Teresa. 'Irish. Arrived in Glasgow afore the war. First thing we had tae do was catch her and make her wear shoes!' The newcomers look at the two older women, unsure whether or not to laugh.

'Have ye ever heard such a foul slur in yer lives?' Teresa brings a cup and saucer from the sideboard. Pours herself some tea. Points a finger. 'That will give yer an idea what I've had t' put up wit', from the day I moved inter this close. And that's over t'irty years ago.' She sits down with a sigh, turns to Granny. 'Would there be an auld biscuit going spare?'

Some ten minutes later the couple, reluctantly, decide they really should go upstairs and continue with their moving-in. Mohammed turns just before they exit. 'It has been very nice to meet you, ladies. You have made us feel very welcome.'

Teresa looks at her old friend, then the new tenants. 'Granny has been making folk feel welcome at eighteen Dalbeattie Street – you'll not believe me – since *before* the First World War. She's lived up this close since 1910. Now isn't that sumt'ing?'

'Goodness me! Over fifty years!' says Ayesha.

'Are you trying tae make me seem auld, Teresa O'Malley?'

'Jayz! Ye *are* buggering old!'

The room seems quiet, dull even, after the couple have gone. The two friends sit in silence, busy with their thoughts. Teresa sips her tea, the cup seems to chink loudly when placed back in its saucer.

'Sure, an' they seem a nice young couple.'

'They do indeed. They've got things aw' planned. Ah jist hope it works oot for them. Ye sometimes read in the paper aboot bloody toerags causing them trouble, jist because they're no' white.'

'Ye do. That's just what I was t'inking, Bella. Mind you. T'was the same before the war. Even earlier. When the Irish came over lookin' for jobs,' she sighs, 'soon as people heard the accent, the faces would be twisted. 'Tis the way of the world so 'tis.'

'Yer right, Teresa. And there's Irish still coming ower tae this day. And noo we've got the Asian folk as well.' She shakes her head. 'Ah'll tell ye what. There are days when Ah'm roon' that Maryhill Road for the rations, and Ah'm no' sure whether Ah'm in Donegal, or Bengal!'

CHAPTER THIRTY-EIGHT

The Best o' Freens Must Pairt

It's not yet half-past seven as Isabella Thomson sits on a low stool clearing out the ashes from under the range. Her days of kneeling are long gone. As usual her two doors are ajar. She loves listening to the morning noises as the close comes awake around her. It's a Tuesday, so it's weekday noises. One of the other two doors on her landing opens. The voices of Robert and Rhea Stewart, with Sammy and Louise in tow, are heard as they leave their house. Rhea's high heels skitter across the stone slabs, then change key as they step onto the linoleum in Granny's lobby.

'It's jist me.' Rhea's face appears round the kitchen door. 'Eeeeh! This is yer big day the day, Granny. Are ye aw' excited?'

'Dae ye know whit? Ah think Ah am.' She gingerly sits the full ashbox down on the enamelled hearth plate.

Robert looks over his wife's shoulder. 'Can ye be ready for five o'clock, Granny?'

'Any time ye like, son. Are ye thinking we should get there early?'

'Ah am. Ah've a feeling this is gonny be the biggest night in the city since VE Day!'

Rhea turns her head. 'Dae ye think sae, Robert?'

'Ah definitely do.' He looks again at his elderly neighbour. 'Ah think we'll be well advised tae be early, Granny. The parade starts at half-six. Ah'd hate tae struggle through traffic, get there late and find the depot empty. It would be terrible if ye missed your last hurl on a tram.'

'Oh, dis'nae bear thinking aboot. Right, Ah'll be ready and champing at the bit for five on the dot.' Sammy finds a gap between his parents.

'You're lucky, Granny. It'll be great tae be able to say ye took part in the last tram celebrations.'

Louise also pushes through. 'Mibbe you'll get your photie in the paper, Granny. Or, you could even be on the Glesga news on the telly the night, dae ye think?'

Rhea gives her daughter a gentle cuff. 'It's no' Glesga, madam. It's Glasgow if ye don't mind.' Her son and daughter look at one another. '*Eeeeh!* Get her! You say Glesga aw' the time.'

They each receive a featherweight clout. She spots Robert laughing. He is also issued with one. 'See whit Ah've got tae put up wi', Granny?'

The old woman smiles at this family scenario. 'Aye, you've got a hard life, Rhea. So ye have.'

As she listens to the Stewarts going down the stairs, Granny stands up. She looks again at the pink ticket leaning against a wally dug on the mantelpiece. Her eyes home in on the date – Tuesday 4 September, 1962. That's the day. The excitement rises in her once more. Jeez! For the life of me, Ah cannae remember the last time Ah felt like this. She hears a door bang up above. Seconds later there come the familiar footsteps of Agnes Dalrymple. They increase in volume as they step onto the landing, then into her lobby.

'Are ye all set for yer big night, hen?'

'Aye, no' half, Agnes. Fair lookin' forward tae it.'

'Ah'll tell ye, some folk huv aw' the luck. You'll be consorting wi' former Lord Provosts, MPs and other worthies the night, Bella. Ah hope you're putting oan clean underwear!'

'Whit a cheeky bizzum you are, Agnes Dalrymple!'

'Simply in case ye get involved in an accident . . .' she pauses. 'Jist imagine it, Bella. What if you were tae be the last person tae be ran ower by a tram in Glesga! Your name wid live forever.'

'Aye. But *Ah* bloody well wid'nae.'

'Oh! Ah never thought o' that.' The pair, as they often do, dissolve into a fit of laughter. Agnes recovers first. 'You'd be lying therr, swatched in bandages – like yon mummy that used tae be in the pictures. Remember? Lon Chaney junior. Eee! Ah'll tell ye, them fillums used tae frighten the wits oot o' me. Ah'd go and see wan. Then jist efter eleven o' clock oan a winter's night Ah'd huv tae come hame fae the Roxy on ma own.' She looks at Granny. 'Ah'd walk intae the close – they were still gas lit then – and the flame wid be guttering. Remember when they used tae dae that? And the shadows wid be moving . . .'

The matriarch interrupts. 'Dae Ah remember? Mibbe you've no' noticed – Ah've still *got* the buggerin' gas!'

'Oh, aye. So ye huv. Anywye, Ah'm no' kidding, Bella. Ah'd get halfway alang the close, jist approaching the stairs, and Ah'd be looking towards the blackness oot in the back court,' Agnes leans forward, 'because Ah knew fur *certain* the mummy wiz lurking therr. He'd somehow managed tae get oot the Roxy and doon the Maryhill Road in front o' me. Eeeh, Granny. Ah remember wan night, Ah wiz halfway along the close, almost at the stairs, when Ah suddenly heard movement – and the doonstairs lavvy door flew open! Ah nearly drapped oan the spot! Ah thought my end had come, the mummy's got me! So Ah let oot sich a scream – and so did the mummy! It wiz jist Mary Stewart coming oot the lavvy. Anywye. Ah'd normally get aw' the wye up tae the top storey and intae the hoose. Great! That's me safe. Then Ah'd remember. Ye huv'nae been tae the lavvy yet, Agnes. So Ah'd tiptoe doon tae the half-landing and stand ootside the door wi' the key in ma hand . . .' the two of them start laughing in anticipation '. . . listening fur the least wee movement.' She looks at Granny. 'Ah wiz always awfy nervous efter that Mary Stewart incident. But anywye, Ah'd stand facing the door and Ah wid know fur *definite*, Lon is jist behind that lavvy door waiting tae drag me in . . .' Agnes has to break off as she becomes helpless.

Granny eventually manages to say, 'Will ye get oan wi' it.'

'Well. At the finish up, Ah'd huv maself in such a state – Ah used tae jist come back up tae the hoose and huv a pee in the sink!'

'Ye did'nae!'

'Ah did!' It comes out as a squeak.

'If they frichted ye as much as that, why did ye no' stop going tae see them?'

'Whit fur? Ah loved them!'

*　　*　　*

Frank Galloway is already in Granny's flat when Robert and Rhea take the few steps across the landing and join them.

Rhea looks at the uniformed Frank. 'Are you on duty the night?'

He finishes taking a draw on a Senior Service, shakes his head as he exhales. 'No. But Ah thought Ah might be able tae get in and oot places better, if Ah'm in uniform.'

Robert nods. 'Probably a good idea.'

'Ah used tae be at Dalmarnock, before Ah transferred tae Maryhill. So they all know me.'

'Ah!' says Rhea. 'That's how Granny finished up wi' a reserved seat. An inside job, eh?'

Granny sniffs. 'Aye, but dinnae forget the terrible power that Ah have ower men!'

'Are you coming with us, Rhea?' Frank throws the last of the cigarette onto the fire.

'Of course Ah am. There's nae show withoot Punch.'

Robert looks at his watch. 'It's just gone five, folks. Ah would think the earlier we get ower tae Dalmarnock, the better.'

Frank rises. 'Aye, both *The Evening Times* and the *Citizen* are forecasting that the route of the procession will be absolutely chock-a-block the night. What way are ye thinking of going tae get ower tae Dalmarnock, Robert?'

'Through the city centre is definitely oot. Ah think oor best bet is tae take a roundabout way for a shortcut. Oot Parliamentary Road, through Dennistoun on Alexandra Parade and fiddle oor way round the far end of Bridgeton till we get tae Springfield Road. Then up tae Ruby Street and the depot. Whit dae ye think?'

'Sounds good. Should keep us well clear of the route. So

we should miss the crowds lining it – and the diversions the polis will have set up.'

Robert turns to Granny. 'All set, Bella?'

'Aye! Raring tae go.'

Granny Thomson, as befits her status, is to travel in the front passenger seat of the Riley. Rhea and Frank in the back. As Frank opens the rear door, the smell of the leather uphol-stery greets him. 'Oh, my God! Now this is a *proper* motor car. An automobile. Can Ah mibbe borrow the keys from you now and again, Robert? Ah *don't* want tae drive it. Ah just want tae sit in it and read the Sunday papers, while breathing in this gorgeous smell.'

Rhea laughs. 'Ah remember the day we got it, Frank. That was the first thing Ah loved aboot it. The smell o' the leather. And Ah still love it.'

Granny half-turns her head. 'What's Wilma daeing, Frank. Is she bothered aboot the parade?'

'Oh, aye. Not half. She's making her way doon the toon under her ain steam tae watch them. She's wearing her uniform as well. The two of us still have our Corporation Tramways' cap badges. Tonight is the last time we can wear them. From now on all the staff, and any new recruits, just get issued with a badge that says Corporation Transport Department.' He reaches for his cigarettes. 'Not quite the same, is it?'

The matriarch turns her head. 'Youse mark ma words. The day will come when they'll be sorry they done away wi' the trams. Ah was reading an article a couple o' weeks ago. And this fella was saying, aw' they needed tae do wiz build some new caurs. The whole system is still in place. Rails, wires, depots. It jist needed some new vehicles. Stupid idea tae scrap it!'

Frank agrees. 'Most of the auld trams in the city were fifty tae sixty years old, you know. Can you imagine a bus lasting even *half* that time?'

Robert joins in. 'Look at all the cities on the continent that still run tram systems – and no intention of daeing away wi' them. All Glasgow needed was new rolling-stock.'

It's around twenty to six when Frank Galloway, Granny on his arm, saunters into Dalmarnock Depot. His first ten minutes are spent being greeted by former workmates. Eventually they get a chance to look around them. 'My God! It's a hive of activity, Bella.' They are looking over a sea of heads, uniformed staff and civilians. Many of the latter are tonight's passengers. Camera flashbulbs are continually going off. Rising above this milling crowd and the beehive-like hum of conversations, are a line of beautifully restored trams. Paintwork gleaming, they somehow seem aloof, as though aware they are tonight's stars. They range from a horse-drawn, open-top tram of the 1890s, through various models, liveries and styles until they reach the ultimate in tram-car design – the sleek Art Deco Coronations of the 1930s.

To an observant eye, this crowd can easily be divided into three distinct groups. First, or perhaps that should be last, are those attending tonight's ceremony simply to socialise. To 'see and be seen'. The second and third groups can, and should, be taken as one. They consist of folk who love their city's trams and are saddened at their going. The difference between these two groups is slight. Minimal. There are those who have spent their working lives *with* the Tramways Department. The rest have spent their working lives travelling *on* the city's trams. The most amateur of detectives could easily identify these three bands. Those who are here to socialise – the first group – indulge in small talk and barely glance at the trams. The folk who make up the combined second and third bands are very easy to spot. They are all seizing, with both hands, this last chance to walk round, climb aboard, photograph – or simply touch – what has been a much-loved part of their lives for decades. These good citizens know that, after tonight, things will never be quite the same again in their city. Or their lives. Tomorrow they will feel bereft. Isabella Thomson and Frank Galloway are amongst their number.

Frank points. 'That's your one, Bella. The fourth from the front. Do ye remember them like that? With the top deck only partly covered, the vestibules at either end still open?'

'Ah do indeed, Frank. And Ah see it's a "red" tram. They did'nae have numbers back then, as ye know. Ye could tell where a caur was going jist by looking at the coloured band running roond, between the top and bottom decks.' She rubs her chin. 'If Ah mind right, the "red" caurs went tae Queens Park.'

Frank squeezes her arm. 'Spot on! There's nothing wrong wi' your memory, Bella.'

She looks pensive. 'Ah'd nearly forgotten aboot the colours, Frank. There wiz a time when it wiz an everyday thing. Somebody would ask ye, "How dae Ah get tae such-and-such a district?" And ye'd say. "Oh, ye want a white caur, or a blue caur."' She gives a heavy sigh. 'Aye, and after tonight, son, it'll aw' be gone.' She looks sad. 'The whole shebang!'

* * *

It's just after six-thirty when the horse-drawn tram leading the parade emerges from the depot. When the first cheers go up from those waiting, the two greys step higher than ever, as though in response. As the entire route is lined with spectators, six to ten deep on both sides of the road, this first hurrah from those outside Dalmarnock Depot becomes a never-ending cheer which will accompany the procession for its entire journey to Coplawhill Works, over three miles away. There, as the parade ends, those same cheers become a *last* hurrah! The crowd will later be estimated as in excess of a quarter of a million.

The matriarch's tram is fourth of the twenty taking part. She sits upstairs on the foremost seat of the small, open vestibule. Two other folk, a couple, share this area with her. The majority of the upstairs passengers sit in the covered-in section. Entry to this is gained via sliding doors at either end. The two trams in between Granny's vehicle and the leading, horse-drawn car, are both single-deckers. From her seat upstairs, at the front of the first double-decker, she has an unrestricted view of the streets. She is quite aware she has the best seat in the procession.

As each tram passes, spectators wave as well as cheer. Granny responds. She turns to her fellow passengers. 'Eeee! It's like being royalty, isn't it?'

While the column meanders by at walking pace, folk dart back and forth from the crowd to lay coins on the rails. Moments later, when their chosen tram has passed, they make a second dash to recover their 'do-it-yourself' souvenirs. Newly bent pennies.

Granny has an idea. She sits herself at the foremost edge of the open vestibule, looks straight ahead. That's better!

She cannot see the passengers in the covered-in section behind her, nor even her two neighbours. Next, she rests her folded arms on top of the metal panel which curves in front of her. She leans forward as far as she can, then holds her head up. No longer able to see the frontage of the tram underneath her, the old woman feels she's sitting on a balcony, fifteen feet above the city's streets, floating through the evening air. Folk cheer her as she drifts by. Magical! Even better than when Ah was a lassie and first came tae the city. Ma pals and me would go for a long hurl on the tram every Sunday. After nearly sixty years she can still see them; Annie Kenwright, May McKechnie and Jessie Orr. As long as Ah don't turn roon', Ah know they're sitting ahint me the nicht.

It had rained earlier in the day but now, to everyone's relief, it has cleared up and the streets are dry. Not that it will make much difference to the good burghers of Glasgow. Not tonight. They are here to say goodbye to their faithful servants.

The trams have passed Bridgeton Cross and are nearing the Barrowland when they come to a halt, barely half an hour into the journey. Somebody calls up to one of Granny's fellow passengers, that a 'people-catcher' – the wooden-framed safety device underneath all the city's trams – has come loose on one of the vehicles, and is rattling and banging along the cobbled setts. The parade has stopped while running repairs are done. The brightly lit trams quickly become marooned in a sea of spectators who have surged round them. They appear to be under siege. Run aground even. From her unique vantage point the old woman misses nothing, drinks it all in.

The press of the crowd, light streaming out of almost every flat in nearby tenements, residents placing cushions on window sills, so they can 'hing oot the windae' and enjoy the spectacle.

It is during this time that Granny feels, then sees, the first spots of rain falling onto her hands and the sleeves of her worn, bombazine coat. Och, jist a wee spit. Minutes later, she realises her forecast is just wishful thinking as it becomes heavier, steadier. No shower this. She looks up at the leaden sky, shakes her head, mutters, 'You're no' gonny spoil this are ye? Can ye no' leave folk in peace for five bloody minutes?' As though choreographed by Busby Berkeley, umbrellas seem to blossom in sequence amongst the crowd. There comes the sound of steelshod hooves sparking on granite setts, as the greys become impatient to be on their way. At last, after what seems longer than the actual twenty minutes, they get their wish. Amidst cheers, not quite so enthusiastic in the heavy rain, the great parade sets off again.

Granny feels a hand on her shoulder. It's one of her fellow-passengers. 'We're gonny squeeze into the covered-in bit, or go doonstairs tae the saloon. Are ye coming?'

She looks up at him. 'It would'nae be the same inside. The windaes are steamed up already. We'll no' see a thing from in there. Thanks aw' the same, but Ah think Ah'll jist stick it oot.'

'God! Are ye sure? It if carries on like this you'll no' half get wet.'

'Ach, Ah've never died a winter yet! Ah'm no' wanting tae give up this smashing view.'

He looks at her. 'Ah know whit ye mean.' He glances at

the sky. 'It's a shame, but it looks as if it's on for the night. We're gonny go inside. Cheerio.'

Alone. Isolated at the foremost point of a 'red' tram which will never again see Queens Park, Isabella Thomson is carried through the brightly lit streets in the driving rain. Arms folded, she bends forward to take what little shelter she can from the curved, metal panel in front of her. Her feet, legs and most of her front are somewhat protected, but as the car sways into the night, the rain pelts relentlessly down onto her head, back and shoulders. Three times she takes off the black cloche hat – bought so long ago for her husband's funeral – wrings it out, and, with increasingly cold fingers, pins it back on with three kirby grips. The procession makes its slow way along the Trongate into Argyll Street and past Glasgow Cross. Just before the Central Railway Bridge, the Heilanman's Umbrella, it turns left for Jamaica Bridge and onward to Eglinton Street. By now, Granny has long-since stopped looking around. There is no further pleasure to be had from the ride. It is now a battle between her and the elements – and whoever controls them. She will not give up her seat.

Robert and Rhea Stewart sit in the front of the Riley, Frank Galloway in the back. They are parked in Albert Drive, fifty yards from the large, open doors of Coplawhill Works. Frank has lowered a rear window a fraction to allow the smoke of his frequent cigarettes to escape. In the silence the rain drums relentlessly onto the roof of the car, streams down the windows in rivulets. Conversation has long-since become desultory. Robert flicks the wipers on and off now and again.

When he does, all three look through the momentarily clear windscreen until, seconds later, the rain reclaims it, turning it into a post-Impressionist work of art. Light spills out from the open doors of the tramway works onto the waiting crowd, huddling under their umbrellas. For the last hour, numbers have slowly decreased as folk, worn down by the rain, have peeled off now and again and headed for home.

'Jeez-oh! They're no' half late, aren't they?' Rhea breaks the silence once more, leans her head back against the top of her seat. 'If they don't hurry up Ah'll be fawin' asleep.'

'Me tae,' says Robert. 'It's a bloody shame, in't it? Would have been a really special night if the rain had kept away.'

'Ach, it's always the same in Scotland. If somebody plans something that's in the open air, doon comes the buggerin' rai—' Rhea stops. 'Wipe that windae again, Robert.' He does. She leans forward, peers between fresh raindrops. 'It's them! They're here at last.'

Robert starts the engine. 'Ah'll go up as near as Ah can. You and Rhea can go and get her, Frank. Ah'll dae a U-turn when you go in, then we're ready tae head off for home.'

He drives to within thirty feet of the crowd and they sit for a moment, watch the horse-drawn tram enter the large workshops. The roofs of the single deckers can just be seen above the crowd as they float past, then . . . 'Oh, my God! She's still sitting up the front. On her own.' Rhea looks at the two men. 'Ye don't think she's sat there for the whole journey, dae ye?'

Robert shakes his head. 'You know whit she's like. She'll have defied it.'

Frank shrugs. 'You two know her better than me, but I'd

take a bet she hasn't moved.' He reaches for the door handle. 'We'll soon find out!'

As they approach the tram through the bustling crowd inside the depot, Frank takes Rhea by the elbow. 'We'll go up via the driver's platform. It'll be less busy.' They watch as the passengers, unable to break the habit of a lifetime, obediently exit from the rear of the tram. Frank and Rhea climb on to what is, at the moment, the front. The driver turns.

'Hello, Frank! Huv ye come back tae us?'

'James, my boy. How are ye?' They shake hands.

'Are ye still at Maryhill?'

'Aye. Driving a bus of course. Anyway, we'll jist nip up this way. Picking up an auld friend.'

'See ye another time, Frank. Hah! Ah'll be driving a bus maself next week. All the best!'

Frank is first to gain the upstairs. 'Bella! *Bella*!'

She looks up, as though newly wakened from a sleep. Clears her throat. 'Eh?'

Rhea slips by him, lays a hand on her shoulder. 'Aw, my God! You're wringing wet!' She looks at Frank. 'She is soaking tae the skin. Granny, why did ye no' take yerself inside, oot o' the rain?'

'Wiz'nae wanting tae gie up ma good seat.' She is pale, no sign of her usual ruddy cheeks.

'Right! C'mon, we'll get ye away hame and get ye dried oot.' They help her to her feet, support her. Frank looks at Rhea. 'She's shivering. Chilled tae the bone.' He shakes his head. 'Right, c'mon Bella. Let's get ye doon the stairs.' They slowly get her moving, then she pauses.

'Where are ma freens?'

'Whit freens, Granny?'

'Annie and May and . . . oh, aye, Jessie. They were sitting jist ahint me.'

Rhea looks heavenward. 'Oh, we seen them getting aff ootside the depot. Ah think somebody wiz meeting them. Anywye, let's get ye tae the car. We've got a nice big tartan rug in the boot. We'll get ye wrapped in that. Warm ye up a bit.'

'That'll be nice. Ah'm a wee bit cauld.'

Thirty minutes later they step onto the first-floor landing at 18 Dalbeattie Street. Teresa O'Malley has heard the car and stands at her open door. 'Is she not well?'

'She's drookit! Been sitting ootside on top o' the caur. We'll have tae get her clothes aff and dry her, or she'll catch her death.' She turns to Frank. 'My ma and me will see tae her, Frank.'

Robert Stewart turns off the stairs onto the half-landing. 'Come in for a wee half, Frank, while the women are seeing tae Granny.'

'Best idea Ah've heard the night!' As Rhea and her mother help Granny into her house, Frank steps into the Stewarts'.

Forty minutes later Robert and Frank are enjoying a second measure of Bell's when Rhea and her mother come in. 'Well, that's her tucked in fur the night.' Rhea takes her coat off. 'She wiz chilled tae the bone. Whit a stupid thing tae dae. We've hud tae strip her off, gie her a good brisk rub wi' a couple o' towels, then make her a strong, hot toddy. We've re-lit her fire and banked it up fur the night. We'll see how she is in the morning.'

359

Teresa sits herself at the table. 'I'll tell youse sumt'ing for nuttin'. That soaking will do her a power of *no* good. Not at her age. She's eighty-seven ye know. Hasn't got a good chest at the best o' times. Don't know what possessed her!'

'If she diz'nae finish up wi' a bout o' bronchitis, or at the very least a heavy cauld, Ah'll be surprised.' Rhea starts filling the kettle at the sink. 'Anywye, Ah'll look in tae see her afore we go tae work tomorrow. We'll see whit the morning brings.'

CHAPTER THIRTY-NINE

Trouble Diznae Come Alone

I t's next morning.

'Robert! Ah'm jist gonny nip ower tae Granny's tae see how she is afore we leave.'

'Don't be surprised if she's snuffed it during the night!' he calls from the bedroom. Sammy and Louise take a fit of the giggles.

'Robert Stewart! That's a terrible thing tae say. The auld soul.' She turns towards the table. 'That's enough, you two!'

Robert shouts through once more. 'Just trying tae forewarn you, hen.'

She gives a massive tut. 'Ah'm no' needing forewarned, thank you very much.' She looks at the kids. 'Louise, clear the table, will ye? Jist put the dishes intae the sink tae steep. Ah'll only be a couple o' minutes at Granny's.'

It's Louise's turn to tut. 'How come it's alwiz me that has tae clear the table? He should take a turn noo and again.'

'Ah'm a boy! That's lassie's work.'

'Clear the table, Louise. Ah huv'nae time for arguments.

Jist do it *now*!' Rhea watches her daughter rise from the table then, in a greeting, girning voice, proclaim to anyone who'll listen, how unfair life is. She also takes note of the smirk on Sammy's face. 'Samuel Stewart, you can wipe that smile aff yer face. Whit your sister says is right. There's nae reason whatsoever why *you* cannae take a turn at clearing the table noo and again.' She pauses at the door. 'There's gonny be some changes made in here. Soon!'

As Rhea steps onto the landing she hears a considerably cheered-up Louise. 'Hah, hah, hah! You're no' gonny get away wi' it for much longer, Samuel Stewart. You'll soon huv tae be taking your turn, tae.'

'That's whit you think.'

Their mother stops. Steps back into the lobby. 'Naw, it's whit *Ah* think!' She smiles as she hears Robert make another contribution from the bedroom.

'And that's also what *Ah* think. Ah regularly take a turn at washing the dishes tae help your Ma. No reason why you can't do the same, Sammy.'

The boy glowers at his sister. 'See whit you've started, Louise Stewart.'

'Don't care!'

Rhea feels a little apprehensive as she faces Granny's front door. Recalls the state the old woman was in last night. Jeez! Robert could be right. She reaches out, the handle turns! Did we forget tae lock it last night? Jeez! We must have forgot tae lock it efter we put her tae bed. She tentatively pushes it open. The inner door isn't closed, she can see into the room.

'Come in if you're coming! Dinnae be shy.' The matriarch

sits at her table. A cup of tea and a plate with two crusts on it, lies in front of her. All that's left from a slice of plain bread.

'Eeeh! My God, you're up, Granny. Ah thought you'd be at death's door this morning!'

'Huh! You're no' the only yin. Ah felt awful last night when youse put me tae bed. Ah remember thinking tae maself – don't be surprised if ye waken up deid in the morning, Bella!'

Rhea walks over, puts her arms round her, kisses her on the cheek. 'Oh, Granny! Ah really am glad tae see ye up and aboot. How dae ye feel?'

'Och, jist a bit tired. And Ah'm a wee bit sniffly. Ah'm bound tae come doon wi' a cauld.'

Rhea straightens up. 'That's the very least Ah'd expect efter the drookin' ye got last night. You could'nae have got any wetter if you'd fell intae the Clyde!'

Granny frowns. 'Ah've telt ye a thousand million times no' tae exaggerate, Rhea O'Malley.'

'Eh, Rhea *Stewart* if ye don't mind. It's a while since Ah've been O'Malley.'

The old woman laughs. 'Where did Ah get that fae? Ah think the rain must huv seeped intae ma heid.'

Rhea's about to reply, but they hear voices from the landing. Robert has got the kids moving. He looks into Granny's. 'Here's your bag, Rhea. My God! Bella. Are ye up and aboot? Ah'd have taken a bet you'd still be in your bed.'

'Oh! Ah cannae be daeing wi' lying in ma bed. Hav'nae got the time.'

It's later that day. Just gone two o'clock in the afternoon. Ella Cameron, wearing her best coat, turns the corner into Dalbeattie Street, walks slowly towards the close. As she looks along the street a hundred memories flash through her mind. All happy ones. They are all of sunny days. Archie junior and Katherine are always bairns. Playing wi' their pals in the street. Me and Drena and some o' the lassies having a cup o' tea and a cake fae the Scotia. Sitting ootside, taking the sun, killing oorselves laughing at nothing. Archie and me taking a walk doon the toon. Looking intae department store windaes at things we cannae afford. Giving oor minds a treat. Going tae the pictures. Leaning oot the windae looking intae the street while Archie's dinner's cooking oan the stove. The weans playing on the carpet. Ma heart lifting when ma man turns the corner. Hame fae his work. She gives a shuddering sigh. Ah don't care whit anybody says – the forties and fifties wur the best. Skint. Rationed. And as happy as the day wiz long. She feels tearful as she nears the close. Look at me noo'. Forty-three years auld and ma life's fucked! Nothing tae look forward tae. Nothing!

Ella manages to keep control of herself until she enters the close. Drena's door is ajar. 'Oh. Thank God!' She pushes it, swallows hard, tries to stop her voice from quavering,

'Are ye in, Drena?'

'Aye. My you're early. You took a half-day? Irma and me are having a cuppa.'

Ella opens the kitchen door; her two friends look up, smile. She can't hold back any longer. Takes two steps into the room, drops her bag on the floor, bursts into tears. It's so pent-up she can't get it out, can't get her breath. It emerges as big, painful sobs.

It is so instant, powerful, it takes Drena and Irma by surprise. Frightens them with its intensity. Drena is first to react, rises from the table, goes to her pal. 'Jesus Christ!

Whit's the matter, Ella? Whit's happened? Whit's the matter wi' ye?' She puts an arm round her shoulder, takes one of her hands.

Irma goes to her other side, gently rubs her back. 'Oh, *Mein Gott*! What has happened, Ella? I never see you in such a state. Michty me!'

Ella tries to speak, but can't stop sobbing.

'C'mon, come and sit doon. Loosen your coat.' They support her to the table, lower her into a kitchen chair.

'Irma. Get the whisky oot the sideboard and pour her a hauf while Ah make fresh tea.' As they carry out these tasks her friends continually shoot glances at her, talk reassuringly. At last, all three sit at the table with cups of tea and glasses of whisky in front of them, Ella in the middle. Drena lays both hands on top of Ella's. 'Right, whit's caused this? Ah've never, in ma life, seen you in such a state. Whit's happened?'

Ella gulps at the whisky, screws her face up, immediately chases it with a mouthful of tea. She straightens up in the chair. Takes a deep breath. 'Ah've jist come fae the High Court.' They can see, and hear, she's trying to keep from breaking down again. 'Ma boy has jist got sent tae prison fur a year!' A few dry sobs force their way out.

'Oh, my God!' says Drena. 'Whit fur? Whit's he been daeing?'

The deepest of sighs comes out of Ella. She looks down at the table, cannot meet her friends' concerned eyes. 'Aw, him and another two fellas. They've been breaking intae shops, people's hooses . . .' She looks up. 'The other two got sent tae jail for longer than Archie.'

'Oh, Ella! I am so sad for you.' Irma moves her chair closer, strokes her back once more. 'You have never said he was in trouble. This is unexpected.'

Drena looks at her. 'Ah must be honest, Ella. Ah did know he wiz in a bit of bother. Wi' Billy junior being a polis, well, he knew. He never went intae any detail, but Ah knew. Ah wiz gonny let you bring it up. But ye did'nae. So Ah never let oan that Ah knew. And Ah hav'nae told anybody, either.'

Ella takes another sip of whisky, seems calmer now. 'It's wan o' them things. You don't know whether tae talk aboot it or no'. If he hadn't got sent tae prison,' she shrugs, 'Ah suppose Ah would jist have carried on. Not said anything. Hope youse wid'nae find oot.' She looks at her two pals. 'Because, well, it's embarrasing tae tell folk your son's in trouble wi' the law. And noo' it's even worse,' she begins to cry. 'He's in the jail.'

'Oh, Ella. Everybody roon' here knows you're a hardworking woman – and a bloody good mother. There's nae blame attached tae you, hen. Or Archie. He's a good faither . . .' She pauses. 'Did he go doon tae the court wi' ye?'

'Naw. Archie's washed his hands o' him. He says he's a grown man. Thinks he knows everything. Runs aboot wi' a lot o' toerags. As far as his faither's concerned, he's made his bed – so he can lie in it!'

Drena has a lot of sympathy for his father's opinion, but doesn't want to upset Ella any further. She says nothing, just sits holding her hand.

Ella looks at her. 'Ower these last few years, Drena, you don't know how many times Ah've thought aboot oor two boys. You and me huv been good pals. When they were laddies, so were they. Their faithers are hardworking men, and they are great pals. We live up the same close. How can wan o' them finish up a polis – and the other wan finish up in jail?' She gives a dry sob. 'They jist seem tae huv taken completely different paths.'

The answer comes into Drena's mind . . . because it's in his nature. But yet again, she says nothing. There's no point. 'What dae ye think Archie senior will dae now?'

'Ah'll tell ye in wan word. Nuthing! He telt Archie straight a couple o' days ago. "If ye get sent tae jail, don't expect me tae come and see ye." Dae ye know whit else he said, Drena. He said that when he's due oot, he'd better arrange wi' the authorities tae get hostel accommodation . . .' She falters again. 'Because he's no' letting him back intae the hoose.' Ella sobs. 'He says if he comes tae the door he'll throw him doon the sterrs. So whit can Ah dae?'

Drena looks at her. 'Ohhh, Ella. Every life goes through bad periods noo' and again. This is yours, hen. Ah know it feels like the end o' the world at the minute. And if it wiz any other kind of problem, you know that Archie wid support ye. But it's the boy. And his faither huz taken against him. You'll jist huv tae come doon tae see Irma or me when ye want somebody tae talk tae about him. All Ah can say, Ella, is that this is probably the worst day. Believe me, in a way it's a bit like when ye have a death in the family. As time goes on, things get a wee bit easier. Being at court the day – on your own – and him getting sent tae prison. This has been the worst day, hen.' She puts her arm round Ella's shoulder, kisses her on the cheek.

Irma leans forward, kisses her on her other cheek. Ella sits and sobs for a while. Ten minutes later, red-eyed, she says her 'cheerios'. Makes her way up the stairs. She has to get the dinner on for her husband and daughter coming in.

* * *

It's two hours later. As she comes into the close, Agnes Dalrymple is humming 'Oh! Sweet Mystery of Life'. Her bag is heavy tonight. There's a few extra tit-bits in it. For Bella. Help her get ower her bad experience at that tram thingummy yesterday. She comes onto the first-storey landing, opens Granny's outside door.

'It's jist me, Bella.' No answer. She raps the inner door. 'Bella!' Waits a few seconds. '*Bella*!' She's certain she heard movement. Pops her head round the kitchen door . . . There it is again! Agnes looks towards the recess bed. 'Are ye in your bed?'

'Buggering *aye*!' It's meant to be emphatic, but she hasn't the strength.

Agnes goes to the side of the bed. 'Eeee, Bella! It's no' like you tae take tae yer bed. Are ye no' weel?'

The old woman lies on her side, the covers pulled right up as far as her ears. She keeks out between blankets and bolster, fixes Agnes with a beady eye. 'Never felt better in ma life!'

'Bella! You're terrible, so ye are.' As Agnes finishes speaking, they both hear the sound of footsteps entering the close. The matriarch's fingers appear above the covers, pull them clear of her ear for a moment.

'That's Rhea. Go an' tell her Ah want tae see her for a minute.'

Agnes takes the few steps into the lobby. Stands at Granny's front door. Moments later the old woman hears voices. Rhea appears at the side of her bed. Agnes hovers behind.

'Whit's going on? You were right as rain, this mornin'.' Granny's hand still shows above the covers, Rhea takes it in both of hers. The old woman's voice is low. She clears her throat.

'As the day went on Ah began tae get sniffly. Ma nose running. By the middle o' the efterninn, well, Ah jist felt rotten. No' very well at aw'. So Ah've came tae ma bed.'

Rhea can tell this conversation has been an effort. 'Will Ah send fur the doctor?'

She shakes her head. 'Nae doctors. Ah'd like wan o' yer toddies. A guid strong yin.' Rhea pushes a few strands of white hair back off her forehead.

'Okay. Agnes, will you bank her fire up while Ah make it for her?'

'Of course.'

Thirty minutes later, a propped-up Granny manages to finish the toddy. Exhausted, she needs the help of her two neighbours to get her comfortably settled under the covers again.

'Ahh, that wiz guid! Oh! Will ye light yin o' ma gaslights for me afore ye go. Ah like a wee bit light on if Ah'm no' feeling weel.'

'We'll see how ye are in the morning, Granny. If you're nae better, it'll huv tae be the doctor.'

'Aye, we'll see . . .' The two women watch her eyes begin to close even as she speaks. Her breathing becomes steady. They step away from the bed, walk round to the lobby.

Agnes sighs. 'Ah weesh she had'nae went on that last tram carry-oan, yesterday.'

'Aye, me tae. But she wanted tae go, Agnes. She wiz determined.'

'Oh, Ah'm no' blaming anybody, Rhea. Ah did'nae mean it like that. Ah jist weesh she had'nae wanted tae go. Had'nae been so keen.'

369

Rhea smiles. 'We know whit she's like. There's nae arguing wi' her when she makes her mind up.'

The voice from the room is faint. 'Ah can hear youse, ye know.'

Rhea and Agnes laugh, look at each other with eyes that are instantly full. 'Okay,' says Rhea, a catch in her voice. 'We'll jist go oot ontae the landing and talk aboot ye.'

'Ah'll still hear ye.'

CHAPTER FORTY

Connections

A beautiful September morning. Sunlight streams in through Frank Galloway's top-storey windows, falls onto the corner of the table where he sits, obligingly illuminating last week's *Sunday Post*. Which he hasn't yet finished. He stretches both arms out in front of him, yawns. God, I love mornings like this. He hears Wilma turn the handle on the outside door, feels a tingle of anticipation. He folds the paper, turns his head to watch her come into the room.

'Hi yah!' She walks into the single-end, swings the shopping bag up onto the table, blows her cheeks out.

Frank looks at her. A couple of tightly curled strands of hair have, as usual, escaped from under a kirby grip and fallen onto her temple. Funny how it never seems to be any of her brown hair. It's always the very fair ones from the side. Must be more springy than the rest. He watches her take her coat off. 'Whit's aw' this puffin' and blowing we're getting?'

'You'd be puffin' and blawin' tae, son, if you had climbed up tae the tap storey wi' a full message bag!'

Frank puts on an exaggerated, tough guy persona. 'Listen, kid. Ah could carry the bag – and you – and still no' be peching and blawing like you are.'

'Huh! Who dae ye think ye urr. Johnny Weismuller?'

'Watch it! Or Ah'll be oot o' this chair and show ye!'

'You and whose army?' She giggles as he leaps out of the chair, chases her round the table, easily catches her. He wraps his arms round her. She looks up at him. He kisses her.

'Wilma Ballantyne. I thought you'd maybe like to know. Since you moved in here, even when you were just my lodger, you've made me as happy as the day is long.'

Her eyes sparkle. 'Oh, Frank. Me tae. You're the best thing that's happened tae me since . . . well, ever! *Oh*! Wait till Ah tell ye. Ah gave Auntie Maggie a ring fae the call-box on the Maryhill Road. Ha! And would ye believe it? Ma mother says she wid like tae see me!'

'She would, would she? Ah hope you're not gonny fall for that, Wilma. I really wouldn't be happy at the thought of you being alone wi' her. Ah think she's capable of anything. Will you promise me? Under no circumstances will you go and see her. She'll ask you to come back. You'll say "No". And I really think she's capable of seriously assaulting you.'

'No, Ah'm no' interested in visiting her, Frank. Ah've telt Auntie Maggie she can tell her that.'

'I'm glad tae hear it, Wilma. I don't think you should ever go over tae the house on your own. She's a nasty piece o' work. You've finally got away from her, and I think she's really mad about that. Keep well away from her. Promise?'

Wilma nods. 'Aye, Ah promise. She's hit me plenty of times in the past.' She sighs.

'And one last thing, Wilma. If you're ever in here on your own and she knocks on the door. As soon as you open it and see that it's her, don't speak to her. Immediately slam the door shut and lock it. Got it? Right! That's enough o' yer mother. We're on a week's holiday, kid. It's been long lies and cuddles every morning. So let's finish in style. What aboot getting aw' togged-up the night. Ower tae Stromboli's for a meal. Then a taxi tae Le Bar Rendezvous for a wee dance. And much later, sometime in the wee small hours, I shall waft you back hame tae Le Single-end, in another taxi!'

'That'll be lovely, Frank. Oh! And mair news. Granny must huv got a right chill on Tuesday. Agnes next door was saying she seemed tae be fine this morning, but later on she's hud tae take tae her bed. They're keepin' an eye oan her. If she gets any worse they'll get the doctor in.'

Frank shakes his head. 'Aye. And I'll take a bet she'll have been telling them she diz'nae want the doctor bothered. Anyway, I'll drop in tae see her later oan.'

Wilma starts emptying her message bag. 'Ah got some nice sliced beef fae yon cooked-meat shop, doon the other side o' Queens Cross. And fresh-baked rolls fae Ross's Dairy. So we'll huv a nice wee cuppa and a sandwich aboot two o'clock, eh?'

'Sounds good tae me, darlin'.' He reaches for the *Sunday Post*. 'Ah'll try and get this finished.'

Wilma speaks. Tries to keep her voice steady. 'Seeing as we're going oot the night, we should huv a wee nap efter we eat. No' jist forty winks in the chair. We should mibbe, eh, go tae bed for an hour. Huv a proper sleep. Freshen up. After aw', we're oan holiday, aren't we?'

Frank rustles the paper to attract her attention. She looks at him. He stares at her . . .

'Whit?' She has the grace to blush.

'Ah'll gie ye "whit?", ya brazen hussy! We'll jist go tae bed for a wee sleep. Aye. Ah know whit happens when you get me intae that recess bed in the middle o' the efterninn. Wi' the door locked. Naebody tae bother us. You *cannot* get enough of it, Wilma Ballantyne!

Though she's aware she's blushing, Wilma stands her ground. 'Well Ah don't care, Frank Galloway. Ah find it extra nice in the efterninn. Anywye. It's your ain fault – you've got me tae like it so ye have. So there!' She continues to blush.

He laughs. 'Aww! That's the nicest thing anybody has ever said tae me. Ah'll tell ye what Ah'll do, Wilma. I'll just keep going for ages and ages withoot finishing – so as you'll be coming non-stop and really enjoying yourself.' He watches as she tries to say something, but can't get it out. She grows weak with suppressed mirth. It proves so infectious he can't help but join in. At last, she manages to speak . . . 'Oh, goody!'

It's quarter to eleven when Frank and Wilma alight from a cab, outside Le Bar Rendezvous. The lovely day has turned into a mild September evening. Dry, with a soft breeze. The neon sign casts its glow onto them as Frank pays the cabbie. Wilma takes his arm for the few steps needed to bring them to the door of the club. They pause while Frank takes a final draw from his cigarette, then flicks what remains over towards the edge of the pavement. As they enter the club, the cigarette end is taken by the breeze, rolled off the pavement, into the gutter. There, kept alive by that same breeze, its red tip glows for some minutes as though competing with the club's neon sign. It eventually loses out.

Ruth Lockerbie, *proprietrix extraordinaire* – as she's called in Glasgow – sits, legs crossed, on her high stool. The Black Sobranie sends out a hint of Mittel Europa to mingle with the lesser exotica issuing from Capstans and Gold Flakes. She is surrounded by some of her favourite people – Johnny McKinnon, formerly of the Hillhead Bar, with Vicky Shaw on his arm, and Robert and Rhea Stewart of Dalbeattie Street. At just this moment Frank and Wilma enter, stop for a second to look around, decide where to sit. Rhea spots them, waves frantically to attract their attention, then beckons them over. 'Eeee! What are you two daeing here?' Before they can answer, Ruth leans forward.

'Good evening. Nice to see you again. Frank and Wilma if my memory serves me right?'

Rhea's mouth falls open. 'Huv you two been here before?'

Ruth winks at the new arrivals, turns to Rhea. 'They are regulars, darling. Here more often than you and Robert!'

Rhea's mouth refuses to close after this revelation. 'Ye urr not!'

Frank leans forward. 'We urr sot!' The entire group laughs.

Rhea turns to Ruth. 'Ah, but Ah bet ye don't know that they live up oor close?'

It's Ruth's turn to be surprised. 'Do you really? Now I *didn't* know that.' She looks at Rhea. 'I don't suppose George knows either, does he?'

'Naw. Oh, let me tell him, let me tell him!' They smile as Rhea goes into one of her excited turns. 'Where is he? Oh!

There he is, George! GEORGE!' She attracts his attention. He's talking to a couple sitting in one of the banquettes. He waves back in acknowledgement, stands up, obviously cutting short his conversation with the customers.

Ruth leans forward. 'Excuse me, Rhea Stewart. Would you mind not interfering with my husband when he's busy with our public relations. That's Hugh Fraser, the son and heir to The House of Fraser department stores.'

'Och, so he owns a couple o' shoaps! This is mair important. This is Dalbeattie Street!'

George joins the company, greets Frank and Wilma. 'Hello! How are you two?'

They don't get the chance to answer. Rhea tugs his sleeve. 'George, you're never gonny believe this. Frank and Wilma here, they live up oor close. Number eighteen.' She turns to the newcomers. 'George lived at number eighteen tae. In the close. Whit's now Drena's hoose.'

'Well, isn't that amazing,' says Frank. 'I'll tell you, Dalbeattie Street's got a lot tae answer for!'

'Which flat do you live in?' asks George.

'The single-end on the top storey.'

'Ahh! Don't tell me . . .' George taps his temple. 'Donald McNeil's old place!'

'That's right. The lady next door, Agnes, often talks about him. A very nice man, seemingly. A Highlander if I mind right.'

'Awww! He wiz. Aye. Donald wiz a lovely man,' agrees Rhea.

While this discourse about the alumni of number eighteen has been going on, Ruth, Johnny and Vicky deliberately turn their heads, in unison, to left and right as though following a tennis match. The Dalbeattie Street veterans ignore them, until Johnny McKinnon dramatically claps a hand to his forehead, then intones, 'Ohhh! Ah'm gettin' a buggerin' heidache!'

It's quarter to one in the morning. Frank and Wilma, by invitation, have stayed in the company for the rest of the evening. The time has flown. No one is ready to call it a night.

Ruth puts an arm round Rhea's shoulder, leans close to her ear. 'Do you think Frank and Wilma might like to come back to Agincourt Avenue with us?'

'Oh, Ruth! Ah wiz hoping you'd say that. Ah want tae see their faces when they walk intae your flat for the first time. Ah bet ye their mooths will faw wide open!'

'Rhea, darling. You have such a way with words.'

'Ah know!' Rhea uses her right forearm to make an exaggerated bosom adjustment. 'It's a gift!' Seconds later she has to steady Ruth, when she realises the strange noises she's making are because she's choking with laughter and is about to topple off her stool.

Forty minutes after that, Rhea takes great delight in watching the reactions of Frank and Wilma, as they step into Ruth's stunning Art Deco flat.

It's later still. Sometime after three in the morning. Robert's 1949 model one-and-a-half litre Riley, glides through the city's empty streets, taking the four of them home. *The* flat is the sole topic of conversation. Wilma and Rhea snuggle together in the back. Wilma reaches a hand out, sleepily strokes the leather upholstery. 'Ah'll tell ye what, Robert. Leaving Ruth and George's flat, then driving hame in your car – mmm, the feel and the smell o' the leather – oh! Ah'm quite convinced we've been transported back tae the thirties. Their flat is magic, Rhea, in't it?'

'No' half. Ah never get fed-up wi' it. Ah must try and see it some day when Ah'm sober!'

CHAPTER FORTY-ONE

Sent For

'Good morning!' Dr John McNicol pushes Granny Thomson's door wide open, strides in.

'Morning, Doctor' is said in unison by Teresa O'Malley and Drena McClaren who are both in attendance.

'What seems to be the trouble?'

Teresa is rather nervous. It was she who 'sent for the doctor'. Dr McNicol is known to have little patience with time wasters – especially when it's *his* time they're wasting. She watches him lay his Gladstone bag on the table.

''Tis herself, Doctor. She got soaking wet at that tram t'ing last week. She's had to take to her bed so she has. And getting worse so she is. So we've had to send for yourself.'

'Uh-huh.' He walks over to the recess bed. Granny lies on her side, facing out towards the room. She opens one eye.

'What's this then, Isabella Thomson? Not like you to be needing my services.' He gives her the fleeting smile which most of his female patients delight in. To use Ella Cameron's description: 'He jist switches it oan and aff like a light so he diz.'

'You're the doctor, John. You tell me!' Her voice is weak. She is one of a select number of his patients who are allowed – or have the nerve – to call him by his Christian name. The on/off smile makes another appearance. Teresa and Drena look at one another, mouths open.

'Oh! It's cheek I'm going to be getting, is it?'

'Ah huv'nae the strength.'

'Right! I'll have to have a wee look at you, Isabella. Can you manage to roll onto your stomach for me. I need to give you a good sounding, starting with your back.' He has been holding his stethoscope in his hand. He now hangs it from his neck, preparatory to assisting her to turn onto her stomach.

'Ah hope you're gonny warm that stethothingummy afore ye use it.'

'Seeing as it's you, I will. And I'll warm my hands, too.' Teresa and Drena watch in disbelief as he, at Granny's bidding, steps over to the range and proceeds to warm his hands. When he returns to his patient it's to find she has dozed off. She wakens when he starts his examination.

Eventually John McNicol straightens up, takes his stethoscope off, holds it in his hand. 'I won't beat about the bush, Isabella. I believe you're in the early stages of pneumonia. It's the hospital for you, my girl.'

The old woman shakes her head. 'Nae hospital for me, John.'

'Mmm, I thought you might say that.'

'John. This . . .' she gasps for breath, 'is maist important.' Her left hand appears from under the covers, points. 'Bring a chair. Ah huv'nae the energy . . . talk loud.' Her voice fades.

Drena pulls a chair out from under the table, slides it along the linoleum towards him. She and Teresa watch as he sits at the side of her bed, rests an arm on the covers, holds his head to the side so his ear is close to her. When Teresa and Drena see his attention is all on his patient, they softly shuffle forward. In case they miss anything. Their eye-witness bulletins will be in great demand the length and breadth of the close. BBC and STV? Eat your hearts out!

What little talking she has done since the good Doctor arrived has already used up most of Granny's dwindling strength. Her breathing is laboured as she gets ready to speak . . . 'Ye must listen.' He leans nearer. 'Now this isnae me being awkward. Ah'm eighty-seven. There's nae betterness for me.' She looks him in the eye. 'Ah want tae go in ma ain bed. If ye send me tae hospital, tae die in a ward fu' o' strangers, Ah'll nae forgive ye, John.' He can see she's on the brink of tears. Frightened. He also knows she's right. She won't get over this. She has had chronic bronchitis which is new approaching acute. Her age is against her. This pneumonia will most certainly take her – in or out of hospital. Now she has made her wishes clear, she looks intently at him, her eyes searching his. He reaches out with both hands, takes her left hand in them. 'Isabella. When I took over that wee surgery on the Maryhill Road, not long after the war, you were just about the first patient to join my panel.' The wee smile lingers longer than normal. 'There was no health service then—'

She finds the strength to interrupt. 'Half a croon for a consultation, John.' He waits while she sucks some more air into her lungs. 'Three and six if ye came tae the hoose.'

The smile still lingers. 'Yes, indeed. They were tough days.

Anyway, Isabella,' he looks into her eyes, gives her hand the gentlest of squeezes, 'you know I wouldn't send you to hospital against your will. If you wish to remain in your own bed, in your own corner, that'll be the way of it. Is that what you want to hear?'

She nods. 'That's what Ah want, John.' It's almost a sigh.

He rises from the chair. 'Right, my dear. Now, after all that rousting about when I was examining you . . .' He glances at Teresa and Drena. 'I'm sure the ladies will fetch you maybe a wee drop of broth, or even just a cup of tea. You have to keep taking liquids, Isabella.' Granny watches him go to the table, put the stethoscope into the scuffed Gladstone bag. He lifts it and returns for a moment to stand at her bedside. They look at one another; the doctor and the patient. An old woman and her friend. It's a special look. Private. John McNicol feels this could be their last consultation. She knows it is.

'You will *not* be going to hospital. That's my promise to you. Bye for now, Isabella.'

She manages a smile, raises the fingers of the hand which lies outside the covers. John McNicol gives her his on/off smile. Then takes his leave.

It's very early the next morning. Still dark. Granny Thomson comes wide awake, certain she heard someone in the room. Expects to see one of her neighbours. There's no one there. She looks towards the windows. Still black dark. Must be early. She turns her head slightly, looks at the luminous hands of the alarm clock. Och, jist ten tae five. My! Ah must have had a guid sleep. This is the best Ah've felt for days. The room seems poorly lit. Each evening, since she took to her bed, the last thing Rhea does for her is light one of the gas lamps. It's left to burn all night. She looks at it. It seemed tae be aw'right last night. Now, it's as if it has been turned down. The flame is'nae high enough tae make the mantle glow like it should. It's nae stronger than a single candle. Mibbe the pressure has dropped at the gasworks.

She lies for a while in the half-dark, thinking. Soon, her eyes begin to close and she starts to doze. Minutes later, or so it seems, she's again wakened by movement in the darkened room. As she is still lying on her side, facing outward, she becomes aware someone is standing close by the bed. She narrows her eyes to see who it is. The weak glow from the gas and the first glimmer of daylight slipping past the old blackouts, are enough to let her see her visitor in silhouette. Whoever she is, she is quite short and has a head of curly hair. A pale shaft of light finds a gap in the wartime blackouts, illuminates the outline of a head and shoulders. Those are blonde curls!

'Is that you, Jane?'

There's a giggle which she hasn't heard for many a month. 'Yes, Granny. Have you forgot me?'

The old woman tuts. 'Dae ye think Granny would forget her wee pal?' She makes the decision to ask straight out. 'Whit have ye come for, hen?'

'I've been sent, 'cos you know things will be all right if you're with me.' As the child speaks the gas flame burns brighter, the mantle begins to glow, the room is lighter. She can now see the child's face whenever she turns her head to the right; towards the light. All of a sudden it feels so good to be lying in bed, talking to the bairn. There is no fear. The old woman looks down.

'Ah see you've still got oor kaleidoscope, hen.'

'Uh-huh. Nobody else gets to look through it, Granny. I've been waiting for you.'

'Aww! Noo isn't that nice. But Ah've been no' weel, Jane. Ah dinnae think Ah've got the strength tae get oot o' bed and get ready tae go wi' ye.'

Jane laughs. 'Don't be silly, it's easy-peasy.' The old woman watches her transfer the kaleidoscope to her left hand, then hold out her right. 'All you do is take my hand, Granny.' She gives her little-girl shrug and the blonde curls bounce like always. 'And that's it. All done!'

'Och, well.' Isabella Thomson turns the covers back, reaches out and takes the child's hand.

CHAPTER FORTY-TWO

Hail and Farewell!

The black Rover 90, having left Langside behind, turns right onto Pollokshaws Road and heads for the city. Fred Dickinson looks at the dashboard clock. 'It's just gone ten, darling. Shall we get ourselves parked and have a wander round the shops? I'll tell you what. If you see something you really, really like, I'll treat you.'

Ruby Baxter looks at him. 'Fred. You don't have to always be buying me thi—'

'Are you trying to spoil my fun? I get great pleasure from treating you.' He takes his left hand off the steering wheel for a moment, places it on top of hers, which are clasped in her lap.

She looks out the window, watches Glasgow folk going about their business. Women doing their shopping with kids in tow. Van drivers making deliveries. It suddenly enters her head, just how lucky she is. She squints against the mid-September sun. From out of nowhere, an idea comes to her. 'Do you know what I'd like to do, Fred?' She doesn't wait for his reply. 'Take a wee run up to Dalbeattie Street for half an hour. Introduce you to Granny Thomson. She'll be pleased that we're getting married soon.'

'Yeah. I've never met the old soul, but I sure have a lot to thank her for.' He grins. 'Haven't I?'

'I'll never forget it,' says Ruby. 'There I was, giving Granny all my worries. Well, what I thought were worries. Then she took one of her fey turns. Basically told me, "If you don't marry this man, you're stupid. Go and tell him, now!" That was when I dashed next door to the Stewart's, rang you up—'

He interrupts. 'And I received the best phone call of my life. Heard you say, "I will! I'll marry you, Fred." It'll be nice to meet her. Thank her for making you see sense. When you lived there, you used to talk about Granny more than anyone else.'

Ruby laughs. 'Hah! I bet I did. We didn't always get on, you know. Especially at first. Many's the time we were at daggers drawn! But eventually, we reached an understanding.' She laughs again. 'That I should do what I'm told!'

Fred turns his head. 'I most definitely have got to meet this woman. Get some tips.'

The Rover turns in off the Maryhill Road, stops outside 18 Dalbeattie Street. 'She'll want us to have a cup of tea, Fred. A dish of tay as she calls it. And a couple of biscuits. It's mandatory.'

They step onto the first-storey landing. 'This is her.' Ruby points to the middle of three doors. Fred looks at the brass nameplate and letterbox. 'F. Thomson' is almost polished away. They hear footsteps.

'Oh, it's you, Ruby.' Drena McClaren has opened the O'Malleys' door.

'Hello, Drena! I thought you lived in the close?'

'Ah, do. But, eh . . . You'd better come in a minute.'

Ruby looks at her. She feels the smile freeze on her face. Gets a funny feeling in her stomach. Somehow she knows. In fact, absolutely *knows* there's something bad going on. Drena turns, walks back into the O'Malleys'. Ruby follows, Fred behind her. The lobby is dark, gloomy. The kitchen is . . . sombre. Someone sits in a fireside chair, back to the window, in shadow.

'Hello, Ruby. Nice tae see ye again.'

'Hello, Rhea.' She'd got to like Rhea while she'd lived here. 'Are you not at work, today?'

'Naw. Eh, Granny died this morning!'

She wouldn't have expected to – Granny and her were certainly not close friends – but Ruby bursts into tears. Finds herself standing in the middle of Teresa O'Malley's kitchen with tears running down her face. She's also set Rhea off. Ruby manages to bring herself under control.

'Oh, God!' She gestures towards Fred. 'I was bringing Fred up to meet her.' She gives a big, shuddering sigh. 'And now it's too late.' Tears come again. 'Of all the days to choose for a visit.'

Rhea has managed to compose herself. 'My ma called in to see how she was this morning. She has'nae been well. She'd taken pneumonia on top of aw' her other troubles.' Rhea dabs her eyes. 'It wiz aboot seven when Ma found her. She must have not long slipped away. She was still warm. Probably went roon' aboot five or six this morning. She's still in the recess bed if you want tae see her.'

Ruby stands for a moment. Thinking about it. 'No. No, I don't think I will, Rhea. I'd rather picture her exactly as she was the last time I was in her company. Sitting at her table with the tea things out. It's perfect.'

'Look at the time!' Drena glances at the clock on Teresa's mantelpiece. Ruby and Fred sit at the table. They both have a whisky in front of them. It's standing beside their third cup of tea.

Drena looks around, 'Right! Who's here? Teresa, Rhea, Irma, Agnes, Irene. We'll huv tae wait till Ella gets here before we start. We hud tae phone her doon at Cakeland. She should'nae be long.' Drena turns towards Ruby. 'We'll no' include you in the meeting, Ruby. Simply because ye don't live in the close anymair. Nae offence or anything.'

'No, of course not. None taken. I suppose this will be about the funeral arrangements?'

'Jayz! More like the lack o' them,' says Teresa. 'She knew she was going, you know. She felt it was near. In spite o' that, she'd made almost no arrangements. Did ye know she had the Gift?'

'Oh, I certainly knew that,' says Ruby. 'I had first-hand experience of it.'

'She did get all her policies together. Showed me where I could lay me hands on them when the time came.' Teresa stops to wipe away a few tears. 'Oh, Jayz! Youse don't know what a miss she's going to be for me . . .'

'You're no' the only wan.' Agnes Dalrymple dabs a dewdrop from the end of her nose.

'Yah. Me too,' says Irma. 'Whenever I want good advice, I always go to the Granny.'

All heads turn at a sudden noise. Ella Cameron comes bustling through the door, leans her shopping bag against a leg of the sideboard. She straightens up. Looks at the sad faces of her assembled friends. Granny's friends. They're all looking at her. Looking for a lead. She clears her throat. 'Well . . .' she bursts into tears.

Drena goes to her, also starts crying. They embrace.

'Aw! Drena. Can ye imagine the close withoot her? It'll no' *be* eighteen Dalbeattie Street anymair!'

'Can we have a bit of order, please.' Teresa takes it on herself to get things started. 'I might as well get to the point, girls. We haven't begun yet t' make arrangements about burying herself. Haven't phoned an undertaker or anyt'ing. Bella was good at giving all of us advice, but she could have done wit' some herself.' She has their attention. The room is quiet.

Ella looks at her. 'Is there a problem, Teresa?'

'I've tallied up her policies. She would have been foine – if she'd died round about 1930! They come to a grand total of thirty-eight pounds, all told.'

'Oh, my God!'

'We'll be having door-to-door collections round the street. Everybody knew her. But I don't t'ink we'll get any more than we normally get. Enough to buy some nice wreaths. Not enough to bury her. And she wanted t' be buried. But there's no family lair. Her man was cremated.'

Drena poses *the* question. 'Urr we talkin' a pauper's funeral here?'

Teresa looks sad. 'Can't see any other way. There are no relations. She out-lived them all. There's no money. She never had a bank account in her life.'

Agnes Dalrymple intervenes. 'Well, Ah'm not having that! Ah'll pay whatever's needed, even if it takes aw' ma savings. Ah'm no' huving ma lovely pal going tae a pauper's grave!'

'You're a good soul, Agnes,' says Irene Stuart. 'I can manage twenty-five pounds.'

'Ladies! May I make a suggestion? Would you allow me to pay for the funeral?' All heads, including Ruby's, turn toward Fred Dickinson. She looks at him. A surge of tenderness wells up in her. She reaches her hand out, places it on top of his.

'But, Jayzus! You didn't even know her, mister, eh, Fred.' says Teresa.

'I didn't,' Fred agrees, 'but Granny did me a big favour. She told Ruby here she'd be a fool if she didn't marry me!'

'And Ah'll tell ye whit,' says Drena. 'Granny wiz right!'

Fred blushes. 'Thank you very much. Okay, to business. I'll phone Lambert's the funeral directors, over in Hillhead. Anthony Lambert and I are fellow Rotarians. When I tell him the situation and, of course, put pressure on him, I know he'll do me a good price.' Fred glances at Ruby. She has continued to look at him. He leans towards her, whispers, 'Are you all right?'

She lifts her head higher, looks into his eyes. 'Fred Dickinson. You're just wonderful!'

'Oh, thank you. Anyway.' He turns back to Teresa. 'Now, so that we will know who's doing what, would you like to write this down? I'll tell Lambert's I'll take care of the coffin, buying a lair at the cemetery, pay for the padre, eh, the vicar, and, let's see, six cars for mourners to follow the hearse?' he pauses. 'Oh! And for the funeral tea afterwards.' He scratches his head. 'Shall we say the City Bakeries function rooms on the Byres Road? Now, are you quite sure there are no relations? I don't want to be stepping on anyone's toes.'

'There are definitely none, Fred,' says Teresa. 'I remember, oh, about two years ago t'was. She was telling me some cousin had died. He was the last. Now. What do ye want us to do wit' the money from her policies and what we'll collect round the street? Will we send it to you?'

He shakes his head. 'Use it for flowers or some such. Oh, I'll tell you what else,' says Fred. 'A headstone. We'll get a nice stone for her.'

'Goodness me,' says Ella. 'Dae ye realise, Fred. Altogether, this is gonny cost you aboot four, mibbe even *five* hundred pounds!'

'Thank you for pointing it out, but please, let me worry about that, ladies.'

Rhea knocks on the table. 'Before we close this meeting,' they hear the tremor in her voice, 'we owe a big vote of thanks to these two. Do youse realise if Ruby had'nae taken a notion tae come ower here the day tae introduce Fred tae Granny, Agnes would huv hud tae spend aw' her savings tae keep Granny oot o' a pauper's grave?'

Ruby speaks. 'I've been wondering about that. Fred and I were going up to town to do a bit of shopping. Then, out of the blue I got this, well, *urge* to drive up to Maryhill to see Granny. Let her meet Fred. Just popped into my head. Don't know where it came from.'

Teresa can't wait. 'Well I do!' She nods her head in the direction of next door. ''Tis straight from the woman lying on the other side o' that wall. You can take it from me – Isabella Thomson would have no intention of lying in a pauper's grave. There ye are, now.' She sits down.

'Aye! Ah'd take a bet you're right.' says Agnes.

Rhea comes in again. 'Ah wid'nae be surprised if that's whit happened, Ruby. Granny will huv put the idea intae yer heid.'

Ruby laughs. 'I've been sitting here thinking about it. That's the only answer I came up with!'

'Right, folks.' Fred rises, Ruby follows. 'Normally I'm at the office, so I suggest, if you wish to get in touch over any problems, that you ring Ruby. Mornings are the best time to be sure of catching her. She'll be on Langside 4262.'

Ruby turns to Rhea. 'And you'll be in the phone book, won't you?'

'I am. So you and me can be the point of contact.' Rhea stands up. 'Ladies. Can I say once again: we owe a *BIG* debt of gratitude to Fred here. This is a lovely thing he's daeing for Granny.' There are cries of 'Here! Here!' from around the room.

'But may I remind you, ladies.' Fred rubs his chin. 'Agnes was prepared to pay for it all! Okay. Seeing as you're on the phone, Rhea, would you mind if I ring Anthony Lambert right now? It'll get things started. Oh! And most important. You'll need a death certif—'

'I rang Dr McNicol this morning,' Rhea interrupts. 'He came oot right away. Says the certificate can be picked up from the surgery any time.'

A few minutes later Fred comes out of Rhea's. Ruby and Rhea stand talking on the landing.

'Right. I've given Lambert's the green light.' Fred looks at Rhea. 'There's one other matter. As you've heard this morning, I never got to know the Great Lady in life. Before we leave, I'd like to go in and pay my respects. I take it she's presentable?'

'She is, oh aye. Ah'll take ye in. Are you sure you're no' wanting tae see her, Ruby?'

Ruby shakes her head. 'No. The last time I saw her was the day she told me I should marry Fred. That will be a nice memory.'

After a short while, Rhea and Fred emerge from Granny's single-end. He sighs. 'Well, I can now put a face to the Queen of Dalbeattie Street. Anyway, we'd better get ourselves away.'

'Thanks again, the two of you,' says Rhea. 'That's such a kind think you're daeing, it really is.'

Fred has already started to descend the stairs. He raises a hand in acknowledgement. Ruby says her goodbyes and follows him down to the car.

As the black Rover pulls silently away from the pavement, from the corner of his eye Fred can see Ruby is half-turned in her seat, looking at him. 'What?' he says.

'Granny was *so* right about you, Fred Dickinson.'

CHAPTER FORTY-THREE

The End of Two Eras

'Huv ye ever seen such a turnoot in your life?' Ella looks at Drena.

'Ah have not.'

They stand on the pavement to the side of the close mouth. Next to them are Dennis and Teresa O'Malley. Robert and Rhea Stewart are nearby. As the undertaker's men slide the coffin into the hearse they, along with the rest of number 18's residents, watch the matriarch being readied for her last journey. Rhea leans over towards the two pals.

'Ah think the whole of Dalbeattie Street's oot.'

'Aye. Not far off,' says Drena. She looks at the waiting cortege: hearse, six cars and two single-decker Bluebird coaches. As she does, her eye catches someone amongst the spectators. 'Aw look, Rhea. There's Ken fae the paper shop. That's the first Ah've seen him since he retired.'

'It looks like he's got the best suit oan. Ah think we should mibbe ask him if he'd like tae go tae the funeral. He's known Granny fur forty years or mair, ye know.'

'Good idea, hen. Away and ask him.'

Rhea crosses the street to where Ken stands amongst the many lining the pavement.

'Hello Ken. Jist spotted ye there. You're very welcome tae come tae the service *and* the funeral wi' the rest o' us. There's room oan wan o' the coaches if ye huv the time.'

'That's nice of ye, Rhea. Ah was gonny come tae the church service anyway. Could'nae let Bella go withoot paying ma respects.'

'Jist come across the road wi' me and join the mourners. You'll know everybody.'

Once back with her neighbours, Rhea walks over to join Frank Galloway and Wilma. 'Ah know it's awful short notice, Frank. Could you dae us a wee favour? Would you be able tae get up in the church tae say a few words aboot Granny? Jist something short. Off the cuff.'

'Oh, thanks a lot!' He smiles. 'Have you any idea, Rhea, how many days rehearsal it takes – to say something off the cuff?' He manages to keep his face straight as her brows knit together while she tries to work that out.

'Aw! Ah did'nae know that, Frank. Whit it was, some of us were huving a cuppa in oor hoose this morning, and Robert wiz wondering who we could we ask tae give a thingummy, a eulogy.'

Frank shrugs. 'Ah would have thought Robert himself would be the best man for the job. He's good wi' words.'

She shakes her head. 'He says if it had been for anybody else, he could huv done it nae bother. But he's too close tae her. She really huz been like oor Granny. Robert and me were born in number eighteen. We've known her since we were weans.'

Robert joins them. 'Do ye think you could manage it, Frank?

Ah would love tae do it maself,' he shakes his head, 'but Ah'd never get through it. Ah'd choke up before Ah got halfway.'

'Well,' says Frank. 'You do realise, Ah've known her for less than two years? So Ah'd just have tae speak about the Granny I know. Do you have any basic facts aboot her? You know, when and where she was born, stuff like that?'

'Got it aw' ready for ye.' Robert pulls a folded sheet of paper from his pocket. 'I did this for myself, just in case you said you couldn't do it.' He hands it to Frank. 'Funnily enough, I felt you'd be a good choice *because* you've only known her for a wee while. It might actually be a help. Anyway, Ah'm sure you'll do her justice, Frank.'

He tucks the paper into his inside pocket. 'Ah hope Ah live up tae your expectations.'

With a bit of hunching-up, the mourners from 18 Dalbeattie Street manage to fit themselves into the six limousines. Then more cramming is required when four former residents turn up. Ruby Baxter, George Lockerbie plus Marjorie and Jack Marshall are squeezed in by being split up and each allocated as an extra passenger for separate cars. 'Jayz!' says Dennis O'Malley. 'Like kippers in a box we are!' Those friends of Granny's from nearby closes or other streets board the Bluebird coaches in a more leisurely manner.

During the car journey and even in church, Robert Stewart notices that Frank is busy, continually writing, scoring-out, then rewriting as he prepares his last-minute eulogy. Then, time runs out . . . The minister looks around. 'I'd now like to call on one of Isabella's neighbours to say a few words about her. Frank Galloway, please.'

Wilma watches her man rise, make his way to the pulpit. She's aware he's nervous, simply because he wishes he'd been given more notice. She watches him climb up, take a creased sheet of paper from his pocket. The scribblings-out and notes in the margin are clear to see as he unfolds it. He pauses to let an outbreak of coughing subside.

'Isabella Thomson was her Sunday name. "Granny" to most of us. Especially to those of us lucky enough to live at eighteen Dalbeattie Street. Today, the fourteenth of September, 1962, we are here for her funeral service. We're all sad because we're not going to see her again. But I think it's more than that. We'll never see the like of her again!' Frank pauses, looks around the congregation. 'And that's why this service should also be a celebration. To mark her long life. Eighty-seven years! That's a good run by any standards. And on the whole, for most of those years, she enjoyed good, robust health.' Frank has now visibly relaxed. 'Granny was born in Girvan in 1875. Came to Glasgow at the turn of the century for work. And, as girls did back then, she went into service. I remember her telling me, she loved this city from the day she set foot in it. She moved into her single-end in Dalbeattie Street when she married Frank Thomson.' He looks up. '*That* was in 1910! As we all know, she also loved her wee hoose as she called it. Especially its first-floor windows . . .' He pauses to let the laughter subside. 'From those windows, she kept an eye on the comings and goings in our street for more than half a century! Can you imagine that? Her life, however, wasn't all fun and frolic. She certainly had her share of sadness. She lost a child just hours after birth. Then the biggest loss was the death of her husband, Frank Thomson in 1918. He was one of millions of folk, world-wide, who died in a terrible flu epidemic. Or as Granny would point out – a pandemic! That's what you call something that is much, much bigger than an epidemic.

'Even late in life the tragedies didn't end. In January of this year, she was very badly affected by the loss of little Jane Marshall, the child of neighbours.' Frank inclines his head towards Jack and Marjorie. 'That was a shock and a sadness for all of us. But none more than Granny. She had always called Jane her 'wee pal'.

'My own relationship with this great lady,' he looks at the upturned faces, 'hasn't been nearly as long as I would have liked. But let there be no mistake – in her own way, Isabella Thomson *was* a great lady!' Many heads nod in agreement. 'I moved into number eighteen last year, after my wife died in an accident. I was, to say the least, depressed. However, I soon got into a routine. Many a night I'd come back to the close, usually after midnight, ready to face a cold, empty house. I'd approach number eighteen, look up, and Granny's windows would be lit with the pale light from her gas lamps. I'd give her a knock, and finish up sitting at her hearth into the wee sma' hours. The twin lamps glowing above us, a grand fire in the grate, and herself plying me with many a dish o' tay. She was a wonderful help. A comfort. A sounding-board. She'd let you get things off your chest. Or help you put them in perspective. I know she did that for most of us over the years.'

Wilma watches, her eyes moist, as he folds up his piece of paper, clears his throat.

'So there you are, folks. And I haven't told any of the stories to highlight the fact that Granny was fey. We could all give first-hand evidence of that.' Yet again, numerous heads nod in the congregation. 'So may I finish by saying, God rest her and bless her. As I said earlier, we'll not see another one like her. Thank you.'

As Frank steps down from the pulpit a smattering of applause breaks out, then just as quickly fades as some folk 'shush' for silence – or others suddenly remember where they are. The minister reclaims his pulpit, looks at the assembled mourners, smiles. 'I can't say I blame you! There has been many a time over the years when I've thought, why shouldn't a well-delivered eulogy receive some applause? Anyway, thank you very much, Frank. A lovely tribute.'

At the cemetery six women: Teresa O'Malley, Agnes Dalrymple, Rhea Stewart, Drena McClaren, Ella Cameron and Irma Armstrong – Granny's pals – take hold of the blue cords and lower the matriarch into her grave. When the cords go slack, they let go, then listen to the thumps as the heavy tasselled ends beat a tattoo on the lid. They look at the untidy coils, the brass plate with 'Isabella Thomson' engraved on it. Next, her neighbours throw clods of damp brown earth into the grave. Watch it clatter and scatter over the coffin, somehow feel it's disrespectful. Tears are shed. But they are of sadness, not sorrow. If they were to compare notes at this very moment, uppermost in their minds would be the thought that never again will they walk into her single-end, breathe in the smell of gas burning in a mantle, of mothballs and Sloan's Liniment, of cheap perfume masking the stale sweat of an old woman who doesn't own a bath. No longer find her sound asleep in her chair, the kettle singing on the edge of the range. To know that in a minute or two she'll come awake, clear her throat, and ask that perennial question . . . 'Have ye time for a dish o' tay?'

* * *

There's a low respectful hum of conversation in the upstairs room of the City Bakeries – which won't last for long. Those from 'the close' sit at the long, top table. Another fifty or so are seated at circular tables, six to each. The catering is silver service.

Teresa O'Malley lifts her fork, looks at the back of it, nudges Agnes Dalrymple. 'I used to t'ink the cutlery really was solid silver, ye know. Until I got me first pair o' specs. Then I realised them marks on the back just said 'epns'. They weren't real hallmarks at all.'

'Ah know. They're jist silver plated.' She leans over to Teresa. 'Ye know why they did that, don't ye?' She carries straight on. 'So that if any toffs fell oan hard times, they could sell their silver and replace it wi' the plated stuff. And naebody wid know the difference because o' the phoney marks!' Agnes sits back, sniffs, adjusts her bosom.

'Do ye t'ink so?'

'Know it fur a fact.'

'Here's the waitress coming wit' the sherry.' Teresa looks at Agnes. 'Will ye be huving a wee drop?'

'Bloody sure and Ah'm no'! Be orange squash fur me. Wan drop o' that, Teresa, and Ah'd be back oan the slippery slope!'

'Good for you, girl.' Teresa squeezes her forearm.

Irene Stuart sips her sherry, turns to Mary Stewart. 'Well, that was a nice send-off for the auld soul. No more than she deserved.'

'Yes, indeed. Are you going tae take advantage of the offer tae have a wee item from the house, Irene? You know, as a wee remembrance.'

'I'll tell you what. Let me know when you're going in and I'll come with ye.' Irene sighs. 'Ah know Granny said long ago that when the day came folk could take whatever they wanted. But it's still gonny feel like we're picking ower her stuff.' She looks at Mary.

'Ah know exactly what ye mean. But she's got nae family. The factor will be sending up some carriers tae clear the hoose in a few days. Them lads will sell anything that can be sold, and the rest will just get dumped. So if there's a wee bit o' china or an ornament that you've always liked, Irene, ye might as well take it as a wee keepsake. Tae remember her.'

'Aye. If ye look at it like that, Ah suppose you're right.'

'Oor Robert and Rhea. Do ye know what they're taking?' She laughs. 'Her auld kettle!'

'Jeezus-johnny! It's as black as the ace o' spades wi' always sitting on the range.'

'Oh, they're not gonny be using it. Or cleaning it. It's just gonny sit up on the shelf so as they'll always remember aw' the dishes o' tay.' The conversation falters; they look at one another, eyes moist.

After a moment, Irene manages . . . 'Och, that's nice. That's nice so it is.'

It's quarter to four. The decision has finally been made to evacuate the City Bakeries function rooms on the Byres Road. The Bluebird coaches await.

Frank Galloway looks up into the sky. 'It's not a bad day for the middle of September, Wilma.'

'No' half. It's often the most settled month of them all, in't it?'

He's about to answer, but Robert and Rhea, followed by

401

Ruby Baxter, Ella and Drena, spill out the door of the bakery department, onto the pavement.

'Well, that's it Ah guess.' Drena looks at her watch. 'Oor auld pal will be covered up by noo and settling intae the soundest of all sleeps.'

Ella looks at her. 'Jeez-oh! Drena. Ye sound like a poet talking.'

'It'll be the half-boatel o' sherry – not me!' She turns to Ruby. 'Ah know we've already said it, but will ye thank Fred once again when ye get hame, Ruby. It's so good of him to pay for this.'

They are interrupted by a clatter of high heels. 'Crivvens!' says Irma. 'Now I am in the fresh air . . .' she leans on the wall. 'Oh, mammy daddy! I think I also have too much sherry.'

Archie Cameron puts his arm round her waist to support her. '*Hast du zu viel getrunken*, Irma?'

'*Ganz bestimmt*, Erchie!'

Billy McClaren takes up post on her other side. '*Komm*, Irma. *Schnell nach dem autobus.*'

Ella looks at Drena. 'Ah think them three huv hud a schnapps too many, Drena. We'll aw' be back doon the Bunker before the night's oot!'

Rhea is looking at the cars. 'Robert, that's baith oor parents got on.' She turns. 'Anyway, Ruby. Ah'm sure we'll be bumping intae you and Fred at the Bar Rendezvous noo and again.' She pauses, '*Oh*! Ah *knew* Ah had something tae tell ye. She points at Frank and Wilma. 'These two came intae the Rendezvous a couple of Saturdays ago. If you'd been in that night you'd huv made up the full set. It's time Ruth wiz changing the name tae the Bar Dalbeattie!'

'Oh, I'm sure we'll eventually all turn up together one

Saturday night.' Ruby looks at her watch. 'Well, I'm going to hail a cab. I'll see you all again. Bye!' They watch the ever-stylish Ruby sashay off. Her expensive, long blue coat sways from side to side as she strides along the Byres Road and the sun begins to dip behind its chimney pots.

'Are you two coming?' Ella looks at Frank and Wilma. 'Better no' hold up the cars for too long.'

Frank turns to Wilma. 'It's as nice a late afternoon as you could ask for. Do ye know what? I fancy a nice daunder up the road. Get a bit exercise. What dae ye think?'

'Why not. It is lovely.'

'We're just gonny walk hame, Ella,' says Frank.

'Oh, that'll be nice. Ah weesh Ah hud the time tae join ye, but Ah've got a pile of ironing tae dae, then get the dinner oan. Enjoy it.'

Ella is the last to climb into a car. Frank and Wilma wait until they pull away, followed by the coaches. They stand at the kerb, smile and wave as the small convoy goes past. Wilma laughs. 'That's the bairns away tae the seaside.'

Crossing the Great Western Road they set off up Queen Margaret Drive. Wilma takes his arm. 'This is nice, Frank.' She looks at him. 'You're awfy quiet. Still sad aboot Granny?'

'Well, of course it's that. But . . . it's sort of more.' He presses her arm to his side. 'The whole afternoon something has kept coming into my mind. It just won't go away.' He takes a deep breath. 'It's only ten days since the last tram ran in the city. Granny took part in that parade. And because of it, caught pneumonia. To the folk who live up oor close, especially the older ones, the death of Granny Thomson will be the major event of this month. This year. And rightly so. For most folk

403

in Glasgow, the end of the city's trams will have been the main thing.' Wilma can tell he's trying to find the right words. 'Now, how can I explain what's been spinning round in my head all day?' He pauses again. 'Because I'm a tram driver who happens to *live* at eighteen Dalbeattie Street – and had a lovely friendship with this special old lady . . .' He gives a sad smile. 'I feel strongly that I've just seen the end of *two* eras. And for me they're both big losses. All day I've been trying to sort these thoughts out in my mind. Just ten days in September – yet life won't be quite the same any more.'

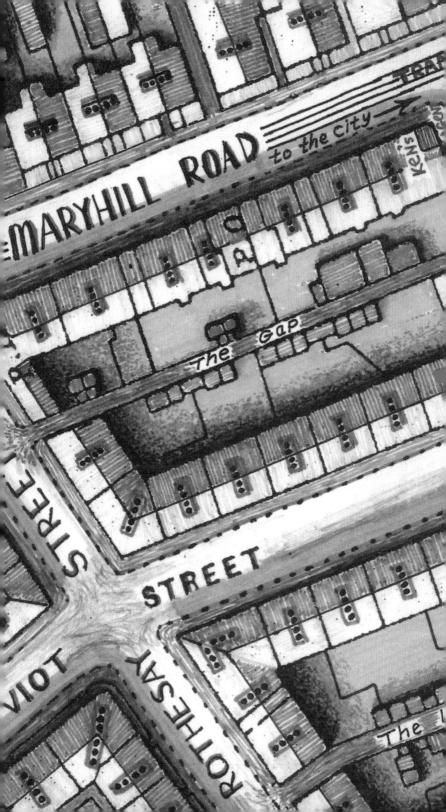